A CRUEL SEASON *for* DYING

A CRUEL SEASON *for* DYING

HARKER MOORE

Published by Warner Books

An AOL Time Warner Company

Mysterious Press books are published by Warner Books, Inc.,
1271 Avenue of the Americas, New York, NY 10020.

Visit our Web site at www.twbookmark.com.

An AOL Time Warner Company

The Mysterious Press name and logo
are registered trademarks of Warner Books, Inc.

Printed in the United States of America

First Printing: June 2003
10 9 8 7 6 5 4 3 2 1

Library of Congress Cataloging-in-Publication Data
Moore, Harker.
A cruel season for dying / Harker Moore.
p. cm.
ISBN 0-89296-774-9
1. Police—New York (State)—New York—Fiction.
2. Japanese Americans—Fiction.
3. New York (N.Y.)—Fiction. I. Title.

PS3613.O559 C78 2003
813'.6—dc21   2002029596

To angels past and present—Louise Ann, Charles, and Elle . . .
and to Gerry and Ike—the best of friends in this life, or any other

ACKNOWLEDGMENTS

The author would like to thank Dr. Karen Ross, Herbert Erwin, Gerrie Singer, Robert Aberdeen, Lisa Cordon, Dr. Alfredo Suarez, Bill Troy, Stirling and Migo Nagura, David Spiess, Dr. Hugh W. Buckingham, Rabbi Barry L. Weinstein, Jim Churchman, Chuck Farrier, and others who helped lend an air of authenticity to James Sakura's fictional world. Any errors or creative interpretations are the author's.

Thanks also to Mel Berger of William Morris and his assistant Donna, and to editors Jackie Joiner and Colin Fox. A special thanks to Barbara Alpert for helping to make it all happen.

A CRUEL SEASON *for* DYING

PROLOGUE

The man's ear, an inch above the chest, listened for the silence. No
breath. No beat of heart. His mouth longed to suck up the brilliant
light now seeping from the pores. Passing from his too human vision.
A firefly pinched between the fingers of God.

There was a reverence in the manner in which he cleansed the body.
And a meticulousness—depositing the soiled toweling and alcohol
wipes into the garbage bag he'd packed. Rolling and safeguarding the
Visqueen that had lain beneath the body.

Now he straddled the waist, pulling the torso up toward him,
angling the pale shoulder into his chest. In death there was a kind of
clumsy resistance that made his work difficult, though not unmanage-
able. Carefully he rotated the torso farther to the side so that hips and
legs remained parallel, the head in profile.

The scalpel slipped easily into flesh as though through softening
butter. There was no blood. The time of bleeding had passed. He
inserted his latexed fingers into the deep pocket he'd made, severing
more cleanly skin from muscle. The wound was precisely under the
shelter of shoulder blade.

Twisting the body to the opposite side, he made an identical incision. He bent the torso forward, head to knees, and slowly inserted the
sharp projections of cartilage into the open slits, careful not to damage
the tissue. Cradling the juncture of flesh and feather, he released the
body back, flat against the bed. Arranged the arms and hands.

He got up from the bed and retrieved the camera, loading a fresh
roll of film. Through the Nocta's lens the body seemed satisfy-
ingly less human. He snapped the first photograph. The split-second
illumination from the flash burned the white skin whiter, made the
dark recesses of the body blacker. He focused on a crevice, the point

where armpit fit chest. *Click*. Then down the long thin line of shadow tucked from groin to ankle. *Click*.

He danced at the foot of the bed, moving from one side to the other. Clicking, clicking in rapid-fire succession, shots from a gun, the artificial explosions from his camera mimicking the natural explosions of dry lightning jumping through the uncurtained window. *Big light. Little light*. The whole of the room emitting a kind of cosmic warning signal.

CHAPTER

1

In the beginner's mind there are many possibilities, but in the expert's mind there are few. Driving through dark streets to the scene of murder, Detective Lieutenant James Sakura repeated the words to himself, an important reminder of weakness as well as virtue.

If not for his special FBI training, he would still be home in bed lying next to Hanae. But on Friday evening he'd been called to the apartment of Luis Carrera, a dancer with the Metropolitan Ballet, who'd been found in circumstances that suggested more than an ordinary murder. Now, less than seventy-two hours later, a second victim had turned up over an art gallery in the East Village. The investigation had been officially transferred from the precincts to his Special Homicide Unit.

At three thirty-seven on a Monday morning, there was relatively little traffic on the Bowery. Sakura raced through intersections, running lights like beads collected on string. When he turned off on St. Marks, homicide and radio cars were already jamming the street. He pulled his own car halfway onto the sidewalk and got out.

The month had been colder and wetter than was normal for October, and tonight's rain waited in an indeterminate sky that seemed to feed on light. Despite the damp chilliness, a collection of street people from the nearby park had gathered at the lines of yellow tape. One of the patrolmen, canvassing for witnesses in the crowd, spotted Sakura and walked over.

"Are you first officer?" Sakura flashed his gold detective's shield.

"No, sir. Frank Kramer's first. He's inside."

Sakura felt relief. Kramer was a good cop, a twenty-year veteran who knew how to protect a crime scene.

Inside the gallery detectives from the local precinct stood talking to the chief of detectives. Lincoln McCauley's presence at the murder scene was an indication of the importance that was being attached to the case. Sakura waited as McCauley detached himself from the group and walked over.

"You made good time." The chief of detectives reached into his pocket for the case that held his cigars. "Crime Scene's still photographing the bedroom."

"Have my people been called?"

"On their way." McCauley parked an unlit cigar securely in his teeth. Put the case back inside his jacket. "Dr. Linsky's been notified too."

Sakura nodded. Linsky had been the medical examiner at the murder scene on Friday. Calling him tonight would insure continuity.

"Have you been upstairs?" he asked McCauley.

"Yeah, Jimmy. I've seen worse. But never anything like this."

Sakura understood. Certain things weren't measured in blood.

＊＊＊

In the bedroom the smell of dead incense was a cloud existing at eye level. It crawled into Sakura's throat, recalling the death scene on Friday, feeding his awareness of what waited for him on the bed. He fought off the image. This room and what it contained had to stand apart. Later, when he could reconstruct every detail in his mind, then the two murder scenes could be compared. By then, anything that was different should shout at him as loudly as that which seemed the same.

The room, apart from the bed, appeared to be, if anything, too normal, without even the usual clutter of cast-off clothes. There was no sign of a struggle. A collection of clay figures stood undisturbed on a shelf. Canvases on the walls hung straight. There was no blood spatter on the rugs or wooden floor. Not a piece of furniture seemed to be out of place.

Sakura turned to the bed. It, too, was neat, seemingly undisturbed by the nude body that lay on top. There was no illusion of sleeping. The man on the bed was dead, with the overwhelming sense of flesh vacated. The arms were arranged, hands crossed over genitals tucked between the legs. The blue eyes, half open, fixed in an expression that Sakura had observed many times. *Of course* was what the eyes seemed to say, as if dying brought the solution to some very simple riddle.

The spent sweet smell of incense was stronger near the bed, concentrated in the charcoal letters scrawled across the wall. The same ashy residue stood out darkly on the victim's chest in a pattern of roughly concentric circles, with other lines coming down.

Sakura moved closer. The bedspread beneath the body was a gray, heavy silk. Against its dull luster, the small blood pools forming beneath the shoulders were nearly invisible. Leaking from incisions cut into the victim's back, the stains were only apparent because he'd known they would be there, overshadowed though they were by the large white wings that stretched across the pillows.

He stared at what had once been human on the bed. For some detectives, the motive in finding the killer was a kind of sanctioned revenge, and Sakura knew veterans who spoke sentimentally of victims in forgotten files who still cried out for justice. For him, it was simpler. Murder, the most heinous of crimes, was the most disruptive of social order. To restore balance, one must find and punish the killer.

Looking at the winged corpse, the indecipherable writing, he suddenly understood what it was about these crime scenes that most unnerved him, what had kept him awake at Hanae's side each night since the first murder. It was not doubt that he could do the job, but a much more primal fear. In the undisturbed room, in the weird and careful ritual, lay a precise if bizarre logic, the signature of a mind that, in its own twisted way, craved order as much as his own.

✺

The living area had the same studied spareness as the bedroom. Artwork dominated. A few large canvases, mostly abstract, arranged on pale glazed walls—collections of small ancient-looking objects on glass and wrought iron tables. The Crime Scene Unit had begun their work in the rest of the upstairs apartment, and fingerprint powder like drifting volcanic ash lay everywhere on the living room's hard surfaces. A single sooty shoe print marred the bleached wool carpet, like an artifact or an omen.

Sakura stood inside the doorway observing the man on the sofa. Jerry Greenberg was, according to Kramer's report, the victim's business partner and lover. He sat hunched forward on the gray leather cushions in a classic pose of mourning, elbows on knees, the heels of his palms pressed hard against his eyelids. He wore jeans and a turtleneck sweater, which showed above the collar of the outdoor jacket he had not taken time to remove. He did not seem aware of the heat in the apartment or that anyone had entered the room. Sakura walked over.

"Mr. Greenberg . . ."

An indistinguishable noise, a simultaneous sucking in of breath and grief, shuddered in the fabric of the jacket as Greenberg pulled himself up, his blond head thrown into relief against the abstract painting behind him. He was thinner than Sakura had first imagined, and the vague slackness of sudden shock made his face appear older than the thirty-six listed in Kramer's report. The pale eyes seemed unnaturally large, as if he had to concentrate to keep them open.

"I'm Lieutenant Sakura, Mr. Greenberg," he introduced himself. "I'm sorry for your loss, but there are questions I have to ask."

Greenberg swallowed once, nodded.

"As I understand it," Sakura began, "you've been away for the last few days. You arrived here from the airport around one forty-five this morning."

"Yes, I've been on a buying trip. I was supposed to fly home tomorrow." Greenberg's voice was unexpectedly deep and resonant. It made his simplest statement sound important. "But I finished up early and managed to get a flight. . . ." The words trailed off.

"What happened when you got here?"

"I came straight up to the bedroom."

"The downstairs door was locked as usual?"

"Yes."

Sakura nodded. As with the Carrera apartment, there had been no sign of forced entry. "So you came upstairs, and you saw Mr. Milne," he prompted.

"Yes," Greenberg said again, "but I couldn't make sense of it. I mean, I didn't even know it was David at first. It wouldn't register. . . . Then I just knew he was dead."

"Do you have any idea who might have done this?"

Greenberg shook his head. He was no longer looking at Sakura.

"Could you have done it?"

The gray eyes flashed upward, indignation penetrating the grief. "What kind of question is that?"

"Direct." Sakura didn't smile.

"I loved David."

"That doesn't disqualify you, Mr. Greenberg."

Greenberg had pushed his hands into the pockets of his jacket. Now one of them came out. "This does." He held up a boarding pass.

Sakura took it, read the time and flight number. "May I keep it?"

"Of course . . . check it out." Greenberg's voice had developed an undertow of belligerence.

Sakura did not react, slipping the boarding pass into his pocket. "Perhaps Mr. Milne invited someone up here this evening," he said.

Greenberg's eyes flashed again, but his answer was calm. "David and I were faithful to each other."

"But you had friends?"

"A lot of them. Everyone loved David." There was no irony in the statement.

Sakura held the man's eyes. "Were you or Mr. Milne, or any of these friends, into any kind of religious or ritualistic . . . activity? Something that could get out of hand?"

Greenberg didn't flinch. "I know no one who could have done *this*."

Sakura let it drop. "We'll want a list of those friends," he said, "as well as lists of your artists and clients. . . . You get a lot of traffic in the gallery?"

"Yes." For the first time Greenberg nearly smiled. "David was a sculptor," he said. "The problem was he had rheumatoid arthritis. He started the gallery when he couldn't continue to work. He liked finding new artists and helping them. Even when our people made it uptown, a lot of them would come back here and do shows for us."

Sakura listened, letting him finish. "I think you would have to agree," he said, "that there is a certain artistic element to what happened in that bedroom. I ask you again. Can you think of anyone who might have done this to Mr. Milne?"

"No." Greenberg was shaking his head violently. "And I find it disgusting that you could call what I saw in there . . . artistic."

Sakura watched him. There was a suggestion of performance in all Greenberg's reactions. The man was very self-aware. It did not follow, however, that the emotions had to be anything less than genuine.

He tried another tack. "Does the name Luis Carrera mean anything to you?"

"No," Greenberg said, looking up again. "Should it?"

Sakura did not answer. The truth was, he'd been hoping for some easy connection between David Milne and Friday night's victim, who'd also been homosexual, but Greenberg's denial seemed real. And with no personal link between the gallery owner and the dancer, it seemed more probable that the killer was targeting gay men at random.

"It's important," he said finally, "that you don't talk to anyone about the details of Mr. Milne's death. Especially anyone from the media."

Greenberg nodded.

"One of my people will drive you to headquarters for a formal statement. You can wait here till we finish; then get whatever you need. The building will have to be sealed for a few days."

Greenberg stared, and Sakura could read in the man's face exactly what he was thinking. That a few days would do nothing to change the enormity of what had happened.

"I'll want to speak with you again," he said, "so make sure we know where you can be reached. If anything occurs to you before then"— he pulled a card from the inside pocket of his jacket—"this has my number. And don't forget what I said about talking to anyone about the details of what happened here tonight. That would damage our chances of finding Mr. Milne's killer, and you could be charged with obstruction of justice for interference in a criminal investigation."

Greenberg's eyes had gone blank again. He took the card without looking. Kept it in his fingers.

At the door Sakura turned back. The man had not changed position. His stricken face, made paler by distance, seemed frozen and flat, floating like an icon on the painted surface behind him.

Beneath the corner of Thirtieth Street and First Avenue was the realm of the dead, the basement morgue that handled Manhattan's homicides. Colder and damper than the outdoor October, the morgue was a fluorescent-lit underworld where toe-tagged bodies waited like hitchhikers along the steel-lockered corridors for attendants who would wheel them into the cutting room. Fortunately for Sakura, the hierarchies of city bureaucracy reached even beyond the grave. Bodies with clout moved to the head of the line.

Still with a weekend between the two murders, Sakura had yet to receive even the most basic toxicological or lab reports. And Saturday's autopsy on Luis Carrera had failed to establish a cause of death. Earlier at the Milne apartment, he had tried to question Linsky, but the medical examiner had remained determinedly closemouthed, deferring any discussion of his findings to this morning's autopsy on the gallery owner.

The procedure had been quickly scheduled, and Linsky, as was his custom, had shunned the protective "bunny suit" for more traditional scrubs and apron. The son of Russian émigrés, the medical examiner possessed the preciseness of an old-world technician. It was not unusual for the apron to remain virtually spotless throughout the most involved procedure. A starched white lab coat would replace it as Linsky exited the swinging metal doors.

The cutting room was silent except for the shuffling of the attendant and Linsky's monotonous droning as he talked through his external examination for the overhead mike. Some medical examiners played taped background music on the theory that sound helped to dampen the brain's response to odor. Linsky took no such mercy. A detective was present to preserve the evidential chain. The smell was part of the job. For the moment Milne's body remained unopened. It lay face-down on the stainless table, the two shoulder wounds like butcher cuts in tallow.

". . . A pair of wounds are present on the posterior chest wall, parallel to the spine and deeply incised into the underlying skeletal muscle." Linsky continued to speak for the microphone. "The incisions are approximately five to six centimeters in length. Margins are sharp and even, suggestive of a small knife or a scalpel-like instrument. Lack of

bleeding into adjacent tissue indicates the injuries were made post-
mortem. Bruising about the mouth and around the ankles and wrists is
consistent with the use of duct tape.

"You seem to have a question, Lieutenant Sakura?" The M.E. had
cut the mike and was looking at him through the plastic visor shield.

"I was wondering about the fingernails," Sakura said.

"The lab work isn't in yet for Carrera. But I saw no obvious skin
fragments beneath his nails or Mr. Milne's here . . . if that's what you're
asking."

"You said that the bruising was consistent with the victims struggling *after* they were bound?"

"Yes . . . after." Linsky's voice betrayed a bit of impatience. "Otherwise, we'd expect to see more bruising or abrasions. On the hands for
instance."

"That's what puzzles me," Sakura said. "Why didn't they struggle
before he taped them? Why just let him do it?"

The medical examiner was notoriously reluctant to speculate. A
moment passed while he appeared to weigh the worth of the question.
"Perhaps these were bondage situations that turned into something
else," he said finally. "Or given that these victims were both relatively
small men, it's possible they felt sufficiently threatened physically that
they just didn't fight. . . . I don't know, Lieutenant."

"Neither do I," Sakura admitted.

He watched as the attendant helped Linsky turn the body. Faceup
again on the table, David Milne was suddenly real, the body somehow
more human than it had appeared last night in the bedroom. Sakura
felt an odd pang of impersonal guilt, as if the indecency of the forensic
procedure and his own silent witness could take as much from the
dead man as the killer.

Milne was small, with that adolescent boniness that Sakura associ-
ated with some gay men. His chest was pale and hairless. The killer's
charcoal drawing stood out below the nipples, more smudged and
faded since last night. Linsky obliterated it further. Pressing with one
hand against the sternum, he began the thoraco-abdominal incision.
First the long shallow curve through the pectorals from one shoulder
blade to the other. Then the straight deep line from breastbone to

pubis. With the Y-shaped cut gaping open, Linsky peeled back flesh and cartilage from the rib cage, then crunched with the cutters through the breastbone to the pale milky sac veiling the organs. Standing behind the medical examiner, Sakura could identify the lungs and liver above the snaky loops of intestine. With the layers coming away, it was easier again to think of Milne as just a body. The smell resisted abstraction.

The process continued. Linsky removed the organ tree, transferring it to a metal sink. He proceeded to extract his samples, inspecting and weighing the organs. Sakura thought the medical examiner looked no more satisfied than he had at Carrera's autopsy. He waited for a moment when the M.E. ceased speaking for the mike.

"You still don't know how they died, do you?" he said.

Linsky turned to him. "No, Lieutenant Sakura, I do not. The needle marks on the arms are suggestive, but on Saturday, when I opened Carrera, I found no damage to the organs. And the basic toxicological screens turned up nothing beyond a common pain medication, an anti-inflammatory, and an antidepressant."

"And Milne . . . ?"

"The organs, as you've heard me say, appear normal."

"You said the needle marks were suggestive—"

Linsky cut off the implied question with a look. "It is my intention," he said, "to push through a much wider range of tests on blood and tissue samples from both victims."

"When?" Sakura asked.

"As soon as possible, Lieutenant. I don't like mysteries any better than you do."

✤

In Kyoto the Japanese instinct for elegance and restraint had been tempered by the realities of day-to-day living in the simple home of Hanae's parents. The cages of their daughter's finches had shared space with the family, bedding and clothing stored beneath the raised *tatami* floor, a large *tansu* holding most of the family's smaller treasures. Rooms were created with screens that could easily be moved. And though Hanae's marriage had taken her from one crowded island to another,

James Sakura had made a promise not to deny his wife when she'd asked to bring her birds.

Since he had come home, Sakura had spoken little more than a dozen words to Hanae; they had not touched. The touching would come later when they drew back the *tsutsugaki,* the quilt cover that was a wedding gift from Hanae's parents, and lay together for the night. For now, he was taking immense pleasure in sitting on the *tatami* rug of their living room and watching his wife move from one cage to another. When he was working on a major case, the birds, as well as Taiko her dog, kept as irregular hours as he and Hanae.

She reached and closed the last of the cages that held her beloved finches. He watched her place a seed in her mouth and move her face against the metal cage. *Tee-tee-tee.* She made a kind of trumpeting sound, and the dominant bird came closer to pluck the seed from between her teeth. Then she walked over to a worktable and removed a cloth shrouding a mass of clay.

At first her fingers moved lightly over the surface of the bulky shape. Then they constricted, working the mass deliberately. The arms that slipped from her kimono sleeves appeared startlingly naked, and Sakura thought that the flat of his wife's hands seemed too plump and childish for her slim delicate fingers.

"You and Taiko should find other work," she said without turning.

"We enjoy watching you." He reached to scratch behind the dog's ears.

"And what do you see?"

"That your fingers are too long for your hands."

"And . . . ?" She turned then, fixing him with her sightless eyes.

"That my wife is naked beneath her kimono."

"Japanese men do not lust after their wives."

"I'm American."

At this Hanae laughed. "You are right. Sometimes I think that except for your thin face and lidless eyes, there is little of your Japanese ancestors in you." She returned to her modeling, the light from the *chochin* reflecting in the blackness of her hair.

"Did you go to art class this afternoon?"

"Yes, I'm still working on the birds. Ms. Nguyen is a very patient teacher."

"What is *this* you're sculpting?"

"I am not sure. My hands will tell me when they are ready."

He knew it was a lie. The bust was going to be a surprise for Christmas. He could recognize his features already forming in the crude mass.

She moved her fingers deeper into the moist clay. "Vicky called today."

"And how do they like Minneapolis?"

"She said it is not Manhattan."

"Not a very good review," he said. "You're going to miss her, aren't you?"

She nodded. "I've never had a friend like Victoria."

"You'll find someone else."

She shrugged. "I have a lot to keep me busy."

"I can see that." He stood and walked behind her, his hands resting on her shoulders, his thumbs finding the nape of her neck. "It looks like a head."

"It will be." She let her hands fall into her lap. "How is your investigation going?"

Despite his efforts, she had sensed his mood. "This appears to be a serial case," he answered. "They are always difficult."

She dipped her hands in the bowl of water, then wiped them with the towel. "Have you spoken to Kenjin?" She turned her face up to him.

The question had surprised him. A moment passed when even his breath was silent. "No," he said. "I haven't talked to Michael for a while."

"I think this time you may need him."

"He won't come back, Hanae."

"But it is not impossible?"

"Michael was cleared of any wrongdoing. It was his decision to resign."

She pulled him down to her, taking his face in her hands. "Tell me about that night."

He had no wish to reopen the wounds that had scarred, if not healed, in the time that had passed. But his wife's instincts were a deep, slow-stirring sea. He did not question the tides that moved her.

"A suspect was killed," he said to her.

"This much I know, Jimmy." She waited.

"The suspect didn't have a weapon," he said finally.

She sighed, as if the knowledge were a release. "But Kenjin shot him."

"Michael thought the man was firing at us," he explained. "He believed he saw a powder flash."

"What happened?"

"Backup arrived. Barney Edleman saw right away we had a bad shooting. He pulled out a drop piece he had under the seat of the patrol car."

"A drop piece?"

"A gun that couldn't be traced. Michael said no. But Edleman said he was crazy, throwing away his career for someone like Robby Hudson."

"What did you say?"

"Nothing. I watched Edleman wrap Hudson's hand around the grip, then wipe his own prints off the barrel before he tossed it in some trash. The report read that the weapon was found in the search, that the suspect must have dropped it as he fell."

"Kenjin allowed this?"

"I was the officer of record. It was my name on the report."

The pressure of her fingers softened on his cheeks. "And Kenjin resigned."

He shook his head. "It was a couple months later that the offer came for me to attend the program at Quantico. That was when Michael resigned."

"Because you accepted?"

"Because Michael was afraid I wouldn't. I had lied to keep him on the force. He would never resign as long as I was there. And he knew I understood that."

Her hands still cupped his face. He reached for them, took them into his. "Michael changed after the shooting, Hanae. He didn't trust himself. He was trying to regain his balance."

"He was depending on you."

"Yes. But I failed him. My lie betrayed him more than the truth."

"The guilt you feel is foolish, my husband. As is your anger. You chose once for Kenjin. In the end he chose for himself."

"I didn't like what I did. I still don't. But Michael was a good detective. He should have remained on the force."

"Your faith in him was greater than his own. But time has passed," she said. "Will you ask him to return?"

His wife's commands, ever gentle, rested in the guise of questions.

☗

Father Andrew Kellog measured an extra finger of bourbon into his glass and walked to the parlor window that gave a view to the street. He had thought he'd heard Father Graff's Jeep, but pulling back the curtain, he could see nothing outside but the dark and silent patch of failing neighborhood. The black pane of glass breathed coldness, and he stepped back, pulling the robe tighter around him in the under-heated room. The living quarters at St. Sebastian were as old and unre-modeled as the church itself. And while a lack of change might be deemed a virtue in a building that mimicked twelfth-century Gothic, for the two priests assigned to the outmoded Brooklyn rectory, the neglect meant mostly discomfort.

He took a sip of the drink, then shuffled like the old man he was becoming to the recliner in front of the TV. He should be thankful for the archdiocesan attention, which the younger priest's assignment to St. Sebastian represented. But charity was in as short supply as faith and hope in his heart—virtues lost not through some brave battle with temptation, but drained away softly in the acid rain of years. Was it the world that had changed, or had he? Was it time or the devil that had curdled his soul?

As always, he regretted the bitterness of his thoughts, and in all his more honest moments, he acknowledged that he was not cut out to be a pastor, and in the old days never would have been one. Now, with the shortage of priests, men more than twenty years younger than he were getting their own parishes, better and richer parishes than St. Sebastian. Thomas Graff, he knew, would be presented just such a plum for his work in parish renewal.

He reached down to the space heater and turned up the dial, welcoming the warm blast of air on his feet. On the television the news had ended, and a cop show, decades old, was playing. The violence seemed stilted, infinitely less real than the daily dramas that played in

the nearby streets. He keyed in the time on the remote: *11:52* in glowing blue-green appeared in the corner of the screen. Surely, Father
Graff had not forgotten that it was his turn for early Mass tomorrow.

He frowned, sipping again at the drink, allowing a memory of the
old days when the church had been full. Perhaps the chronic bad
weather had something to do with it, but even with all Graff's efforts
there seemed to be fewer and fewer people scattered in the pews.
Though Marian's husband, of all people, had been there this morning.

Light rose and skittered across the curtains. This time, unmistak-
ably, he heard the sounds of the Jeep. In a few moments Thomas Graff
came into the foyer. Despite the cold, he wore no coat over athletic
pants and jacket. He looked boyish with his duffel bag and the baseball cap riding his fair hair. With a pang of what he acknowledged as
jealousy, Father Kellog thought of how quickly the women, young and
old, had taken to Father Graff.

He watched the man take off his cap as he came into the room. The
priest greeted him and smiled.

"Cold out?" Kellog sought conversation.

"Pretty cold." Graff nodded. "Mrs. Callahan thinks it'll snow before
Christmas." He was unfailingly pleasant. A subtle condescension.

"You saw Mrs. Callahan?"

"Her daughter asked me to drop by and bring her Communion. I visited a friend after that." Graff looked at his watch. "Later than I
thought," he said. "Mass tomorrow. I better get some sleep."

Father Kellog nodded his good-night, watching as the younger man
bounded up the stairs. Thomas Graff was not quite as youthful as he
appeared, but he kept fit, running most mornings he didn't say Mass.

The hall clock struck midnight. The deep chimes seemed incomplete and ominous. He looked down into his drink, finished it. He
picked up the remote, settling back in his chair. Flipping through the
channels, he searched for a movie in black and white, putting off bed
and the silence of his cold room.

CHAPTER

2

Sleep fell away like leaden weight. Sakura's eyes snapped opened. 5:47 in the morning. He reached to switch off the alarm before it sounded, and settled back down under the sheets. Turning toward Hanae, he saw that against the stark white of the pillow, her black hair spread like fine dark silk. He bent and kissed it, inhaling its scent. Rain. Not city rain. But the rainfall of his childhood near the sea.

Slowly he lifted the covers and sat up, swinging his feet to the *tatami*-covered floor. Standing, he caught his reflection across the room. The watery gray light drained the remaining color from his already too pale skin. He moved his hand down his chest, loosening his pajama bottoms. His naked image always surprised him.

He remembered another day, another reflection. He had been visiting his Kyoto cousins; his uncle Ikenobo, a Shinto priest, had traveled from Nagasaki. It was early spring and his uncle wanted him to make a pilgrimage to Fushimi Inari with him. Thousands of vermilion-colored stone *torii* marked the path as they climbed up the steep mountain to the shrine. It was a difficult journey, but he wanted to please his uncle and was anxious to offer prayer at the holy place. However, when they neared the summit, he became both confused and disappointed. Beyond a single large *torii*, there was nothing at the mountaintop but a pile of stones. He searched his uncle's face, but it was empty of all expression, as fixed as the stones before him.

He moved closer. A glint of pale sunlight flickered in his eye. Resting at the center of the stones was a mirror, reflecting blue sky, the green edges of trees, clouds moving as in a dream. A single bird soared across the silver glass. Again he looked at his uncle, who had waited below. Their eyes met. Then his uncle raised his hands to his chest, made three quick claps—*kashiwade,* the highest sign of respect at a Shinto shrine.

With the sharp explosions still ringing in his ear, he understood why Uncle Ikenobo had led him to Fushimi Inari. Shinto was more than worship or ritual. It was experiencing the universe itself. He bent over then, examining his eight-year-old face in the round mirror. And this, too, he had understood.

The day he had earned his gold shield as an NYPD homicide detective, he received a letter from his uncle Ikenobo. His uncle wrote of *honne,* one's true intentions, and *tatemae,* expected behavior. He prayed his nephew would always know the difference, and hoped that the two would not often be at war. As he had shifted the pages, a *konusa* leaf fell to the floor. The leaf had been used by his uncle to scatter drops of water to dispel *tsumi*—impurities of wounds, blood, death—an inevitable part of his job as a police officer.

Yet he knew his uncle understood the other reality of his job. The reality that had made him ultimately choose police work—his need to restore order to the universe. To create harmony out of chaos. This principle of renewal was as much a part of Shinto as avoidance of *tsumi.* Had not this concept of restoration been the driving force that had led his uncle as a young monk to Suwa Jinja? The ancient shrine with its hundred-year-old gates and sanctuaries, with its clear stream and sacred grove of trees, had been for the burned bodies and scorched souls of the people of Nagasaki a place of purification after the horrors of the bomb. His uncle had embraced the impurities of war in order to reconcile human existence with the changing world. He believed this letter had been Uncle Ikenobo's way of letting him know he understood why he had chosen the life of a cop.

In the mirror he saw that Hanae had awakened and was smiling. "You look like a cat with a belly full of cream."

"I am satisfied."

He walked toward the bed, climbing back under the covers. "And why are you so satisfied, Wife?"

She reached up and pulled his face close to hers. "Because my husband is such a good lover."

He laughed. "You're a wicked woman."

"The alarm has not gone off."

"I shut it off. It's already after six."

Her lips closed over his, her tongue slipping easily inside his mouth. "My husband will be late this morning."

The apartment in SoHo was tiny. Detective Walter Talbot sat forward on the lumpy sofa, trying to visualize that the person standing in front of him had killed two men. But the image wouldn't hold. In part because the twentysomething dancer had sad, innocent eyes. But mostly because he had a reasonable alibi.

Philippe Lambert, who shared this dinky walk-up with three other dancers, claimed to have stayed late in the theater after a performance on the night Carrera had died; he returned to his apartment with two of his roommates immediately afterward. Of course, it was a fool who said you could tell a killer by his eyes. And alibis, like promises, were made to be broken.

"I want to help," the dancer was saying. He was pacing in the small space that served as living room and kitchen. "It's just that I answered all these questions in my statement."

"As I explained on the phone, Mr. Lambert, jurisdiction in this case has been transferred to a Special Homicide Unit. We're reinterviewing everybody involved in this case."

Some of the tension seemed to drain out of the dancer. He sat down in a peeling chair. One of two that matched the table. A fifties dinette set in gray and blue. On top sat a carved jack-o'-lantern.

"Let me summarize," Talbot picked up the thread. "You said Mr. Carrera had not felt well, that he called Thursday morning to say he wouldn't be coming in to the studio, or attending the performance that evening. Then when you couldn't reach him all the next day, you went to check at his apartment."

The brown eyes closed shut. "It was horrible."

"How did you get in?"

"I have a key."

"You found no evidence of forced entry?"

"No." The eyes went wide.

"That suggests that Mr. Carrera knew his killer, or invited him in. Do you have any idea if he might have been expecting anyone that Friday?"

"No. Most everybody was at the performance."

"Who was he seeing socially?"

"You mean, who was he sleeping with?"

"Yes."

"He was sleeping with me."

"Only with you?" He watched carefully for the reaction.

"I believe so," Lambert said easily enough. "Luis was not promiscuous."

"Does the name David Milne mean anything to you?"

"I don't think so. . . . Is he a dancer?"

"Mr. Milne owned an art gallery in the East Village."

"You're talking about that other guy who was murdered?" Lambert caught on quick. "Are you saying he was killed . . . like Luis?"

"I haven't said that at all, Mr. Lambert. And repeating that kind of rumor could be considered interference with a police investigation. You understand?"

"Sure." The eyes said he was shaken.

"You have no idea who killed Mr. Carrera?"

"No."

"He didn't mention anyone new? Someone he'd just met, perhaps?"

"No, he didn't. The truth is, Luis was becoming more and more isolated."

"Why was that?"

"He could get pretty depressed. Luis was a huge star before he injured his back. You know his history?"

"I know he defected from Cuba."

"Luis came here as part of an international troupe—the hottest thing going in the Cuban National Ballet. Castro caused a big stink when the State Department gave him asylum. Luis had been trained by the Russians. Was supposed to be the next Baryshnikov."

"And was he?"

"Yes, until the injury. Lumbar compression. He couldn't do the lifts. Of course, the good side of his not being able to dance the major roles was that he threw himself into teaching the younger dancers in the company. Helping people like me."

"So, he was liked by the younger dancers."

"By everyone in the company. And that's really saying something."

"Why?"

"The company is a very small world, Detective Talbot. You're together all the time. There are a lot of petty jealousies."

"But not with Mr. Carrera?"

"I guess there might have been a lot of envy at the beginning. But not later."

"Still, he must have had *some* enemies."

Lambert sighed. "Well, there was one person that Luis had a problem with. You could almost call it a feud. But it wasn't serious."

"I'd still like to hear about it."

"At the end of last season"—Lambert relaxed in the chair—"I got my first solo. I think Luis was more excited than I was. He wanted everything to be perfect."

"But it wasn't?"

"Andrea . . . she's one of the wardrobe assistants. Sometimes she likes to monkey around with the costumes. Just some little change here or there. Nobody cares that much. But it always drove Luis crazy, her 'fixing' things in the middle of a run. It was a superstition with him. He thought it was bad luck."

"And this Andrea 'fixed' something during your performance?"

"Opening night. She changed the drape on my tunic. There was so much tension already. Luis chewed her out good. He could have a real Latin temper sometimes. But by the next day, he'd always forget he'd been angry."

"But this time was different?"

"Not for Luis," Lambert said, "but Andrea got into a real snit. She put a dead chicken in his dressing room."

"Are you talking voodoo?"

"Santeria. Andrea liked to rag Luis about being Latino . . . a peasant. Andrea claims she's descended from the czars."

"And how did Mr. Carrera react . . . to the chicken?"

"He said he'd left Cuba to get away from that shit. Told her to leave him alone."

"Was that the end of it?"

Lambert shook his head. "Andrea was enjoying it too much. She made a sort of altar near the dressing rooms—candles and stuff, scraps of fabric that could have been from Luis's old costumes. She was playing with his head."

"And Luis?"

"He made a point of ignoring it. But I know it got under his skin. He didn't need any more bad luck. He seemed more depressed after that."

"Because of what she was doing?"

Lambert sighed. "No. I think it just finally came home to him that his back wasn't going to get any better. That he was never going to make it back to the top." He looked away for a moment. "To tell you the truth, Detective Talbot," he said finally, "when Luis didn't answer the phone that day, I was afraid he might have killed himself."

⁂

Talbot walked up a back stairway to an old section of the building. The floorboards cracked under his feet like kindling. It seemed the annex was not used much except for storage. Perfect domain for the colorful costume mistress to hold court in its dingy corridors. Philippe Lambert had told him the woman's eccentricities were tolerated because she was one of the best in the business.

He knocked on the door. From inside he could hear music. Something sultry and thrumming. He knew enough to tell that the lyrics were in Portuguese. He knocked again. Harder. The singer sang on. He reached and twisted the doorknob.

The room was a carnival sideshow. Christmas lights were strung across the ceiling and along the seams of the walls. An assortment of old dolls crowded the seat of a battered wicker chair. The mummified remains of a small monkey swung from a tasseled cord; he thought of *Sunset Boulevard* and Gloria Swanson. The monkey shivered at the end of the rope, and the Portuguese chanteuse sang on.

"Like Latin music?" The voice was deep.

He turned. She was at least six feet tall and too old to have blond pageboy hair. This time Veronica Lake came to mind. The hair, not the face. This face was hard and almost ugly. One hand was on a hip; the other rested on a chaise. It was an orchestrated pose.

"I don't know much about it." He drew out his detective's shield.

"I could teach you." She smiled, showing off remarkably pretty teeth, taking his badge into a large hand with bloodred nails. She dropped her eyes and examined his identification. The false eyelashes were impossibly long. She glanced up. "What can I do for you, Detective?"

"I'm investigating the death of Luis Carrera."

She shrugged her shoulders. "Sad thing about our little Cuban."

"I've been told that you and Mr. Carrera had difficulties."

She laughed. Too loud. "That's a nice way to put it. He hated me. Though, I rather liked Luis. Despite his age, he still had the tightest ass in the company."

She moved for the first time and he noticed she walked with a limp. She bent, tossing several pillows off the chaise. "Here, take a load off your feet," she said, heading for the straight-back chair in front of a vanity table, settling in her length. "Got that thing for looks. If I get in, I can't get out."

He obliged her, sitting on the edge of the lounger. "What was the nature of the problem between you and Mr. Carrera?"

"Mr. Carrera?" She laughed, checking herself in the mirror. She turned back around. "Fidel had a fit when the Pope visited Cuba. He hates the Church. Doesn't like competition from God. Or his saints." She winked. "Ever hear of Santeria? It's a mix of voodoo and Catholic."

"I've read something about it." He played along.

"I'll bet you do a lot of reading, Detective Talbot. You look like the studious type."

This time he smiled.

"A lot of Cubans practice Santeria. But the way I see it, if it worked, they'd have gotten rid of Castro's ass."

"Did Luis practice Santeria?"

"Fuck no. Luis didn't believe in anything but ballet. But that didn't mean I couldn't have a little fun with him." She took up one of the bottles from the dressing table.

"Luis had a boy toy. His protégé." She arched her penciled brows. "After the back trouble, Luis took Philippe Lambert under his wing." She winked again. "And bingo, Philippe gets to solo one night last season. I don't even think it was a full ballet. I can't remember anymore. But the upshot was that Philippe had a less than stellar performance, and Luis had to blame somebody. He picked *moi*. Claimed I screwed up Philippe's costume."

"I've heard you like to make certain creative alterations."

"I'm a frustrated costume designer. But blaming me for Philippe's crappy debut was a crock. The kid was just plain scared. And it wasn't like his career was ruined."

"What happened?"

"I was halfway pissed and decided to play a little joke on Luis. I put a dead chicken in his dressing room. I didn't know he'd go ballistic." She looked down at her hand still holding the perfume bottle, twisted a ring on an index finger. "I didn't know he was going to turn up dead."

"Did you kill him?"

She shook her head and lifted her long skirt. There was no attempt at realism. The knee joint and calf were no more than metal braces, nuts, and bolts, adjoined to a laced-up orthopedic shoe. The whole device was attached to the stump of a thigh by leather straps. "I don't do much dancing myself." The laughter was false.

He waited a moment and forced his eyes away from the thickly muscled good leg. He noticed it was shaved clean under the sheer stocking. "Where were you the night Luis was murdered?"

She turned to a CD player in the corner. The music had stopped. "An alibi?" She met his eyes. "After the performance I went out with a couple of friends. Drank some red wine, smoked a little dope. I didn't get home till almost four in the morning. I can give you names."

He nodded.

"The truth is, Detective Talbot, the only thing I ever wanted to do to Luis Carrera was fuck him. But you can see I have another problem." She raised the knit skirt higher so that he could see the outline of a penis, a spongy sac of testicles beneath sheer panties. "Since the accident the dick doesn't work much better than the leg."

⁕

The damp October wind sneaked in every time the doors of St. Sebastian's parish hall were opened, sending shivers up and down everyone's spine, teasing the Japanese lanterns into a ghostly dance. An unplanned, though not an entirely unwelcome, effect at a Halloween party.

Trick-or-treating wasn't what it used to be, and most of the parishioners had jumped at Father Graff's suggestion that the parish host an old-fashioned party to keep the kids off the streets. It was the priest's favorite holiday, he had to admit, after Christmas, of course. In a frenzy of activity, he had resurrected some vintage decorations from an old storeroom—papier-mâché jack-o'-lanterns, die-cut witches on brooms, grinning black cats with honeycomb legs, and yards of crepe paper streamers—conceding to the giddy ladies who'd helped him that everything was a bit faded and ruined. But didn't it all contribute to the general atmosphere of spookiness?

A couple of galvanized tubs of water held crisp red apples ready for bobbing, and a huge, jaunty scarecrow admonished all who entered:

> Quickly don your mummer's suit
> When the horned owl begins to hoot.
> Steal softly out and don't be late
> For Hallowe'en seals your fate.

Father Kellog lifted his smiling devil's mask to the top of his head. The mask, his singular concession to wearing a costume, somehow didn't seem incompatible with his long black cassock. He glanced around the hall. There were more parishioners here than he'd seen at Mass in months. He checked his watch.

"Did you expect him to be on time?" Agnes Tuminello had come up beside him and set down a tray of sandwiches. She noted the dripping candles and decided the plastic tablecloth would have to be sacrificed after tonight.

"Yes, I did expect him to be on time." He fought to keep an edge of anger out of his voice. "This Halloween party was his idea."

"I'm sure he's at His Eminence's kissing his ring."

His instincts told him Graff was more than likely kissing something else of the Cardinal's. "He better show. I'm too old for this sort of thing."

The housekeeper rolled her kohl-lined eyes. Mrs. Tuminello had grudgingly settled on a fortune teller's disguise, but was now pulling off one of her gold-coin earrings. The costume was for the children, not for Graff, she reminded herself again. "Have you eaten?"

"Not hungry," he said, distracted by a small scene playing itself out in one of the ancient hall's dark corners. The usually reserved Dominick Mancuso appeared to be arguing with his wife. His arm rose and fell in a kind of restrained anger, his head shaking in mute protest. It was a strangely cinematic moment.

🔱

Eight-year-old Lucia Mancuso threw back her head provocatively and laughed. The sound of a tiny crystal bell. She struck another pose and the camera clicked. *Magic child.* He breathed the words to himself. *Magic child* . . . The flash exploded, bleaching the tableau for an instant of all color.

Outside the lens she fell in and out of focus, and Tony Paladino felt faintly light-headed, a fire growing in his belly as if he'd taken a shot of whiskey. He grasped the edge of a folding chair, fighting the electric buzz in his ears. There was an astringent taste at the back of his throat.

Lucia was moving again, coquettishly twisting her body in her bright red-and-black ladybug costume. Her homemade antennae waved like small arms from atop her dark head.

"Like this, Uncle Tony?"

"What?"

She put her hands on her hips and scowled. "You weren't paying any attention."

"Yes, I was, Lucia. Do just what you were doing."

She gave him an exasperated look, then struck her pose.

"Good girl." *Click.*

"You know, Uncle Tony, Daddy says I'm not supposed to be alone with you. Or let you touch me."

He lowered the camera. "Your father never liked me, Lucia. He never wanted me to marry your aunt Barbara. I wasn't good enough for his baby sister."

"But I like you, Uncle Tony."

He smiled. "And I like you, Lucia."

He began raising his camera again, but didn't complete the motion. An iron hand grasped his shoulder, pulling him away from Lucia, out of the church hall, down the steps, onto the street.

In the haze of moonlight, Dominick Mancuso looked ugly. Bigger than he was. Less human. In fact, there was a rawness about everything. When Tony reached to unlock his brother-in-law's grip, he half expected to encounter a large hairy paw. He felt flesh.

"You"—the hand that had been on his shoulder now pointed a finger at him—"do not touch my Lucia."

"For God's sake, I was taking her picture."

"I don't want you near her or Celia. *Capisce,* Antonio?"

"I *capisce.*" He shook his head, walked a few paces away so that he stood directly under one of the streetlamps. "Barbara is crazy. And if you and Sophia believe that shit she told you, you're crazy too."

"Just stay away from my girls."

"I'm still married to your sister."

"That I don't understand."

He laughed. "She can't get enough of my cock."

This time Dominick's hand did feel like an animal's. Hard and angry, it drove into his jaw until he tasted blood. He reeled backward from the blow, but he caught himself before he could fall. Through what seemed like smoke, he watched his brother-in-law turn and move up the stairs, back into the church hall.

For a moment he stared at the black blank expanse of closed doors. Then his vision cleared and he looked to his feet. He kicked a small rock across the wet pavement, waiting for the sound of its landing. He loosened his hold on his camera's leather strap around his neck and stroked his jawline. It was sore, but there was also a slight fleshiness that had not been there six months ago. He was getting soft. He needed to start hitting the weights harder. Tighten up. Ease some of the tension.

He took out a handkerchief and spat, rubbing away a small drool of blood from his chin. Raking his hand through his hair, he straightened himself. Barbara would become suspicious, think that something was wrong if he didn't get back in there with her and his kids, at least for a little while longer. Whatever the cost, he needed to keep Barbara happy.

⁂

The West Side bistro was as bright and artificial as a hothouse, a jewel box that glittered on the wet uptown sidewalk. The man sat inside, alone at a window table. Ghosts from his coffee shivered in the black wall of glass as he drank from his cup, staring past his reflection to the apartment building on the other side of the street. The building's glassed-in foyer was another lighted box. Behind its double doors Geoffrey Westlake stood, backlit by the yellow glow from the lobby.

A taxi pulled to the curb. The man watched the figure push out into the night and walk down the few steps to the pavement. For a moment before Westlake ducked into the cab, he was completely visible in his own amazing light, which poured out from him like a beacon.

The taxi drove away, and the man set down his cup. He was acutely aware of the pressure of the leather straps, the feel of what they held against his back. Once thawed, ligament, skin, and muscle had begun the inevitable process of decay. With his heightened senses he could smell the soft beginnings of rot that seeped above the collar of his jacket.

Droplets of rain had gathered on the window. They crawled past his face in black centipede tracks. He picked up the cup again, wishing instead for the cigarettes he'd given up since the accident. He acknowledged the human craving before he banished it. Eyes closed, he willed himself to relax. There was risk involved in the plan tonight, but no special need to hurry. He'd been watching Westlake long enough to guess where he would go.

He threw a couple bills on the table and left, walking the blocks to where he'd found a space for the bike. The Harley from day one had been a good investment. In the rain-soaked streets, it gave him an added maneuverability.

When he arrived, Marlowe's was relatively uncrowded, despite that it was Halloween, and he stood exposed for a moment inside the door.

Geoffrey Westlake was here as he'd expected. Normally, the model chose a conspicuous table, but tonight, for the first time, he sat drinking alone at the shadowed side of the bar, the light from him burning into the dimness.

In the instant he'd made the decision to remain, Westlake turned toward him, watching his approach, as if, despite the months of careful invisibility, they were suddenly working some mutual radar.

"Hi," Westlake said as he slid onto the stool next to him. "Haven't seen you around."

"I haven't been around." The lie came easily. "But I recognize you from your commercials. You do nice work."

Westlake's eyes went down to the camera bag he'd set on the floor. "You a photographer?" He looked up. "I could use some new publicity stills."

"Anytime." He made the word an obvious invitation.

Geoffrey Westlake smiled back and killed the remainder of his drink.

⁊

"Gad-ri-el." He spoke the syllables separately and distinctly, gathering his focus. It still amazed him how vibrations made in air could so nearly capture essence. But his name had been the first thing to come back to him that night, when the world had cracked like an egg. And he had remembered.

"Gadriel." For a moment the grief and the loneliness he had felt that night returned, and he was there again, trapped within the blackness of the tunnel. He pushed away the despair. "Gadriel." His name three times spoken, transforming him, grounding him in the present reality of black ceramic tile and gleaming fixtures.

He looked around the bathroom. The sublet was as posh as Westlake had bragged, the bath as large as some entire city apartments. He sat down on the sleek toilet and took off his cap and shoes. Grabbed a towel from the warming rack and spread it out over the floor. Standing in its center, he removed the rest of his clothes, rolling them into tight tubes that he stuffed into the camera bag along with his other things.

He turned toward his image in the mirrored wall, the reflection of his human shell at once alien and familiar. Tall and naturally thin, he would appear ectomorphic to anyone seeing him with clothes. Actually, he was well muscled and fit again after the long months of rehabilitation. Before going out tonight, he had once again shaved his armpits, chest, and pubis. And standing completely still, his nude body in its leather harness seemed as perfect and white as marble against the backdrop of black tile.

He walked closer to the glass, running his hands over the hair he had lacquered against his skull. Light streamed through his pores, nearly obscuring his features.

"Trick or treat." Westlake's amused voice came from the other side of the door. "I've got your drink out here."

He said nothing. But stepped aside, and carefully picking up the towel like an inverted tent, he shook out over the bowl any fibers that might have come from his clothes. He flushed, watching the water spiral down.

He had been careful to touch nothing in the room, and now he put on the latex gloves. Much later, with his shoes on again, he would wipe the tile floor of any footprints. He stooped down to the camera bag, unzipping another compartment. When he rose, the gas mask was on his face. Even to his own eyes, he looked like a monster in the mirror.

CHAPTER

3

Avoiding the elevators, which were always slow and crowded, Sakura walked down the hallway from the chief of detectives' office to the stairwell. Let the door suck closed behind him like an air lock.

His meeting this morning with Lincoln McCauley had gone as well as could be expected, given the atmosphere of official panic that always developed around this kind of case. This morning's *Post* story had not helped with its lurid speculation that a new serial killer might be preying on the city's gay population. Worse, it was obvious that the leaks had begun. He had to expect that the press would put two and two together, but the *Post* article had gone way beyond what could be gleaned from public record. Witnesses, such as Greenberg and Lambert, had apparently begun to talk. Or his own people. When the precinct detectives working the Carrera and Milne murders had been subsumed under the Special Homicide Unit, he had given them all the usual speech about leaks. But it was nearly impossible with the number of people involved to keep a case with this sort of media appeal completely under wraps.

Serial murder, even in this city, became a tribal thing, a public airing of primitive emotion. What he feared was the kind of media circus that had surrounded "Son of Sam." Even when there was nothing happening in the case, the New York media had hyped the story for ratings, virtually assuring that the killer would strike again. The papers had generated a kind of mass hysteria that had fed on itself, affecting everyone's judgment, including that of the police.

If Carrera and Milne were simply the beginning, if bodies continued to turn up, then sooner or later the most sensational details would leak. And then no rational explanation of the difficulties involved would suffice to explain a lack of progress. For the moment at least, he could count on the chief of detectives. But if a scapegoat became necessary, McCauley would not have the slightest hesitation in cutting him loose. They would prosper together, or Sakura would sink alone.

Not that he had any intention to sink. Pressure from the top was part of the job. He could handle it. What he hated was failure, and having to face that the odds of his failing were high. His training had prepared him to understand how difficult it was to solve a case where the victims were chosen at random and the murders motiveless in any ordinary sense. With little physical evidence and no witnesses, he had almost nothing that could lead him to the killer. The ritual element of these deaths was the strongest thing he had to go on—a window on the landscape of the killer's obsession.

This killer's ritual struck him as something . . . *personal* was the only word he had for it. But a serial almost never murdered people he knew. His victims were not subjects but faceless objects to be slotted anonymously into the fantasy that was driving him. The fantasy was what substituted for motive. So it was the fantasy that he must try to understand. He had to feel his way into the killer's brain.

His people, meanwhile, were going through the mechanics of canvasses and interviews. They would check out all the religious cults and hate groups that targeted gays, along with the recent releases from mental institutions. A waste of time and manpower in his estimation. This killer was a loner, not the member of any group. And too organized to be crazy—at least in a legal sense.

What he would have to consider was going proactive, especially when they'd worked up a profile. There was no doubt that many serials monitored their cases in the media and often liked to insinuate themselves into the investigation. The outrage that was already building in the gay community might be used to construct a trap, a series of police meetings with various interest groups where the killer might show up. A signature on a petition list might ultimately be cross-linked with other information that developed.

On the landing below him, a door opened. Footsteps went clambering down the metal stairs. He waited for a moment, then followed them downward. At the eleventh floor he stopped, passing through the door to the brick-lined hallway that led to the Special Investigation Division and the controlled chaos that waited inside Major Case. In the squad room he signed out, picking up the keys to his department car. There was time to check in quickly with his unit before heading out to his appointment at the university.

Zoe Kahn hailed from an unfortunate section of Queens. A fact that she took no pains to hide. Humble beginnings looked great when you made it big. And Zoe intended to make it. She owed it to God for the heavy dose of good looks and brains with which he'd seen fit to endow her. And she was not afraid of hard work. Zoe feared nothing.

A handy trait given her current position as police beat reporter for the *Post*. And her intention to climb. Cable news contributor was the next logical step, and she'd been looking for a story that could get her an invite to the talking-head circuit. She figured she might have found it.

Two fairly prominent homosexuals murdered in the city in the space of three days, and some sort of psycho ritual performed on the bodies. Homosexual thrill killings à la Cunanan, or a serial's opening gambit. Either way it was juicy, though the serial angle had the better potential long term. Her headline this morning had screamed: SERIAL KILLER STALKING CITY'S GAYS? The question mark thrown in to cover her ass.

Her cell phone rang, sounding eerily in the basement garage.

"Here," she spoke into the unit.

"He's on his way down," the voice said.

"Thanks." She flipped the phone closed and nestled back into the shadow of a concrete pillar, going over the moves in her head, the questions she wanted to ask. Not that she really expected Sakura to give her any real answers at this stage. She'd been through this dance with him before. A former deputy commissioner's daughter murdered with plenty of mayhem and sex in suitably high places—a Special

Homicide Unit case that had made her reputation on the police beat. So in a way, she supposed, she owed Sakura. He had played the case close but straight. He never lied, or even stretched the truth overmuch. He just didn't tell you a goddamn thing until he was good and ready.

She knew his reputation with his men. Respected, if not beloved, for a harsh but scrupulous fairness, and a competence that made everyone around him look good. Her own appraisal was a cold man, but not without his passions. His eyes betrayed him with an intensity that could burn like dry ice. She'd felt their sting more than once. It was the same look he no doubt used to intimidate police witnesses into silence with the press, with that spiel of his about obstruction of justice.

The elevator opened, disgorging passengers. She watched Sakura separate from the pack. His figure distinct. Ridiculously tall for an Asian.

His height always surprised her, as if mentally she'd been trying to cut him down. Truth was, she found him attractive. Something in that deliciously cruel mouth and the way he never seemed to notice that she was an extraordinarily beautiful woman. That was the hook, the thing that got under her skin. She and Sakura were colleagues of a sort, both with their little tricks of intimidation. Except that hers never seemed to work on him. She had a fantasy of interviewing him entirely in the nude. See if he could ignore her obvious attributes then.

"Lieutenant Sakura." She stepped out in front of him. "The Carrera-Milne murders. Is it your belief we're dealing with a serial?"

To his credit, his reaction to her presence here was cool. He walked past her, shaking his head, as if her question itself were foolish. "Your article this morning was premature, Ms. Kahn. We have two deaths. It's simply your assumption they're related."

"My article stated that the condition of both bodies suggested a ritualized murder of some kind." She managed to match her stride to his, despite the confines of her skirt. "Are you denying a ritual aspect to these deaths?"

He had reached his car, and now he stopped and faced her. "I don't know where you're getting your information."

She smiled. "But you're not denying it's accurate?"

His key was in his hand. He fitted it in the lock.

"What about the gay community?" she said to his back. "Don't people have a right to be warned of the danger?"

"I feel certain, Ms. Kahn, that you'll continue to take care of that." He had spoken as he opened the door. He climbed in while she continued to pepper him with questions.

"I'm not ready to say anything about this case." He spoke mildly. "You can contact the Public Information Section. I'm sure they'll have a statement."

He started the engine and backed out. She stood watching, as his car moved away and disappeared up the ramp. Her little ambush had accomplished its purpose. News out of no news to feed tomorrow's cycle. She ran the lead in her head: *In an interview yesterday Lieutenant James Sakura of the Special Homicide Unit did not deny a bizarre ritual aspect to the recent murders of Metropolitan Ballet danseur Luis Carrera and David Milne, co-owner of a popular Alphabet City art gallery. Sakura, however, refused comment on widespread speculation that his budding investigation may be dealing with a serial killer targeting members of the city's prominent gay community.*

She smiled her satisfaction, tossing back her signature blond mane and tugging her short skirt into alignment. Whether he liked it or not, Sakura was set to play the star in the little morality tale she was about to spin for the city's hungry readers. The problem for the lieutenant was that, this time out, he might prove to be no more than a shooting star, or the kind that finally collapsed on its own brilliance. That crack of his about the department's Public Information Section was a symptom of his contempt not only for the press but for the way the game was played in general. An impressive clearance rate had so far protected Sakura from the jealousy of his betters, but goodness and light could get you only so far when you operated in a shark tank. And she, for one, was betting on the sharks.

🙢

James Sakura thought Dr. Simon Whelan looked like a gnome. The linguist was an aging scholar, sitting at an ancient desk behind a disorganized accumulation of books and papers. His shock of white hair was startling above almost transparent blue-gray eyes. The single incongruity, tacked to the wall behind the professor's desk, was an out-of-date calendar displaying a smiling Vargas-like beauty advertising Jose's Cantina, El Paso, Texas. Sakura watched as the linguist's untidy head bobbed against the backdrop of the señorita's ample breasts.

Whelan spoke directly to the black-and-white photographs of the crime scene walls. "No spaces between the letters." He rotated the shots toward Sakura, tapping a finger against one of the series of ash-drawn letters. "They're words, freestanding words."

"Not just random strings of letters?" Sakura looked at the photographs he'd examined a dozen times before.

"No, the letters follow graphotactic rules." The professor leaned back into his chair. "Permitted sequences of letters. Vowels occurring in appropriate places. Some fairly standard consonant patterns. . . . Say them, Lieutenant Sakura."

Sakura read off the words that had been written over the victims' beds.

Whelan's laugh was electric. "They're a mouthful but still pronounceable within the context of certain rules of the English language."

"What do they mean, Doctor?"

"Linguists are not magicians, Lieutenant Sakura." Whelan shook his white head in a parody of modesty. "But I think we may reasonably assume that the killer is an English speaker and that these foreign-sounding words are Anglicized versions of words from another language, probably Indo-European or Semitic. The *k* and the *q* sounds, which we see here, frequently occur in both those language groups." He paused, stopping the flutter of his birdlike hands. "There is something else you might consider, Lieutenant. These words may have significance beyond their denotative meaning. '*Kasyade. Jeqon.*'" Whelan literally sang the words.

Sakura waited.

"The *sound* of the words, Lieutenant. Perhaps it is the sound and not the meaning that is important. Especially if the words are attached to some ritual."

Sakura placed a folder next to the black-and-white shots of the walls. Although Whelan had been informed that his visit was connected with the recent homicides, he'd purposely withheld the photographs of the victims' bodies. Now he opened the file and slid color prints of the two murdered men toward the language expert.

The reaction was surprise, as though the professor were wondering if the range of human behavior could support such conduct. He frowned. "What besides murder is this man doing?" Then in answer to his own question, he blurted out, "Why, the devil's making angels!"

The cell phone sounded in Sakura's jacket. He fished it out, flipped open the case. "Sakura," he responded.

"We just found number three." Kelly's voice in his ear.

There was less street activity than might have been expected in front of an apartment building where murder had been committed only hours before. A single patrol car and a crime lab van stood parked near the curb. The uniformed officer who'd remained outside turned as an unmarked sedan pulled up, stopping in midstreet.

The man standing outside the corner bistro watched as a tall figure exited from the front seat, holding a badge aloft, his identity obvious from media reports. In the failing sunlight his skin shone with the pale translucency of Asian flesh, his thinness lightly masked by a navy topcoat he'd worn against an afternoon grown blustery and colder. His black hair was stylishly cut, his eyes intent under delicate slashes of dark brow.

There was an elegant deliberateness, a sense of concentrated intelligence that marked the detective's actions. One leather-gloved hand pinned the badge to his coat, then reached to tame a maroon tie carelessly blown against the plane of his starched white shirt. He glanced over his shoulder briefly, then turned his attention to the entrance of the building.

The man watched the detective mount the steps, his focus already moving into the interior, to what lay in the bedroom upstairs. Murder had thrice been committed. He had upped the ante on Lieutenant James Sakura.

The third victim's apartment, like the others, showed no evidence of a break-in. Sakura entered, thinking that there was terrible irony in serial murder. With each death came another layer of impressions, a new set of clues. Hope that at last there would be something that would lead to the killer. Yet nothing seemed different in Westlake's apartment, except for *BARAKEL* written above the bed.

The meticulous order of the bedroom was the same. So was the nude body, the wings splayed like blades of scissors. As with the first two victims, there was that quality that seemed to transcend death. He searched for something to ground the scene. But nothing could anchor what was in this room to any world he understood. Westlake's features were relaxed, almost beatific, seeming to welcome what must have been a horrific death. The nude body appeared genderless, sterile, unviolated in what was usually a sexually motivated crime.

Sakura reminded himself that the grotesque tableau was a map to the killer's mind, a reaffirmation that the murderer himself was a kind of victim, a slave to the complex fantasy that was driving him to do the things that he did. He stilled his own mind, reducing his focus to the key questions: What had taken place here? Why had it happened the way it had? Who would have committed these crimes for these reasons?

One of the techs, emerging from the bathroom with the black light, interrupted his thoughts.

"The guy's real careful, Lieutenant. He's not taking off the gloves. But I think he might have spent some time in the john this go-round. Smears all over the countertop. Maybe some good enough partials on the mirror."

Sakura nodded. It was a long shot, but clear prints sometimes came through latex. "Tell Murray to take plenty shots of that bathroom," he said. "Black-and-white and color. And—"

"Yeah, Lieutenant, I know. We'll look for all the pubes." The tech went back into the bathroom.

"Linsky shown up?"

Sakura turned at the sound of Lincoln McCauley's voice. "He's been notified."

The chief came through the bedroom door, bent over the corpse. "This one gay too?"

"Unknown. Officer Sanchez is still questioning the friend who called it in."

McCauley grunted. "Look at him. Pretty as a picture."

"Mr. Westlake was a model." Sakura followed the chief's eyes back to the body on the bed. One thing was sure. There was little gross physical difference among the three dead men. All had been small framed, fine-boned. And with the genitals tucked neatly between the thighs, any one of them could have been mistaken for a particularly boyish female.

The chief stood up. His eyes leaked a predatory look his recently acquired polish couldn't contain. His smile was nasty. "You're a hot item, Sakura. Of course the press is a whore. Can turn on you at any time." He removed a cigar from the case he kept in the inner pocket of his jacket and began working it between his teeth. "They're calling our killer a serial. Targeting gays. Talked about ritualized aspects in the murders." He spoke around the cigar. "Read the *Post,* Sakura?"

"I saw it."

"Have you now. Well, it seems you may have a leak you need to patch, Lieutenant." He unplugged the cigar. "I'm out of here. Call me after you hear from Linsky."

Sakura watched McCauley's back as he moved out of the room. He had no illusions about his relationship with the chief of detectives. They didn't like each other.

He walked over to one of the windows facing out onto the street. A taxi below had screeched to a halt, the driver shaking his fist at a woman crossing against the light.

"Well, I'll be damned, Lieutenant. If it ain't 'Miss Assistant D.A.' herself." Murray had poked his head out of the bathroom just in time to catch Faith Baldwin jaywalking.

Impervious to the cold, she didn't have on a coat, and Sakura watched her body glide inside the man-tailored suit as though she wore nothing at all. A wisp of chestnut hair was momentarily trapped inside the frames of glasses she didn't need, but in true Baldwin style used only for effect.

"Think she's a dyke?" The other tech joined them at the window.

"She's got big enough balls. But I figure her for a nympho. Fire under all that ice." Murray laughed, began reloading his camera.

Sakura turned away from the window. Of one thing he was sure—Faith had balls, but she was no dyke. Their eight-month affair more than five years ago was proof of that. It was a relationship both had agreed to keep secret, and Faith had been more than discreet. In public, the assistant D.A. had made a show of barely tolerating him, her game of high indifference seeming only to intensify what happened between them in bed. His fingers went to his wrist as he recalled the last time they'd made love. Faith had used his own handcuffs on him. It had been a kind of insanity that had both frightened and excited him.

He looked up at the sound of her cool, uninflected voice. "What do we have here, Lieutenant Sakura?" Her green eyes, cool too, met his straight on.

"Something quite unpleasant, Ms. Baldwin."

"Such decorum, Lieutenant." She unlocked her eyes and glanced over at Westlake's corpse.

"I take it this is an official visit," he said.

She moved fractionally closer. "The D.A.'s office always takes a keen interest in the work of the NYPD."

He stood still, just breathing, inhaling her fragrance.

"I hope you won't disappoint me," she said. "I expect a case I can win, Lieutenant Sakura."

🔻

Three bodies in less than a week. Another day of mobilizing the task force—officers borrowed from other commands to canvass yet one more neighborhood.

Tonight, alone in his office, Sakura was beginning to feel the special fatigue that went with frustration. He had little real hope for the smudged latents they had pulled today from the mirror in Westlake's bathroom, and a second session with Greenberg this evening had gotten him nothing new. The gallery owner, whose alibi checked out, had denied talking to the press and could still provide no connecting link between his partner and Carrera.

Nor did Greenberg know of any connection between his partner and Geoffrey Westlake; though like many others in the city, he had certainly been aware of the model's work as an actor in TV ads. The evening news had played it big, with commentary voiced over running clips of Westlake's commercials—local celebrity, a Halloween-night victim of what they were now all calling a gay serial killer.

Geoffrey Westlake's friends and associates had apparently had little compunction about outing him after his death. Zoe Kahn would have plenty of company in tomorrow's morning editions. Sakura could only hope for some time before any more details leaked. They had already suffered the first of what would certainly become many false confessions. A copycat could be next.

For a moment he let himself give in to exhaustion, and closing his eyes, he massaged his temples. Above him the banks of fluorescents buzzed like insects. One tube, going bad, enhanced the illusion of tiny frenetic wings beating between him and the light.

In the black behind his eyes, an image of Faith arose, as if it had been waiting for the moment. He had managed to avoid working with her all these years only because she was avoiding him too. Apparently, her interest in this case was too great for any consideration of personal feelings. Faith had always had a way of attaching herself to high-profile cases.

But a case high powered enough to advance a career could also blow up in your face. There could be nothing worse for a prosecutor than failing to convict a man whom the media had painted as a monster and a threat to public safety. Faith was, as she'd said, counting on him not to box her into a trial without a solid chance of conviction. Her trust in him was flattering.

And the truth was he trusted her too. Not that she would cover his errors or make excuses to the press for his mistakes, but neither would she stab him in the back. Faith had no sentiment, but she did have integrity. Their past emotional involvement would never be allowed to affect her professional judgment. She was the best the D.A.'s office had, and he should be grateful she was on the case. He had just not been prepared for his own visceral reaction.

He opened his eyes, studied his hands white with chalk from the blackboard. He hated getting chalk on his fingers. The dryness made his flesh plump up, feel tight and lifeless. He took out his handkerchief, the one Hanae washed and ironed and made sure he was never without, and rubbed his hands. He noticed that the white dust had made perfect tracings of his fingerprints. What he needed was a trip down the hall to wash up, but he was not yet ready to concede another day's defeat.

With so little to go on, he'd been concentrating the efforts of his people on reconstructing the last few weeks of Carrera's and Milne's lives. But despite extensive interviews, nothing had been discovered which tied the two together or suggested why either might have been targeted for murder. Canvasses of the neighborhoods had so far produced neither witnesses nor suspects, and the days had gone by in a blur of paperwork adding to no result. With today's discovery of Westlake's body, the process was repeating under the intensifying scrutiny of the press. Not that it mattered. Press attention was an annoyance, not a goad. He needed none beyond his own drive.

He accepted his ambition. He had thrived on testing himself for as long as he could remember. That his need to excel might spring at least in part from the unusual circumstances of his youth was not something he usually examined. The past was the past.

He had no real memory of his mother or his early life in New York. His first clear memories were of his bed in the house on Hokkaido, the smell of the sea, and the sight of his grandfather's prize roosters strutting in the little yard.

In many ways the years in Japan had been his happiest. And, certainly, sending little Akira to be cared for by his grandparents must have seemed to Isao, his father, the most rational solution to the problem of a motherless two-year-old. Who else was there to care for him? His mother, Mai, a student like his father, had been third-generation American. Her father lived fairly near in New Jersey, but her own mother had died nearly as young as she from the same heart condition.

In the house on Hokkaido, the existence of his father had played like an undertone to the rich sensory mix of his child's life on the rural coast of Japan. There were photographs and letters to his grandparents, with always a word for him. And then the one short summer visit when he was almost seven.

His father had returned for *O-bon,* the Feast of the Dead, when the ancestral spirits of each family were honored. What he remembered most about that visit was the joy of his grandmother as she prepared for the festival, cleaning and dusting, hanging out the red lantern that would guide the spirits home. It had seemed to his child's mind that it was his father she was guiding, as much a spirit to him as his long-dead ancestors.

But his father had at last appeared, very tall and real, with gifts for everyone and fruit and flowers for the family altar. It had been a good time, and at the end of the week, they had attended the celebrations in the nearby city. Amid the food, and the dancing, and the fireworks, his father had helped him place his little raft with its paper lantern among the others on the river. It was *Toro Nagashi,* the floating lanterns meant to comfort the spirits as they left again on their way.

His father was to leave the next day, and he woke to a change in the house. Anger in his grandfather. Tears from his grandmother, which were more than the sorrow of a son's parting. His father had taken him aside in the garden and revealed the story of his secret life, like offering up a peach. It seemed he had remarried and become a United States citizen. Even after the training in his specialty was completed, he would not be returning to Japan. And he, Akira, must also return to the land of his birth. Someday soon he would be sent for to live with his family in America.

And so with this promise, his father had once again disappeared from the ordinary course of his life, leaving him as one marked amidst the chaos he'd created.

Letters arrived with photos now of the blue-eyed wife and the children. A son, Paul, only two years younger than himself. And Elizabeth, the three-year-old daughter. But no word of when Akira was to join them. It would be four years before that summons came.

He shook his head, an unconscious gesture of denial. He had read somewhere that Japanese emigrants more quickly than any other group lost their language and their culture. This might seem odd in a society where ethnic identity was so strong, but it was simply a fact that *Japaneseness* was not easily sustained outside the unique context that created it.

And though it was so with his father, whose own Japaneseness had fallen so easily from his shoulders, it was not exactly so with him. Certainly, he was American, not only by birth but by conviction and choice. And yet, if James Sakura believed anything at all, he believed that some essential element of his being had been forged in those misplaced years on Hokkaido, that his *tamashi,* the core of his soul, was Japanese.

He realized he had been refolding the handkerchief in his hand, duplicating Hanae's pattern. And now he tucked it back inside his breast pocket. He reexamined the chalkboard, for what seemed the hundredth time, hoping to discover somewhere in the tidy display of his writing, something of the spirit of his killer. Despite all manner of modern detection, was it not a man's *tamashi* that must ultimately betray him?

If a serial killer had a soul? It was a question he'd once half jokingly asked at an after-hours bull session at Quantico of the instructor who'd asserted in class that serial killers were not fully human. Serial killers had souls, Dr. French had replied, but their consciences were undeveloped, and as sociopaths, they were as incapable of moral judgment as a two-year-old. Sakura had not agreed, and yet her answer had disturbed him. It disturbed him now.

He was shaking his head again. There was more than enough that was troubling about this case without dragging in the intangible. Like the ease with which the killer gained access to his victims. His boldness in killing them in their own apartments, where he apparently remained for hours, performing a ritual that included cleaning and posing their bodies. According to Linsky's estimate, Milne had died late on Sunday night. Was it only luck of one sort or another that had prevented Jerry Greenberg's earlier than scheduled return from interrupting the murder of his lover?

The killer's luck had held again last night. An electronic card system let residents in and out of Westlake's building. The model had been noticed by one of the other residents leaving at around nine o'clock. No one had seen his return. But with no sign of forced entry, it seemed probable that the killer had been someone he'd brought back to his apartment.

Sakura picked up the jade disk from his desk, a good luck talisman, a gift from his uncle Ikenobo on his seventh-year *matsuri,* when he was brought to the local shrine to be blessed. Rubbing its smooth surface, he swiveled in his chair to study the photographs tacked around the chalkboard's wooden frame. Borrowed photos were juxtaposed with crime scene close-ups of each of the three victims. Greenberg had provided a small color snapshot of David Milne. Carrera and Westlake were represented by eight-by-ten black-and-white posed publicity stills. The gallery owner, the dancer, and the model. If, as now seemed likely, all were victims of a serial killer randomly targeting gays, then what particular set of circumstances had placed each of these three men in whatever territory their murderer considered his hunting ground? And what was the unwitting set of cues that had pushed the killer over the line and made each man's selection as a victim inevitable? What had each man done or said that singled him out, fitted him for the passive role inside the killer's fantasy?

Johnny Rozelli's familiar laugh rang out in the squad room. Sakura turned from the blackboard and looked through the glass that fronted his office. Talbot and Rozelli, two of the four detectives from his unit, were still working the keyboards. With this third murder his Special Homicide Unit was being expanded into a task force, McCauley allowing him to handpick from among the available officers. He was confident in his people, and yet there was still that void he always felt in moments like this one. He was not himself immodest—he understood his own value well—but Michael Darius had something that went beyond ordinary cop instinct, a gut-level ability to quantum leap the facts that had little to do with either logic or training. He looked at the stack of files littering his desk. Would Michael see something in this jumble that he continued to miss?

He rose from his chair and walked to the floor-to-ceiling window, which was the dominating feature in the tiny eleventh-floor office. Beyond the plaza the Municipal Building loomed over Chambers Street, its collocated towers topped by the statue *Civic Fame*. Bracing his hands against the black glass, he dropped his head and breathed deeply, as if he could inhale the night. Then closing his eyes, he let his head fall back on his shoulders. His next breath held a single soft sound. *Hanae*. His wife's name. His mantra.

This time of evening in lower Manhattan, the streets were mostly empty. The Fulton Street Market not set to stir for hours. The canyons of Wall Street deserted. The man had little trouble finding a space for his cycle near the rental garage to which he'd trailed his quarry. Plenty of time to get himself in place.

He held his breath now, bracing his arm for the shot. The infrared image that was Lieutenant James Sakura shimmered like heat waves in the scope, the mounted lamps on either side of the Nocta triggering with a soft electronic pop that was hidden in the traffic noise drifting from the Brooklyn Bridge. The flash itself was intense, if invisible to human eyes. The detective, pausing on the pavement, had no awareness of the camera not twenty yards away.

Still irradiated by the scope's built-in searchlight, Sakura walked the remaining steps to the entranceway of a nearby building. With his key in the lock, he turned back to the street, as if for the first time sensing something not quite right in the dark. The lamps flashed again in a whisper, catching the tired smile that mocked his apprehension. Caught him again as he disappeared through the door.

The man breathed out slowly, resting for a moment against the cold brick at the mouth of the alley. The effects of the drug he had taken last night had long since worn away, and the desire of his human shell for food and rest tugged at the edges of his consciousness. He had not eaten for more than twenty-four hours, had not slept.

He had, of course, been aware that the dead bodies would draw police and press attention. There was no way to avoid that. And though he might resent the unavoidable human dimensions of the mission he had set for himself, he could not afford to ignore them. He had waited since before dawn in the streets outside Westlake's building. Had been drinking coffee in the bistro across the street when the first police vehicles had arrived. He'd already paid the bill and stepped outside as Sakura had emerged from his unmarked car.

It was an opportunity to learn what he could of his adversary, and he'd followed the detective as he'd left the crime scene and gone back to Police Plaza. It had been a matter of parking the Harley in sight of the ramp from which Sakura would have to exit the underground lot . . . and waiting. A very long wait as it had turned out. But he had kept the vigil through the afternoon and evening, till the detective's car did at last emerge onto the street, then trailed him here to the apartment building where he apparently lived.

For a moment hunger nearly overcame him, and he considered giving in. But there might be more he could learn tonight. He closed his eyes, denying the flesh, repeating the syllables of his name till exhaustion vanished. A car went past. A tug sounded from the river. Then with the Nocta safe in the bag, he went looking for a suitable building.

For a long moment, Sakura stood without moving inside the *genkan*. The small entryway, with Hanae's marriage kimono suspended over the low *tansu*, was for him both an ending and a beginning—the curtain that fell each night, closing off the outer world and opening the private world that was his and Hanae's alone. But tonight the outside world would not be stilled. Even before he'd removed his coat, the cell phone was ringing inside his pocket.

"Lieutenant Sakura." Simon Whelan's voice on the line. "They told me I'd just missed you at your office. I hope you don't mind my calling."

"No, Dr. Whelan, that's why I left this number with you." He was surprised to hear from the language professor so soon. "Murder investigations don't follow nine-to-five schedules."

"I'm sure they don't, Lieutenant."

"Unfortunately, we do indeed have a third victim."

"And a new word on the wall?"

He spelled out the letters written in Westlake's bedroom. "So what have you found out, Dr. Whelan?"

"Not me, Lieutenant Sakura. My good friend, Dr. Haim Isaacs at Yeshiva. Remember when I said this morning that your killer was making angels? Well, he's also naming them. Kasyade and Jeqon are names of angels found in an Apocryphal text called *The Book of Enoch.*"

"The wings seemed obvious. But this confirms it. You said Apocryphal text?"

"Material excluded from authorized translations of the Bible."

"So whatever the killer is doing," Sakura asked, "might have something to do with religion?"

"Possibly."

"What about the markings on the chests?"

"I haven't found anything yet, and Haim said he didn't see any connection with *Enoch*."

"I'd like to see this book."

"I'm sure Dr. Isaacs would loan you his copy."

"Thank you, Dr. Whelan." He got out his notebook and was jotting down the Yeshiva professor's number.

"Lieutenant Sakura!"

"Yes, Doctor?"

"But how could I be so forgetful," the man was saying. "Haim said these are not just the names of any angels. He wanted me to make it clear that the names on the walls are the names of *fallen* angels."

✦

The man had scaled the last section of the building up to the roof like an experienced mountain climber. In truth, he didn't like heights. Although, it wasn't heights so much he feared but falling. He forced himself to look down now. A dull darkness gave way to a denser blackness.

He swallowed a hard knot of saliva and inched backward from the edge. From beneath his foot a stone unsettled itself. He breathed the cold air and stretched his arms wide. The thick skin of his leather jacket glinted weakly in the moonlight, and he imagined himself a large bat unplugging itself from its nighttime roost.

Behind and above him the bridge soared. A line of cars winking into Brooklyn. He bent and, unzipping his bag, retrieved his camera. This rooftop would give him the vantage he needed. He circled around some air venting to the other side of the building. From here it seemed he could see the entire universe.

He looked out. The aura surrounding the silhouetted figure came as a shock, and he caught himself before he could fall. He held his breath, hearing the roar of blood inside his head. His fingers trembled as he brought the Nocta up to his face. Even with the scope he was having trouble focusing, but he knew what he was seeing. He clicked the lens once before the light exploded.

⚶

The warmth of the bedroom seemed an indulgence to Hanae, so long accustomed to a house that was cold in winter. She dropped to kneel beside Jimmy and began the process of centering herself in *hara,* drawing her mind to the point below her navel that was the exact physical center of her body.

Her husband, fresh from his bath, lay facedown, his head resting on folded arms, his back draped with the traditional cloth that would veil his skin from her touch.

The cloth was white, a fact she could sense in its steady surface vibration, so different from an object that was a buzzing red, or cooling blue beneath her fingers. But the visual aspect of color remained an impenetrable mystery. She could not even begin to imagine what it must be to sense color with the eyes. This was her small regret for having been born blind. The greater loss was that, despite the intimacy of her fingers with its contours, she would never actually see her husband's face.

She emptied her mind. Her heart already open, she began with his head and neck tonight, rubbing and pressing where worry and fatigue had disturbed the natural flow of *ki* through the channels.

"Feels good." He spoke once as her hands flowed to his shoulders. Then, "Uhhh, that one is sensitive, Hanae," when she had moved to his back. "Where are you?" he said in another moment. Jimmy liked to have her name the *tsubos,* the fixed points on the channels where *ki* could be taken in or released.

"You should not speak," she said. "Empty mind is important for the receiver as well as for the giver of healing."

"I want to know," he insisted.

"*Mei-mon,*" she answered. "The gate of life."

"Because . . . ?"

"Because it is so near *jin-yu,* the seat of inborn energy." Her fingers flowed to the place. "*Mei-mon* and *jin-yu* are each connected with the life force inherited from the parents. In only a few hours, you will return to work. Restoring the proper flow of *ki* here builds stamina."

Now, at last, she could feel him smile. "I thought it was *shi-shitsu* that did that."

"That *tsubo* is also near *jin-yu*," she answered. "But its name implies another kind of stamina."

"If I remember correctly," he said, "'*shi-shitsu*' translates roughly as . . . *sperm room*." He rolled over beneath her fingers.

"I am not finished."

"I feel much better. I want to hold my wife."

She lay down beside him, naked again beneath her kimono as no proper Japanese wife. He held her, stomach to back, his chin resting in her hair. Not speaking at first, which was always the way of his unburdening.

"There was another body today." He broke the silence.

It explained the blockage of *ki*. She turned toward him, her hand cradling his face. She could sense his eyes searching, blinder than she was in the dark. "Have you spoken yet to Kenjin?"

"No."

"You must ask him to return."

"I don't know," he said softly.

She felt his tension increasing again, building in the muscles of his jaw. "He is your friend," she said. "He wears *on* with no offense." The concept had no real English equivalent. The closest translation was debt of gratitude.

"And I wear mine with none," he said.

"Then, my dear husband, perhaps it will be a calm sea you cross."

She had thought him long asleep when he reached for her. She turned toward him, slipping from her kimono. She was eager as always for their lovemaking. It was a joy to *see* Jimmy, not just with the tips of her fingers on his face, but with the full feel of him, body to body. In these moments he was completely hers, wholly apprehended.

He began tonight with gentleness, kissing her deeply. But soon he was like raging water carrying her to that place of peace. She moved with his thrusts, the light behind her lids a growing pressure. At the moment of her climax, she was the light, consumed in the grace of their union.

The solution ran off like thin blood. The excess dripping into the steel pan as the man hung the photographs to dry. His fingers appeared detached from his hands, moving like small white worms in the brothel red light of the developing room.

But that was only an illusion, for his flesh pressed against him with increased vigor. No matter how often he bathed, he could smell himself. The odor of decaying fruit. And the feel of it. That, too, was more acute than ever. Arms. Legs. The sack of skin attached to muscle. The connection of tendon to bone. The flush of blood. He had an absolute consciousness of every cell in his body. Every molecule. Every atom. Every nucleus of every atom.

That the level of communion with his physical self had grown these last months did not surprise him. Nor that he had plunged to the very edge of sensation. It was an expected consequence of awakening.

What was still a mystery to him was if there were others of his kind who had awakened. Or was he the only one on the physical plane fully conscious of what he was? It made the burden greater. But no matter, he knew what must be done.

He looked down at the last of the prints floating in the pan. A blowup. A tight profile. It was unquestionably the best shot taken from the roof. His single perfect happiness in so many months.

"Zavebe," he whispered to the photograph.

CHAPTER

4

The men's room in the basement morgue had the feeling of a crypt and smelled like fake maraschino cherries. Sakura splashed his face with water from the tap and wondered who had decided that a germicidal disinfectant should cloy your throat with the sweetness of sugared fruit. There were no paper towels in the dispenser. He pulled the handkerchief out of his pocket and dried his face, observing himself in the mirror. He looked hollow-eyed in the greenish light that brought out the sallowness of his skin.

The autopsy on Westlake, which he had just witnessed, had proceeded identically to those of the first two victims. Dr. Linsky had insisted on delaying any discussion of the case to a meeting that was to follow in his office. Folding and replacing the handkerchief in his pocket, Sakura headed there now.

The medical examiner was already waiting for him in the small but miraculously neat space. He sat behind his desk, its surface clean except for a stack of current cases and a framed portrait of a young and pretty wife—mail order from Moscow according to department rumor. Sakura took the chair offered him, plunged in. "What did the lab come up with?"

Linsky looked at him. "Nothing that could be the mechanism of death."

The overpreciseness of language was interesting. The medical examiner was making a careful distinction between the mechanism, or agent, and the cause of death, the actual physical effect of that agent within the body. Obliqueness was not Linsky's style. He was enjoying this. The case had risen to the level of his interest.

The M.E. surprised him by asking, "Have you found any evidence that the victims knew each other?"

"No," Sakura admitted. "And so far, there's no indication that any of the victims were into weird sex."

"I see." Linsky settled back in his chair. "Death is always a messy business," he began again. "The body releases its fluids. Lividity indicates that these victims died in their beds, and yet the bedclothes are pristine except for the small amount of blood leaking from the incisions he made to insert the wings. There's no doubt the killer cleaned up, including washing the bodies. We found traces of alcohol and cotton fibers."

Sakura nodded. "Part of his ritual," he said. "Or a concern with eliminating physical evidence."

"He wasn't totally effective. There were still some traces of adhesive on the skin."

"Semen?" Sakura asked.

Linsky shook his head. "I doubt there ever was any. The reports were all negative, including the oral and anal swabs."

Sakura was only marginally surprised. Serial murder was usually a sex crime, but it was not all that rare for the killer to fail to ejaculate at the scene. "You said the lab didn't find anything that could be the mechanism of death," he said. "But I believe you know what killed them."

Linsky actually smiled. "*Know* is too strong a word," he said, "but there is virtually no substance that can remain undetectable to a complete battery of tests. By process of elimination, the killer must have injected something that is *too* detectable. A substance that can hide in plain sight."

"What kind of substance?"

"A potassium compound. Most probably potassium chloride."

"You said it could hide—"

"There's potassium in every cell of the body, Lieutenant. The moment that death occurs, the cells begin to break down and potassium is released in massive quantities. Whatever amount the killer injected is going to be masked by that."

"And the cause of death?"

"Heart failure. Potassium is vitally necessary for cell functioning, but only within a certain range. Too little or too much and the result is the same, arrhythmia and cardiac arrest. There is no physiological damage to the heart. The muscle simply stops pumping."

"It seems a strange way to kill, especially if you're not trying to hide the fact that your victims were murdered," Sakura said.

Linsky shrugged. The gesture was oddly elegant in the starched coat. "Potassium chloride, as you probably know, is one of the drugs used in lethal injection. Perhaps there's some significance in that."

"There were two needle marks," Sakura remembered. "Was the second injection also potassium chloride?"

"Very unlikely. One injection would be quite sufficient."

"Then what?"

"Lysergic acid diethylamide."

"LSD?"

"Yes. We found high levels of the drug in the first two victims."

"It could be coincidence," Sakura thought aloud. "There's a lot of LSD use. . . . But injected by the killer?"

"It would logically have to be injected first. Potassium chloride kills very rapidly."

"But why would the killer give them LSD?" Sakura asked.

"I only work on bodies, Lieutenant. It's not my job to know what the murderer is thinking when he kills them."

Sakura nodded. That job description was very precisely his. "How soon can we get the blood work on Westlake?" He looked at the medical examiner.

"It's top priority, Detective Sakura." Linsky managed to sound collegial. "I'll call you as soon as I know something."

Sakura left the morgue and headed back to police headquarters for yet one more unpleasant task. Since yesterday's discovery of the third homosexual victim, the serial-killer story had spread to every media outlet in the city. Pressure on City Hall from the gay community was increasing by the hour. A press conference had been scheduled for later this morning, at which he would have to speak. It was a duty he accepted with any high-profile case, but he didn't have to enjoy it.

Zoe Kahn smoothed her tight French twist, draping her black cash-mere coat over the back of the seat. She sat near the front of the auditorium, a gray room, that had the effect of making everyone feel trapped in the blankness of a television screen. She'd arrived early at One Police Plaza when talk of a hastily thrown together press conference was still in the rumor stage. Crossing her legs, she resettled her purse on the floor. A green knit dress ignited the gold in her hazel eyes and contrasted with her bright red lips, only recently collagen enhanced for the second time. Zoe took considerable time with her appearance. Nature had been generous, but she wasn't leaving anything to chance.

The press conference was going to be well attended. Extra folding chairs were being brought in. Everyone was hungry for the latest on the murders now that the count was up to three. She turned and spotted Ralph Gunner, from *Left Hand*, a gay-activist rag. She blew him a quick kiss.

The hall quieted as Phil Doss came up to the podium. Doss was the typical media-relations flunky who didn't have a straight answer for anything. He droned on for a few minutes, then introduced the chief of detectives. Zoe didn't especially like Lincoln McCauley, but she admired his grit. Men with far greater gifts had failed in the system. Long hours in a gym had squeezed the chief into the confines of a dark designer suit, but his beefy face seemed to explode from the starched collar of his shirt. He remained a relic, a throwback to the decades when the Irish had predominated in the hierarchies of the New York City Police.

The chief read a tersely prepared statement, his voice holding an edge that was more than bureaucratic irritation. He warned against the press corrupting what he called "the purity of the investigation." Then flatly refusing questions, he passed the mike to James Sakura.

Center stage, she knew, was not a place the gold-shield detective relished. Yet he appeared cool, in control, almost indifferent. That could spell trouble. A cop without passion could mean a cop who didn't care. Zoe knew that wasn't true, yet perception was everything. He was talking about setting up meetings so that the public could communicate more directly with the police. This was more than assuaging gays; the investigation was going proactive, she realized. Cast out the net and see what you drag in.

But for her, playing the gay trump card was wearing thin. She knew if the story was really going to get hot, heterosexuals had to feel threatened. Thanks to her sources, she had gotten a tip on the West-lake murder almost as soon as it was called in. The head start meant an exclusive with the model's mother. But everybody was fishing in the same pond now. Maybe she needed to go proactive herself. Bait the killer, draw him out, like Breslin had done with Berkowitz.

Unfortunately, Sakura wasn't giving her much that was new. She glanced over her shoulder. Gunner was standing, breaking protocol, asking Sakura if the victims had been straight, might not the killer already have been apprehended. The atmosphere iced over. Sakura seemed to stiffen, but neither his tone nor his words betrayed any weakness.

"The race, gender, creed, or sexual orientation of any victim has never impeded the aggressive actions with which the officers of the NYPD pursue an investigation," he said.

In those few moments when he'd spoken, some unplayed script, some ill-defined undercurrent, seemed to lend a great importance to everything. McCauley stepped back, away from the podium, absorbed by the grayness of the room. Perhaps the rumblings she'd heard about the Palace Guard wanting to replace Sakura with an officer of higher rank were true. The bureaucrats were capable of almost any idiocy. But Lieutenant James Sakura was the best the department had.

⚜

Gray clouds hung in the sky like drapery. The traffic was never really light, but for a gloomy Thursday afternoon, it moved along smoothly enough. And after the rigors of this morning's press conference and a sandwich snatched while going over the latest reports on his desk, Sakura did not entirely regret this time away from his office. He would not regret it at all if this afternoon's interview panned out.

Last night on the local TV newscasts, a police hot-line number had been run beneath updates of the serial-killer story, reaping the mixed blessing of so much public attention. Shortly after the program a call had come in, a man insisting he had information he would only give Sakura. The screener had made the judgment to transfer the call.

Sakura had spoken to the man, a bartender who claimed he'd seen Geoffrey Westlake on the night he'd been murdered. He hadn't liked the man's tone, which impressed him as both overeager and evasive. He'd refused to give more details on the phone. But Sakura had long ago learned not to make snap judgments about a possible witness, especially based on a single telephone conversation. He had agreed to a meeting this afternoon, and a subsequent check of the cab company records confirmed that a fare picked up Halloween night at Westlake's building had been dropped off at the bar.

Crossing Columbus Avenue, Sakura turned off on Sixty-seventh and pulled the unmarked department car onto the curb. Taking the vehicle identification plate from behind the visor, he tossed it on the dash. He got out and walked the half block to Marlowe's, a popular neighborhood pub that catered to soap opera actors and newspeople from the nearby ABC building. This time of afternoon the lunch crowd had cleared and the place was fairly empty.

Sakura took a seat at the bar. "I'm looking for Jack Trehan." He flashed his badge.

"You got him, Lieutenant Sakura." The bartender had an over-groomed look that made it hard to place his age. "Fix you something?" He smiled with capped teeth, indicating the bottles behind him.

Sakura shook his head. "You said you had something that could help us."

"About Geoffrey . . . yeah." Trehan waited.

"You knew Mr. Westlake?"

Now the bartender shrugged. "We weren't close. But he came in here a lot. And sometimes, when it wasn't too busy, we'd talk."

"What about?"

"Acting mostly. I'm an actor." The smile stretched wider.

"You do commercials too?"

The bartender made a noise. "Commercials are a bitch to get."

"But Geoffrey got commercials?"

Trehan nodded, leaning in, his elbows on the bar, an insider imparting information. "A while back," he said, "year or two after he started modeling, Geoffrey lands this pilot that gets picked up as a series.

Good part, second banana to Byron Shelton, the comic who's supposed to be the next Drew Carey."

"But . . . ?" Sakura picked up the cue.

"But the sitcom never made it to the air. Shelton got arrested for exposing himself to little girls in the park. Too bad for Geoff's big break. Still, he and the show's producer got pretty chummy." The smile became a smirk. "He's the one who started Geoffrey in commercials."

"Was it generally known that Mr. Westlake was gay?"

"Depends on what you mean. He wasn't out of the closet, but people in the business pretty much knew."

"You said this morning that Mr. Westlake was here on Tuesday night. Was he with anyone?"

Trehan frowned, faking concentration. "It was slower than I expected that night, being Halloween and all, but the weather was so crappy. Some of Geoffrey's friends came in, but that was later. After he'd left."

"And he left alone?"

The bartender was smiling again, the tension of the scene having played to his direction. He pointed to the far side of the bar. "Geoffrey was sitting there," he said. "It was dark, and I was busy filling orders for the tables. But I saw this guy sit down next to him."

It was obvious where this was going, and Sakura allowed himself to hope. "Did you know this man?" he asked.

"No." At least Trehan didn't string it out. "I finished with the drinks and figured I'd take his order. Only he's gone already. And so's Geoffrey."

"Can you describe him?"

"Yeah." The flatness of the answer betrayed him. "I'd say he was tall and thin, but he had on a big outdoor jacket that made it hard to tell. I thought the coat looked too big for him."

"Hair?" Sakura asked.

"Difficult to say." Trehan shook his head. "Remember, it was pretty dark in here. And he was wearing a Yankees cap . . . and dark glasses. I couldn't see his eyes."

Certainly an anticlimax. "One of my people will call and set up an appointment with a sketch artist." Sakura took refuge in habit.

"Sketch artist, huh?" The bartender seemed pleased with the notion.

"Also, I'll want a list of those friends of Westlake's you mentioned. And anyone who was here that night who might have gotten a better look at this guy."

"Sure," Trehan said, but his tone was dismissive. "Like I said, Lieutenant, he wasn't around long enough to even order a drink. You think he was the killer?"

"I don't know," Sakura said, refusing the man satisfaction. But the truth was, that in his gut, he did. Just as he was certain that any composite based on the bartender's vague description would be virtually worthless. The killer had exposed himself, but he'd been reasonably careful. And lucky. Beginner's luck. He wondered how long it would hold.

⚜

Gil Avery never imagined anyone would want to photograph his birthmark. But this nutso did. Seemed to get off on it too.

"How's this?" Gil asked from his position on the cool white sheets. He'd twisted his torso so that his hip became the dominant feature in a landscape of flesh.

The photographer nodded from his spot at the foot of the bed.

Wasn't much for talk. In fact, Gil could count the number of words he'd spoken since he'd picked him up. *Click.*

"Yes," he finally said in a breathless voice. "Yes, yes, yes."

A litany of yeses. *Click. Click. Click.* A run of spiky clicks like teeth chattering. The whir of the roll like a toy train. Gil went with it. Let the photographer's momentum pull him along. It was a weird kind of power just lying back, posing like some god. Knowing some guy wanted to take pictures of you. Make memories. It was as close to immortality as the young model was likely to get, and the pleasure of it leaked to every cell. Slowly Gil found himself getting hard, and the freak hadn't even touched him.

⚜

Today's overcast had not broken, and dead night air clung to the window like paper wrapping. Sakura tried to be grateful for the new fluorescent tube that shone uncompromisingly upon the growing stacks of DD-5's on his desk. A major problem in this kind of investigation was the sheer amount of data it gathered, and the task force was generating a blizzard of reports. Critical connections could be missed because no one person possessed all the facts. For as long as it was possible, Sakura was determined to know everything.

Computerizing things helped, and Walt Talbot was good at that. The detective was in the process of setting up a program that would help identify potential suspects. Of course, the trick was to keep up with the paperwork. Organizing, categorizing, feeding the information into the proper files.

He smiled, thinking of Talbot. The detective's cool had been thoroughly shaken Tuesday by Philippe Lambert's sin of omission. Obviously, the members of the ballet company had long ago disregarded the birth gender of Andrea, alias André Wilitz, and felt no compunction to inform the uninitiated. At first Andrea might have seemed a dream suspect—an impotent homosexual transvestite with a decidedly artistic bent who had had an ongoing feud with Luis Carrera at the time of his death. But there were several factors that disqualified Wilitz as the killer. In addition to an alibi that checked out, the wardrobe mistress was nearing sixty and an amputee.

Lambert's alibi had also cleared him of Carrera's murder, and by implication of those of the other two victims. He had indeed been in the theater for the Thursday-night performance and had returned immediately after to his apartment with two of his roommates.

As for the Westlake murder, some fairly clear prints, other than the victim's own, had been found in the model's bedroom. The prints, though, were undoubtedly female and belonged, most likely, to the maid who'd been in to clean. The partials from the bathroom were more tantalizing, but as he'd expected, had too few points of identification to be of any use.

The crime lab was working on identifying the adhesive left on the victims' skins and would prepare a brand list of the corresponding duct tapes. But trying to trace the point of purchase would be a long shot. And they could forget the potassium chloride. It was a common compound, which the killer could have picked up virtually anywhere.

Spectrographic analysis of the substance on the walls had indicated that it was ash from incense burned at the scene. The same for the symbols on the chests. The next step was trying to pinpoint the brand, though knowing whether it was commercially or liturgically distributed was less important than understanding why incense had been used at all. Why not something as simple as a marker? Because incense fit with angels?

According to the crime lab, the white wings were swan wings from a genus that was plentiful along the East Coast. They had not been preserved in any chemical way, but had perhaps been frozen. Unless the killer was keeping a pen of the birds to be used as they were needed, which seemed unlikely in the city.

A tap at his open door caught his attention. Adelia Johnson poked in her head. One of his unit regulars, she'd come to him from Sex Crimes, where she'd worked a fair number of cases involving repeat rapists. A serial rapist, as someone once remarked, was a serial killer who hadn't yet worked up the guts. To a large extent, this was true, which meant that, like her partner, Kelly, Detective Johnson was one of very few task force members with actual experience dealing in serial crime.

"We're ordering pizza. . . ." She let the words hang. A question. Her white smile blazed.

"No, Delia . . . thanks."

The detective's head disappeared. He listened to her footsteps moving back down the hall. A light tread for such a substantial woman.

Sakura slid open the bottom drawer of his desk. He had not yet reached the point of succumbing to junk food. He removed his tea things, swiveling the chair toward the console behind him, where a kettle of water stood on a small hot plate. He switched it on, heating the water to be poured into the small porcelain pot, anticipating the scent of tea.

The phone rang. His direct line. He lifted the receiver. "Yes."

"Lieutenant Sakura." Dr. Linsky's voice.

"You have the results on Westlake?"

"Yes, I do. His electrolyte levels show the same pattern as the others."

"Consistent with his being given potassium chloride."

"That is precisely the way to put it." Linsky sounded approving. "It is consistent."

It was as definitive a statement as Sakura could expect. "What about LSD?" he asked.

"There was also LSD in Mr. Westlake's system."

Three victims out of three. Surely beyond coincidence. "What would be the effect of an injection of LSD," he asked, "in contrast to ingesting it?"

"The effects would be the same," Linsky answered, "especially with the large dose that these three apparently received. The difference is the speed with which the effects would begin. With injection, it's nearly instantaneous."

"Mental distortions? Disorientation?"

"It all depends. The effects are highly variable. Experience with the drug generally allows the user to function in a manner approximating normality."

"But if you don't understand what's happening . . ."

"Paranoia usually results. But in any case the effects are variable. Even an experienced user can get a very nasty effect . . . feel he's losing his mind."

"What about the physical effects?"

"LSD is neutral to systems other than the brain. And interestingly, once the receptors in the brain have all been engaged, taking more of the drug has no effect. One can't actually overdose."

"But there are deaths with LSD."

"The result of impurities, some substance the drug was cut with. Significant impurities would have shown up in the blood work, but there was none of that here. Which leads me to suppose that the killer may be manufacturing the drug himself. It's a relatively simple process."

Sakura was silent. The question remained why the victims were being injected with LSD at all. Apparently, like the bizarre ritual of the incense and the wings, and the death by cardiac arrest, the psychoactive drug also served some aspect of the killer's fantasy. But there was nothing to be gained by raising this point with Linsky.

"Thank you, Doctor," he said, "I appreciate your getting back to me so quickly."

"I am not as fond of late hours as you are," the M.E. responded, "but I told you I didn't like mysteries." He paused for a moment. "Just remember to keep in mind, Lieutenant, the caseload under which the coroner's office labors in this city. It will take me some time to compile the official reports."

"Of course." Sakura smiled. This was vintage Linsky. The autopsy results were public documents. The M.E. was assuring him that he would withhold filing on Carrera and the others as long as possible to keep the forensic details from the press.

Sakura hung up the phone. The water for his tea was boiling. He would have a cup and work awhile longer. He had read his last report for tonight, but there was one more thing he wanted to do before leaving. He poured the water into the porcelain pot and reached across the desk for the folder of crime scene photos.

✳

Alone in her Quantico office, Dr. Wilhelmina French sat entombed at her desk six stories beneath the Virginia earth. *Still under sea level* was her private joke, a reference to the geography of her native New Orleans, where only a complex system of levees kept the Mississippi and Lake Pontchartrain from creating a second Venice. Willie was a true native of the Crescent City, a descendant of the town's original French and Spanish settlers. She was blessed or cursed, depending on the vagrancy of the weather, with thick black hair that charmingly curled or frizzed. Her magnolia skin was flawless. Tim, her sometime lover, called her only half playfully a goddess. Most times she, too, felt that energy that prompted him to say it. Other times, like tonight, she was filled instead with an edginess that was close to desperation, the sudden coldness of a life crowded not only with professional accomplishments but also with *what ifs* and *might have beens*.

She looked down where the yellow light from the desk lamp cut a sharp circle in the windowless dark. Her hands on the computer keyboard moved inside the glow, punching out the final draft of the report that might very well determine her professional future.

In the last few years, in addition to her teaching duties at the academy, she had traveled the country on weekends and holidays, in the weeks between semesters, interviewing and testing every currently incarcerated serial killer. She had surprised even herself with the level of cooperation she had managed to obtain, not only from prison officials but from the men and one woman who were the objects of her research.

But then, many serial killers were above average in intelligence and as fascinated with their own pathology as any psychiatrist. Her study, more rigorous than any that had preceded it, had not provided any great surprise, supporting current theory that a constellation of factors both genetic and environmental created a serial killer. But its sheer exhaustiveness would establish beyond question her complete credibility in the field, a credibility she would have to draw on when the real thrust of her research became apparent.

And the seeds of that research were here in the words that glowed on the screen, not hidden but plainly imbedded in the conventionality of her results. She had documented in the killers' own words, in their carefully collected histories, the primary role of fantasy in their development, from an early inability to connect with the world to the inevitable first act of murder.

Serial killers started small. They started as children. Fire starters, bed wetters, animal torturers who progressed, it seemed, inevitably to homicide. She was determined to learn everything about the process. And then she wanted to short-circuit it. She believed it was possible to reprogram the malfunctioning circuits in the limbic brain. Convincing the government to let her test her theories was another matter altogether.

She mistyped a sentence and cursed. Leaned back in the chair. As always when she was feeling sorry for herself, she imagined the wry face of Dr. Krieger. He had called her "Joan of Arc" and warned her of what life would be like if she persisted in her attraction to controversial areas of research. But in the end it had been he who had arranged for her graduate work in Switzerland, where work with psychoactive drugs was still possible. Her mentor was dead now for two years, but she knew what he would say: *Plan ahead, but solve today's problems.*

One thing at a time. Finish the report now. Think about the next step tomorrow. Or, maybe, rest now and finish tomorrow. It had been a very long day.

She saved her work and reached to shut off the computer but dropped her hand. Her brother's still unopened letter sat on her desk just beyond the circle of lamplight. She didn't need to open it to know what it said. Would she be coming home for Christmas this year? Their father had asked. She really should give Mason an answer. She could telephone or type out a letter. Her brother remained impervious to e-mail.

She was still sitting motionless, her thoughts wandering backward, when the fax machine signaled a document coming through. She turned gratefully to the printer.

First page. She recognized Jimmy's precise writing. *Take a look at these and call me tomorrow.* She grabbed at the pages that followed. Blowups of crime scenes. She placed them side by side on the desk. Swung the lamp to light them.

Willie had seen a lot of dead bodies, murders of the worst kind. Dismemberments. Mutilations. Women and children mostly. Always it was the details that stayed with her—the exposed whiteness of a thigh, a mouth frozen open in a scream. These nude male bodies disturbed her in a different way. Not a visceral reaction but a purer kind of fascination that made her uncomfortable.

She looked at the clock. *Call me tomorrow.* Just like Sakura to leave her with a million questions. A student's revenge. Her best student. Her inscrutable friend. She loved to tease him with that one, but it was this quality in him she loved best. Perhaps inevitably, people had become for her little more than specimens, far too easily pigeonholed. Jimmy remained among the few exceptions.

Her fingers hesitated on the phone. She could probably still catch him at the office.

⁂

There was no reason for him to keep the mask. In fact, he should have thrown the obscenity away since it only served as a reminder that Thomas Graff had never shown the night of the Halloween party. But

that was the point precisely. The garish red image of the devil's face
was a most effective device to stoke his anger, keep warm his resent-
ment of the priest's intrusion into his life. He didn't want to like Father
Graff. Didn't want him to save St. Sebastian. He would gladly go down
with the ship he'd never wanted to captain. At this stage of his life, his
heart had no room for a champion of good deeds. It was a sin he was
willing to live with.

He had already taken Graff to task on the Halloween party, but
certainly not to his satisfaction. The priest's excuses, though they
seemed genuine enough, his mea culpas, though sufficiently sincere,
still rankled. In reality, he should have been pleased by the man's
absence, since such events were part of his grand agenda for parish
renewal, and his no-show insinuated a lack of commitment to the
cause. And he'd offered no alibi for his associate's truancy, though the
ladies were ready enough with forgiveness and with endless explana-
tions for the children, who fawned over the priest as much as they did.
He remembered hearing a rumor somewhere that a young Thomas
Graff had been engaged.

The outer door opened and closed. He glanced up at the clock.
11:05 in the night. Almost tomorrow and Graff was just returning to
the rectory.

"Father Graff . . . ," he called from his study.

"Father Kellog, you're still up." Graff paused before the open door,
his briefcase in his hand.

"It's late."

He glanced at his watch. "I lost track of time. Mrs. Ziober insisted
I stay for supper, and the table talk sort of turned into another meeting. There were some really good ideas thrown around."

"Thrown around . . . ?"

Now he set his case down and walked into the study. "Father Kellog, I know we don't see eye to eye on a lot of the parish-renewal program. But I promise in the long run—"

"What I don't see eye to eye is your conduct. You act more like a
businessman than a priest."

"I am a businessman, Andrew, for the Church."

"But you are God's priest first."

He bowed his head, then looked up. His eyes were clear and shock-ingly steady. "I know. I came late to my vocation, Father Kellog, but I have not forgotten why I entered the priesthood."

"Then I won't have to remind you again."

"Good night, Father, in the future I'll mind the clock more carefully."

Despite his best intentions to go home, Sakura, on his second cup of tea, sat skimming the canvass reports for the neighborhood surround-ing Westlake's building. The phone buzzed.

"Jimmy?" Willie's voice.

He stopped reading and smiled. "Good evening, Dr. French."

"I'm glad I caught you. These damn photos of yours would have had me up half the night. . . . Is this your case?"

"Yes."

"You could have faxed me the autopsy reports. I can't even tell how he's killing them."

"I wanted your impressions of the scenes first."

"Not fair, Sakura. What he's doing to the victims is at least as impor-tant as how he's leaving the scenes."

"Humor me."

Her response was an expressive exhalation. "Where's this happen-ing?" she asked him.

"In the victims' bedrooms. All three were homosexuals. No forced entry. We think they were random pickups. No evidence that any of them knew each other."

"The level of control is amazing. He's organized as hell and he's not hiding the bodies." She fell silent, and he imagined her studying the photographs.

"The scenes are so structured . . . ," she began again.

"I've thought about that a lot," he said. "The killer could be staging the scenes, trying to make us believe it's a cult. But where's the blood? If he's smart enough to pull this off, he's smart enough to make a better show of it."

"I think it's posing—the structure of the scenes is part of his signa-ture. He's using the victims as props to convey his message."

"But then what's the message?" he said.

"Those wings are certainly suggestive."

"Swan wings," he said. "Confirmed through the lab. It seems the birds are plentiful all along the Coast. But we've no idea how he's getting them."

"The obvious symbolism is angels," she said, "but he could be operating on a deeper level. Wings could simply indicate that he believes he's liberating the victims in some way. From their homosexuality maybe. The hands placed over the genitals could support that."

"Liberation could be part of it," he said, "but the ritual is definitely connected with angels. The letters above the beds spell out names of fallen angels."

"*Fallen angels.*" She echoed his words. "I'll have to think about that. . . . What's the sexual assault?"

"None that's apparent."

"It's possible he's impotent or masturbating later. Is he taking souvenirs?"

"Not body parts. There's no mutilation except for the incisions to insert the wings. He could be taking clothes or something else, but so far there's no indication of anything missing."

"You need to check carefully on that," she said, "but my guess is he's taking pictures. Maybe even video. He's an artist. He's going to want to record this in some way, to help sustain the fantasy."

"I should have thought of that."

She fell silent again. Then, "Do we know what the symbol is on the chests?"

"Not a clue."

"You still haven't told me how he's killing them, Sakura."

"Injection with potassium chloride. He's stopping their hearts."

"God . . . that's a new one."

"So's his whole MO," he said. "I've talked to Lawrence at the field office. There's nothing even close in the computers, and that includes all the states that keep records."

"I can't believe he hasn't killed before," she said. "Serials this organized take time to get up to speed. Where the hell did he come from?"

He had no answer.

"Jimmy . . . what is it you're still not telling me?"

He smiled at her sudden intuition. "Did I forget to mention that he's injecting the victims with LSD before he kills them?"

There was an indeterminate noise on the line. "You didn't forget to tell me that."

"Maybe I was afraid when you knew, you wouldn't be able to think about anything else."

"Bastard." She was laughing now. "You think I'm that obsessed?"

"I need your help, Willie."

"Injecting them with LSD. I can't believe it."

"What I need to know is *why*?"

"Right." She had caught his soberness. "I can imagine one reason," she said after a moment, "but it's really out there. You need to give me a little time to think about it. And fax me your reports . . . and the VICAP forms. Hell, fax me everything you've got. Forget the conventional wisdom that a profiler can have too much information."

"So you wouldn't mind giving me a little help?"

Her laugh rang again on the line. "Sarcasm doesn't suit you, Sakura."

⋔

Gothic spires, needles penetrating the pillow of darkness, soared above the exoskeleton of flying buttresses. Beneath, vaulting arches doubled and tripled upon themselves, competing in a controlled but maddening race toward the heavens. The whole structure was an exercise in opposing forces, the impossible resolution of an exquisite geometric conflict.

Michael Darius stared at his work, his intense blue eyes surprising in his naturally tanned face. His Greek Welsh heritage made for an interesting, if not conventionally handsome, combination. He ran his hand through his dark wavy hair; then with all deliberateness his fist came down hard, skin split on impact. Shadow, wood, table, shimmied, but the cathedral remained intact. His model possessed the same engineering integrity as the original in Chartres.

He sucked at his wound, tasting the iron in his blood, inhaling the scent of raw wood that flavored the rough skin of his carpenter's hands. It was an unorthodox test, but one he executed each time he completed one of his models. Of course, there was risk in what he did, but that instant before his fist fell was as exhilarating as it was frightening. Walking the tightrope between success and failure always made him light-headed. But it was his pain, not his victory, that gave him the giddiness of a first-time drunk. The pain was real, more substantive and more important to him than the building. It made him human.

From the adjacent bedroom a bubble of blue illumination, a flickering ghost from the television set, spilled into the dark corners of the workroom. The reflection danced in his peripheral vision, accompanied by the droning libretto of late-night news functioning as a kind of mantra, pieces of his environment sensed rather than seen or heard.

It wasn't until the disembodied voice spoke the name he himself had spoken hundreds of times that he became fully aware of what he was hearing. He froze, forgetting the pain, willing his brain to register exactly what the reporter was saying. . . . *Serial murder . . . homosexual victims . . . task force headed by Lieutenant James Sakura.*

A large bead of sweat ran from his hairline down the center of his face. He walked over to where he'd left the remote lying and hit mute.

It was then he heard the knocking. For a moment he considered ignoring it, then walked to the entrance. Jimmy Sakura was standing at his door.

"Jimmy." He moved back into the living room.

Sakura closed the door.

"It's after eleven."

Sakura nodded in agreement.

"You been home today?"

"Not yet."

"Hanae can't like that."

"Hanae understands."

Darius smiled. "Does she?"

Sakura walked to a chair but didn't sit. "Have you been keeping up with the news?"

Darius almost smiled again. "If you mean the serial killer . . . the answer is no."

"I like order." Sakura's face remained expressionless.

Darius smoothed his hair back from his forehead. His widow's peak make him look like a vampire. "Now there is chaos," he said.

Sakura nodded.

"The universe is a very nasty place"—Darius moved to a stack of his jazz CDs and began reading titles—"and unpredictable." He turned. "Go figure, my partner of three years, a man of infinite taste and judgment, is a lover of heavy metal."

Sakura ignored the comment. "Three bodies. No connection," he said.

"They were all gay."

Sakura shrugged.

"What's the M.E. giving you?"

"As many questions as answers."

"The lab boys?"

"Negatives."

Darius turned back to the CDs. "You would think you'd prefer classical." He moved a couple of the cases. "So what have you got, Jimmy?"

"Nude bodies with no sexual assault. Taped, gagged, but no sign of struggle."

Darius reached for a specific disc. "Willing victims . . ." He tested the logic of his words. "What about cause of death?"

"Induced heart failure. Injected them with potassium."

"Why didn't he just slit their throats?"

"He could have. He had a knife. But he was after something else. It seems he also injected them with LSD."

Darius looked up. "What's this guy into?"

Sakura pulled photographs from the folder he'd been holding.

Darius set the CD back in place, reached for the pictures. He looked down. In an instant his face went wide, then closed in on itself.

"It can all be fixed. . . ." Sakura broke the silence.

Darius glanced up. "What can be fixed?"

"Your coming back. They've made it clear I can have anyone I want."

Darius tossed the photographs onto a table and walked over to a gym that took over most of the space near the windows. He squatted on the bench, grasping the handles of the horizontal bar, pulling down until it touched his trapezius muscles.

"Hanae says I need you on this case."

Darius began to pump the bar, controlling the weight, letting his lats do most of the work. "You really ought to get one of these, Jimmy. Put some muscle on that skinny body of yours."

"He's going to kill again."

Suddenly Darius released the bar with a slam, and for a few moments it swung crazily back and forth like an empty trapeze. It seemed he'd forgotten that Sakura was even in the room as he looked down at his fingers splayed across the padded seat. Then he raised his right arm and made his hand into a gun, aimed, and fired.

"Hudson was nothing, Michael."

Darius slowly lowered his arm. "Nothing is nothing, Sakura. Now get the fuck out of here."

It was very late, but for the moment the man was enjoying how the moon threw the outline of the long row of windows onto the hardwood floor. He closed his eyelids and inhaled deeply. His obliques responded, tucking themselves higher inside the wall of his chest.

His scent was even stronger when he worked out. Rotating his head, he sniffed the damp of an armpit. Then he ran a hand between his legs, pulling up on the moist fleshy sac of his testicles. Bringing his fingers to his nostrils, he noted that the odor of his groin was slightly different. The smell of his sex seemed essentially more organic.

He walked away from the windows and moved to a floor-to-ceiling mirror. Behind him, in the moonlight, the massive hulk of his exercise equipment crouched like an alien beast. Chrome glittered like eyes. He flipped a light switch. The sharp contours of his body were instantly excited by the cool fluorescence overhead. He saw a skeleton overlaid with taut muscle. Pale, hairless flesh held the neat assemblage together. It was an attractive, well-disciplined package, this body bag. Except for the scar that ran from the Vastus lateralis to the Vastus medialis of his right leg, he might have considered himself a perfect specimen.

He flexed his chest, admiring the ladder of muscle that descended from pectorals to waist. He'd always used his body to great advantage, especially in his youth, in that second decade after the war in Southeast Asia. In the eighties, he had been part of an elite special ops unit, whose goal was to kidnap members of the Vietnamese politburo and coerce them into revealing the truth about American MIAs and POWs. Although the mission failed, he had gained invaluable knowledge and developed remarkable skills in the service.

It still seemed ironic he'd ended up in the army after he'd dropped out of college. The last place he figured he would have set course was the armed forces, since his stepfather, a man he hated, had been military and had ruled his life with an unyielding authority until he was gratefully shuttled off at eight to his grandfather.

His eyes moved back to the whiter ribbon of flesh that was the scar. No matter how desperately he tried, it was impossible without examining the photographs he'd taken to remember how wonderful life had been those few precious years before the accident. That singular horror of the head, rolling across the floor of the car, eclipsed all other memories.

He touched one of his pale nipples. Since his awakening he'd begun to suspect that there was more than an element of capriciousness in the cycle of death and rebirth that the Fallen had to endure. And he wondered if, in another lifetime, he had been a woman.

But this was to be his last lifetime on Earth. His hand reached out to the image of his face in the glass. "Gad-ri-el . . ." He drew out the name, moving as he did to the bathroom, to the medicine cabinet, to the vials lined on the shelf like small soldiers. He reached for one, and a package containing a fresh syringe. He tore away the paper and angled the needle into the cap of the bottle. In moments the LSD would take effect, take him down, down into the dark, now-remembered abyss.

CHAPTER

5

Hanae, ignoring her breakfast, sat turned to the window instead. Something about the pressure of the light that came through to her this morning was akin to that internal light that beat behind her lids—a harmony of vibration that kept darkness at bay.

In the two weeks that had now passed since Geoffrey Westlake's murder, no new victims had been found. But despite, or perhaps because of, this, the media had chosen to concentrate on a lack of police progress in the case. Jimmy's newspaper crackled as he folded it, the sharpness of the sound an indication of his displeasure. Sometimes he would discuss with her what he'd read that had disturbed him. But today, as with so many days lately, he was silent.

At last she heard the clink of his knife and fork. He was eating his bacon and eggs.

The bacon. The smell of it made her queasy, though less now than when she had removed it from the microwave. She welcomed the nausea as a sign; then with a gentle act of will, she pushed the sickness away and finished her bowl of miso. The proper nutrition was important.

"You did not have to get up this early." Jimmy's voice.

She smiled, turning her face toward him. "You were not home for supper last night. I wanted you to have a good breakfast."

It was Jimmy who rose first, taking the empty dishes to the kitchen. She heard him scraping the plates, putting them into the dishwasher. She got up from the cushion as he came back into the room.

"I'll try to make it home earlier tonight." He walked over, bent to place a kiss on her cheek. An American husband.

"I have my class this afternoon," she said.

"It's freezing outside."

"I will be fine. Mr. Romero is picking me up."

"Good," he said. Jimmy liked the driver. His fingers, which rested on her shoulder, moved down her arm to touch her hand, and were gone. The outer door closed. She heard his key turn in the lock.

At her side Taiko stirred, claiming her attention. She reached to pat his head. The dog's increased protectiveness had been one more sign that the miracle she'd long awaited was at last happening inside her. She had as yet said nothing to Jimmy. With the case absorbing so much of his attention, there never seemed a time that was right.

⁂

Sakura scanned his notes, then looked up at the members of his Special Homicide Unit who had gathered for this early-morning meeting in his office. The four detectives who made up his regular team acted as a semiautonomous group, functioning inside the Major Case Squad of the Special Investigation Division. At present they formed the nucleus of the task force that had been placed in charge of the triple-murder investigation. Adelia Johnson sat next to Johnny Rozelli, Pat Kelly next to Walt Talbot. However, the seating arrangement was something of a false readout. Johnson was more comfortable with Kelly; the two younger male officers more compatible.

Pat Kelly was the veteran of the group. A cop's cop who'd worked hundreds of homicides, who as a precinct cop had even seen time on the Son of Sam case. Working homicide, Kelly had once said, scarred a detective for life. Most of Kelly's scars were visible.

"Well, Lieutenant, think he's finished? It's been two weeks since the last one." A chain-smoker, Kelly rolled an unlit cigarette between his blunt fingers.

"Maybe three was all he had in him." Sakura riffled through his notes, waiting for Kelly to comment. The fifty-six-year-old had apparently had another sleepless night. The skin under his eyes appeared bruised. Only Kelly's mind was spared the insults he perpetrated on the rest of his body.

Delia Johnson spoke instead. "You know you don't believe that, Lieutenant." The detective had great instincts.

"Maybe we're not dealing with a serial." Sakura's gaze made a round of the table. "Maybe there's some connection among the victims we're still missing."

"They're all queer, Lieutenant," said Rozelli. "That's the only connection. This one's going to kill again. Just give him some time." The latest arrival in a long line of Rozelli cops flashed his patented smirk that made even the toughest perps nervous.

"I agree with Johnny," said Talbot. "I think we've got a bona fide serial who's cooling off." Talbot, the junior in the unit, had made gold shield after the Kasavettes case. He'd been able to sidestep the nasty window dressing and had gone straight to the heart of the crime. *Creative visualization,* he'd explained when pressed how he'd solved it.

Sakura hoped the killing was over, but he doubted it. Sometimes serials started to feel they were losing control and attempted to stop acting on the fantasy. Inevitably, they failed and killed again. For the police it became a kind of waiting game. He checked his notes once more and looked up. "I'm concerned with how much is getting out to the media. I don't like how they latched on so quickly to the ritual aspects of the case."

"Come on, Lieutenant." Rozelli was standing, fidgeting with the lapels of his designer sport coat. "They're just guessing. They got nothing important."

There was a moment's silence before Sakura spoke. "We will not allow anyone to take this case away from us." It was the nasty truth, but the press could be every bit as dangerous as the killer.

Ms. Nguyen had brought dozens of sculptures for Hanae to feel during the first weeks she attended art class. Some were copies, like the Rodin. Others were originals done by Janice Nguyen herself. It was a way of orienting her senses, Ms. Nguyen had said. Hanae complied meekly, not wanting to offend her young instructor's good intentions. That she had internal vision, that her fingers had been her eyes from the first, Ms. Nguyen might not understand.

Then there came that moment when the instructor walked to Hanae's table, saw the cool lumps of clay obeying Hanae's fingers like so many small children. "I'm sorry," she'd spoken quietly, understanding at last Hanae's extraordinary abilities. "I was most foolish."

Hanae frowned now. The clay had a will of its own this afternoon. She pinched the point where the wing joined the body of the bird. *Better,* she thought, massaging a loose piece of clay between her thumb and middle fingers.

"I've been watching you since I started this class," his voice came from her right, slightly behind her. "What you do with that clay is amazing."

Taiko, at her side, beat a tattoo against the hardwood floor. She turned toward the male voice. "Thank you. It is something I enjoy."

"How long . . ." He stalled.

". . . Have I been blind? Since birth."

"I guess that was a pretty rude question," he said. "It's just that what you do is so remarkable. Birds, huh."

"I have finches."

"Sorry, name's Adrian Lovett."

"Hanae Sakura."

"Japanese, right?"

"Yes."

"Didn't figure you for a native." He laughed. "Well, I better let you get back to work. Nice meeting you, Hanae. . . . Did I say that right?"

"Yes." She felt herself smiling.

Nearly nine P.M. It had been another very long day. Endless paperwork and countless task force meetings. Departmental feathers to be soothed. James Sakura shut his computer down and sat in the relative quiet of his office, trying to work up the energy to go home to his wife as he'd promised.

Three bodies in one week, and now two weeks of hell waiting for the shoe that never dropped. But it would drop. And though he knew it was foolish to put the extra pressure on himself, he could never get over the feeling in these situations that with only a little more police work he could prevent a death. That for somebody out there now who was living and laughing and breathing, the clock was running out.

He sighed. He would leave in a minute. He wanted to be home, in fact, but it seemed so infinitely difficult to pass through the gauntlet of small tasks that were required to get there. So he reached for his headphones instead and hit the button of the Discman. The Red Hot Chili Peppers boomed in his head, blotting everything out.

He closed his eyes and leaned back in his chair.

Behind the wall of noise lived an eleven-year-old in the last of his boyhood summers. Darkness gathered at the edge of the sea and rolled beyond him into blackness. He stood on the shore, listening to the sound of the surf, feeling already in the cooling ocean breath that first touch of change. Had he, in fact, been its agent? Had there been some fatal magic in his gesture, when kneeling in the sand, he had set his little handmade boats with their daring candles on their imaginary journey to his father?

For only a few weeks after, the summons to America had come. His father had at last prevailed upon his wife to bring his firstborn son into their home.

The story of his father's second marriage, which had come so quickly after his mother's death, had been gradually pieced out through the years. Susan was a nurse whom his father had worked with in the course of his medical studies, and they had become friendly after his mother's death. As his grandmother perceived it, Susan had used his father's loneliness to trap him and steal his soul. The woman had purposely become pregnant, forcing the honorable Isao to marry her and remain in America with their child.

His grandmother had been very wise, but her vision of her own firstborn was clouded by love. There was truth in her portrayal of his father's second marriage, but it was not the whole truth. His father was no more a victim than was anyone in this life. If he had strayed from his Tao, was it not his own feet upon the path?

His own belief was that misery was most often self-imposed and certainly contagious. A truth which his eleven-year-old self had been very soon to learn.

The light from them was everywhere, everywhere he looked, thin yellow auras pulsing in the sodden air. No streetlamps needed tonight on Christopher Street. Not for him.

The man found a parking space for the Harley, made sure the side compartment that held his equipment was locked, and walked. The Fallen surrounded him, bumped him, eyed him, but he was alone.

Last night the drug had failed him, calling forth not the glory of the vision he'd regained inside the tunnel but vivid memories of his human life before the accident. Tonight he felt only the pain of loss, belonging nowhere, a creature neither of Heaven nor of Earth. He longed for human comfort. And the peace, no matter how false, of the life he had had before his awakening. He wanted *not to know*.

But he did know. That there was no happiness that lasted, no love. That the forgetfulness he craved tonight was a trap. That forgetting, that denying his mission, meant dying not once but again and again, reincarnating over and over, with no more chances to escape the flesh he had once desired above all things but was now his prison. This was the war again from before men and time, and he was a warrior, hunting MIAs in another kind of jungle. An irony in a life of ironies.

The bar he went into was filled with the light of the Fallen, but a murky light, dulled by alcohol and drugs, by the lust that was a sign of the real union lost. The dance went on around him, broken and maimed, a sad reflection almost beyond bearing tonight. He bought a whiskey at the bar and walked it to a shadowed table where there was less chance of being approached. He needed to think.

He swallowed half the drink. He had no choice but to go on. The question was how long he could remain safe in this city. He had been careful, but eventually he might make a mistake, especially with Zavebe.

He could get out now, leave the life of this human shell behind. He could move to another city. He had plenty of money from the insurance settlements. But where better for his research than New York? Given his real enemy, the police were gnats.

Gnats with bullets, he reminded himself. This was spiritual war fought on an earthly plane. Capture was unthinkable, a double prison truly beyond his bearing. And his death the most ironic of failures. Still it seemed crazy to consider leaving.

No, *he* was crazy. But was he? He wished that he were.

He knocked down the last of his drink. Got up. Pushed through the gathered bodies, through the luminescent fog of sickly light and smoke. Back on the street, he headed toward the Harley, giving up the search that was less than halfhearted tonight.

As always the aura of a great one came as a shock—the overwhelming brilliance anchored but uncontained by the black seed of flesh in which it dwelt. The boy at the center of the brightness stood at the edge of the sidewalk. Eyes darting, trolling the cruising cars, he half lounged, half danced along the curb, shopping grimy adolescent cool, as if the thrift shop jacket and dirty jeans were mere affectation.

He made an instant decision, closing the distance between them, heading off the blue Volvo pulling to the curb. The boy, already leaning toward the fleeting invitation of the car, jerked upward toward him in a small moment of anger. But changed his mind and smiled.

Hanae shut her eyes to concentrate the light. A blind woman's sight carved from darkness. Yet she had trouble focusing. The only illumination she could gather was a thin anemic veil that seemed threatened by shadows hovering just inside the limits of her inner vision.

That she was incapable of drawing in the light probably had to do with the current of complex emotions that flowed through her. She reached and touched the place where the child was growing. Happiness should have ignited the flame inside her. But yet she struggled.

Nori. Nori would ease her mind. At least for a time. She inserted the cassette and listened to the pleasant sounds of her cousin's Japanese litany as it crackled off the tape. The research trials at the laboratory were going well despite Dr. Murasaki's interference. Nori had no patience with the male-dominated system that afforded her entrance into the biomedical field only because of her impressive academic achievements.

Murasaki wants me to trade my lab coat for a dark dress that covers my knees. To shuffle behind a husband who will expect nothing beyond the breeding of intelligent children and clever shopping.

Nori at twenty-four was dangerously close to becoming a Christmas cake—an unmarried girl past desirability.

I cannot love Hiroshi. Nori's tone betrayed an uncommon sadness. *My heart yearns to, but my soul will not allow it.* Her voice hardened. *His words are earnest, but he will become my father, should we marry.*

I . . . Nori faltered. *I had a dream.*

Hanae moved closer to the machine, her fingers adjusting the volume.

I am walking down a long corridor. There is just enough light so that I do not stumble over my own feet. My shoes make cricket sounds against the floor. I am myself, yet I am not.

A cold, wet wind ruffles a long line of curtains hung on metal rods, but their hems do not touch the floor. I can see that each drape hides a small enclosure. One of the curtains billows, and I see two shoeless feet dangling. I am conscious of my hand pushing against the fabric.

She is young. Her black hair chopped short, with thick bangs covering her brows. Her face is snow white. Her mouth red with thick lipstick. Her head slumps against a naked shoulder, and her tiny body swings against its own weight. Stockings pulled tight by a garter belt cover her plump legs. She is dead, yet her fingers fight the edge of a pale corset, binding her like a kind of orthopedic device. She struggles to cover her exposed vagina.

Tears fall from closed lids. She is clearly embarrassed by the immodesty of her own death, by the shameless display of her body.

I am horrified, but I cannot resist. I push at one curtain after another. Behind each a young woman is hanging, tugging at the corset to hide herself. I accept this as some kind of ritual suicide, but there is ambivalence. . . . Nori's sigh. Then, *Hanae, what does the dream mean?*

She snapped off the recorder, pressed her mouth into a hard line. She would have to reply to her cousin. She must tell Nori that her dream was no more than a mirror of her fear of marriage to Hiroshi. Her family expected such guidance, but she did not always want to see beneath the mist that shrouded the mountain.

At four, behind her blind eyes, she had *seen* her grandmother fall— the missed step bringing her to the ground, her head hard against the stone lantern in the garden. It had been her first prophetic vision. One that had brought tears to her eyes and had caused her mother and father to think she was ill. She had had a fever, her body on fire like the

fire beneath the lids of her eyes illuminating the death of her grandmother. Over and over she had repeated her grandmother's name, begging to see her.

"Bad dream." Mama-san had whispered those words in her ear.

But she had not been sleeping. Only in her bed playing with her
favorite doll.

Later that evening, when her uncle had come to the house, she
knew his words before they were spoken. And after, her mother had
taken her into her arms, holding her so tightly that she could feel her
frightened heart against her own chest. For a time she harbored a
child's guilt, never certain whether her vision had made what had happened so.

Taiko stirred. She ran her foot down the length of his spine. What
would he make of the new one? She shook away the thought. She did
not have Dr. Blanchard's confirmation. Yet she had known the last
time, even before she'd seen a doctor.

But she had lost the baby. After only three months she had miscar-
ried. The life slipping away in a small flood between her thighs. Jimmy
had been more concerned with her own health than the loss of the
child. But she was inconsolable for months. And later a softer sadness
had settled inside her, which she had hidden from Jimmy, and most of
the time from her own awareness. Except when she visited the little
shrine to Jizo she had constructed in her heart and made offerings in
remembrance of her *water child*.

She should not wait for the doctor's appointment to tell Jimmy. She
should tell him tonight. She listened for the door of the *genkan* to
open. Silence. Lightly she touched Taiko's head with the tip of her toe
and sighed. Her husband was once again late.

"Why don't you pack it up, Lieutenant?" Pat Kelly's nicotine-wasted
voice caught Sakura off guard.

"What's your excuse, Kelly?"

"Nothing waiting for me at home."

Sakura picked up his cup, took a sip. "Cold."

Kelly came into the office, slumped into a chair. He fished inside his jacket, unplugging a cigarette from a crumpled pack. "So what're you thinking?" He hitched an unlit unfiltered between his teeth.

He stood and walked to the window. "I don't like this waiting."

Kelly grunted. "He'll ante up soon enough."

"I know." He came back and sat down behind his desk.

"Lorenzo." Kelly chuckled. A smoker's laugh.

Nate Lorenzo. Captain Nathan Lorenzo. An NYPD cop accused of hiring a hit on his wife. His first murder case. A case no one else wanted to touch. Taboo. Even Internal Affairs had played it soft.

"Excuse my language, Lieutenant, but it took big balls to go after Lorenzo."

"It was my job."

Kelly shook his head. "There're ways to do the job, and then there're ways."

"I know only one way."

"That's what I mean, Lieutenant. This serial ain't got nothing on Lorenzo. You'll get him."

"I don't feel so confident, Kelly. It's been two weeks."

Kelly shrugged, nursing the cold cigarette. "Can't figure a crazy."

He picked up the jade disk. "Something is about to happen."

"That's the only way we get moving. The only way we get the son of a bitch off the streets."

"Somebody will die."

"Somebody always dies, Lieutenant."

"It feels bad, Kelly."

The vet half stood, stuffing the worked-over cigarette into his pocket. "That's how you and Darius got along so well. God knows nobody else could."

"What do you mean?"

"Those feelings you two get."

No, he didn't have Darius's instincts. "I'm not like Michael."

"Closer than you think." Kelly grinned. "You just don't know it." Fully rising from his seat, and with what was an extraordinary gesture, he reached across the desk and clasped his arm.

Sakura looked down, covering the old detective's hand with his own. When he looked up, the air glinted between them. Then he felt the vet's hand slip from beneath his. The sergeant grinned. It was as close to a real smile as he would likely get from Pat Kelly.

⋔

The room had a sour coldness, but Jude Pinot, standing near the bed, had begun to peel off his clothes. His eyes were shut, which somehow made it easier. Even in the darkness he hated to look at this dump, a flop he shared with two other guys. Holing up to sleep like bats in the daylight. Flittering back and forth at night.

At least in the house in Jersey, things had been warm and clean. He could still see his mother, if he wanted, like a movie inside his lids. On her hands and knees, scrubbing at old linoleum more chipped and faded than she was. Working away, as if it were the germs she always talked about that had left him with bruises and broken ribs, instead of that bastard she'd married.

The image scrolled in his brain, her hands come dripping with gray water from the bucket. The same spindly hands that tended him after the beatings. Huge white spiders crawling on his skin with old washcloths wrapping ice, binding his wounds with bands of yellowed adhesive. Treating him at home. Not because of the shame. Not even because of the fear. Because emergency rooms and hospitals were full of germs that could kill you. She'd kept him safe from germs, if nothing else.

Jacketless and shoeless now, he pulled off his shirt and tossed it into the corner, breathing in the mattress funk of night sweat and spilled semen. Reminding himself it was freedom he inhaled. That the hustling wasn't forever.

"What's that?" He'd turned to see the john taking something from the bag he'd been carrying.

"Camera." The man showed him. "I want to take some pictures."

"Whatever." He shrugged. "You paid for the night." He walked into the bathroom, thinking it was funny how things worked out. Gil and Chad had been gone since this morning, faceless extras in some porno flick they were shooting out in Jersey, of all places. He'd turned down the gig because he hadn't liked the idea of doing it on camera. And he never crossed the Hudson. A symbolic thing with him. Never going back. Weird that he'd ended up starring in his own little freak show tonight.

He unzipped his jeans, deciding to think of nothing, finding the softened edge inside his brain, the place where the dope he smoked had nestled and spread. The floorboards creaked. The john had followed him into the bathroom. His penis still aimed at the toilet, he turned, saw what he saw.

His body reacted, moving ahead of his mind. Something . . . the mask . . . registered. The canister coming up to spray. He fought at first, holding his breath, his hands protecting his face. But the attempt at flight was a gesture, like most everything else in his life. At the end it was pleasant to surrender.

CHAPTER

6

There was an old stink of fast food and stale sex in the small room. You could have easily missed *ASBEEL* printed in ash on the dirty wall, if not for the flood lamps the techs had set up. The cold illumination made the body on the mattress appear romantically spectral rather than dead. What the light made of the rest of the room was less forgiving. The only relief in the dingy, cramped space was a tangle of color in an old poster thumbtacked against a closet door: BARBRA, THE CONCERT.

The killer had been slumming, thought Sakura. Except the young victim looked no different from the others. Attractive, fine-boned, lean. The muscles of his body defined more by life on the streets than workouts at any gym. The boy's mouth was fixed in a full-lipped pout, as though he were somehow put out by this final, unfortunate turn of events.

The swan wings jutted out whiter against the soiled mattress ticking, the boy's delicate fingers cupping his sex in a gesture that seemed oddly modest. In another reality the ash markings inscribing his chest might have been a testament to some primitive rite of passage.

The snap of Linsky's gloves stopped Sakura's thoughts.

"Injection marks?" he asked the M.E., his words punctuated by frigid puffs in the underheated room. He could see the wings, the drawing, a new name written on the wall. He needed confirmation of what his eyes could not so easily discern.

Linsky lifted the victim's arm. "He was a user. Heroin, I suspect." He inspected the groin and between the toes. "Fairly new at it, it seems."

He pulled at the skin on the inside of the elbow, isolating the site where two fresh-looking marks appeared. "I can't be positive, but these look like what we've been seeing. We'll run the complete battery of tests. I can't be specific, but I think this one's been dead for less than twenty-four hours." The M.E. moved to the other side of the room and motioned for the gurney to be brought in.

Sakura took another look at the corpse. The cooling-off period was over.

"Seems our killer wasn't as selective." McCauley walked up behind him and bent over the body, looking down at the slim wrists. The bruising from the duct tape was clear. The chief of detectives stretched back to his full height, glanced around the room. "This is a rat hole. The kid working the streets?"

"Unconfirmed. But Talbot is talking to the roommate who found him this morning."

McCauley took out a handkerchief and held it against his face as though he feared contamination. "Who's this Dr. French you're bringing in?"

"Forensic psychiatrist. Consults on serials for the Bureau. She was one of my instructors at Quantico."

McCauley nodded. "An agent?"

"Independent."

"Good. We don't need the FBI to tell us how to run things. You know jurisdiction is a sacred cow, Sakura. How good is she?"

"The best."

McCauley finished with his handkerchief, stuck it back in his pocket. "I said you can bring in whoever you need. If Dr. French can help you get this son of a bitch off my streets, more power to you. I want him. Now."

He watched McCauley walk out of the room, peel off the latex gloves, and deposit them into the plastic bag the techs had provided. *Now,* the chief had said, but Sakura had not understood it as an ultimatum. At least, not yet.

⁂

Hanae sat before the small Buddhist altar she had brought with her from Kyoto. She was preparing for meditation and was thinking about

Willie, who was arriving today in New York. Willie, a Catholic who struggled with her religion, had once joked after reading a book on Japan that the Japanese must surely be the pack rats of religion, tucking away bits and pieces of spirituality to pull out what was needed at the moment.

She had laughed and admitted it was true. It was a common saying that every Japanese had a Shinto wedding and a Buddhist funeral, a generalization that was both more and less than accurate. The actual situation was more complex. Taoism and Confucianism, even Christianity, were all part of the religious and ethical mix in Japan.

Today she must be a Buddhist. Offering her thanks for Willie's coming. Meditating on why Willie's arrival should bring such a sense of relief. Certainly, she liked Willie very much, from the time when Jimmy had attended the academy at Quantico. She remembered how strange she had thought it at first when her husband had become so familiar with one of his teachers. It was different in Japan, where the rules of hierarchy proscribed a formal relationship between a teacher and student. But also unlike Japan, where friends met in restaurants rather than sharing meals in their homes, Jimmy had invited Willie to their small Virginia apartment for dinner.

She had been so nervous preparing that meal. And Willie had come early. But after a short introduction, Jimmy and their guest had taken their drinks to the adjoining living room, where they'd sat and joked about people and cases and things that had happened in class. It had been very pleasant to hear Jimmy laughing about the work that he always took so seriously. But that was the effect of Willie on everyone. Listening to their words and their laughter, she had forgotten her nervousness about the food. So the meal was a great success. And she and Willie had themselves become close over those long months at Quantico.

So, naturally, she was happy Willie was arriving today. Willie was her friend. And Willie was a window that opened on Jimmy's working world. Willie would tell her the things about his job that Jimmy would not—the dangers and the pressures from which he believed he must protect her.

But that was not all of it. She wanted more from Willie than a wife's small and secret pathway into her husband's hidden life. She wanted

Willie as part of this case for the same reason she wanted Kenjin. She feared this case. She forced herself to form the word in her mind. She *feared* it, had feared it since Jimmy had first been placed in charge, although she had at once understood it as both a great challenge and opportunity. But it was not that she thought Jimmy needed his friends' help. She feared he would need their protection.

Was this one of her presentiments of danger, or something small and foolish? Was she afraid that the more successful Jimmy became in his work, the less important she would be to him?

She had never resented Jimmy's dedication. Her husband was indivisible. No split existed between what Jimmy was and what he did. It was this wholeness in him that she loved, a wholeness that had encompassed her since the day they had met. There was no moment of his life, she knew, of which she was not a part. And so it would be with their child.

Foolish, foolish, Hanae. Was it not simply change that she feared?

She sat upright on the cushion, making a place for stillness. For a long time she remained, contemplating the Noble Truths that all is impermanence, that suffering results from an attempt to confine the fluid forms of reality in the rigid categories created by the mind.

The telephone rang.

⋔

The apartment building was an oddity in the city. One of a handful of grand Victorian ladies passed down through a family both rich enough and eccentric enough to resist the pressures toward going condo. The lobby was L-shaped and cavernous. A march of white columns in blue gloom. Carved marble fireplaces more than two decades cold.

A single shaft of late sun pierced through heavy draperies, falling in a hazy spotlight where Hanae Sakura sat in her red coat on one of the faded sofas. Dust motes like frenzied ghosts danced in the beam, whipped up by Taiko's tail beating a welcome on the carpet.

Michael Darius had come in from the street and was crossing the lobby toward them, Hanae's eyes tracking as if she could see. He shifted his tool bag to his other hand and leaned down to pet the shepherd.

"You should have called," he said to Hanae.

"We have not been waiting long." She reached out a hand to settle the dog. Her pale face, veiled in sun, canted upward to Darius.

He sat down in a chair by the side of the sofa, his knees cutting the light.

"You're making cabinets?" she asked him.

He smiled. She could smell as well as he the sawdust clinging to his work clothes. "Shelves," he said, "for a private residence. Rosewood. Very nice."

"You always do beautiful work."

He smiled again at the double edge. Small talk was impossible between them. "Jimmy came by here the other night," he said.

She didn't answer. She was sitting perfectly still.

"I don't want to go back to police work, Hanae. Besides, I'm a better carpenter."

"Is this what you believe?"

"Yes. And there's always the law. . . ." His words ran out in silence. "Do you want to come up?"

"No." She smiled. "Jimmy phoned before I came here. They have found another body, but he has promised to try to be home for a few hours tonight." She got up from the sofa, bringing Taiko to his feet. His harness jingled like muffled bells. "I'm going to have something special prepared."

Darius stood too. He towered over her. "I'm sorry, Hanae, that I can't do what you want."

Again her head tilted, following his voice. The black almond eyes were laughing now. "Be selfish, Kenjin. Try to remember what you want."

Michael Darius entered the bedroom like a man visiting a grave. He walked slowly, approaching the bed, still perfectly made, stopping paces from its padded edge. The thick mattress with its custom sheets and coverlet kept well beyond his reach. As if the bed were a trap.

He stood very still, his glance going to the paintings, to the photograph his wife had abandoned with the other things on the vanity. Allowing the memories to come. Aware of the scent that had enveloped him from the moment he'd entered. The odor of civet and roses that still lingered.

He turned and walked out, closing the door behind him *for the last time*. Knowing as the vow was renewed that it would not be kept.

He went to the kitchen and fixed himself a sandwich, as if the routine of living were a cure that might someday take hold. He took his plate to the living room and set it down on the table. The photographs still lay where he'd thrown them the night of Jimmy's visit.

He pushed the plate away and pulled the eight-by-tens toward him, laying the shots of the crime scenes like a game of solitaire, placing the victim close-ups side by side. Three gay men, very similar in body type. Die-cut fodder for the killer's sick fantasy. The homosexual context seemed obvious, even glaring. So why didn't he buy it? What made him so sure that the obvious here was wrong?

As always when looking at dead bodies, thoughts of his sister could not be avoided. And the time away from police work had taken away the blunted edge of routine. Elena's murder, when he had been in high school, came back with renewed force. His discovery of her body. The strangeness of the way his consciousness had split between horror and a numb objectivity. It was the numbness that had remained. His only interest, the pursuit of justice for the man who had done it. A part-time yardman, quickly apprehended, who had returned to rob, and only incidentally to rape and murder his sister.

Her killer's conviction had brought some satisfaction. But inside, the numbness persisted. Emotion was a distant reflex, a relic he could examine, even mimic, but not anything he could feel. That had changed for a while with Margot.

He returned his attention to Sakura's victims, focusing on the symbol, dark against the hairless chests. The ash-drawn pattern was tantalizing, somehow familiar. He stared at it, reaching for the memory that would make sense of the ragged design. He closed his eyes, shutting out distraction, but the drifting fragments that played inside his head refused to coalesce.

Why was he doing this? He stood. And picking up the plate of food and the photographs, he returned to the kitchen. But it was only the uneaten sandwich that made it into the trash.

✦

The night sky was flat and opaque, the river air misty with reflected neon. Cold light and a colder wind. It shuffled off the water, blowing away the traffic noise from the nearby tangle of approaches that fed the Brooklyn Bridge. It crawled against his skin, chilling him despite the leather jacket. Michael Darius threw his cigarette down, crushing red sparks with his foot. The butt was the third he had left in the alley.

The wind blew harder, pushing him farther into the darkness, the river smell mixing with fading smoke and the layered odors of garbage. Always a little rot left behind. Seeds of deterioration planted in brick and concrete, breathed back day after day.

It was long after eight when Sakura finally appeared, materializing through the fog that rose from the grillwork near the curb.

He crossed the street, falling in step behind. "Jimmy . . ."

Sakura turned on his heel, his face a pale triangle floating in the fall-out from the streetlamp.

"Damn it, Michael, where the hell did you come from?"

"Over there." He threw a shoulder toward the black gap of the alley. "I took a chance on catching you."

"You been waiting long?"

"Yeah."

"I thought you'd stopped smoking."

Darius snapped the lighter shut, thrust it back into the jacket, and exhaled. "I did," he said.

Sakura made no comment. The logical question was why Michael was here. "Have you eaten?" he asked instead.

Darius shook his head.

✦

Two in the *genkan*. Hanae listened. Two removing their shoes. Tonight was good. Like old times. She rose to her feet as they came into the room.

"I brought someone." Jimmy's happiness was in his voice.

"Welcome, Kenjin." She smiled, fixed on his breathing, on the sound of Taiko's wagging tail beating out its greeting.

"Where's Willie?" Jimmy asked.

"Right here," Willie answered for her, her rough-pleasant voice moving toward them out of the kitchen. "This is my third beer, Sakura. You plan to starve me? Or just get me drunk?" She had stopped at Jimmy's side. "Hi," she said. The word directed at Kenjin.

"Dr. Wilhelmina French"—Jimmy made the introduction— "Michael Darius. . . . Michael was my partner."

Hanae listened. Kenjin was standing very still, the protectiveness he always wore pulled tightly about him. A cloak against this stranger. "Dr. French," he said.

"Willie was one of my instructors at Quantico," Jimmy continued the introduction. "She led my group the last nine months when we profiled actual cases."

"Jimmy helped us track down a serial."

"Please sit." Hanae indicated the table. "The pot is hot and waiting. We don't want Willie to starve."

Shabu shabu was a one-pot meal. Peasant fare. A meal to be shared among friends. Together she and Willie brought the small warm bottles of sake from the kitchen, the platter of meat and vegetables to be cooked in the charcoal-heated pot that was placed at the center of the table.

"Everything is wonderful, Hanae." Willie spoke to her from across the table. "Especially the pickles."

Jimmy laughed.

"What did I say?" Willie asked.

"You explain it to her, Michael," Jimmy said to him. "I remember you said the same thing the first time you tasted Hanae's *tsukemono*."

She wondered for a moment if Kenjin would not answer. But he did. "In Japan a housewife who makes good pickles," he said, "is also supposed to be skilled in the art of making love."

Willie made a noise. "So how can you tell that a *man* is a good lover?"

"All Japanese men are good lovers," Jimmy said.

Even Kenjin laughed at that.

They had rejected the sofa and chairs in favor of cushions on the *tatami*. In a circle, cross-legged, Sakura, Darius, and Willie French now sat. An interloper might have assumed that meditation was in order, but the posture was an illusion. They'd been discussing murder for almost an hour.

Sakura watched as Willie drew in her legs, resting her chin on her knees while she shifted the photographs of the four victims into chronological order. The cumulative effect of the layout was so powerful it almost blunted the intellect.

"Killing by injection is rare," she said, staring at the eight-by-tens. "Especially outside a hospital setting."

"But the medical component is strong," Sakura said.

"Possibly. He certainly knows what he's doing with the potassium. And how to handle a scalpel." She stood now and began pacing. "Two weeks roughly between Westlake and Pinot," she said. "Still Pinot feels more opportunistic than the other kills. Maybe it's the kid himself. A street hustler is different from an art gallery owner or a dancer in the Metropolitan Ballet. Makes me wonder if he couldn't hold back any longer. Exploded, grabbing at whatever he could get." She stopped, looking down. "Yet he's still as organized as hell."

"But don't organized serials hide the bodies of their victims?" Darius asked.

"Usually," she answered him.

"So maybe he wants you to see what he's doing." Darius intercepted her stare. "The murders seem staged."

"Not staged, staging would be for us," she said. "He's posing the bodies. And the posing is for him. Whatever he's doing, he needs to do. It's intrinsic to his fantasy."

"And what fantasy is that, Dr. French?" Darius was still looking at her.

"His focus on homosexuals is primary, I think, and placing the victims' hands over their genitalia is a strong message. Of course, the wings are indicative, and the fact that he's writing the names of angels on the walls . . ." She stopped and sat back down on the cushion, aware perhaps that she hadn't really answered his question.

Sakura reached into the manila envelope and pulled out the black-and-whites that showed wider shots of the murder scenes. He pointed to the ash-drawn letters scrawled over Carrera's bed. "The names of *fallen* angels," he added.

"The battle between good and evil." Willie seemed grateful for his intercession. "The cosmic imagery fits with LSD use," she said. She glanced down at the photo he'd singled out. "Maybe he perceives homosexuals as *fallen* men."

"And killing them is punishment?" Darius asked.

"I don't think I'd call it punishment," she said. "I'm still impressed by the lack of violence. I think *fallen* doesn't translate as evil in the killer's mind, but rather as disadvantaged in some way."

"Something he's got to fix," Darius said.

"Yes." Willie seemed pleased how Michael had finished off her hypothesis.

Darius nodded and rose.

Sakura collected the photographs, replacing them into the envelope, then stood too.

"Understanding the fantasy is paramount," he said. "I have an appointment with Dr. Isaacs on Friday. He's the Hebrew professor who discovered that those words were the names of fallen angels. I want to see what else he has to say and get his copy of this book *Enoch*."

"Sounds like a plan." Willie rose now to stand next to him. "Nice to have met you," she said, extending her arm toward Darius.

They shook hands like adversaries, and Sakura was remembering uncomfortably all that he'd told Willie about his ex-partner back at Quantico. He felt guilty again, as he had earlier tonight when making the introductions. Perhaps he'd given Willie some kind of unfair advantage. But then, he had never expected the two of them to meet.

✦

What Zoe liked best about having sex with him was that she didn't have to fake an orgasm. Of course, she never had to fake an orgasm. She could come at will. But sometimes she just didn't want to. Depending on her partner. But with him, she always came. In multiples.

Why this was so, she never really analyzed. He wasn't the best-looking man she'd ever slept with, or the best lover. She'd had better in both departments. But if she'd had to pin it down, it was that he just damn loved screwing her. She still giggled remembering the story he'd told her of how his uncle Vito would treat him to an ice-cream sundae every Saturday when he was growing up. He'd dreamed of putting that first spoonful in his mouth all week. He said she was like that ice-cream sundae.

She rode him now. Her fingers cupping her breasts. Her long legs astride him, bearing in. A smile opening her mouth so that her white teeth showed bright and perfect. She bent over, her hair falling like a veil, to lick his closed lids.

He twisted his head to the side and moaned, "Oh, baby . . ."

"You're sweating like a pig, honey."

"Shhh . . ."

She lifted up, angling her hips, grinding him in deeper.

"Yessss . . ." He exploded and she laughed in pure joy. Better than her own orgasm was watching his.

She lay with her head on his chest, circling his nipple with the tip of her tongue. He tasted salty, and his heart lumbered against her ear.

"Did you come?" he asked, rubbing his fingers in her hair.

"Why do men always ask that?"

He grunted.

She lifted up, her hazel eyes half lidded. "What's up?"

"What?" He rolled over onto his stomach.

"What's up with Pinot?"

"Same shit."

"After waiting so long, you'd have figured he'd be more particular," she said. "Pinot was a street punk."

He turned over. "Obviously, social background ain't part of our killer's agenda."

"So what did he look like?"

"Who?"

"Pinot."

"The little whore looked just like the pretty dancer, the sweet gallery owner, and the darling model."

"You're nasty. So politically incorrect."

"Crap."

"I like you in spite of your flaws." She stretched up to kiss him. "Did he do the same thing to the body?"

"Same damn thing." He sat up, rolled his legs over the side of the bed. "Every time I go to one of these scenes, I feel like I've been to Catholic benediction with Mama Rosa."

"Catholic benediction?"

"The asshole burns incense. Uses it to write mumbo jumbo on the walls. Doodle on the victims' chests."

"Interesting . . ."

"You got anything to drink in that refrigerator, Zoe, besides fancy water?"

"Johnny Rozelli, I pegged you for a Perrier man."

CHAPTER

7

Willie French had been up before six A.M., swilling coffee, searching for something unrumpled from her partially unpacked wardrobe. She had taken a taxi to Police Plaza, arriving early for introductions to the members of Sakura's regular unit.

She sat with his team now, in the first row of chairs set up in the eleventh-floor operations room, where blowups of the victims and crime scene photos decorated the walls. This morning's meeting had gathered a majority of the task force members, most of whom had never worked a serial case. Despite the popularization of profiling in the media, it was not a process that was well understood. Hardened homicide cops assumed they knew everything about murder. It was always a tough crowd.

She flipped through her largely unnecessary index cards, jettisoning the niceties of her opening remarks. As Jimmy completed her introduction, she rose to take his place at the front of the room.

"He's male and he's white," she plunged right in, not particularly loudly. She saw the faces come up, focusing to catch her words. "Statistically speaking, women don't commit serial murder, and serial murderers rarely kill outside their race. He's at least in his thirties. These are complex crimes, indicating a level of confidence impossible for a beginner. We should expect a criminal record. And whether he's been charged with it or not, it's almost certain that he's killed before."

The direct approach, as usual, seemed to have worked. She had their full attention.

"His intelligence is obviously high," she went on, "but the formal education level is more tricky. College or self-taught would be my guess. He fancies himself an intellectual.

"He appears confident, even arrogant. He may dress casually, but he's not sloppy or scruffy. He's a control freak.

"His victims are gay men, which suggests that the killer may be repressing his own homosexuality. He may be in a relationship with a woman, or even currently married. But expect a history of failed relationships. He may be impotent, since he's leaving no semen.

"He's nocturnal, killing at night," she continued, "so it's possible he's holding down a regular job. Maybe something in the arts from the look of these crime scenes. Or he could be working some dead-end job, because he can't break into the arts. Either way, he's probably not very successful, and angry with that lack of success. He's developed a paranoid scenario to explain his failure.

"On the other hand, he knows how to use a syringe and a scalpel, so he might be in a medical field. A paramedic or a nurse's aide who believes he knows better than the doctors.

"The religious content of these murders makes me believe that we're dealing with an individual who's had strong religious influences, at least in his early life. Who still feels the pull of his spiritual background.

"I know it's New York"—she smiled—"but he's probably using a car. He's packing a lot in his murder kit. The wings, incense, syringes, the tape, his cleanup paraphernalia. Possibly a camera. The vehicle might be a van, probably black or dark blue. . . ." She came to a dead stop. "You seem skeptical, Detective Rozelli."

All eyes turned to the detective, who rose to the bait. He stood, looking amused, the very symbol of unspoken doubt.

"Well, yeah . . . you know"—the words tumbled out—"I mean, I understand this profiling can be pretty specific . . . but the *color* of the car?"

"Profiling is both an art and a science. Some say it's *all* art." She waited for the undertow of comment. "There is always a creative element to evidence assessment," she continued. "But a thing like the color of the car is based on statistics. It's simply a fact that compulsives favor darker cars."

"And this guy's a compulsive?" Rozelli obliged her, continuing to play the foil.

"The cleaning and ritual posing of the bodies are compulsive behaviors," she said. "And it appears now that he's injecting the victims with LSD, which I believe is an extreme extension of his need for domination and control.

"But it never hurts to be skeptical, Detective Rozelli." She watched as he took his seat, then looked out to include them all. "The profile I just gave you is based on years of experience with serial-murder cases. So give it due weight. But don't let it limit your thinking. If a piece of data doesn't fit, that's the piece I want to hear about. The important information is what you're *not* expecting—the clue that puts everything in a new light. Profiling is just the best we can do"—she paused—"while we pray for an eyewitness."

A round of laughter broke the ice. The questions went on for an hour.

The park today had a hemmed-in feeling for Willie. A bleached-out thickness of air. Against the bleak wintery grayness, Hanae's favorite red coat stood out like a pool of blood.

"How did things go this morning?" Hanae turned to her as they walked along the pathway lined in bare-armed trees that seemed to pray for snow.

"They went well. I like the people in Jimmy's unit. And he seems to have assembled a very impressive task force."

"I am glad you are here."

Hanae's words sounded heartfelt, and Willie wondered, as she had last night, how much the pressure of a serial case was affecting Jimmy's life at home. She opened her mouth to ask but didn't.

"It's lucky for me that I could get away," she said instead. "I don't know how much Jimmy's told you, but the killer is injecting his victims with LSD. I had to be part of this case."

"And you don't mind missing Christmas with your family?"

She laughed. "You wouldn't ask that if you knew my family."

Hanae shook her head but smiled. "You said you had a good place to stay in the city."

"A friend's apartment. In the Village. Dr. Jamili and his wife spend winters away." She shivered.

"Are you cold?" Hanae's sensitivity was amazing.

"Yes, I am a little. But it feels good. I don't get outdoors enough."

"Taiko and I come here often."

"I like watching you together. He's a wonderful dog."

"Kenjin said I needed a dog."

"Darius?"

"He said I was too much like my birds. Jimmy had mentioned a dog many times. Kenjin insisted, then helped me through the training."

"Michael is . . . unusual."

"Attractive."

"No. I mean . . . that's not what I was saying, Hanae."

Hanae had stopped on the trail, letting Taiko sniff something on the ground. Her depthless eyes seemed to search Willie's. "You know . . . what happened?"

"The shooting thing . . . yes. Jimmy told me about that back at Quantico. I got the idea he felt he'd deserted Michael."

"I believe that is how Jimmy felt. And then it was worse after what happened with Margot."

"Who is Margot?"

Hanae's hand moved on the dog's harness, and the three of them resumed walking. "Margot was Kenjin's wife," Hanae said. "They met in law school. I do not think she was happy when he decided to become a policeman."

"Are you saying his wife left him because he didn't become a lawyer?" Willie asked.

"There were other things." The smooth brow furrowed, fine line crazing in porcelain. "Kenjin can be difficult. But it was very cruel, her moving out so suddenly without telling him she was pregnant."

"Michael has a child?"

"He has sons . . . twins." Hanae answered. "I do not know how often Kenjin sees them."

"Why do you call him Kenjin?"

"It is difficult to translate . . . old sad wise one."

"It fits," she said. "I'm not sure why, but it fits."

Hanae nodded. "Do you have time to go somewhere else?"

"Sure."

The sidewalks, when they left the park, were thick with early Christmas shoppers. The crowd parted for Taiko, efficient more than polite. Willie had to slow her normal breakneck pace, matching it consciously to the dog's, as he matched his to Hanae's. It was Hanae who actually led.

The library was a small private one with an extensive collection in braille. The building that housed it was early twentieth century, the typical Beaux Arts town house of the district. Willie registered the interior as modern, not as cold as some. She walked behind Hanae through the security posts, past the checkout desk to the stairs.

"Second floor?" She turned to Hanae, wondering if there were an elevator.

"No. It's this staircase I wanted you to see."

She turned back, really looked at what was in front of her. In this city you forgot to do that. There was too much, so you saw nothing.

Illuminated by a skylight, the staircase glowed, curving and sinuous. Simple, but magnificent, it made you think of a snake. Except it was a snake you wanted to touch.

"It's beautiful." She reached out, stroking the warm wood.

Hanae's hand moved next to hers. "It is his soul you feel inside." The soft voice spoke at her shoulder. "It was Kenjin who made this."

Dr. Isaacs's office was a small and crowded sanctuary. Haim Isaacs himself was a big man, bearded, balding, and jolly. More like a secular Santa Claus than a Hebrew scholar.

"Please sit, Lieutenant Sakura." The professor's beefy hand indicated a well-loved chair.

"Thank you for seeing me."

His eyes went just short of twinkling. "My pleasure. I have no sense of shame. I am what you call a show-off. I enjoy talking about what I know."

Sakura laughed.

"So, you want to know about angels."

"Yes," he said. "Understanding angels may be critical to apprehending this killer."

The professor nodded.

"A serial killer is not like other murderers," Sakura said. "Most killers murder people they know and at least have superficially rational motives for what they do."

"Jealousy, greed, hatred." Isaacs enumerated emotions, which in another context might have been labeled sins.

"Yes. But serial murder is different. The killer murders to satisfy a well-rehearsed script inside his head. This particular killer's fantasy seems to be about transformation." He removed the crime scene photos from a folder and spread them across the desk.

Isaacs sat, looking at them for a moment, then stood and moved to the window, examining the remnants of a cold and dreary afternoon. "Dr. Whelan seems to believe your killer is making human beings into angels," he said. His words settled against the glass in a fine mist.

"But why *fallen* angels?" Sakura asked.

"Your victims were all homosexuals. Let's start there." Dr. Isaacs walked back to his chair. "Angels are androgynes, beings that are neither male nor female. Your killer may believe that homosexuality, which is the union of *like* to *like,* is closer to the androgynous state of angels."

"So you're saying that in the killer's mind, homosexuals are more like angels than heterosexuals."

"Yes," he answered.

"And through ritual murder, he's transforming homosexuals into angels?" Sakura said.

"Exactly. The wings are symbolic of his success."

"But why *fallen* angels?" he asked again.

"According to *Enoch,* the fallen angels were punished because they took on human bodies to sleep with the daughters of men. They were anything but homosexual. It seems something of a contradiction."

Sakura frowned. "So where does that leave us?"

"I don't know. Maybe the names are not attached to the bodies and are simply the killer's statement against heterosexuality. Those names, Lieutenant Sakura"—he smiled—"may be no more than the graffiti of a very angry man."

Sakura maneuvered through tight traffic, recalling the spread of prints he'd just moments ago reviewed with Dr. Isaacs. Black-and-white stills from some godless universe inhabited by a madman. And with the images of the hellish photographs came the odor of incense used by the killer. Strange, until today the scent had never evoked that other incense that precisely demarcated his life.

It had been three years and his California home was still alien to him. As were his stepmother, Susan, and his half brother, Paul, and his half sister, Elizabeth. From the very first day when his stepmother had given him her too-quick smile, he understood he was an outsider. With his father so involved with his practice, it was Susan who cataloged his days; it was Susan who had finally decided that he was to be called James, believing that Akira was too cumbersome for teachers and friends. He was certain she had also declared that his father was to be Ike instead of Isao.

Nine-year-old Paul was more difficult to read. Moody and intense, his father's second son was like a desert mirage. There and not there. But seven-year-old Elizabeth was as bright and open as the sparklers he had once lit on festival days in Japan. She had almost made his life bearable.

He had fought the irony. For so long he had wanted to live with his father, but when his wish had finally been granted, he'd despised his new life.

Sakura pulled into his space in the underground garage. For a moment he sat and watched the keys dangle from the ignition. He reached for the crime scene photographs. The ancient incense came to him fresh, along with the face of his father.

He had returned from school to find Isao slumped on the edge of his bed, seemingly trapped in his American doctor's suit. When his father spoke, the words slapped like an open palm. His grandmother was dead.

The trip back home was a dream, flying in over the ocean. He'd descended through the blue labyrinth of sky, weaving blindly in and out of clouds. Mountains pierced the cold mist. Snow like fresh cream shrouded hills and rooftops. But home could not be the same. His greatest happiness was gone. And he'd come to pick through her ashes for her bones, to bury her inside the dark, cold earth of a Buddhist cemetery.

Chrysanthemums, the color of pale sunlight, stood in stark contrast to the black dresses of his aunts. For a moment he stared at the single pearl, like a milky tear, hanging in the hollow of his aunt Otoko's throat. Unlike the other female relatives, his grandmother lay dressed in a white kimono, folded right over left, a mirror of life, marking her passage from this world. But the flesh of her face seemed luminescent and smooth, her hair, pulled back into a tight knot, as black as in younger days. Her lips moistened, she appeared almost alive.

He watched her taken away to have her flesh transformed to soft ash, her death-breath turned to pale smoke. He sat with his family to eat the first meal, but each morsel was a stone falling through the hollow of his chest. Then at the close of the ritual feast, his grandmother's ashes were presented to the family, and with clean chopsticks each relative passed the remnants of bone one to another. He made his arm iron so that he would not tremble as he passed a fragment of bone to his uncle Ikenobo.

Then yellow-robed monks chanted and prayed as his grandmother's remains were placed inside an urn. Incense burned, filling the air so thickly he thought he would vomit.

Sakura gagged now, dry heaving into his handkerchief, wiping a rivulet of saliva from the corner of his mouth. He counted breaths, his head leaden against the seat rest. "Nakamura." He spoke his grandfather's name inside the cavern of the squad car. After the funeral he had begged to stay behind with his grandfather. But Isao had refused.

Back in California he had overheard one of the few arguments between his father and Susan. She couldn't understand why her husband had not allowed his son to remain in Japan. Certainly, this arrangement would have been better for everyone concerned. His father's voice had been low but angry when he answered that California, not Japan, was Akira's home now.

In the days that had followed, he had grown more sullen and quiet. He lost weight and his grades fell. In desperation, his father sent him to a therapist. And although he had hated his sessions with

Dr. Ambrose, the psychologist became his savior in the end. He recommended that James be sent away for a time.

The boy from Hokkaido had been lost the day his grandmother died. A veil had fallen between Akira and the child who would grow to be the man.

⁂

Michael Darius fit the key into the lock of Luis Carrera's apartment, still uncertain if he really wanted to become a part of what had happened behind this door. Early this morning when Sakura had first slid the key across his desk, he could only stare at it. Finally he'd picked it up, put it into his pocket, got up, and walked out without saying another word. He'd had no choice. His very presence at Police Plaza had betrayed him. He was infected with the old disease—his allegiance to Jimmy, and his need to drive evil back into its hole.

He stepped under the yellow crime scene tape and moved inside. He reached back and closed the door, conscious of the dull thud of wood meeting wood. The blinds were closed against the watery late-afternoon light, but even in the semidarkness it was easy to make out the sooty leavings of the Crime Scene Unit.

He closed his eyes, willing himself to forget what he had seen in those photographs, what he'd heard Willie French say the other night at Jimmy's. He had to come into this naked, free of the weight of facts and opinions already laid out.

He opened his eyes and examined what had once been Carrera's home. The living room was spare, except for the walls. Ballet posters and photographs covered most of the space. Most photos showed Carrera himself in publicity stills or candid shots with other dancers.

But the back injury in Linsky's autopsy report had probably meant that Carrera would have never again achieved star status. And he wondered if this had anything to do with what had happened. Had Carrera wanted to die?

He thought of the photograph he'd seen of Carrera lying dead in his own bed. Ironically, death seemed to have bestowed on the dancer something he'd never been able to achieve in life. The white wings appeared natural rather than abstracted, sprouting from his shoulders rather than affixed by some mad killer's hand. Even the unforgiving photography had been unable to hide the waxy translucency of Carrera's flesh. With his long fingers chastely folded over his groin, he seemed poised to fly, transform into some purer, rarer entity. *Now I begin,* the image in the photograph had seemed to say.

He shook his head to dispel his thoughts and moved toward the bedroom. The air grew notably denser, so that he seemed to be breathing through layers of gauze. The smell was distinctively Roman Catholic. He'd served for only two years as an altar boy, but the scent that had flaunted pagan harems in the face of Christianity's God was something he'd never forgotten. He raked his tongue against his hard palate, scratching the tickle of spicy staleness.

He supposed it was that faint odor of the incense that drew him first. Then it was the metallic stink of blood. But what had Jimmy said? That he'd never worked a homicide with less blood. In the end, however, when he stood in the bedroom, he was able to determine with absolute certainty that what had drawn him in was the murderer's own scent.

He thought peaches. Furry, fleshy peaches left in the hot summer sun too long. Allowed to linger in a bowl, forgotten until their odor refused to be ignored. It was a scent that evoked waste. Terrible tragic waste. Yet it was a scent with which he'd grown familiar. A scent he'd smelled a thousand times. An odor so intimate that at first he'd failed to notice, failed to recognize as the odor of his own flesh.

CHAPTER

8

Geoffrey Westlake's bedroom was a showplace, a bigger, more expensive version of David Milne's room above the gallery. But no longer much to look at, as far as Willie was concerned. No body. No blood at all in the stripped-down bed. Only the ash writing and finger-print powder in random black smudges remained.

Willie watched as Darius disappeared into the vastness of a walk-in closet and hoped he was getting more out of these murder scenes than she was. Antagonism remained in the air, a natural rivalry, professional as well as personal, with the additional complication of Jimmy's expectation that they actually like each other. It was the demand inherent in the blind-date refrain: *He's got such a good personality.* Well, Michael Darius wasn't a blind date, thank God, and his personality left a lot to be desired. But that she would have expected. Jimmy's confidences about his former partner had prepared her for the moroseness that seemed to be his essential characteristic. But Jimmy had also said that Darius had the best investigative instincts he'd ever seen. Jimmy wanted him on the case. That was what was important.

Darius emerged from the closet, stood next to the bed, appearing to study the letters that spelled out *Barakel* on the wall. From the doorway she studied his back. Its blank tenseness was a message clearer than words. Any small impression of agreement reached at Jimmy's place the other night had been pure illusion.

She walked back into the living room, leaving him alone to do whatever it was that he did. On a chrome console table a framed photograph of Geoffrey Westlake held place of honor against a mirrored wall. Model's ego, she thought, displaying his own portrait. But crossing the room to get a better look, she noted the dedication scrawled across the bottom: *Rob, Love always, Geoff.*

Rob would be Robert Lindel, the apartment's actual owner. She had read about him in Jimmy's background files. Lindel was a wealthy businessman in his sixties who spent his winters in Palm Springs, a self-described patron of the arts who'd taken a friendly interest in Geoffrey Westlake's career. The sublet he'd offered at such a nominal fee, he'd explained as a business transaction. A fair exchange to have someone he trusted watching over his things.

It was obvious from the photo what Lindel's real interest in Westlake had been. *Love always.* No . . . probably not that. But maybe what he'd called it. A fair exchange. Value for value.

The door to the hallway was open. A man walked in, small and rigidly poised in a heavy black suit that made him look like a butler. His gaze went over her sternly, made a quick inventory of the room.

"I'm with the police," she explained. "Is there some problem, Mr. . . . ?"

"Babcock. I'm the manager of this building. Lieutenant Sakura promised to inform me whenever anyone was to enter Mr. Lindel's apartment."

She put on a smile. Better than making trouble for Jimmy. "I'm sorry," she said, "but I'm sure you can understand—"

"What I want to know is when that bedroom can be repainted," Babcock cut her short. "Mr. Lindel's been upset enough by . . . what's happened." The officious little eyes slid past her. Darius had entered the room.

"How long had Geoffrey Westlake lived in this apartment?" he asked the manager.

"Mr. Lindel left for the Coast at the end of the summer," Babcock answered readily enough, dropping the posturing. "But Mr. Westlake had been staying here for a couple months by then, living here for all practical purposes."

Darius nodded. His eyes were an intense shade of blue. They made him look Black Irish rather than Greek. "Have you any idea where Mr. Westlake lived before that?" he asked the manager.

Babcock frowned, having to admit that he hadn't.

"Thank you," Darius said. A clear dismissal.

She watched the manager leave, then turned to Darius. His own gaze was inward, and she wondered what he was thinking. One thing was clear. He didn't just not want to be here with her. He plain didn't want to be here. And he wouldn't be, except for this noble macho pissing contest he was having with Sakura. And yet the case engaged him in spite of himself. His intensity betrayed him.

The blue eyes focused, catching her stare. She didn't blink. She could piss with the best of them. And it was Jimmy, not she, who had suggested they view some of the crime scenes together.

"You find anything?" she said.

"No."

"What took you so long then?"

He didn't answer.

"You don't like me very much, do you, Mr. Darius?"

He surprised her by smiling. It changed his whole face. "I don't like psychiatrists."

"Afraid of what we'll see?"

He laughed.

She took it for a yes.

"Pinot's next," he said.

She looked at her watch. "Sorry. Can't go. I'm supposed to meet with Jimmy. You want to come?"

He shook his head but made no move to leave.

She left him, closing the door behind him. She could admit he was attractive, as Hanae had said, but *fucked up* in her clinical diagnosis. She had been with men who'd had a certain edge. Michael Darius was bristling with spikes. The kind on which you could impale yourself.

✦

Hanae walked out of Janice Nguyen's studio into the cold. She felt somewhat like an unfinished butterfly in the cocoon of her red coat. Her knit cap, pulled over her ears, muted the steady whir of the wind. She settled one gloved hand into the shelter of a pocket, the other fixed on Taiko's lead. She breathed in the chilled air. What she loved most about the cold was the retreat into warmth. Opposite sensations tucked one into another like an old letter secreted inside an envelope.

"Coffee or hot chocolate?" Adrian Lovett asked, matching her steps as she walked down the stairs.

"Tea."

"*Tea*, of course." She heard the sharp *zip-zip* of his jacket. "There's a little place right around the corner. We can even sit outside, if you think Taiko would be more comfortable. . . . Up for a short walk?"

"I love walking. I walk in the park at least twice a week."

"Central Park?" She could hear the muffled slide of his hands into gloves.

"Yes, Taiko and I need the exercise."

"When did you get him?"

"Soon after I moved to the city. A friend of mine thought it would be a good idea."

"Have Taiko, will travel."

"I don't . . ." She'd turned toward him.

"A stupid joke. Old American television show."

The metallic jungle of Taiko's harness made high-pitched notes as they moved. The afternoon sun stretched cool skeleton shadows across the pavement, and dry leaves scratched the cement in a wild game of hopscotch. From behind someone laughed, a perfect sound, like a single egg cracking. Hanae shivered.

"Cold?"

"No, I love cold weather."

"We don't have to sit outside."

"No, it will be fine. Taiko will like that better."

"Well, here we are." She felt his hand touch the center of her back, direct her toward a table.

He ordered her a pot of tea and a cup of black coffee for himself.

"Are you enjoying the class?" she asked, pulling off a glove, lifting her cup.

"Very much. But I'm not very good. I'm doing it mostly for therapy."

"Therapy?"

"To relax. My job gets a bit stressful at times. I'm a Web designer, and all my clients want everything yesterday. But I can't seem to get anything done until after the sun goes down. I'm what you'd call a night owl."

"A wise bird."

"I don't know about that. I read somewhere that owls are stupid."

She laughed. "I have become something of a night owl too. I cannot sleep until my husband comes home."

"What does he do?"

"My Jimmy is a policeman."

"Jimmy . . . as in Lieutenant James Sakura, NYPD?"

"Yes."

"Big case he's working on."

She nodded, taking another sip of tea.

"I'm separated," he said. "One son."

"A son"—she could feel herself smiling—". . . how old?"

"Eight next month. He was a Christmas present."

"Will you see him for his birthday?"

"Actually, my ex and I are good friends. I pretty much get to see Christopher whenever I want"—he took a swallow of coffee—"but what I can't figure is how you sculpt the way you do?"

She removed her other glove, set it down with the other. Taiko was running his muzzle against her leg. "May I . . . ?" she asked.

Then she reached across the table, taking his face into her hands. A small muscle jumped in his neck, flinched as though she'd surprised him. Her palms pressed lightly against the bones of his cheeks, the ends of her fingers learning the texture of his skin. At first she moved tentatively, like the uncertain landing of a small insect, then her hesitancy gave way to a steely strength. A sculptor's hands seeking to mold the contours of his jaw and chin, setting in place the curves and planes of his features. Her thumbs resting at last inside the deep wells of his eyes.

"You are older than I thought," she said, letting her hands fall into her lap. "And your eyes are green."

⁂

GAY KILLER RELIGIOUS FANATIC? the cover headline screamed. Willie, waiting for Jimmy in his office, picked up the *Post* from the wastebasket near his desk. It was last Thursday's edition, and the article had featured disturbingly accurate details of the incense burned at the scenes. She tossed the rag back in the trash.

"Hi." Jimmy came in and sat down, offering her tea.

"Thanks." She accepted. She had found the morning exhausting.

"How are you and Michael getting along?"

"Okay." She watched him preparing the tea. "I can't say that visiting the Milne and Westlake crime scenes has given me any brilliant new insights. Darius may have something. . . . What about you?"

Jimmy gave a negative shrug. "We had a couple of names come up with Walt's cross-check program."

"Oh . . . ?"

"A few people on the Milne gallery list turned up as signers on petition sheets from the neighborhood action meeting. It's what you'd expect. We're checking it out, but none of them seem good for the murders." He poured hot water over the leaves in the pot.

"I don't guess we've had any results yet on the bartender's composite?" she asked him.

"All the wrong kind. The sketch could fit at least a quarter of the population."

"You get back the lab work on Pinot?"

Jimmy nodded. "Same pattern, including the LSD. Only difference, he was positive for marijuana. Trace of heroin."

He poured out tea for the two of them, handed her a cup. She watched him sip. The only man who didn't look silly with a tiny cup in his hand.

"I'm still waiting to hear your theory," he said, "about how he's using the LSD."

She smiled. "What do you know about brainwashing?"

"I think you might have talked about it at Quantico. I'm not sure how much I remember."

It was an invitation to go on. Jimmy never forgot a thing.

"Well, *washing* is not the best metaphor for the process." She settled back in the chair. "Computer terminology works better. Reprogramming the brain . . . erasing old patterns of thought and behavior, replacing them with new ones."

"I remember your mentioning the Hearst case."

She nodded. "Spoiled heiress Patty transformed against her will into machine gun–wielding Tanya. Nice trick, even if the jury didn't buy it."

"But you believe she should have been acquitted?"

"Patty Hearst wasn't guilty of anything more than possessing a human brain," she said. "The jury just didn't want to accept how quickly and profoundly a person's reality could be changed by some-one with the knowledge and ruthlessness to do it."

She drained her cup, set it down on the desk. "You don't like that idea, do you, Jimmy? You think you could have resisted."

"Are you saying nobody could?"

"No. And certainly if you understand the process, that's a defense."

"Make me understand it."

"The human brain is designed to accept certain kinds of *software*," she said. "If the software is properly structured, *and* presented at the appropriate time, the brain will imprint the program—no questions asked."

"What do you mean . . . *imprint*?"

"Although we don't generally call what we do to our children brain-washing, we're all programmed into modes of thought and behavior by our parents, society, and whatever culture we're members of. From infancy on we build up a functioning model of the world, that little bubble of personal reality we so stubbornly mistake for the real thing."

"But the model can be changed?" he said.

"It can be modified as we process new information. But the core realities that we develop early in life are extremely difficult to change."

"But the Hearst case implies that they can."

She nodded. "The subject must be returned to the infantile state. In the case of Patty Hearst, the SLA ripped her violently out of her old life, then isolated her for months in a dark closet. Functionally, she was returned to the womb and made totally dependent on her captors for all her most basic needs. First food and warmth. Later love and approval. Finally even sex. Every biosurvival circuit in her brain was disengaged from the rich American heiress model and reprogrammed to respond to the Symbionese Liberation Army model instead."

He reached for the pot, poured more tea for them both. "What's this have to do with the killer?"

He'd always known when to do that, she thought, even in class. Reel her in and return her to the bottom line. She picked up her cup, feeling the heat of the liquid. "The SLA did it the old-fashioned way," she said. "There's a faster method of reprogramming that's more like a conversion experience. Like Saul becoming Paul on the road to Damascus."

His own tea sat ignored. "LSD?" he said.

"Theoretically," she answered, "LSD can chemically break down imprints. If the experience is carefully structured, a new set of imprints can be put into place while the subject is still in the vulnerable state."

"And that's what you think the killer is doing?"

She leaned forward toward him. "The wings, the writing, the symbol on the chests, it could all be part of what's technically called the *set,* part of the structuring. Think about it, Jimmy. Isn't that what all serial killers crave? For the victim to become part of the fantasy. He's programming them to actually share that reality tunnel he's trapped in."

The audacity of it registered in his voice. "You don't really believe that's possible?"

She shook her head. "The subject's attitude is critical to the process. I can't imagine that the victims are in any mood to cooperate. Not that it probably matters."

"Meaning?"

She watched him lift his cup, drink the steaming liquid.

"Meaning he's probably psychotic," she said. "It's only what he believes that counts."

⁂

The reception area of Physicians Plaza was at war with itself. The walls, tempered into a cool institutional gray, were fractured at irregular intervals with canvases of bold color and erratic line. The man, waiting for his three o'clock appointment, decided the raised and crusty pools of red pigment in the largest of the abstract paintings reminded him of drying blood.

He brushed back the cuff of his sleeve and checked his watch. It was now three-thirty, but he was a forgiving soul. His regular orthopedist had taken a last-minute ski trip with his family for Thanksgiving, and an associate was going to see him. He had never seen Dr. Kerry and was slightly disappointed he wouldn't be seeing Hendrick, since this was probably his final checkup. He'd already gotten clean bills of health from Dr. Patel and Dr. Skidmore.

He heard his name called and looked up to see a pretty blond nurse standing at the entrance to the examination area.

"I'm Diana Tierney"—she smiled—"Dr. Kerry's nurse." She opened the door wider. "I'm sorry for the wait." She apologized over her shoulder as she led him down the long hall.

"No problem," he answered her breezily.

She opened the door to exam room 3. "It shouldn't be too long."

"Just grateful Dr. Kerry was able to fit me in."

"We help each other out around here." Another smile. "Any problem with the leg?"

"None at all," he reassured her.

"Doing the exercises the therapist showed you?" She was studying his chart.

"Graduated to full body workouts," he boasted.

"Great. Wish all our patients were as conscientious." She reached for the paper sheet. "If you would remove your pants and cover your legs with this."

"Of course," he said.

He glanced around the room. The walls were sage green. He thought he might have been in this room before, but couldn't recall ever seeing the painting over the examination table. Another abstract. This one smaller than the ones in the waiting room. No blood here.

He heard the voice first. Telling Nurse Tierney something about another patient. Then the sound of the door opening. The first thing he saw was the hand, beautifully manicured, extending toward him, taking his own into its soft dry palm. Then the voice again. Introducing himself. Saying something about the fine progress he'd made. Now he drew back the sheet, running the cool tip of a finger down the pale and puckered flesh of his scar.

The man looked up, finally focusing, forcing his other senses to shut down. Only his eyes fed. Inhaling, swallowing, ingesting the light exploding like a nova from the physician's head. Pouring out from the sockets of his eyes, the narrow nostrils of his nose. Spilling from his open mouth, from between even white teeth.

He willed himself to breathe air, his heart to pump. Blood through vessels. *Stay in control,* spoke the small voice inside his head.

More than a year ago, he had met Luis here. A patient like himself. Never, even in his dreams, had he expected to find another.

✧

Almost a week now since Pinot and nothing learned from his death. If there was a different feel to the murder of the young hustler, it was a difference of degree, not of kind. Sakura threw down the report he'd been reading, a completely unenlightening interview with one of Pinot's roommates. Perhaps it was only the dry simplicity of the reporting officer's prose, but Gil Avery seemed singularly unaffected by the death of a boy with whom he had shared a room. Life seemed to mean so little to these lost children. Even their own. Had Pinot cared about the waste of his years at the end?

He had worked through lunch, and without a break his efficiency would begin to suffer. He boiled fresh water and poured it into the pot, the pleasant fragrance of his grandmother's favorite *gyokuro* sending him back to Hokkaido.

The island was Japan's northernmost. He had grown up on an unspoiled Pacific coast—cold in winter, but with summers of unimaginable beauty. The family farm grew rice. But his grandfather's delight was in the breeding of *chabo,* ornamental bantam chickens.

It was his grandfather's birds that had raised the dilemma of the fox. *Kitsune* lived everywhere on Hokkaido, carnivores whose main sources of food were insects and fruit. But it was a hard winter that last year of his boyhood, and one particular fox had discovered his grandfather's chickens.

The *kitsune* were sacred to the goddess of rice, and his grandfather paid as much homage to the *Kami* as anyone. But his chickens were sacred too. So Grandfather declared that the fox's actions in this case were *Kunitsu-Tsumi,* a hazard that must be taken care of for the good of the community. Which meant that he, Akira, was given the duty of dealing as he could with the fox.

According to Shinto, animals had spirits that were *mono,* which meant they could sometimes be mischievous and cause trouble for humans, as it was now with *kitsune* and his grandfather. So he went to the place in the woods where he had seen fox spoor and made offering of *inarizushi,* rice-stuffed tofu, which was the favorite food of the foxes that were the messengers of the goddess.

But the spirit of his adversary would not be soothed, and two more of his grandfather's chickens disappeared. So now he made a wooden trap and baited it with the least valuable of the hens, and he placed the trap at dusk in the forest near the trail where he knew the fox would pass.

In the morning all was well with the birds. His grandfather smiled. But his own heart was heavy as he went with his noose to the forest.

Kitsune was there, very fine in his winter coat, pacing in the small cage, where chicken blood stained red the drifts of snow. So many years ago, he thought now. But the image so clear. And the feeling.

He raised the tea to his lips, letting its astringent sweetness soothe the memory. He had done what he had to do, the duty he owed his grandfather. And immediately after, he had gone to the shrine for purification.

But locked in its wild eyes, in the moments before the rope, had he not in his boy's heart envied *kitsune* his freedom?

✾

The lightbulb on the second-floor landing was out. Michael Darius stood in the unwholesome dark, knocking on the door to 23. He got no answer—as expected. According to the girl who rented the room below him, the guy who was living here now was out most nights. He reached into his pocket for the pick, adding illegal entry to his sins.

The apartment inside was cold and incredibly tiny. Paint peeled in scabs from the discolored ceiling. It was amazing what people would put up with to live in this city. Westlake, when he'd stayed here, had been working regularly as a model. But the money, no doubt, had gone for restaurants and clothes. He must have jumped at the invitation to move into Lindel's apartment.

Had it been only after the move that Westlake had been targeted by the killer? It was the question he had come here hoping to answer. A call to the actors' union had gotten him Westlake's old address, which was still in their files. But now that he was here . . . He looked around at the scarred and mismatched furniture, at the personal possessions of a stranger. And felt nothing.

At least he was alone. It had been difficult with Willie French looking over his shoulder. Even now she remained at the periphery of his vision, her beauty with the bluntness of a threat. He couldn't let that matter. And with her or without her, it had made no difference. Milne, Westlake, and then alone at the Pinot murder scene, he'd come away with nothing more than that same haunting uneasiness he'd first experienced in Luis Carrera's apartment.

There was nothing of that here. And nothing left of Westlake, even if it were still his name on the lease. Crazy, that even this dump could be a sublet. As much as he loved this city, he doubted that he could stand for long to inhabit such circumscribed space.

He turned off the light, walked to stand for a moment at the grimy, curtainless window. Across the narrow street was the facing glass of an abandoned building—a level black eye, blank and obvious, staring back.

⁕

Except for the task force meeting the first thing this morning, Sakura had been at his desk all day. He held a cup of coffee in his hand. He was past the refinement of tea, beginning to feel the physical effects of bad food or no food, and too little sleep. Rest and nourishment caught on the run between bouts with information.

He was imbedded in data. Forms multiplying like bacteria filled his office, along with petition lists and surveillance photographs from the latest community action meetings. He took another swill of the coffee and set the mug down. Pulled over the tabloid that Kelly had left on his desk. The papers were still filled with speculation about the homosexual killer, but since last week's article on the incense, nothing more of real substance had leaked. That much was good at least.

"Your taste in reading has changed." Michael's voice from the door.

He looked up. "Just trying to keep on top of things."

Darius walked over to sit in the chair in front of his desk. "Anything new?"

"Pinot seems to have been something of a departure, more a victim of opportunity. But I don't know what that means."

"What did that professor say?"

"Isaacs? He had some complicated theory. Thinks the killer is targeting gays because he believes homosexuals are more like angels than straights."

"What . . . ?"

"Isaacs thinks," he went on, "that the names on the walls might not have any direct connection to the bodies."

Darius's mouth twisted. "It's obvious the killer is naming them," he said, "and believes the victims somehow embody these fallen angels."

"I agree." He picked up his coffee. Nodded at the cup. "Want some?"

Darius shook his head, taking out his cigarettes instead. "I found something," he said.

Finally the explanation of why Michael was here. He waited while he lit up.

"Turns out Westlake had been staying at Lindel's for only a few months." Darius blew out smoke. "I just made a visit to his old apartment." He stopped, drew hard again on the cigarette.

"You going to make me suffer for this, Michael?"

"No." He took something out of his pocket. "There was an abandoned warehouse across the street from Westlake's old room. It was easy enough to get in. I found this."

"In the warehouse . . ." Sakura picked up the plastic bag that Darius had tossed on the desk and held it up to the light. There was a torn fragment of printed cardboard inside.

"It's part of a film carton," Darius said. "A piece of the end flap. See the letters?"

". . . IE 36."

"The *H* in front is missing. It's HIE 36. High Speed Infrared. Thirty-six exposures. The same film we use for surveillance."

"He's stalking them."

"Westlake at least." Darius leaned back in the chair. "I saw what looked like tripod marks in the dust by the window."

"We haven't been going back far enough in their lives." Sakura was thinking aloud. "There may be other things we've overlooked. It seems like he might have backlogged the first three. He stalked them and killed them, one right after another. Then almost two weeks pass before we get Pinot. Tomorrow's a week without a DOA. What's he doing?"

"I don't know," Darius said. "I'm just afraid we might be making a lot of unwarranted assumptions."

He smiled at the diplomatic phrasing. "We, Michael? You mean Willie and I. . . . You two getting along?"

"Sure."

Sakura wondered what complexities that single syllable was meant to cover. He hadn't gotten any more today from Willie. "Are you coming for Thanksgiving dinner?" he said.

"What time?"

"Around one is good. I plan on coming in for a few hours in the morning. It'll be a skeleton crew and some backup for the guys working the parade route. You haven't forgotten what it was like to work the Macy's crowd?"

Darius didn't answer but reached to crush his cigarette against the inside of the trash can.

Sakura shook his head. "You're the only one I let smoke in here."

"Kelly smokes."

"Not in my office," he said. Then, "I'll get a warrant to search that warehouse first thing Friday. . . . And thanks."

"For what?" Darius shrugged. "There's nothing there. That piece of box top was behind some lumber in a corner. He had to reload the film in the darkest place he could find. Probably used a changing bag, but it's awkward under any circumstances."

"There must be footprints."

"In the dust . . . yeah. Looks like some kind of work boot."

"There could be fingerprints too. If not in the warehouse, we might get at least a partial off this." Sakura was looking at the torn sliver of cardboard. "It's another long shot with all the professional photographers in this city, but we can try to get a lead from the kind of film. And who knows what we might turn up in a canvass. Let me dream for a few hours. We could get lucky."

Darius had this way of reacting, his eyes narrowing, hovering on some border of change, as if in the next second, he was as likely to laugh as cry. He did it now, tilting in the chair, his lips twisting in a cynic's version of a smile.

"You're right, Jimmy, there's something about all of this that we're missing. We find what it is; we get him. And luck won't have anything to do with it."

⁂

Glass stretched uninterrupted across the rear of the house, exposing a kitchen constructed of granite and wood. Sections of stainless steel, copper, and porcelain glinted like small constellations. The man was close enough now in the dark for his breath to fog the window. He inhaled. The thin crust of fresh frost could not obscure the rich smell of decaying leaves underfoot. He crouched lower behind the tangle of thick bushes growing near the outside wall. The doctor had been relatively easy to follow to his Forest Hills home.

He pressed closer, pushing less important layers of sound into deeper recesses of his brain. Gone was the weak skitter of insects in the cold soil, the beat of his own heart. He concentrated on their voices, his vision tracking, moving beyond the reflections in the glass to the flesh inside.

The daughter looked like the father. Blond, blue-eyed, and pretty. With the kind of skin that would freckle in the sun. He heard her giggle. Her father had pulled one of her pigtails. The son was more like his mother. Darker, with deep-set eyes. Eyes that could show hurt.

"I thought you two were going to make the salad." The mother's voice was unexpectedly rich.

"We are, Lylah. Can't you see how hard we're working? Aren't we, Emmy?" Kerry whispered conspiratorially to his daughter.

"The only thing you two are doing is making a mess. Right, Jonathan?" The mother was seeking an ally of her own.

"Yes, Mommy," the young boy said, looking for confirmation he'd given the right answer.

"Come on, the spaghetti's almost ready." The woman sounded more tired now than annoyed.

"We're almost done." Emmy tore furiously at the lettuce.

"It's getting late and you two haven't even had your baths." Lylah shook her head in mock exasperation.

"We don't need to take a bath tonight," the girl begged. "No school tomorrow."

"But there's lots to do before we leave for Aunt Penny's Friday morning."

"Daddy, please come with us to Aunt Penny's," the daughter pleaded.

"Sorry, sweetie." He planted a kiss on the top of her head. "I'm on call, and I've got to get a speech ready for a seminar. Besides, we'll get to carve up old tom turkey together before you leave."

Even under the bleaching effect of the fluorescents, the doctor's aura was blinding. The man crouched, mesmerized, thinking how he'd spent over a year tracking the first ones, making meticulous plans, then orchestrating their awakenings—*one, two, three.* Luis, whom he'd found at the clinic. David, whom he'd known before but rediscovered on his first gallery visit after the accident and his own awakening. And Westlake, he'd seen on TV.

Then came Pinot. And now Kerry. He shivered with the deliciousness of his good luck, the joy of beating God at his own game.

CHAPTER

9

Agnes Tuminello pressed her back against the wall and hid in the shadows of the second-floor alcove. She wouldn't have been here in the rectory at all, if she hadn't felt guilty about her little holiday with her daughter Connie's family, leaving poor Father Kellog with nothing but leftover turkey these last two days. And so she'd come this evening with a pan of her special lasagna, only to be drawn from the kitchen and up the stairs by the loud voices.

Never before had she heard Father Kellog speak in such anger. She closed her eyes, clasping the Miraculous medal that hung from a thin chain around her neck, asking God to deliver them from such evil.

"You do not respect my authority. You do not respect me. You do not respect—"

"God? Oh, I respect God, Father Kellog. Because I know how dirty He can play."

"You blaspheme."

She cringed at Graff's nasty laughter.

"I've never failed to do my duty," the younger priest said. "I've never missed Mass. Or confession. I have listened to enough pettiness and foolishness, have smelled enough death and despair to last a lifetime. What more, old man, what more do you want from me?"

Then suddenly Graff was out of his room, flying down the stairs, flinging wide the front door, running away from the rectory into the street.

When she dared, she could see downstairs through the opened door that rain had begun to fall. She should go down and close the door, but she could not move, could not let Father Kellog know she'd been on the landing, listening.

A small noise, and she saw the priest standing outside Graff's room. For an instant he clutched the wall for support, then his hand reached for the banister. She wanted to go to him, comfort him, but she must not.

She watched him pad slowly down the stairs, shut the front door, and enter his study. A bit of shuffling, the squeak of a spring from his favorite chair, then nothing. She glanced up at a nervous skittering. Squirrels in the attic or, worse, mice. Behind her the wall creaked, an old house rattling its bones. Then slowly she stepped from her hiding place, stiff from having remained still so long.

A band of weak electric light fell across the hall carpet from Father Graff's suite. The priest had converted the larger sitting room into his bedroom, and the bedroom into what Mrs. Tuminello referred to as his "secret room." Standing in the hall, she now vowed never to enter the priest's room again. Never to dust the furniture or change his bed. The rugs would go unvacuumed, the floor unpolished. It would be her small revenge against Graff for upsetting Father Kellog. For now, she would just shut the door. However, what she glimpsed through the gaping door caused her resolve to punish the priest to instantly evaporate.

Her hand fell away from the doorknob, and she stood transfixed, eyeing the long, dark fissure in the far wall. In his haste and anger, Father Graff had been careless, had failed to lock the door between his two rooms. All the doors inside the rectory had old-style locks. A rusting assortment of skeleton keys found in the hall desk drawer might or might not fit any particular lock. On the door between his bedroom and his private room, however, Father Graff had installed a sturdy dead bolt, explaining to her that he would be responsible for any cleaning that had to be done inside. She had complained to Father Kellog, but to no avail.

Now she slowly crossed the bedroom, stopping before the partially opened door between the rooms. She began a Hail Mary, but it died just as she stepped inside the smaller room's threshold. At first she attempted to make sense of the collection of shapes and patterns in the dimness. Then she felt a brush of cold against her cheek. She jumped, watching a brass chain swish back and forth from a bulb in the ceiling. She pulled the cord. Red light flooded the room. *Hell* was her single thought.

Her eyes took in the eely coils of discarded film, the stainless trays of clear liquid, the hump of a camera. Then her focus moved to the collection of blown-up prints, gleaming black-and-white photographs, suspended like grotesque laundry, one piece after another, from a taut drying wire.

⁘

The cobwebs in William Kerry's head lifted gradually but completely. He remembered the fear, slick and cold in the pit of his stomach. Then he remembered why he'd been afraid.

Flat on his back in the darkness, still naked from his bath, his wrists and ankles bound together with tape, he threw his head from side to side on the bed. He couldn't see anyone in the room now. But God, oh God, why hadn't he acted on his impulse to drive into the city on Friday morning as soon as Lylah had left with the children?

He lay quiet against the bedspread for a moment, his pulse racing with adrenaline. He concentrated on the nubby feel of the fabric on his skin, tried to slow his breathing. He had to think. There was a clock on the nightstand. It showed he had been out only a few minutes. The odorless gas he'd been sprayed with had to be something harmless like nitrous oxide. He was okay. He hadn't been hurt. The man was probably a burglar who specialized in houses like this. Damn good at it too, or the alarm system would have worked.

A laugh escaped. He was flirting with hysteria. But it was a good sign that the guy was a professional. It meant he didn't make mistakes. It was only the rank amateurs who screwed up and killed people they found at home.

So what was he going to do now? Just lay there? The man was probably still in the house. With the nearest house so far away, it wasn't any use to scream. And anyway, he didn't want to make this guy mad. Still, maybe he shouldn't wait to do something. He could wiggle his way across the bed and throw himself on the floor. His wrists were hog-tied in front to his ankles, but he could still drag the phone off the nightstand, punch out 911. . . . What was that smell? Shit, it was strong.

He fought to get higher on the pillows. The man was in the room. Had been there all the time, in the shadows. *Naked.* The man was naked. That was the fact his brain had forgotten to register. The *burglar* who had come at him from the deeper darkness of the closet had been nude, except for the gas mask . . . and the leather straps.

The mask was gone now. The face it had covered was strangely familiar. And the leather was some kind of harness. The man turned, putting a small plate with a cake of burning incense down on Lylah's desk. Folded on his back was a perfect pair of wings.

"Oh, my God." The words had escaped without volition. The ones that came next were babble from some autonomic center in his brain. He listened to them as a spectator, knowing already they were useless.

"What do you want . . . money? There's a safe. You can have whatever you want. Just, please, please, don't hurt me." He was digging his heels in the mattress, arching himself higher. Not wanting to see but having to. Having to know what was coming, because imagining had to be worse.

The man hadn't spoken. He stooped down, got something from a bag on the floor. Walked toward him with a rolled-up piece of plastic and a small leather case in his hand.

Please . . . no . . . please . . . no . . . please . . . no. The adrenaline had taken over now. He was moving, skittling like a crab across the covers. The man was strong. A hand clamped his shoulder, pulled him back across the bed.

The case was on the nightstand, open. It held a pair of syringes. Something inside him gave up fighting. "Who are you?" he asked.

The face above him smiled. "What I'm going to show you, Dr. Kerry, is who you are."

The last of summer. Leaves along the highway already growing brittle, whispering like children in the dark. The man could remember the drive to the city. Too often, like tonight, he dreamed of it. The good part about it was Marian. In the dream he could see her, could hear her laughter. That night she had laughed like the old Marian before her obsession with the Church. Her head thrown back. Her blond hair whipping her face and throat.

She'd been turned toward him, still smiling, when he'd gone around the curve, half looking. Although it wouldn't have mattered. The oil on the road was invisible in the darkness, the loss of control inevitable at his speed. He remembered his first startled impression of the truck jackknifed along the shoulder, I beams jutting from its broken trailer. Remembered the Land Rover spinning, the sickening uselessness of trying to steer. And the noise of Marian's screaming, slow motion like the rest, cut off in the moment of impact.

They said it was impossible. That her head had been gone in that instant, smashed beyond recognition. But real or not, he knew it was her head he had seen bouncing at his feet on the floorboard. Not pain but surprise in her eyes.

His own pain he didn't remember, not even in his leg. He felt only the constriction of his chest, and the gathering blindness that might have been the blood flowing from the head wound into his eyes. The tunnel was what he remembered next. The light at the end. And Marian, miraculously whole, moving ahead of him. In the dream it was real again. The tunnel was here and now. He fought the pull of Earth. The claim of new flesh. He cried for Marian to wait, clawing, scrabbling his way minutely toward the light.

The barrier was a subtle thing. Invisible. Sensible only in his inability to make any real progress. And in the moment when he finally understood that he could not follow Marian, he had remembered . . . remembered who he was.

He sat up, gasping for the air to fill his lungs. A cold, sour sweat filmed his body, the flavor of tears. He sat rigid and still, trying to hold on to Marian in the moment she had turned to him smiling. But that part of the dream was gone, and he jammed his palms into his eyes to block what came instead.

He increased the pressure of his hands, fighting away the image, thinking of that moment in the hospital when he'd first come to consciousness, of the confusion that had been but a momentary blessing. For that split second he had remembered nothing of the accident or the tunnel. It was his last human moment, when he had only wondered why he had not awakened in his own bed, wondered where was Marian.

Her name forced the horror back, just as it had that day. The insanity of her death, a vacuum that sucked him back to the tunnel and the knowledge that could not be escaped. He was *ma'lak Elohim,* to give it the name he had read so long ago in the ancient Jewish texts. He was a fallen angel, one of a host who had rebelled in their desire to experience matter.

It was all allegory, of course, for concepts beyond human terms. But close enough. Though what his grandfather's books had not explained was the true nature of the punishment for such an unnatural desire—a karmic justice to fit the crime. The Fallen had been granted their wish for human bodies . . . forever. Barred from Heaven, they remained trapped eternally in human flesh, in body bags, prisoners of the cycle of death and rebirth.

But one . . . he . . . Gadriel . . . had cheated God. He had not died, to be reborn with the memory of who he was, lost or fading in an infant's brain. Paramedics had arrived at the scene and resuscitated his body. He had returned to Earth *awakened.*

In the long months of rehabilitation, he had had time to reflect on the hopelessness of his condition and to think of what might be done to free himself and the other Fallen. And he discovered that he could identify the others of his kind by the auras that shone about them, an essence that human flesh could not contain.

At last he had begun to plan. He would find and awaken the most powerful of the Fallen, duplicating for them his own awakening experience. Armed before death with the knowledge of their true identities, they would be prepared to fight reincarnation. Resisting the pull of Earth, they could remain instead in the place between, gathering in strength, till enough of them had assembled to destroy the barrier and regain what had been lost.

He let his hands drop. Sat in the dark with his breathing, waiting for the clearing of his vision. After a moment he got up and threw on a robe. He walked into the familiar red glare of the darkroom and lifted one of the prints from the developing tray. This one had been taken before the moment of awakening, and the eyes of what had still been William Kerry stared back at him in horror.

CHAPTER

10

The room was bright, expensive, perfect. The charcoal letters, an offense. Nearly a foot high, they crawled brokenly on the wall above the bed. *Rumel* was what the letters spelled out, and Sakura spoke the name aloud. He had read the passages in *The Book of Enoch,* the ones that mentioned the fallen angels. The first four names that the killer had written had been listed as leaders of the rebellion against God. He figured the name Rumel would also be among them.

In the harsh morning light, Dr. William Kerry didn't look like an angel. He looked like a man who'd gotten used to being dead. The wings were obscene. The drawing on his chest a primitive horror. Circles, lines. It still meant nothing to Sakura.

Like most of the rooms in the house, the bedroom had floor-to-ceiling glass. From where he stood near the bed, Sakura could watch members of the task force working with borough detectives in a grid search of the grounds.

"You about through in here?" McCauley had appeared in the doorway.

He turned. "Almost. Has Crime Scene finished with the rest of the house?"

"Yeah." The chief came in, following the path of least disturbance. "SOB disabled the alarm before cutting the glass in the kitchen. He was wearing gloves as usual." McCauley had moved to look at the body. "Poor bastard."

He turned back to Sakura. "You saw the press out there," he said.

"Fucking vultures. They sure as hell made you, Lieutenant. Got to figure this one is connected with the others. It's no longer just some psycho offing gays in the city," he growled. "A doctor with a wife and kids
murdered in Forest Hills. You can guess what kind of shit they'll be
printing now."

"Dr. Kerry's practice was in Manhattan," Sakura said. "It's probable
he was targeted there." He looked at the chief of detectives. "The killer
is precise with a scalpel. He's comfortable injecting drugs."

"The clinic . . . ?"

"It's a possibility," he said. "We'll start interviewing the staff immediately." He took the handkerchief out of his pocket and picked up a
framed family photograph that was sitting on the desk—William
Kerry and his family. "Mrs. Kerry is on her way home," he said to
McCauley, "but it's his nurse I want to talk to."

"You thinking the nurse might know the doctor better than the
wife?" The chief was watching him.

Sakura set the picture back in place. "I think it would be a mistake
to assume that the killer has completely broken his pattern."

⁂

Diana Tierney's prettiness was blurred by the tears she had been
shedding. Her cornflower blue eyes were red, her face puffy. She'd
been torturing the same Kleenex between her fingers for the last ten
minutes. She looked down now, noticed her hands, and placed the
overworked tissue on a nearby table.

"I'm sorry to have to ask you these questions now." Detective Johnson's voice sounded too soft for such a large woman.

"I'm sorry I'm not handling this better. . . ." Tierney's voice
trailed off.

"Why did you decide to drive out to Dr. Kerry's home?" Johnson
began the questioning.

"He couldn't be reached. . . ." For a moment the nurse seemed ready
to say something more.

"Why were you trying to contact Dr. Kerry?"

"He was on call and there was an emergency. When the hospital
couldn't reach him, they called me."

"So why did you decide to drive out to Forest Hills?"

She hesitated. "I thought it was odd that he didn't at least answer his pager. I knew he had a paper to write and was planning to work at the house. I got a little worried."

"What happened when you got to the house?"

"I rang the bell, but no one answered."

"What did you do next?" Johnson asked.

"I had a key. Dr. Kerry had given me one when I kept the children one weekend."

"Was the front door locked?"

"Yes, but I opened it. I thought it strange the alarm system was down. I called out."

"And . . . ?" Johnson pressed.

"He . . . he didn't answer." The composure Tierney had tried to regain began to slip away.

"What did you do then?"

"I . . . I thought the house was too quiet."

"But you went in anyway."

"Yes."

"Then what happened, Ms. Tierney?" Johnson was pulling her along slowly.

Tierney took a deep breath. "I looked around downstairs. Everything seemed okay. I didn't notice the broken glass in the kitchen."

"Then . . ."

"I went upstairs. I could see the doors to all the rooms were open . . . except the one at the end of the hall."

"The master bedroom?"

Tierney nodded.

"You entered the bedroom?"

She nodded, fresh tears forming in her voice. "I didn't even know what I was looking at."

Johnson waited a moment. "Did you touch anything in the room?"

"No. God, no." Her chest jumped with a ragged breath.

Johnson waited. "What did you do then?"

"I ran."

"To the neighbors?"

She was crying again, quieter this time. "Yes."

Sakura came forward. "How long have you been Dr. Kerry's nurse, Ms. Tierney?"

She looked up. The sound of his voice seemed to distract her. "Three years."

"Were you friends?"

"We liked each other." Tierney smiled and some of the prettiness returned to her face.

"Did he confide in you?" Sakura asked.

"What?"

"Did he discuss anything personal with you, Ms. Tierney?"

She looked down at her hands, then up to meet his eyes.

"Sometimes," she answered softly.

"What did you talk about?"

"About Lylah and the kids mostly."

"Lylah is Mrs. Kerry?"

"Yes." She moved in her chair.

"Were the doctor and Mrs. Kerry having problems?"

"No." The denial was quick.

Sakura walked away.

Tierney turned to Johnson. "I—" she stopped for a moment, rephrasing. ". . . Did the same person who killed Luis Carrera kill Dr. Kerry?"

Sakura walked back. He stood directly in front of her again. "What do you mean?"

Diana Tierney's face was still swollen, but the play of emotions was becoming easier to read. "Luis Carrera was Dr. Kerry's patient," she said. "He'd been treated for lumbar compression about a year ago. It was a shock when we heard he'd been murdered."

Sakura almost smiled. At last there was a connection between victims. "Was Mr. Carrera still seeing Dr. Kerry?" he asked.

"No, he'd been discharged."

He nodded, turning slightly away from her. "Yes, we believe the same person who killed Mr. Carrera also killed Dr. Kerry. Of course, there are some differences." He closed in on her again. "All the other victims were murdered in the city. Dr. Kerry was murdered in

Queens." Sakura paused. "The others were homosexuals," he said. "And Dr. Kerry . . ."

He left it incomplete, his eyes fixing on hers. He imagined he appeared rather forbidding, his tall, angular body outfitted in a dark suit like a cleric, his Asian features set unforgivingly in his too thin face. For a moment there was no reaction. Then slowly there was a kind of easing of her body, a relaxing of her features, as though at long last peace had settled in, and Diana Tierney seemed no longer willing to be a keeper of secrets.

Having lunched at her favorite nearby restaurant, Hanae entered Central Park at Fifth Avenue and Sixtieth Street through Grand Army Plaza. She could hear voices of children coming from the ice rink as she and Taiko moved along the path. Sometimes her walks took her as far as the Shakespeare Garden, but today she would just cross the Mall and go as far as Bethesda Terrace. She loved to listen to the fountain, *Angel of Waters.*

Despite the exhilaration she usually felt in the cold, she was uncomfortable today in the park. She shivered as the wind blew through the tight weave of her red coat, through to her thick dress and stockinged legs, until it found her bareness beneath. Perhaps it had not been such a good idea to come today.

"I am becoming a foolish woman," she said aloud to Taiko, who sat at her feet next to the bench where she had stopped and huddled. In Japan she had depended on relatives to accompany her, but now, here in New York, Taiko had given her a freedom she had never known in Kyoto.

"Hanae . . ."

His voice had startled her. She hadn't heard his approach.

"I guess I shouldn't be surprised to see you here," he said.

Adrian Lovett sat down next to her, his voice changing level as he bent to pet Taiko. "Hi, boy," he was saying, "you're sure better equipped than we are for this weather." She knew his hand was moving in the dog's fur. "You have a good Thanksgiving?" He had turned to her.

"Very good. We had friends for dinner."

"You fix turkey?"

"Yes. And dressing. I have learned to cook American." She smiled.

"No class tomorrow," he said now. And she had the sudden impression that he might have come to the park seeking her, since they would not see each other tomorrow with Ms. Nguyen still away. A conceited thought. But she guessed that perhaps it was true. She sensed he was lonely, missing having his family together at the holiday.

As if on cue his cell phone rang.

"Sorry," he said to her. She could hear him moving next to her, retrieving the phone.

"Hello," he said. "Oh, hi." His voice softened. "No, I'm in the park . . . with a beautiful lady." He laughed. "It's my son," the words directed at her. "He doesn't believe me. . . . Yes," he said into the phone again, "it is very cold. But I *am* in the park. And I'm sitting with Hanae Sakura on a bench. Here, tell her hi. . . ." He had put the phone into her hand.

"I . . ."

"His name is Christopher," he reminded her.

She lifted the phone obediently to her ear. "Hello, Christopher," she said.

"Hi," the child's voice said.

She offered the phone back to Adrian.

"See," he was saying to his son, "you should know better than to doubt your old man."

"Do you have children?" he asked when finally he'd hung up.

"No," she answered too quickly, making it sound like a lie. "I'm pregnant," she heard herself confessing.

"That's wonderful."

Joy from the mouth of this stranger. She had told him before she had told anyone else. Before she had told her husband. The wrongness of it cut her like a knife. But it could not be taken back.

"It really is cold today," he said. He had seen her shiver.

"Yes. I had better get home."

"Me too." He stood up.

She hoped he would not offer to walk with her.

"Will I see you in class next week?" he asked instead.

"Yes, next week." She smiled again and got up. She could feel his eyes watching as she and Taiko walked away.

Sakura looked around the Manhattan apartment. There was an instant impression that no one lived here. No pictures, no books, no little collections of anything cluttering the surfaces of tables. No traces of anyone's life.

It had been relatively easy getting Diana Tierney to confess that the first call she had made in her effort to locate Kerry had been to this apartment. After all, she was probably the only person other than a succession of lovers who even knew of the apartment's existence.

For the first year after she'd begun working as Kerry's nurse, she had been completely ignorant of his double life. Not even after Kerry told her about the midtown apartment did she suspect. If she thought anything, she imagined he was having an affair with a woman. She had never guessed the reality, until one of his lovers did the unspeakable and showed up at the clinic.

What had happened next, she'd said, she would always remember. Kerry had coolly asked not to be disturbed as he ushered the man into his private office. And he could have left it at that. But after the man had gone, he called her. She never understood why, but he told her everything. She believed he needed to confess to someone, and she was convenient. He had smiled after, saying he felt better that she knew, and hoped . . . She had stopped him then, reassuring him that he didn't have to ask for her loyalty. He had it.

She just felt he was carrying around enough baggage. She didn't want to add to his burden the possibility of whether or not his nurse was going to expose him. Besides, she liked Bill Kerry.

Sakura moved into the kitchen. The cabinets were bare and the refrigerator was empty, except for some wine and bottled water. A single roll of paper towels stood near the spotless sink.

In the bedroom the chest of drawers held only a sweat suit, socks, and underwear. In the closet were shoes and a single change of dress clothes. A box of Kleenex was on the bedside table near a phone. He picked up and listened for the hum of the dial tone. Replacing the receiver, he snapped the edge of one of the latex gloves he was wearing. The sound seemed unnecessarily loud in the small space.

Kerry fit the pattern. Despite the wife and kids, the doctor was a homosexual, or at least bisexual. And despite the fact that he was murdered in Forest Hills, he had likely been targeted in Manhattan. The doctor must have been tailed from the city and watched. How else would the killer have known that Lylah Kerry and the children would not be home? Except for the forced entry, the killer was still running true to form.

And now at last they had gotten a break—a connection between two of the victims. And Milne? Hadn't he had crippling arthritis? Could he also have been one of Kerry's patients? He would need to press hard on the staff interviews and background checks. And they'd need a list of Kerry's patients and a printout of his appointment schedule for the weeks prior to his death. The clinic seemed to be the nexus.

✦

Sakura found Willie still working in her assigned cubicle, a glass-fronted box smaller than his own office at the periphery of the Major Case squad room. She was reading the latest DD-5 interviews with the clinic staff and eating pizza that the task force detectives had ordered in. She wiped her hands on a paper napkin as he walked into the office.

"Hi, Jimmy," she greeted him. "Want some? It's pepperoni." She indicated the cardboard box on her desk.

"No thanks." He sat down.

"You got any leads on the lover?" she asked. His visit today to Kerry's Manhattan apartment had been followed by a canvass of the building and surrounding neighborhood.

"An elderly woman on Kerry's floor claims to have seen 'a nice-looking young man' going into the apartment once or twice," he said. "Her description was pretty vague. White. Average height and weight. Twenties or thirties. Brunet. Doesn't sound like the bartender's composite."

"What about the wife?"

"Lylah Kerry claims complete shock at her husband's double life. I'm inclined to believe her."

"Well," she said, "we did get one significant piece of information from the nurse. Kerry treated Carrera. That's a solid link between two victims. The killer may be connected to the clinic."

"Maybe. But the administration is fighting us on patient information. They were adamant that none of the other victims, including David Milne, had ever been treated there."

She looked down at the reports she'd been reading. "Nobody from the clinic staff stands out so far," she said. "But I'm going to have the Bureau run checks on all the names. See if anything shakes out."

"Good." He knew he didn't sound hopeful.

"I know it's not likely since we're dealing with orthopedics," she said, "but I'd like to see if any of the clinic staff has ever worked in a psychiatric area."

"You're thinking about the LSD."

"Yes. Except that there's a problem with that, Jimmy. The kind of therapy that I told you about has been illegal in this country for decades. That's why I did my graduate work overseas."

"Couldn't some doctor be using the drug anyway?"

"Could be. Which brings up another possibility."

"That a doctor could be the killer."

"You mean a psychiatrist?" She smiled. "I know we're all supposed to be a little nuts, but no . . . I was thinking of a patient. It's no secret that a dose of LSD can send a prepsychotic personality into full-blown psychosis. The patient screening was rigorous in the sixties when therapy with the drug was still allowed, but if there's a doctor out there using it illegally and doesn't quite know what he's doing . . ."

". . . He could have pushed a patient over the edge."

"It's just a theory, Jimmy."

"What have I got but theories?"

"And even if it was true," she went on, "it's doubtful that anyone's going to step forward and own up to creating this monster. It would be professional suicide for a doctor to admit to using the drug without governmental approval."

"Who gets permission to use it?"

"Very few people," she said. "I can make some discreet inquiries, see if anyone in this area has a grant to work with the drug."

"Thanks," he said. Then, "Dr. Linsky confirmed that Kerry was never gagged. No bruising around the mouth. No residue from adhesive."

"That's interesting."

"Yes. It's taking a chance, even with the nearest house so far."

"But I can understand why he'd take the risk, since I believe he has a need to interact with the victims."

"You're saying he wanted Kerry to be able to talk back."

She nodded. "It may have been at least part of the reason for killing him out of the city. The isolation was a luxury. And it fits with the LSD. The drive to share the fantasy, to bring them into his world. He needs to have them understand what he's doing."

"I wish we understood it." He looked at her. "You hear anything from Michael?"

"Me? No . . . I haven't talked to him since Thanksgiving at your place. Why?"

"I called him a couple times today," he said. "Left a message."

"And he hasn't called back. Is that unusual?"

"No."

"I know," she said, weighing the words, "that you think he's an asset—"

"You haven't seen him at his best," he interrupted.

"That I believe."

"Michael's good, Willie."

"And you're not? It's barely a month since the first murder. You know as well as I do that serial investigations take time."

"Time's what I haven't got."

⋔

There was proof enough in the increased sales of the *Daily News* and the *Post* that the city at large was following the gay-killer story. But the kind of mass hysteria that had surrounded Son of Sam had not so far developed in the general population, and this perceived indifference to "the open season on gays" was not to be silently tolerated.

Tonight's gathering in Chelsea was the latest in the police outreach efforts that served a dual purpose. The man standing in the back of the room was well aware of both. The meetings were meant to give a more positive focus to the fear in the community and diffuse the anger building against the police. They were also a lure to trick the killer into exposing himself.

It had been simple enough, however, to avoid the surveillance van parked not far from the building's entrance. There would be officers inside taking pictures of everyone who entered in hope of some obvious match with that pitiful composite drawing that had appeared in the city's newspapers. Plenty of the men here wore jackets and baseball caps. But he was not one of them. A simple overcoat tonight. And hair unlacquered and combed.

He gazed around, trying to pick out the undercover cops in the hall, noting instead how the whole room glowed with the lesser lights of so many auras. So many of the Fallen in this small space, but none with the brilliance of a great one.

The newspapers were well represented, responding to the news of yet another murder. He recognized the *Post* reporter whose sensational speculations had made him smile. They were all so totally wrong in every basic assumption. The media . . . the police. It had been obvious, even before tonight, that the police had nothing. He was careful and had left no physical evidence. But it went beyond that. They had no way to apprehend him in their minds, much less in their reality—no template for what he was doing. They were hunting a serial killer. A man killing other men. How could they ever catch what they couldn't understand? He could sense their frustration. Could almost feel sorry. Especially for James Sakura.

The lieutenant had not appeared to referee tonight. The meeting had begun with fiery speeches and complaints from the locals, then an unctuous spokesman from Public Information had given a reassuring talk with a warning about picking up strangers.

The good part had started with the questioning.

What exactly was being done to catch this monster? a community leader had asked. Mr. Public Information had responded with a numbing litany of procedure, leaving out, of course, the proactive tactics of this meeting.

Another firebrand from the audience, most likely a police plant from Anticrime, was speaking now, charging everyone to sign the petitions for action at the tables in the back of the room, petitions that would then be carried directly to the mayor.

More likely straight to Police Plaza. The man smiled. There was a moment's hesitation, the impulse for audacity was strong. But in the end he did the smart thing. He left without signing his name.

"Enjoying the circus?" Faith Baldwin's even voice cut toward Sakura through the deep shadow backstage. He'd spoken to her briefly in the past three weeks, but he hadn't seen her since Westlake's apartment. He turned from the proceedings in the hall to watch her walking toward him. Her ivory blouse glowed faintly in the stray luminescence from the stage lights, ghostly, till the rest of her appeared, destroying any illusion of disembodiment.

"You never know with these proactive things," he said. "Procedure is procedure because it's worked somewhere in the past." He turned away again, focusing on the last few signers at the petition tables.

"I thought we had a new wrinkle till I got the scoop on the doctor's secret life," she spoke again.

"Who told you?"

She shrugged, a movement in the periphery of his vision. "Were you trying to hide that bit of information from the D.A.'s office?"

"That's not why I asked." He turned to look at her.

She shrugged again. "The lowdown on Kerry was everywhere. . . . You find anything interesting in his apartment?"

He gave up. He knew why the truth about Kerry's sexuality had so quickly disseminated through the system and the press. The leak was official . . . beneficial to the department.

"Jimmy . . . ?" she prodded. "Any leads?"

"Nothing," he said.

She came closer. "You've done well these last five years."

That scent she wore insinuated. Pictures flipped through his head. A snapshot gallery of the two of them in bed . . . the things they'd done.

"It was interesting, hearing you'd come back from Japan married."

"I'm sorry."

She laughed. That perfect laugh, completely genuine. "A little late, Jimmy. But I got the point."

He forced himself to remain looking at her. A hunger, unwanted, ran inside his nerves, jumping the void between neurons.

"Ha-na-e." Her lips moved, carefully forming the syllables. "That's it, isn't it? I've heard she's as pretty as her name."

He owed her this moment of torture.

"Lieutenant . . . ?" Talbot had appeared. "Oh, excuse me, Ms. Baldwin—"

"What is it, Detective?" he cut in.

"It's just that we're wrapping things up and Doss thought you might say a word to Mr. Felton."

He knew he looked blank.

"Mr. Felton's group sponsored this meeting," Talbot explained. "Public relations, Lieutenant."

The lesser, it seemed, of two evils.

"Tell them I'm coming," he said.

⚜

The tiny bar near Zoe's old neighborhood was perfect for clandestine meetings. She settled comfortably in the padded high-backed booth with its faded maroon and gray vinyl. The place, as always, was populated with a few grizzled and slack-cheeked men, too ornery to be home asleep, too old to give her any real grief. Only the occasional territorial stare, as if her appearances here were a disturbance, an unwelcome reminder of things long in the past.

She was halfway through her first drink when Johnny showed up. He came back from the bar with a bottle of beer and a refill of her cocktail.

"You look tired," she said.

"Interviews." He slid in across from her. "Feels like I did a million of them today."

"In Forest Hills?"

"Everywhere." He took a hit on the beer. "Sakura wanted to start right away, tracking down the clinic staff. I think I might actually be glad they're stiffing us on patient lists."

It was obvious from his attitude what the net result of the interviews had been. "Kind of interesting," she said, "that the doc was murdered here in Queens."

"Yeah, but his clinic's in Manhattan."

She waited, sensing there was more.

"The Kerry job was a break-in." He took a swig of the beer.

She sipped her own drink. Johnny had just confirmed the rumor that was circulating in the media. "Copycat?" she asked him.

He shook his head. "Trust me," he said, "this was the same guy."

She knew what that meant. There were distinctive details at the crime scenes known only to the police and the killer—details that little Zoe would kill for. But Johnny Rozelli wasn't dumb. She could not make a frontal approach. At least not verbally.

She smiled to herself, remembering how embarrassed she'd been when at the age of eleven her breasts had seemed to blossom overnight. She had slumped around for months, her mother and grandmother wearing themselves out with admonishments to stand up straight. She had hated the stares and the giggles of the boys at school, until the day it somehow dawned on her that the stares held awe and the nervous laughter was a mask for something else. Her breasts held power. She had used them like a weapon ever since.

She had reached across the table to stroke Johnny's hand. Now she sat up, molding her back to the worn and cracked vinyl. At the withdrawal of her fingers, Johnny looked up from his drink.

She took an impressive breath. "I thought we had another break in the killer's pattern," she said. "Kerry didn't read gay. But the guys at Public Information set us straight."

Johnny grunted disapproval. "Sakura didn't like that. Hell of a way for the wife and kids to find out what the old man's been up to."

She shrugged. "Good story outing the doc. But better if we'd had some suspense, a few days to play the angle that he'd started offing straights."

"Bite your tongue, Zoe. We've got enough trouble as it is."

She smiled, reaching again for his hand. "Poor Johnny." She let the words hang. Then, "Sure wish I had something hot for tomorrow."

He pulled free of her grasp. "I've told you too much already. Want to cost me my job?"

"Course not, baby." She filled her eyes with concern. "You know you haven't given me anything really hard."

"I don't know, Zoe." He leaned back, unaware of her double entendre, shooting his cuffs through the sleeves of his gray Armani. It was a habit he had. She watched him realign his cuff links.

"Just one thing," she pressed. "How'd you cop so quickly to the fact that Kerry wasn't exactly Joe Citizen?"

He picked up his beer and finished it. "His nurse tipped us on an apartment that the doc was keeping in the city," he said finally. "A place to shack up with his boys." He slid up from the booth. "You ready for another one?" He pointed to her drink.

"No, I'm fine. . . . Any line on who the doc was boffing?"

He smiled, sizing her up, and shook his head appreciatively. "You're a piece of work, Zoe."

"You too, baby." She smiled back. The headline he'd just handed her was all she'd get tonight. At least in the way of a story.

Michael Darius knew he was dreaming, the way some people know they are dreaming. Knew that he was lying cold and sweating in his bed. But he let the awareness slip, surrendering to the immediacy of what was happening behind the thin flesh of his eyelids.

Jimmy Sakura was running in the darkness behind him. Darius could hear his partner's labored breathing, the soles of his shoes slapping the filthy concrete. Sakura had called out his name once, and each separate letter had seemed to make its own distinct sound. So that *Da-ri-us* became something drawn out and vaguely foreign.

He'd turned back then, but Sakura was lost. Eclipsed by the night, denser now in this side street, away from city lights. The smell of rotting garbage was thick in his nostrils, and the image of a white one-eyed cat pulling something long and stringy out a dark cavity registered in his brain.

He stopped. Caught his breath. Gazed upward to the net of fire escapes crisscrossing the failing buildings. Beneath the high blank bubble of reflected urban neon, the craze of metal stairways descended like Escher drawings into the alley. He lowered his sight, scanning a patchwork of doors and broken windows that opened on his left into an abandoned warehouse. He had lost track of the halo of acid green light, bobbing ahead of him, moving with the same jaunty rhythm as Hudson's surefooted gait.

He had just decided that maybe Hudson was hiding somewhere in the warehouse, when he caught sight of him again, stepping out of the darker shadows with a *Here I am* confidence. He was dressed in black leather, his head seeming to float on his shoulders, disembodied, the intense light from it pulsating like a large animal's heart. For a split second he thought he could glimpse Hudson's teeth through the brilliance, giving him a cocky, welcoming smile.

The dream, which never changed, was always both more and less than the reality. The imagined smile, a point of departure, when the dream became clearer than what had actually happened—Hudson's empty hand coming out from inside his dark jacket, fingers exploding like Roman candles.

What would always remain infinitely certain, then and after, was Jimmy Sakura's scream as he'd lifted and fired his gun.

He sat up straight in bed and reached for his cigarettes. Avoiding Sakura's phone calls was avoiding the obvious. He'd have to go see him tomorrow.

CHAPTER

11

A full complement of the city's newspapers littered Sakura's desk, all with screaming headlines about the latest victim in the gay serial murders. He sat forward in his chair, remembering this morning's confrontation with the chief of detectives over the leaking of Kerry's homosexuality to the press.

You're damn right I let Phil Doss give it to them. At least McCauley had had the good grace to appear uncomfortable. *The gay-rights people are already halfway up my ass. You think I want to make room for the rest of the population?*

Sakura hadn't bothered to answer. He had made his point. A Pyrrhic victory for Lylah Kerry and her children.

In the wake of his silence, McCauley had gone on offense, insisting that Public Information had said nothing to the media about Kerry's apartment. So how had the *Post* so quickly come up with the love nest story? *Better plug your own leak, Sakura.*

He squeezed his lids shut in a weak attempt to zap out the pain growing behind his eyes. The pressure inside his head filtered through his defenses and he reached for his cup of tea. It was no longer hot, but he took a lukewarm sip anyway and fished in the drawer for some aspirin. The last resort. He hated pills.

Outside the glass-fronted office he could see the change of shifts in Major Case. He looked down at his desk and picked up the petition lists that had been gathered at Sunday's community meeting. Columns of signatures snaked down legal-size sheets—small, scratchy scrawls barely legible alternated with big, bold styles that were more print than cursive. He rubbed his eyes. He couldn't dismiss the possibility that the killer's signature might be inscribed in the clutter of penmanship on at least one of these lists. Most serials liked to insinuate themselves into the investigation. It was another way to embroider upon their fantasies.

He let his head roll back onto his shoulders. The case was going nowhere. And if he despised his own ineffectiveness, it was in great part due to the reservoir of tragedy that murder left in its wake. William Kerry's death had added a widow and two young children to the growing list of living victims. It was becoming a killing field.

Frustration, anger, and guilt were a lethal mix, and it was eating him alive. He slammed his fist down on his desk. The edition of the *Post* featuring a photo of Kerry's love nest sailed to the floor.

Darius appeared at his door.

"Tea?" he offered as Michael came in. "I could use a fresh cup myself."

"No . . . thanks." Darius pulled a chair in front of the desk and sat staring at nothing. "I can't do this, Jimmy. I have commitments for several projects."

"The carpentry work?"

"It's what I do." Darius looked at him. "Besides, you don't need me."

He didn't bother to rebut the point of Michael's work. They both knew it was an excuse.

"There's just no reason," Darius went on. "You've got a serial offing gays. I've got no special insight. You're the one with the training."

Michael was never petty. The Quantico jab stung, but was an indication of something deeper. It meant that the case disturbed him.

Darius stood. "I'm sorry, Jimmy."

"It's okay."

For a moment Darius seemed frozen in place, but then he was gone.

He tried not to feel disappointed. It had probably been wrong to involve his former partner in this case. He was, as Michael had said, the one with the training. The problem was that they kept running into blank walls. They had nothing really, except for Willie's profile. And now, with Kerry's murder, the killer had expanded his comfort zone, branching out from the city to the boroughs.

Calling in Darius had been simply an attempt to gain an edge. Now he was left with the playbook. Until something clicked. Or unless Kelly was right and he had an edge of his own.

🔺

The man sat in a pew near the rear of the empty church, the second time he'd sat here in the last few weeks. He didn't know why he'd come, either then or now, although today was Marian's birthday, and this morning's trip to her grave had been completely unsatisfying. Standing there in the dreary coldness of the cemetery, he hadn't known what else to do or where else to go. And like a sleepwalker who suddenly discovers himself stranded, he had found himself sitting inside St. Sebastian. Perhaps all along he had been fooling himself about his detachment from his human life.

He breathed in the heavy silence. He was alone. So totally alone. And any extreme isolation was dangerous. It affected judgment. The police were not stupid. Lieutenant James Sakura was not stupid. And he had been pushing the limits with his hasty awakenings of Pinot and Kerry.

He should awaken Zavebe and move on. New York had proved a fertile hunting ground, but there were other cities where he might expect to discover many more of the Fallen. And perhaps he had already found the most powerful here.

He rose and moved quietly near the cages of twin confessionals, his shadow looming like a dark and misshapen gargoyle. As he walked past the stand of lit candles and votives, pennies and nickels winked at him from the offertory tray.

A gust of cold wind ruffled the flames and made him turn. Students from Immaculata, the parish elementary school, had entered the church with their teacher and were tramping down the center aisle, two by two. Outfitted in navy-and-white uniforms, the students marched in on saddle-oxford feet toward the main altar in a gait that resembled a loose type of military precision, with a Catholic-school reverence for the Divine Presence. There seemed to be a thin attempt to keep talk to a whisper.

"Lucia Mancuso, you are supposed to be one of God's angels sent to proclaim the birth of His Son, not talk to Anna Marie Gandolpho."

"Yes, Sister Isadore," the girlish voice answered, making a run up and down a musical scale.

The children had taken position in a kind of semicircle before the side altar, where the newly installed Christmas crèche held prominence. He moved out from the shadows into half-light. The child's voice had tickled his ear.

She was neither the tallest nor the shortest girl in Sister Isadore's class, but she was clearly the prettiest. Even from where he stood, he could see her precise, nearly exotic features. The light olive skin that was almost translucent. The dark pixie cap of straight glossy hair. He pressed his hand to his chest, feeling the muscle of his heart constrict and relax. He closed his eyes for a moment, willing his human self to stay calm. When at last he looked again, it was to feast on the light that encircled Lucia's small, perfect head, to devour the aura burning as brightly as any Gadriel of the Cherubim had ever seen.

✲

Hanae touched the small of her back. The pain had settled in a tight web. She'd been sitting at the worktable far too long, fighting the clay. How could she have been so foolish as to believe her skills could match the memory stored in her fingers? She had never attempted a piece as demanding as this bust. She bit her lip. The likeness was to be Jimmy's Christmas gift. She rested her forehead against the cool, raw mass.

She had not been the hoped-for child of Japanese parents. Born a girl in a culture that favored males. Born blind in a society that shunned imperfection. The female offspring of a mother who'd struggled in her pregnancy, who'd almost died giving birth. And more tragically, there would be no more children.

In a country that stressed conformity, her visionless eyes had kept her from being completely Japanese. She existed in her own world. Foreign. *Hanae. Cherry blossom. Blemished blossom.* Yet her blindness had allowed her to define herself, to grow in ways not granted other Japanese women.

Her earliest memories were of her mother's soft coos against her ear, the warmth of her father's hand on the top of her head. Like every Japanese child, she had been spoiled and indulged. Fed sweets until she had almost grown fat. Given toys and puzzles for her little fingers to explore. And when she had asked for a pet, her father had bought her first finch that very day.

She would have liked to explain to her parents that her sightless world suited her, since it was the only one she'd ever known. Yet they would have never understood, for they held themselves somehow responsible for her blindness.

But English saved them all. She had a good ear and learning languages had been easy. Of course, it had been the stilted English of language tapes. But it was good enough, so when the man had asked directions in faltering Japanese, she was able to help.

James Sakura had come from New York to visit his grandmother on Hokkaido. A yearly ritual. But fate, her mother said, had brought him to Kyoto, to the park that day. Hanae always waited there while her mother did the shopping. He was sitting on the bench next to her when her mother returned. For a while the three of them made polite conversation, Hanae acting as interpreter when Jimmy's Japanese failed.

The next day she had asked her cousin to accompany her to the park. She never knew if Nori saw through the pretense of wanting to attend the toy boat races on the lake. But it didn't matter. James Sakura was waiting for her.

The following day her mother went with her. And in what was a bold overture for a Japanese woman, Hanae's mother invited James Sakura to their home for tea. Over the next weeks Hanae saw Jimmy often, storing away each memory, saving up for the time when he would go away forever. Yet before he had left Kyoto, there had been many surprises for both of them. Jimmy had been brought into a case in which she'd played her small part. And Jimmy had asked her to marry him.

That had been five years ago. She lifted her head and, regulating her breathing, centered herself. Once more, her hands reached for the clay. She could feel that the nose was wrong. The forehead too wide, the eye sockets too deep. Jimmy's face. The face she held so clearly in her mind's eye, the face she loved above all others, she could not find in the clay. It seemed as blank to her as the face of a stranger.

She stood up and stretched. Taiko rose too, sensing her restlessness. Her skin seemed too small, her breath too shallow. She reached back and loosened her hair, letting it fall to her waist. In every part of her, there was an unaccustomed energy that she both welcomed and loathed.

She pressed against her abdomen. Jimmy's other gift. Not planned like the sculpture. But unexpected. Now that Dr. Blanchard had confirmed her pregnancy, she had to tell Jimmy. Had to find the right time. But he was so seldom home, and with the increasing pressures of the case, it would not do to have him . . . *Upset?* Was that what she feared? That Jimmy might not want this baby?

Anyone could see they were sisters. The exactness of their features was the same, although the one who waited outside on the steps of St. Sebastian was taller and fairer than the other. And there was a frailness in the older sister, where the other was pure energy.

"You shouldn't have waited, Celia," the dark little one said as she bounded down the steps.

"You know Mama wants us to walk home together."

"It's only five blocks, CeCe."

"Never mind. Where's your jacket, Lucia?"

The girl touched her arms as if to confirm she was without her coat. "Guess I forgot it in the classroom."

"Maybe it's in church."

She shook her head. "I'll get it tomorrow." Lucia hooked her arm through her sister's and pulled her down the last of the church steps onto the sidewalk. "You worry too much, CeCe. Let Mama do the worrying."

The older girl adjusted her backpack. It seemed too heavy for her delicate frame. She coughed, a deep croupy sound.

Lucia turned and frowned. "You getting sick again?"

"You worry too much, Lucia," she said, mimicking her sister, a breathy laugh mixing in with the tail end of her cough.

"You should have gone home."

The girl shook her head, fighting off another spasm.

"Why didn't you wait inside?"

"I did." Her voice was wheezy. "I watched some of the practice. I walked out at the end."

They began to move, arm in arm, down the street. Lucia doing most of the talking, Celia nodding in agreement or shaking her head in despair.

"You know Pete Fazio is in love with you," Lucia was saying.

"He is not. Besides, Jennie Daughtery likes him."

"So. He doesn't give a damn about fat Jennie Daughtery."

"Lucia, that language. Papa would kill you."

"And who's going to tell him?"

Celia looked down to her saddle oxfords, then up at Lucia. A smile lit her beautiful face. It was easy to see that it was love, not intimidation, that would keep her from tattling.

"So when are you going to tell Pete you like him?"

"I . . . I don't." It was a weak denial.

"If you don't tell him, I—" Lucia didn't finish but stopped, turning sharply. Her dark eyes searched the empty street behind her. After a moment she frowned, shrugged her shoulders, and turned back.

"What's wrong, Lucia?"

"Nothing." Lucia had begun walking again, her step quicker, her sister struggling to keep pace. "Come on," she ordered. "It's getting colder."

The man watched from his sheltered position as Lucia's aura, a guiding light in the darkening street, pointed all three of them in the direction of home.

🐦

Hanae pressed the heels of her palms against her eyes, resting her forehead against the stubborn clay. She had no more success with the bust this evening than she had had this morning. Her wrists were stiff, the tips of her fingers numb. But it was her heart that most ached. Jimmy's face could not be coaxed out.

She lifted her head, touching the Band-Aid wound around her index finger. She had injured herself with one of her knives. It was just a small cut, but for some reason the bleeding had been difficult to staunch.

"Have you been working all day?"

She started at the sound of Jimmy's voice, her hands reaching for the cloth to cover the bust. "I did not hear you. You are home early."

He moved closer, planting a soft kiss on the top of her head. "Still won't let me see?"

"No." She turned and let him kiss her full on the mouth. "How was your day?"

He walked away, and she could hear him open a door to one of the birdcages and make a cooing sound. "Why don't they ever have anything to say to me?"

"Maybe they don't know how to speak to a detective."

His laughter told her he understood her not so subtle message. "Michael came in to see me today. He's decided he wants off the case."

"I am sorry. For you. And for Kenjin."

"It was never anything official. He was more or less operating on his own." He moved back toward her. "What's this?" He was touching the finger she'd hurt.

"Nothing. A small cut." She felt his lips brush against the Band-Aid. "I need a bath." He released her hand.

She listened as he walked out of the room. Enter their bedroom. Kenjin gone. Off the case. Like the blood from the cut, it stirred something dark inside. Tonight she must perform *chinkon-sai* to calm the unsettled spirits.

CHAPTER

12

Late Saturday morning. Willie lay curled on the sofa in the Jamilis' pleasant living room, enjoying the fire that burned in the grate. The second-floor apartment looked out onto Washington Square Park, and through the large picture window she could watch the holiday crowds that thronged the Village, despite the awful weather. Christmas was less than a month away, and she had yet to buy her presents, much less mail them to New Orleans. She would have to get out there today, her day of rest as dictated by Jimmy. *Tunnel vision results when you're too close to a case. Give it a rest. Come back with a fresh perspective.* Her own preaching thrown back at her.

It was still good advice. She was a bit burned-out after two weeks of sixteen-hour days working with the members of the task force, talking one-on-one with as many of them as she could, hoping to fill in the cracks of dry reports with something that would break this thing. But it was all with little result.

According to the colleagues she had called, there was no one on the East Coast with a grant for therapeutic use of psychoactive drugs. So that particular theory of a patient "pushed over the edge" through LSD experimentation by a psychiatrist was pretty much a dead end, since there was no way to trace illegal psychiatric use.

There'd been nothing new learned from Kerry's murder, except the doctor's connection to Carrera. No link to any of the other victims. No witness since the bartender who had only glimpsed the probable killer with Westlake. Unless you counted the woman in Kerry's building who'd seen an apparently different man with the doctor at his apartment. Nothing that would change her original profile or provide new insight into the killer's fantasy.

A week now since Kerry's murder. They were all in suspension, consciously or not, waiting. It was a mood as oppressive as the weather, a sullen premonitory coldness that hung about day after day.

As had so often happened since their visits together to the Milne and Westlake crime scenes, she thought of Darius. The intrusion was irritating. His bowing out of the case had not really surprised her. But his abrupt departure had left her with a feeling of . . . *Unfinished business* was the best way she had to describe it. And time after time this past week as she'd worked the case, she'd found herself wondering what Michael's response might be to some thought or theory that occurred to her. She had to admit he was interesting—more than the bitter ex-cop. She was actually sorry she wasn't going to see him again.

A log popped and stirred in the fire. She sighed and sat up. Enough damn rest. And the hell with Christmas. A serial investigation was a full-time thing. She was going to Police Plaza, where she might at least do some good.

The bruised greenish sky had not changed since morning. It leaked a perpetual drizzle that thickened to gray mist shrouding cold stone and pavement. Moving at ground level was a magical act, like breathing underwater.

The narrow side street seemed almost deserted, as quiet as a street in the city ever was on a Saturday in early December. The small figure in the shiny yellow slicker bounded along the sidewalk, hood thrown back, rubbered feet dancing and splashing through every slight depression where rain had collected in the pavement. For the man, following on his Harley, the light bounced too. A spherical glow, lanternlike in the mist, tethered to the dark little head.

The light stopped, disappeared through the door of the small neighborhood pharmacy. He continued down the street, then turned to circle the block. He did not believe in fate, was fully aware of the danger. But this kind of opportunity might not come again.

The mobility of the bike made it possible. That, and the weird muffling effect of the weather. Still, his timing had to be perfect.

She emerged from the store with a little white bag in her hand. He hung back, waiting, as her return trip through the puddles brought her closer to the street. The traffic light went green at the end of the block; cars swept past. He gunned the Harley, curving onto the sidewalk, sweeping her up, arcing into the alley.

She was strong for her age. A good fit for her body. His hand was across her mouth, keeping her silent, his arm pinning her to his chest as she kicked and clawed. With his free hand he reached for the canister clipped to his belt beneath the dark rubber poncho, held his breath while he sprayed her. A good dose before the quick injection that would keep her out for a while.

The drizzling mist, condensing to rain in the narrow brick canyon, fell like a curtain between the alley and street. Still, he was careful, propping her on the far side of the cycle to tape her wrists before removing his poncho.

For a moment as he lifted her, the puppy dog smell of her damp hair evoked a human sadness. In the next moment he had settled her with her arms around his neck, her body hanging limply at his back. He straddled the Harley and put the poncho back on. Beneath its heavy folds, balanced behind him on the seat, Lucia and her light were invisible.

⁂

Tony Paladino was furious. At the weather. At his luck. He knew what he must look like as he walked into the dealership. Wet to the skin and puffing like a bull with a cardiac. He should have gone home to change, but that would have put up Barbara's antenna and made him even later than he was now for his Saturday split.

It hadn't been the best of times at Odyssey Lincoln Mercury. What with the freaky weather bumming everyone out. October and November, usually among the best months, had been lousy for sales. So it shouldn't matter at all that he was late for his shift, but Harris was an asshole who wanted a full complement of salesmen on the floor, even if all that was dribbling through the big glass doors was rain.

"You're a bit late to the dance." Steve Meyer was grinning ear to ear as he walked up. The prominent teeth in his too thin face made him look like a weasel.

"Don't fuck with me, Steve. Besides, you didn't have to stick. What's one less salesman on the floor these days?"

Meyer's grin grew wider. He had something to say but held it. "So what happened to you?" he said instead.

"Fucking flat."

"Too bad."

"Yeah . . . well. For God's sake, what's up? You gonna bust a gut if you don't tell me."

"That Cartier L . . . silver frost with graphite leather interior. I sold it."

"No shit."

"This woman comes in. Didn't look to be more than twenty. Jeans and a sweatshirt. No makeup. No flash at all. Just looking, I figure. You're up, but you're not here, and no way am I letting Jennings take it, even if she looks like she's got empty pockets. So I waltz over sweetly and ask if I can help."

"Is this gonna be a long story?"

"Nah." Meyer brushed off his sarcasm, too wound up in his own bullshit to take offense.

"The little lady wants something safe and comfortable," he went on. "So what the hell, I show her the Cartier L. She gives it the once-over, don't even blink at the sticker price. Just asks if she gets something off for cash. I start to explain how cash don't really matter much the way financing's done today. But then I just say, 'Cash? Yeah, I can take maybe a full hundred off.' And the next thing I know she's writing out a check that her bank clears in maybe five seconds."

Meyer stood looking at him with that damn weasel grin, waiting for the explosion.

"Son of a bitch!" he complied. But his heart wasn't in it. Fuck the stupid commission. There was no way now with that idiot bragging all over the place that the sales manager didn't know just how late he was. And worse than Barbara in one of her moods was Harris asking too many questions.

�֎

The rain had stopped, like skeleton fingers that suddenly cease their tapping. The shades drawn up, the windows stood black and cold, rectangles of blankness in the far wall of the bedroom. From where he stood in the unlit space, the man could see nothing beyond them, as if the city lights had disappeared along with the day's sun. Whatever illumination existed seemed pebbled and sourceless, an ambient trait of the objects in the room. The small yellow slicker at the foot of the bed, alone in the general dimness, maintained a plastic brilliance, sharp angled and bright.

She slept soundly. Dreamless in the dark. Eyes stilled beneath lids. Lashes like spiders against her flesh. He bent his face close, his mouth grazing her lips, parted as though ready to blow a bubble. Drawing in her breath, he could taste its little-girl hard-candy flavor, taste the faint top note of the gas she'd inhaled. A small jumping of her arm, a sigh now and again.

He pulled back, reaching for her wrist, checking her pulse. Her blood flushed rhythmically through a tapestry of tiny vessels. An endless dance of red. He counted beats against the second hand of his watch. Slower than he thought, but certainly within normal range.

A child was new territory. The injections of potassium didn't matter, but he would have to be careful with the LSD. A small girl's brain was different from an adult male's. Everything depended upon precision and timing. He would wait for her to wake naturally. And like a china doll, he would handle her. She was imminently breakable. And he needed her alive, at least until he wanted her dead.

✖

Father Andrew Kellog did not have nightmares, so the vague apprehension that aroused him from sleep was something unusual. For what seemed like an eternity, but was probably more nearly ten minutes, he drifted in a fog of semiawareness, resisting the intuition that whatever had interrupted his good night's rest would have to be sooner or later acknowledged.

Still huddled within the precincts of the comforter, he made himself sit up, pulling the cover around him as he reached for his robe. He had worn his socks to bed, and they gave him some protection as he poked his feet free and slid them into leather slippers. For a minute more he hesitated at the side of the bed. Then relinquishing the old down quilt, he wrapped himself in the robe and shuffled to the window to peer outward, realizing, even as he looked, that it was the church that was the center of his fear.

The building appeared all right. Which was to say it looked as it always had to him, sullen and medieval, its slender spires diminished in the growing decay of the neighborhood. For a fleeting moment as he watched, a light seemed to move behind a window. But was it real, or only headlights reflecting from the street?

He went to the closet and put on his overcoat. He didn't have the patience to put on his boots, but shoes would at least be better than slippers for crossing the yard in the freezing hours before dawn—one more duty to be gotten through in a day.

Outside, it was colder but less damp than inside the rectory. Walking across the yard, his head felt suddenly clear, as if he had decompressed like a diver or an astronaut finally sucking normal air. The light had not appeared again in the window, and he thought of turning back. There was no one in the church. And if there were, what was he going to do about it?

The side door that led to the sacristy was still secure when he reached it, and he wasn't about to walk around the building to check every entrance. He unlocked the door and went in, groping for the switch. The light came on and he listened. He was alone in the sacristy, could hear nothing but silence from the darkness beyond. But the apprehension that had seemed to disperse in the outside air was returning, seeping back inside him with the chilling dampness of stone.

He would just go in for a minute. Just have a quick look to see if anything appeared disturbed. If someone had broken in with an intention to steal, it was the poor boxes they'd go for first.

He walked across the sacristy, aware of his old man's wheezing, aware of cold pipes weeping inside walls. The door into the sanctuary was a deeper blackness. The night outside had been city bright, but the narrow arched windows of the chancel and nave allowed little light through heavy leaded panes. A single candle symbolizing the presence of God burned next to the tabernacle on the altar. Votives fluttered in an alcove. Again he listened, again heard nothing. Whispering a hurried prayer, he inched against the wall toward the switch. In the moment that he hit the altar lights, he heard the muffled footstep.

"Oh, my God," he heard himself say. As, turning, his eyes beheld what hung above the manger, and the naked man in front of him, as startled perhaps as he. In the second when he moved to run, he'd recognized the face. But by then, the blows had started. There was time for submission to the will of his God. Then the floor as cold as ice.

✿

Zoe felt him twist away from her in the same instant the telephone started ringing.

"Yeah," Johnny's sleep-rusty voice spoke into the receiver. "Shit." He jerked up in bed, turned, and began scribbling on a pad. "I'm on my way." He cradled the phone, staring at it for a few seconds.

"Johnny?" She was leaning over, catching a quick look at the address he'd written down.

"I got to go." He was out of bed, ripping away the sheet of paper from the tablet, scrunching it into a pocket as he threw clothes on his naked body.

"What's happened?" She was on her feet, hooking her bra, pulling up her panties.

"We got another one."

"Another murder?" She was next to him. "Who? Where?"

"For chrissake, Zoe, just go back to bed." He moved into the bathroom. She could hear him urinating, then flushing.

"Another gay?" she asked over the running water as he brushed his teeth.

He came out of the bath. The tracks of a wet comb ran through his dark hair. He put his arms around her waist and kissed her. "I'll call you. Lock up when you leave."

"Who, Johnny?"

He pushed her away. "Is that all you can think about?"

"Johnny . . ." She reached out.

"Sorry, Zoe. I'm finished talking." He turned and walked out. The front door of his apartment shut. She closed her eyes and took one long, deep breath.

He hadn't even noticed that she'd dressed while he'd been in the bathroom. She took a brush out of her purse and ran it through her hair. Her mascara had smudged, leaving her with French bedroom eyes. But lipstick was all she had time for. She glanced out the window to the dark street below. He had scrawled an address in Brooklyn on the phone pad. She'd give him a fifteen-minute head start.

St. Sebastian Catholic Church looked like a movie set. Floodlights had been set up around the perimeter of the frozen zone inside, and technicians and extras were everywhere, police being brought in from outside commands on the orders of Lincoln McCauley.

James Sakura had already had his moments alone with the dead. As head of the investigating unit, he remained in complete charge of the area around the bodies. But tonight's vicious murders had complicated an already sensitive case. He could feel the rising panic, like the tug of reins in his hands. Things could start to spiral out of control.

He cursed under his breath. He was letting the pressure get to him. Two more people had died tonight, and still they had nothing. Worse than nothing. Because significant patterns, which had seemed their only insight into the killer's mind, had been broken.

He looked to where Willie stood talking with Detective Johnson. He was glad she was here. He needed her to see this.

"Lieutenant . . ." Rozelli came toward him past the Nativity scene. His eyes held down.

"Yes, Detective."

"Sergeant Kelly wanted me to tell you he's keeping things tight as he can."

"You interviewed the priest who called it in?" Sakura asked him.

"Father Graff . . . yes. Talbot is taking him downtown to sign his statement. But bottom line, he didn't see a thing."

Sakura had gotten as much from the first officer's report. The assistant pastor had returned to the rectory sometime after two A.M. and noticed that the pastor wasn't in his room. A little later, he'd gone to the church to investigate.

One of the CSU techs came over as Rozelli walked away. "The guys are finished with the photos and the sketches, Lieutenant," he said to

Sakura. "We got all the angles you wanted." Charlie Tannehill was hatchet-faced, the kind of forensic specialist who favored graveyard humor. Tonight he seemed nearly as subdued as the rest of them.

Sakura looked at his watch. "Linsky here?"

"Not yet."

"Let's give it some time, Charlie."

"No problem."

"Any word on fingerprints?"

"Same old story, Lieutenant. He wore gloves. Nothing on the candlestick. But I think we may have got a partial footprint."

"Footprint?"

"I think Dearborn's right that our guy's doing this without his clothes on and wiping up the floors. This time there was blood, remember. Head wounds bleed a lot. He stepped in the blood, left us part of a heel. It's not much."

"No, but I'll take what I can get. . . . There's a sink in the back there." Sakura nodded toward the sacristy.

Tannehill's beagle eyes mimicked hurt. "Have a little faith, Lieutenant. We're working on the drain. Likewise in the bathroom."

"Sorry, Charlie. I know you know your job."

Tannehill's gaze went upward. "No problem, Lieutenant," he said again. "Just let me know when you're ready."

◀▦▶

Zoe had the taxi drop her off two blocks away. The area around the church was already being cordoned off. Cop cars were everywhere.

She shoved her scarf farther down over her face, clutched her purse with her camera tucked inside, and walked. It would be tricky, but the church was big, full of nooks and crannies. It cast a wide shadow.

She crossed the street, moving toward a side building, then through a dark breezeway that connected with the left side of the church. The area was deserted. She crouched in some shrubs and waited. Light from inside threw a tangle of color onto the ground as it passed through stained-glass windows.

A side door opened, and she saw a uniform cop coming out. He moved to the rear of St. Sebastian toward another building. A large structure that appeared to be the rectory.

She got up and headed toward the door, hoping it hadn't locked behind him. She was in luck. The door opened. She took a deep breath and entered.

She was in partial shadow, in a small alcove that led into a side altar. Candles flickered, but the main body of the church exploded with light. She could see Johnny talking to another cop about twenty feet away.

She had to move quickly, do what she had to do, and get out. She crouched low, keeping near the outer wall. She was midway down the side aisle when she slid into a pew. All activity seemed to be centered near the main altar and a side altar where a Christmas crèche had been set up. She eased upward, her eyes level with the back of the pew. At first she thought it was just part of the Christmas decorations, until the horror of what she really saw came crashing through.

⁂

"I'm surprised to see you here," Sakura said as Darius walked up to him in the church.

"Willie called. She said I ought to see this."

No answer for that. It was not an explanation he'd expected. "So what do you think?" he asked him.

"I think I'm disgusted for thinking what I see up there is a little bit beautiful."

"I know."

"You know what? That it's beautiful? Or that I think it's beautiful?"

"That you think it's beautiful."

Darius pulled his eyes away. "This the pastor?" he asked. He had turned to the dead man.

"Yes. Father Kellog. Apparently, a secondary victim. He must have surprised the killer."

The priest's smashed head lay in a browning mess, his glazing eyes locked on an image burned into the retina. Darius stood perfectly still, as if filtering something ephemeral through the coppery stench of blood.

"I told Willie I'd just give this a look."

"It's your call."

Darius turned back to the bludgeoned priest lying near the figure of St. Joseph, looked upward to the body strung midair above the manger. The girl's tiny head was slumped against one shoulder. She looked as though she had fallen asleep, strands of her short black hair caught in the white feathers. The familiar ash markings stood out darkly beneath breasts that were no more than ripples in the pale chest. Her hairless mons a small flower enfolded between perfect legs.

"I still don't know if I want to do this, Jimmy," Darius said, his eyes moving to *PENEMUE* scribbled across the wall.

They both knew he lied.

※

Slowly and evenly, against the pull of the weights, the man let his thighs relax and sat up straighter on the padded bench. The exercise area was dim and womb warm. He liked to work out in low light, as close to naked as possible, his concentration centered on the minute workings of his body, the purity of form in motion. But tonight it was a solace that had failed to keep horror at bay.

The images flashed like blades behind his eyes, companions for his memories of the accident. In the gloom of the church, the white old-man face, a death mask turning toward him, its flagging muscles struggling to register the signals firing in the brain. Surprise. Recognition. Terror. The last had stuck. Short-circuited in place by the blows from the candlestick in his hand.

It was pure reaction that had allowed him to so swiftly silence the old man. *Collateral damage,* in the words of the current catch phrase. Kellog, a priest, neither neutral nor civilian. An enlistee on the enemy's side. It was the metaphor of *Enoch* taken too far and he knew it. What was real was that he had killed in cold blood to protect himself from the police. Like that first sin, which had made fugitives of the Fallen, this error, too, would have its karmic price. Of that he had no doubt.

He leaned over, running a hand over the long scar that ran down from his knee, massaging with his fingers the muscle beneath the puckered flesh. There was no denying it, the leg hurt, reinjured tonight in the church when he'd scaled the grappling rope with the deadweight of the girl's body dragging at his back.

He reached for the towel and dried himself, but the scent of anxiety remained, a base note in the odor of his sweat. He could not escape the acuity of his senses. Even as a child his sense of smell had been remarkable. Since his awakening, the degree of sensitivity could become almost painful as the immediacy of the tunnel experience faded and the body fought to reassert itself. And the truth was, he yet loved this prison of flesh.

The admission brought forth a memory of Marian, of how she had looked that first day she'd modeled for him in his studio. Photography had been the one interest he'd retained from his time in the service, and his first critical success had been with pictures he'd taken in post-war Vietnam. But his photojournalism had been sidetracked when the fashion magazines had called. He'd been surprised at first with the offers, but he admired the work of others in the field, and the money was good. And then it had brought him Marian.

Her coming into his life had seemed like an unearned blessing, a sign that the universe could also be randomly good. Later after the accident, he'd looked back on their meeting as something else. A cruel tease dangled, to be snatched away. And yet he had no regrets. What he and Marian had shared was simple human happiness. That was the irony.

He walked to the bathroom and removed one of the vials and a fresh syringe from the cabinet. Marian was dead. Father Kellog was dead. And so, despite the continued existence of his body, was his human persona. The drug was a reminder. It dissolved the bonds that anchored him in the flesh, made it possible to recover some of what he'd experienced in the tunnel.

He went to his bedroom and lay down, letting the needle bite deep. "Gad-ri-el." He spoke the syllables, an invocation to himself. *Gadriel,* he repeated in his mind, over and over, waiting for the drug to take hold, longing for the brief moment of knowing that came before the end, a never-quite-reached memory of the brightness he had been.

This time the programming didn't work. He couldn't keep his focus. The room transformed, pulsed with color. Zavebe appeared in human form, as he had last seen her, her happiness an arrow. The colors warped to blackness. Zavebe remained, an image that floated in the abyss. His own body bag was gone. He existed as a burden of loneli-ness only, as the knowledge of what he had to do.

CHAPTER

13

Zoe felt totally stupid. But she seemed to have no control. She had gone back to the paper, sure. But once there, she'd headed straight to the ladies' room, where the tears had just come. Not sobs, or heaves, or any of that stuff. Just tears. Buckets of them welling from her eyes as she sat curled on the sofa in the corner of the lounge with a roll of tissue, mopping her eyes.

She could have sat in a stall, but she didn't, as if the tears insisted they be at least semipublic. The few women from the early Sunday crew who'd drifted in and out had seen enough in her face not to ask questions. But one of them, probably Rhonda, the new copygirl on the make, had ratted her out to Garvey the minute he'd shown up to oversee Monday's edition. Her editor, who practically lived at the paper, was a red-haired bear-giant of a man, and the last vision you'd expect to appear in the women's rest room. But here he was, in the too, too solid flesh, staring down at her.

"What the fuck's the matter?"

It wasn't concern for her that had propelled him in here. Garvey had, as they said, a nose for the news. He sensed not some personal tragedy, but a story.

"I got a tip on a murder scene," she answered him evenly enough. The tears dried up for the moment. "An address out in Brooklyn."

"Our gay killer?" A heightened interest replaced the aggravation in his voice.

"I thought so. Sakura's team was called out."

"But it wasn't our guy?"

Our guy. She felt the sour bubble of a smile. The way Garvey saw it the paper had a proprietary claim to this monster.

"Are you going to let me tell this?" She allowed her own irritation to show. She never played the vamp with Garvey. Let him see her with her eyes all puffy and red. She liked him, most of the time. He was a stand-up newsman who'd go to bat for his reporters.

"Sure," he said.

"The address in Brooklyn turned out to be a church."

His interest shot up a notch. He kept his mouth shut.

"They were already setting up barricades," she said, "but I managed to sneak around, find an open door in the back."

"You got inside?"

"Yeah." She nodded. "The church was old . . . big. It was easy to hide in the pews."

"What did you see?"

"A little girl." She tried unsuccessfully to hide the crack in her voice. "A little girl hung up with wings above the Nativity scene by the altar."

"Dead?"

She nodded again. A reprieve against speaking. "She was supposed to be an angel," she explained, getting the words out.

"Shit. That's sick." His gaze drifted inward, setting up calculations. "So it wasn't the same guy?" he said.

"There was another body. A priest." She avoided an answer. "His head was bashed in. The cops figured he must have surprised the killer."

"You talked to the cops?"

"No. They never knew I was there. I just stayed in the pews and listened."

"Good girl, Zoe." The calculation tallied up. "The gay killer thing is money in the bank, but a little girl, a priest . . . Christmas. It doesn't get any bigger than that." He had almost said *better.*

"It *was* the same guy." She dropped the bombshell now. The good bomb. The bad would come soon enough.

"What?"

"It was the same guy," she repeated. "Seems he puts wings on all the victims." The tears welled again. She tilted her head back, containing them. "The cops are going nuts," she said. "The gay thing was their only angle. The little girl shoots their profile all to hell."

"Shit." Garvey smiled. "Think what this will do for circulation. Now it's not only the gays. Anybody could be a victim, just like Son of Sam. Nobody is safe in this town."

A tear slipped down her face.

"Goddamn it, Zoe," he reacted. "I thought you, of all people, understood what we do here. We personalize the news, unsterilize it." The slate blue eyes fixed her, not cold, but unrelenting. "Isn't it better to make this little girl's death real to our readers than to leave her bloodless and faceless? I just wish you'd had a photographer."

"I had my camera." She had considered lying, but she was suddenly eager to tell him. "There are the pictures." She pointed to the wastebasket that sat next to the sofa, where gray loops of film coiled amidst the wads of discarded tissue.

"You exposed the goddamn film?" he exploded.

"Yeah, Garvey, I destroyed it," she said. "Why did you think I was crying?"

⁂

For many detectives on homicide, the required attendance at autopsies was the worst part of the job. For Sakura, it was the formal identifications. The sights and smells of the forensic procedure were always horrific, but the victim quickly became an abstraction—the corpse on the table shedding its secrets without further pain. Informing family members that a loved one had been murdered, waiting with them in the unforgiving spareness of the morgue elevator room, was much more immediate and real. With these strangers he intruded, a witness to unguarded emotion, to that first terrible change in lives that would never be the same.

Homicides involving children were the worst. Dominick Mancuso's face leaked hope. Sakura, sitting next to him in the plastic chair, was unbearably aware of the effort that kept the man upright and composed.

A high sucking whine announced that the elevator had lifted from the basement. Mancuso flinched as if he'd been struck, but he rose without speaking and walked with the detective to the viewing window. Standing at his shoulder, Sakura could see the man's haggard face reflected in the glass. The depth of the misery it contained seemed a measure of his own denial—the lie that the pain he dealt with every day never reached beyond his work.

The gurney with its small, sheet-draped body had risen into view. Dominick Mancuso stood hunched and silent. For a very long time, he stared at the doll-like face, studying it so carefully that Sakura allowed himself to wonder if there had been some mistake. But at last a sigh, like air abruptly stirring, rattled itself from out of Mancuso's chest. Tears formed and fell, one and then another down his face.

"Te amo, Lucia." He spoke to the girl behind the glass. *"Dormi in pace, mio piccolo angelo."*

⚶

Sakura let Willie take the lead, while he followed, watching her arm hook around Dominick Mancuso's shoulder as the man's feet trod over the short broken walk, up the slightly uneven concrete steps to the door of his modest brownstone. It was a brownstone in a long string of brownstones that lined the street of the old neighborhood, a neighborhood like many others in Brooklyn that willed itself to stay alive.

Mr. Mancuso stepped up, opened the glass weather door, and fumbled inside his pocket. The nose of a key clicked a staccatoed beat against the brass plate as it sought an opening. Finally it made contact and Mancuso turned the key. For an instant he remained still. There was a kind of painful resolve in the steely way he held on to the door, fighting it seemed to maintain the last barrier against the horror forcing its way inside his home.

In the end he pushed open the heavy door already decorated with a Christmas wreath. Mrs. Mancuso was waiting, like a trapped bird beating against the bars of its cage. Her arms were frantic wings at her sides, her hands balling and unballing the fabric of her robe. Her wild dark eyes, hungry for hope, darted from her husband's face to Willie's to his.

"You have found my baby?" Her hands suddenly quit the fabric, leaving a network of wrinkles, bundles of thin capillaries in her dress.

"Sophia . . ."

She screamed, understanding what terrible message the three syllables of her name held, her body aflame with the misery of what her life was now destined to become. Yet her husband seemed not to want to comfort her, allowing her to feel what she must, completely, inexorably, so that she would never experience more pain than the pain of this moment, so that nothing again would ever hurt as much.

When the hellish fire inside her slowly extinguished itself, Sophia Mancuso seemed reduced to little more than ash. She spilled into her husband's arms and he led her from the room, the muffled noise of their feet sounding against the hardwood floor. Then the soft thud of a door closing.

"It will take time," Mr. Mancuso said softly when he returned. But it was a lie.

"We can come back later," Sakura said.

The man shook his head. "Today is like tomorrow." He braved the truth now. Time would heal nothing.

"Mr. Mancuso, we believe your daughter was targeted," he said.

"I don't understand."

"The killer had been watching Lucia before he abducted her," Willie explained. "He may have been following her for some time."

"She would have said something. My Lucia was smart."

Sakura nodded. "I don't believe she knew she was being followed."

"Or maybe she knew her abductor and did not feel threatened," Willie added.

"Someone we know killed my baby?"

"That's always a possibility in the murder of a child," he said, "that it's someone close to the family. But we believe Lucia's killer was someone she had met recently."

Mr. Mancuso's silence willed him to go on. "This man would not have shown himself to your daughter in a way that would have frightened her," he said, "or made her suspicious. He would appear friendly. Maybe someone who needed help. A handicapped person. Would Lucia help someone in trouble?"

Mancuso nodded. Then his face tightened, his expression hardened. "You know this person." It wasn't a question.

He waited. "There have been a series of murders. You may have heard about them."

"Those gay men?"

"Yes."

"But Lucia . . ."

"Was a beautiful little girl," Willie spoke softly. "But there are reasons why we believe that the person who killed those men also killed Lucia."

"What reasons?" Mancuso's voice had become less controlled.

"The disposition of the bodies is similar," he said.

"My Lucia was raped?" The words exploded darkly.

"No, Mr. Mancuso," Willie answered him. "As far as we can tell there was no sexual assault on any of the victims."

There was no way of avoiding it. Sakura removed a black-and-white photograph from a folder and handed the picture of Lucia Mancuso hanging over the crèche to her father. It was not a gruesome photograph, Lucia hovering over the scene of Bethlehem. Her face peaceful. The wings, full and bright, casting shadows that obscured the nudity.

Mancuso stared at the picture, trying, it seemed, to reconcile this holy tableau with the obscenity of his daughter's murder. In the end his brain erred in favor of kindness, accepting the image's orchestrated beauty, denying the darker truth.

"Angel . . ." His single word.

"The killer places wings on all his victims," Sakura said quietly, taking the photo from Mancuso. "It's important we learn everything we can about the weeks before Lucia disappeared."

"Why is that so important?"

"Because we have to discover how and where the killer crossed paths with your daughter," he said.

"Lucia's life was the same every day."

Sakura replaced the photograph in the folder. "But something changed, Mr. Mancuso."

"I got sick, Papa." Her voice was a light going on in a dark room.

"Celia."

She was an older, fairer version of her sister, dressed in a long flannel gown, her feet bare. On the brink of adolescence, Celia Mancuso was beautiful.

"Hello, Celia." Willie moved closer to the girl, who seemed thinner and paler than she should have been. She smiled. "I'm Dr. French. But everybody calls me Willie."

"That's a boy's name."

"Short for Wilhelmina."

"Are you a real doctor?"

"Yes."

"I've had a bad cold. That's why Lucia went to the drugstore. To get me medicine." Celia isolated the event that had brought Lucia to her fate, had shifted the Mancuso universe.

He walked over. "I'm Lieutenant Sakura, Celia. Do you feel well enough to answer some questions?"

"I'm being brave for Mama," she said. Her skin was slightly mottled, but her large blue eyes told the truth. They were clear as glass.

Dominick Mancuso placed his hands on his daughter's shoulders, gave her a kiss on the top of her head.

"Did you and Lucia often walk around the neighborhood?" he asked.

She stared, her eyes wary. "Yes, but not far. Mostly to school or the park. Usually never past the Fazios' house."

"Did you walk to the drugstore?"

"Sometimes."

"When did you last go to the drugstore together?"

Celia closed her eyes. "Maybe last Tuesday or Wednesday."

"Did you speak to anyone?"

"Of course. Miss Tessa."

"Who is Miss Tessa?"

"She works behind the counter."

"Did you speak to anyone else?"

"I don't think so."

"Did you see anyone you didn't know in the drugstore?"

"No."

"What about outside the store?"

"Freddy Brinks came riding up on his bike."

"Anyone else, Celia?"

She shook her head.

"Would Lucia talk to someone she didn't know?" Sakura asked.

"Lucia would talk to anybody. She was always talking, kind of showing off." She stopped, suddenly aware of how her words must sound. She looked down at her feet, ashamed.

"It's all right, Celia," Willie said.

But it wasn't all right. It never would be. When Celia looked up, she was crying, unable to keep the brave promise she'd made for her mother. "I'm the one who got sick. Lucia's dead because of me."

Sakura stood in the kitchen, obviously the room that got the most traffic. Even here the walls were crowded with religious artifacts. The Mancusos were a good Catholic family.

On the counter near the phone was an envelope of photographs, an entire roll taken of Lucia in her Halloween costume. It was from this set of pictures that the officer filing the earlier missing-person report had taken an identification shot. One glossy color print after another showed the pretty eight-year-old dressed as a ladybug, in bright red-and-black satin, fuzzy antennae bobbing atop her short, shiny black hair. Though it wasn't the costume you really noticed, but the girl. She was clearly posing, smiling for the camera, shouting out for the whole world: *Look at me.* He ran his fingers over one of the prints. *Is that what happened, Lucia? Is that what got you killed? Your fearless eight-year-old heart?*

The photographer was good. He'd gotten it right. Somehow Sakura knew that these images were as close to truth as flesh. Except for one. There was something vaguely disturbing about this photograph, the naked curve of Lucia's shoulder brought up under her chin, her full red lips bowed into a kiss. For all her playfulness and self-possession, this shot seemed coaxed, resurrected not from Lucia's energy but from something inside the photographer.

"Who took these pictures?" he asked as Mancuso walked up behind him.

The man reached for the photographs in his hand. He stared at the top shot for a long moment. When he spoke, it wasn't to answer Sakura's question, but to ask one of his own.

"Didn't you say"—his voice gone cold—"that the killer might be someone close to the family?"

⋔

The woman who opened the door to Agnes Tuminello's home stared at Rozelli's badge as if it were an indecent object.

"I'm Detective Rozelli. This is Detective Johnson. We would like to speak to Mrs. Agnes Tuminello."

"Come in." The woman's voice was husky, too deep for her slight form. "I'm Mrs. Tuminello's daughter, Connie Venza." She closed the door and stood with her arms pressed against the frame as if she needed support. "Mama's not doing well. I don't want her upset any more than she is."

"We understand, Mrs. Venza," Johnson said softly. "We'll be as brief as possible."

Connie Venza nodded, releasing her grip on the door. "Okay if I'm with her when you talk to her?"

"Sure." Johnson smiled.

The room was almost dark, except for the light coming from a floor lamp in the corner. Mrs. Tuminello sat in a large overstuffed chair, an afghan thrown over her lap.

"Mama . . ." Connie touched her mother's shoulder.

"What . . . what has happened?" Mrs. Tuminello's voice rattled with fear.

"Nothing, Mama. Just some people who want to talk to you."

"People? What people?"

"The police, Mama."

"Hello, Mrs. Tuminello." Johnson approached the woman. "I'm Adelia Johnson. And this is Johnny Rozelli."

"Rozelli . . . I knew a Rozelli family."

"Probably some of my cousins." The young detective stepped forward and smiled.

"You are a handsome man, Johnny Rozelli." The woman smiled back.

"That's what they tell me, Agnes." He moved closer, sitting on the sofa opposite her chair. "We're so sorry about what happened. But if we're going to catch the man who did this, we'll have to ask you a few questions." He reached out and took one of her hands.

"Father was such a good man. Who would . . ." She let her head fall back against the soft padding of the chair and closed her eyes.

Johnson waited a moment. "That's what we have to find out—why someone would kill Father Kellog and the little girl."

Mrs. Tuminello kept her eyes closed, speaking softly as though to herself. "My husband passed away two years after Constanza was born. I had to work, but there was no one to keep my baby." She sighed, releasing Rozelli's hand. "Then Father Kellog's housekeeper had a stroke and couldn't work anymore. He offered me the job. He even let me bring Connie to work with me." She looked up and smiled at her daughter. "For twenty-six years I took care of Father and the rectory. And never a complaint. He loved my lasagna." She peered down and observed how her fingers plucked at the yarn of the afghan. "Now I don't think I will make it anymore."

"Mrs. Tuminello, did you know Lucia Mancuso?" asked Johnson.

The housekeeper heaved a ragged breath. "I know the family. I make the Wednesday-night novena with Lucia's grandmother. Last May, Lucia made her First Communion. Like a little bride she was. An angel . . ." Almost immediately she realized the terrible irony of her words. "Oh God," she moaned, her hands closing off her face.

It had been unavoidable. Agnes Tuminello, who worked seven days a week at the rectory, had come onto the crime scene unexpectedly. She had seen lights on and the police cars outside the church, when she arrived at five to start her day. She had gone immediately over to St. Sebastian, gaining entrance through a little-used door the police had failed to seal.

She had seen Lucia Mancuso hanging above the crèche. The girl's body moving ever so slightly, trapped in that falsely beatific pose by the tension of twin monofilament threads. The white wings spread wide but dead in the air.

"Mrs. Tuminello, can you think of anyone who might have done this?" Rozelli asked.

She shook her head violently.

Rozelli reached over and patted the woman's hand. He gave her another moment. "Mrs. Tuminello, we think it was Lucia the killer was after, and that Father Kellog was murdered because he surprised the man."

She looked up, interest in her eyes.

"But we still have to explore every possibility," Johnson said.

Mrs. Tuminello waited.

"Is it possible that someone might have wanted to kill Father Kellog?" Johnson asked.

"No." The word almost strangled her.

"I know how you feel, but this person has killed before, Mrs. Tuminello." Johnson said her next words carefully. "But until last night, his victims had all been men . . . homosexual men."

There was a sharp intake of breath and Mrs. Tuminello's eyes went wide, her face growing red as the implication about Father Kellog registered.

"Get out! Get out of my house."

"Mama, please." Connie Venza bent and placed her arms around her mother. "I told you I didn't want her upset." She looked over her shoulder at the two detectives. "Please wait in the hall."

In a few minutes Connie Venza appeared. Her face seemed older in the yellow light of the hallway. "A few days ago Mama gave me something. I didn't know what to do with it. Until now." She reached into a manila envelope. "Here, I want you to have this."

Rozelli and Johnson stared at the eight-by-ten black-and-white photograph.

"Mama took that picture from Father Graff's darkroom."

⁂

Outside the cutting room Sakura glanced at his watch. There were fifteen minutes before this afternoon's autopsies were scheduled to begin. Linsky always arrived on time and liked to get to work immediately. The bodies would be ready for him, transferred from the storage lockers by an attendant and whoever on the staff was assisting with the procedures. Sakura went in, pushing through black aproned doors.

The remains of Lucia Mancuso and Father Andrew Kellog occupied two tables in the center of the green-tiled space, the priest's ruined skull looking even more ghastly in the cold overhead light. Lucia's injuries were also more apparent, and except for the marked lividity in the lower limbs, and the indentations made by the monofilament, her wounds appeared identical to the first five victims. Sakura was as certain as Darius that a single mind had conceived these murders. But what kind of sick fantasy could include both homosexual men and an eight-year-old schoolgirl?

Rigor had long passed, and Lucia Mancuso, more than any of the dead he had seen, really did appear to be sleeping. She was a very pretty child, and unbidden came the image of her winged body hanging above the crèche. It had taken an enormous amount of planning and athleticism to suspend her from the support beam in that church. It seemed more certain now that the ritual element of these deaths was posing, a statement that the killer felt compelled to make for himself.

Was that what he was doing here? Making a statement as well? He felt shame at the death of this child. If there were any true victims in this world, then surely they were children.

Had he not once been vulnerable, his life and happiness at the mercy of what he believed his father's whims? Certainly, the upstate New York boarding school, with its lonely prospect, had seemed to be the nadir of his journey when he arrived. But he had done well there, arriving to a fall and winter as cold as the ones he had known in Hokkaido. He had made friends. Excelled academically. Gained a measure of control.

His visits home were few, thanks to the face-saving distance. His father called regularly. Elizabeth wrote. He learned to bear his Christmases in California and was rewarded with summer vacations in Japan, where for that short span of time he was once again Akira. Even without his grandmother, these summers were his touchstone, an assurance that in a successful adjustment to America he would not lose himself. He had become content, with only the cloud of his father's expectations of what course he should pursue in college. But that, too, resolved itself.

In his senior year a girl from the nearby town had been brutally murdered. Two students, fellow seniors, were accused and arrested. The boys were not his friends. In fact, he disliked them both, superficially socialized, corrupted by the money of their parents. He could easily imagine them guilty.

Like everyone else in the school, he'd been gripped by the sheer proximity to tragedy—an attraction like gravity, bending objects in space with the mere force of its mass. He was fascinated with the procedures of police work, with the detectives who came to interview them all. The Tao was a web as well as a road, and this death had placed him in the path of his fate. Circumstances made his involvement in the investigation inevitable. His role in the crime's solution set the course of his life. Despite his father's predictable disappointment, and Susan's obvious satisfaction with his choice of career, he had never considered after that time that he would become anything else but a detective with the police.

He stared at the girl on the table. Oblivious, Lucia Mancuso slept on, her lively hair and lashes dark against the marble of her cheeks. As he looked at her now, her father's face in all its pain came back to him, and he considered what the man had said today about his sister's husband, Tony Paladino, the man who had taken the Halloween photographs. He had real doubts that there would be anything more to Mr. Mancuso's suspicions than the bad blood that apparently existed between the two men. Still, they would have to take a look at him. And at someone else who interested him more.

An eight-year-old female victim had hit like an ace dealt from the bottom of the pack. But what if what the bartender at Marlowe's had told him was true, about the comic who'd gotten arrested for exposing himself in the park—the star who'd blown a series in which Geoffrey Westlake had had a featured part? As soon as the autopsies were finished, he'd head back to the office. A call to Hanae to explain why he'd not be home tonight, and then he'd put somebody on tracking down Byron Shelton—the one person who'd surfaced in the investigation with a link to at least one gay victim and a proven predilection for little girls.

CHAPTER

14

It was the meeting from hell, Sakura concluded, as he walked down the hall to the relative peace and security of his own office. Yet if he were Lincoln McCauley, he would have been spitting fire too. His own emotional state was marginal.

What the fuck's wrong with you, Sakura? McCauley had bellowed. *Your Japanese stoicism is wearing thin.*

He hadn't gotten even mildly angry at the racial slur but had focused instead on the chief's use of the word *stoicism*. McCauley's vocabulary was usually less expansive.

His self-control had to do with preempting McCauley's interference. At this juncture containing the chief of detectives meant keeping the three suspects, especially Thomas Graff, under wraps, until the investigation turned up something solid. On a deeper level his apparent passivity was an attempt at Zen posture—to live precisely in the moment. To block a thousand future moments from rushing backward into the present. *When you wash the dishes, think only of washing the dishes.*

The *Post* headline had intruded: NO ONE SAFE! GAYS TO LITTLE GIRLS! McCauley had thrown the newspaper at him, complete with lurid cover. *Find the fucking leak,* he'd shouted, his face ballooning above the starched collar of his shirt. *And haul this bitch's ass in for questioning. For all we know, she might be in contact with the killer. It wouldn't be the first goddamn time.*

The *bitch* was Zoe Kahn, the reporter whose byline hung with the *Post* exclusive, and a couple of other stories that suggested Ms. Kahn was on the receiving end of a very accurate pipeline. For an instant he entertained the thought that her source for this latest story might be Dominick Mancuso. He had shown the man a picture of his daughter, a photograph that closely matched the drawing on the cover of the newspaper. Had told him about the wings on the other bodies. Had Kahn gotten to Mancuso? He hoped not, but she was capable of anything.

Whoever had fed Kahn information had seen crime scene photos, or had been inside St. Sebastian Church that night. And this person knew about the wings. How else to connect Lucia to the other victims? He opened the door to his office, avoiding the light switch, walking over to the hot plate. He needed a cup of tea. Some downtime to think. He felt sure Mancuso wasn't Kahn's source. The leak was closer to home.

✻

Coming to attention, Detective Walter Talbot did everything but salute as Sakura, with a thin folder tucked under his arm, walked into the interrogation room, authoritative and neat in his dark suit and tie. As with most interrogations this one was pure theater, misdirection away from the fact that any suspect not actually under arrest could simply get up and walk.

This morning's improvisation had been hurriedly scripted. The relationship in the city between the Department and the Catholic Church had evolved from a time when the hierarchies of both had been packed with Irish. Although that had changed in the last few decades, the rituals of reciprocal back-scratching remained. This initial session, Sakura knew, might be their only chance to shake Father Thomas Graff before the higher-ups on both sides got involved.

He remained standing as Talbot closed the door. "Lieutenant Sakura"—he identified himself to the priest—"I'm in charge of this case. I'd like to go over a few things in your original statement."

Graff had been picked up very early this morning at the rectory, then made to wait in this room with a grim-faced Walter Talbot, who'd declined to explain why it was necessary to retape the formal statement that Graff had provided on the night of the murder. The priest was studying him carefully, apparently undecided whether complaint or cooperation was the quicker way to end this.

"Is there some problem, Lieutenant?" he asked finally.

Sakura smiled reassurance. His words left doubt. "I hope not."

The priest settled stiffly in the standard-issue chair. "What do you want to know?" he said.

"What made you go to the church Saturday night?"

It was old ground. Graff rolled his eyes to emphasize this. But he answered. "I noticed Father Kellog's door was open."

"Was that unusual?" Sakura asked.

"Yes. The rectory is a barn. Father always closed his door to keep the heat in."

Sakura nodded. "What happened exactly?"

"I was curious." The priest shrugged. "When I looked in, I realized that Father's bed was empty. That's when I saw through the window that a light was on in the church. I thought it was odd."

"So you went to check?" Sakura prodded.

"Not right away. But when I started to take my coat off, I realized how cold it was. Father Kellog would not have gone out unless it was an emergency."

It had certainly been cold that night. Sakura remembered the iciness of the air that had greeted his leaving his apartment after the call, remembered thinking that it would snow before Christmas. Graff was remembering too. His eyes beat rapidly beneath lowered lids, as if the progression of events in his mind had moved beyond simple recall. He opened his eyes as Sakura watched, cutting the process short.

"I understand you knew Lucia Mancuso?" Sakura said now.

"I know her family." Graff's face registered sorrow. "It was such a shock that night. I don't know what was worse, seeing her hanging up there, or Father—"

"What is the Church's position on homosexuality?" Sakura cut in, fast-forwarding the script.

There was a moment of confusion when Graff's face closed in. His lips twisted. "Holy Mother Church says it's okay to be born gay, as long as you don't do anything about it."

Sakura sat down on the edge of the table, inches from Graff's chair. "I would think it would be very difficult for a person to be denied the expression of his sexuality." He watched the wariness in the priest's eyes give way to calculation, a thousand sums and decisions on how, and how not, to react. In the end he said nothing.

The manila folder had remained beneath Sakura's arm. He set it down now on the table, opening it. In the room's dreariness, in the harsh light, the shiny black-and-white photograph seemed garish, the glistening male flesh doubly obscene.

Rage blanked out every other emotion on Graff's face. "Stop that thing." He glared toward the camera, at the technician.

Sakura ignored the demand. "We did not search your rooms." He cut off further objection. "You could say that this particular photograph fell into our hands. We only got a warrant this morning."

Graff swallowed visibly, holding the anger in. He spoke again, calmly, almost with contempt. "I want to make a call." An almost Buddhist imperturbability had taken over his face. What Sakura did not see was guilt.

⁂

Sakura did not watch much television, had never seen the man who was now sitting across from him in the interrogation room. But apparently there had been a time, before his fall from grace, when Byron Shelton's rubber face and trademark shock of red hair had been familiar to anyone who watched the late-night talk shows.

At the far end of the table sat Walter Talbot. Shelton, smoking, slouched in his metal chair. A fair interpretation of a man with nothing to hide.

"So you just look," Sakura responded to Shelton's last statement.

The comic-turned-actor gave him a slow smile, a performance that was at least in part for the camera he'd agreed could record the interview. "That's what I said . . . I just look."

"At prepubescent girls?"

"Yeah. My analyst says I'm attracted to their 'apparent sexual neutrality.' At least he used to say it when I was shelling out the hundred and fifty an hour." Shelton's laugh was unpleasant. "I just like the idea of invisible cunt. I don't touch them or anything."

"That's not what your girlfriend said at your hearing," Talbot spoke up.

"That bitch." Shelton cocked his head slightly in Talbot's direction, crushed out his cigarette viciously in the ashtray that was filling up. "Sheila was pissed because I dumped her. I never laid a hand on that brat of hers. Just once or twice I got her to undress for 'Uncle Byron.'"

"Ms. Davis insisted it was more than that," Sakura said.

"Ms. Davis is a liar." Shelton looked at him. "The charges she filed got dropped." He shrugged. "The network still canceled us."

"I thought the show was canceled because of your arrest on the park incident," Sakura said.

"The little girls? Oh, that all came later. I guess I went a little crazy." The smirk turned on itself.

"The television series"—Sakura went back to it—". . . Geoffrey Westlake was in it?"

Shelton's eyes lit up. "Westlake . . . that's what this is about? You think . . . Christ!" He was looking down now, shaking his head. He seemed genuinely amused. "I saw the papers this morning," he said, "before your guys hauled me in. That little girl . . ." He lifted his face to Sakura. "You're adding two and two and getting five."

"Geoffrey Westlake was in your series?" Sakura returned to his question.

Shelton sighed, shrugging again. "Lenny, the next-door neighbor," he said. "Kid was pretty good."

"You kept in touch with Mr. Westlake?"

"You kidding? I'm a pariah in this town. Nobody from the show would even talk to me."

"That make you mad?" The question from Talbot.

Shelton snorted. "What do you think? I'm wired a little weird, so I'm stupid?" He looked at Sakura. "What do you expect me to say, Lieutenant? My career's in the shit can, so I took out Westlake and a bunch of other queers, threw in a priest and the girl for good measure . . . fuck." He reached for his cigarettes.

Sakura's hand was quicker, covering the pack. "I expect you to tell us the truth."

Shelton drew back, flopped against the chair. "Nobody in this town gives a rat's ass about the truth." He spread his hands. "Look, Lieutenant"—the pale eyes oozed charm—"you know and I know that I don't have to answer your questions. And I'm thinking that I shouldn't till I have a chance to talk to my lawyer. Okay?"

Sakura nodded and stood. "Give Detective Talbot the name of your attorney. Have him call me first thing tomorrow." He handed Shelton his card.

"*He's* a she. Name's Linda Kessler." Shelton took the card and put it in the pocket of his jacket. Smiled and walked out.

Sakura left Talbot and the technician to deal with the recorder, joining Willie and Kelly in the observation room, where they'd been watching through the one-way window.

"What do you think?" Kelly asked him.

"I don't know, Pat. We don't have any real evidence that Shelton ever got physical with any of the little girls."

"No," Kelly said. "But it looks like he's capable of violence. Sheila Davis claims she's got the emergency-room records to show he liked to smack her around. And get this . . . it wasn't another woman he left her for."

"A man?" Willie asked.

"Yeah," Kelly said, "one of the sitcom's producers. Seems Shelton could swing either way if there was profit in it. Used to joke that the casting couch wasn't marked 'women only.'"

Sakura looked back through the glass to the interrogation room, where Shelton had sat coughing up smoke between answers. He thought of the grappling marks that had been found on the support beam of the church, and tried to imagine the comic swinging a metal hook thirty feet against gravity, then climbing the rope with the added drag of Lucia Mancuso's body.

"What do you think, Pat?" He turned the question on the veteran.

Kelly made a noise. "The commissioner's up McCauley's ass for any kind of arrest. I think that sleaze was smart to lawyer up."

🔱

"This is Lieutenant James Sakura, shield number sixty ninety-eight." Sakura looked directly into the eye of the video camera. "Also present are . . ."

"Detective Walter Talbot, shield number seventy thirty-two."

"Present is video technician Herb Dietz. Subject is Antonio Paladino." Sakura nodded for Talbot to begin.

"Mr. Paladino, we want you to understand that you are under no obligation to answer any question. You are not accused of any crime. We asked you to come today to determine if you have any information that could help us in our investigation of Lucia Mancuso's death."

"I understand."

"Did you come here of your own free will?"

"Yes." He coughed, clearing his throat. For a handsome guy, Paladino looked terrible.

"Where are you presently employed?"

"Odyssey Lincoln Mercury. I'm a salesman. . . . I also do a little photography on the side. Mostly weddings."

Talbot made a notation in his file folder. "Mr. Paladino, what was your relationship to Lucia Mancuso?"

"She is . . . *was* my niece." He stared into the camera as if it weren't there.

"How was she your niece?"

"I'm married to Barbara"—he looked back at Talbot—"Dominick's sister."

"Dominick Mancuso, Lucia's father?"

"Yeah."

"Do you have children?"

"Two. A boy and a girl."

"Would you say you were a close family?"

Paladino shrugged. "We got our troubles, like anyone else."

"What kind of troubles, Mr. Paladino?"

"I like to work out. I come home from the gym and the wife thinks I been out with some chick."

"Have you?"

"That's none of your fucking business."

"You're right, Mr. Paladino, it isn't." Talbot made another note. "Any other problems . . . between you and your wife?"

"What does any of this have to do with Lucia?"

Sakura stood. "Mr. Mancuso spoke of some trouble between you and his sister over a neighbor's child."

"Dominick is an asshole."

Sakura moved in closer. "Mr. Paladino, I know this is difficult, and I remind you that you do not have to answer any of our questions. But I have to believe you want to help us find Lucia's killer."

"Yes . . ." He struggled with the word.

"Will you tell me about the neighbor's little girl?"

He ran one of his hands over his eyes, a gesture that seemed to say he was willing to make a fresh start. "It was nothing. I never touched that kid. Her and her mother were crazy."

"Why do you think Mrs. Griffin lied about what happened?"

He squirmed in his seat, a man who had something bad to say, but didn't know how. "I slept with the broad. One time, that's all. She was all over me after that. I told her I loved Barbara."

"So you believe she made up the story to get back at you?"

"Yeah."

"Does your wife know that you slept with Mrs. Griffin?"

Paladino shook his head.

Sakura moved away from the table, faced the one-way window. "Mr. Paladino, where were you Saturday afternoon?"

"At work."

"What time did you arrive?"

Paladino hesitated, as if sensing some trap. "I was pretty late, if that's what you're asking?"

"Why was that?"

"I had a flat."

Sakura had turned back, watching Paladino's reactions. "And it took you almost two hours to fix it?"

"It was raining." The man's eyes shifted farther away.

"And Saturday night? Where were you then?"

"At a bar. Nick's. Having a few beers—" He stopped. "Wait a minute . . . all these damn questions. You think I had something to do with Lucia's death? You think I killed her? Because of what that bitch said?"

"Mr. Paladino," said Talbot, "we have to ask the question."

"Well, I didn't kill Lucia. I loved Lucia. Like my own. I . . . I wished it would have been me instead of her." He dropped his head into his hands, his thick fingers spread over his face like a mask, trying to muffle his sobs.

———✦———

Sakura watched Willie chew on her pencil as she checked the scrawl of notes on her legal pad.

She looked up. "Don't give me that damn inscrutable stare, Sakura."

"Was I?"

She laughed, standing now, walking toward the one-way window through which she'd witnessed the interrogations. She ran her fingers on the ledge, examining the fine layer of dust she'd picked up. She turned. "Okay, let's take them one by one."

"Graff first," he said.

"Looks real good on paper. Fits the profile. A priest. That certainly jibes with the religious elements. And the last two murders take place in his own backyard."

"I hear a *but.*"

"These pictures . . ." She looked down at the spread of Graff's photographs that had just come in under warrant. "I don't think that the man who took these photos is the same one who posed those murder victims in their beds."

Sakura raised his brows. "Why?"

She shrugged. "These photographs are so depersonalized. There are no head shots. Just body parts. And the genitals, they're exploited in Graff's photographs. At the crime scenes the killer hides the sex of the victims."

"I'm listening."

"There's an incompleteness in the photos. An unfinished aspect." She picked up one of the shots. "They're fragmented as though he's not done. But in the crime scenes there's a kind of wholeness. As if the killer had finally achieved resolution."

He removed his jacket, placed it over the back of a chair. "Maybe the photographs are the first stage in the evolution of Graff's fantasy."

"Okay . . ." She waited.

"Graff starts small, takes photographs, pornographic fodder for his fantasy. Then he graduates to the stage where he's actually killing," he said.

"But there's a problem." She was chewing on the pencil again. "The dates on these photographs. There are too many pictures taken after the Carrera murder. I can't see a serial going back."

"Unless we can match any of these body parts to a victim, the best we can do with these pictures is circumstantial evidence against Graff."

"You witnessed the autopsies, Jimmy. Any one of the victims have six toes?" She dropped the photograph she'd been holding. The blond pubic hair was startling against the dusky flesh of phallus and testicles. "Every one of the subjects in these shots has some kind of deformity. None of the victims had any kind of anomaly. Not even a noticeable birthmark among them."

"Milne had arthritis."

She shook her head. "That's different. That happened after years of living. These subjects came into the world . . . *Damaged* is what I think Graff thinks they are."

"And our killer . . . ?"

"*Resurrected* . . . his victims are resurrected. To a higher plane. Perfected. That's why we get angel wings."

"Wings of *fallen* angels."

"Shit, do we have to keep coming back to that." She bit into the pencil. "Forget that for a moment. If it is Graff, and he is so hell-bent on photographing everything, where are the pictures of winged bodies on beds? Serials like trophies."

"I suppose Graff could have hidden them. We're still searching his rooms, and we'll extend the warrant to the whole rectory if necessary," he said. "I wish we could find a grappling hook and some LSD. Or work boots to match those prints Michael found in the warehouse."

"How about some child pornography?"

"That would be nice."

"Because the eight-year-old girl is where we lose Graff," she said, "and pick up Shelton and Paladino."

"Shelton gets high marks, except he's out of shape."

"A bisexual pedophile," she said. "That certainly covers all the bases."

"But . . . ?"

"I don't see Shelton placing wings on bodies," she said. "It's too metaphorical. His mind isn't that elegant."

"We could disqualify Paladino on the same grounds," he said.

"Maybe. But he did take those wonderful Halloween photographs of Lucia. I think there's more to Tony Paladino than meets the eye."

"Both men have a similar scenario with a woman," he said.

"In Shelton's case I think Sheila Davis is telling the truth about her daughter. In Paladino's case I'm not so sure."

"I keep remembering that Lucia was sedated," he said. "Linsky said she'd be conscious but compliant. Was she treated differently from the other victims because she was a child? Or because of a more personal relationship with the killer. . . . But what were you saying about there being more to Paladino?"

She pulled back her wavy hair, fastened it with a band. "I think Tony Paladino is searching for the Holy Grail. The perfect woman. Hence, the screwing around. But he always falls short. Even his wife, whom I believe he loves, doesn't measure up. But Lucia did. I think he was able to project his ideal onto Lucia."

"Lucia was eight years old."

"I know. But Lucia was less than real to him, more a symbol of what could be. In the meantime he played the doting uncle. I don't think he ever touched her. That would have ruined it for him. His sexualization of Lucia was unconscious and specific to her. Besides, I think even if we could convince ourselves that he could have killed Lucia, there's no way he murdered the men."

He stared at her, nodding, wishing more of the puzzle pieces fit.

⁂

For a reporter who'd just scored big time, Zoe Kahn was not in a very good mood. Ordinarily, she would have killed to get inside Sakura's office, but her mind kept wandering to the possibility of running into Johnny—the anticipated confrontation vying with her memories of the crime scene in the church, impressions much more indelible than the never developed film.

And hadn't that been a piece of monumental stupidity, or something much worse? She hadn't guessed she had such impulses in her. And that was scary, not knowing herself half as well as she'd believed. Thankfully, Garvey had taken it in stride, a minor fuckup compared to the overall jazz of an exclusive. NO ONE SAFE! The page-wide banner screaming from the front page. GAYS TO LITTLE GIRLS! Complete with tableau of the winged child suspended over the crèche.

Garvey had called in the artist, who'd mocked-up the whole scene from her description. And that had been good. Talking about it in precise and objective detail had actually helped a little.

But where the hell was Sakura? Was this some cop trick to make her nervous? Well, he could forget it. One thing she knew, she wasn't scared of cops. She was here because she wanted to be, not because the great Sakura had summoned her. She was here because she hoped to get something out of him, especially with rumblings in the pipeline that they'd finally come up with some suspects.

"Good afternoon, Ms. Kahn." He appeared at the door and walked to his seat behind the desk. "Thank you for coming."

He looked awful. Worse than she felt. She nodded, letting him go on.

"I assume you know why I asked you here."

"My story?"

"Yes. And though I understand the argument against a reporter revealing her source, there is one thing I have to know."

"And that is?"

"Are you in any contact with the killer?"

She controlled her expression. It was not the question she'd expected him to ask. Shit, she could only wish the killer would get in touch, like Berkowitz writing to Breslin.

"No, Lieutenant," she said finally.

"I see."

There was a wealth of information in those two words. He knew the leak was close. The question about the killer had been his last hope against part of what was eating him from inside.

"Your source . . . ," he began.

"Don't go there." A command that had sounded like a plea. She said nothing else, and waited.

He waited too.

"Why the little girl, Lieutenant?"

He seemed to sense that this was her question, not the *Post*'s. "I don't know, Ms. Kahn. I don't know why he killed any of them." He used the words against himself, like a knife.

⚓

Sakura stood inside the *genkan,* reaching out to trace the pattern of gold thread slipping through the heavy white silk of Hanae's wedding kimono. It had been a joint decision that it was to be this garment that would hold the honored place in the small entrance hall. The kimono defined what was most essential in life—their bond to each other.

"Jimmy?" Hanae's voice from the living room.

"I am here, Hanae."

She had drawn up the *sudare* and stood in profile against the naked window, one of her hands resting on the ledge, the other near her throat. The floral-patterned kimono she wore looked bright against the canvas of black sky.

"You must be very tired," she said quietly when he'd kissed her.

"Yes."

"Then I shall be the good wife and give you a bath."

He undressed while Hanae made her preparations. He was spoiled by *hinoki* tubs. Cold porcelain was a poor substitute for the fragrant cypress, but Hanae at least had the soap he favored. In Japan he would have soaped and rinsed before soaking.

"Not too hot," he said, walking into the bathroom through gathering clouds of steam.

"Stop telling me how to draw a bath."

He stepped into the tub and sank into the water. Releasing a long breath, he closed his eyes, letting Hanae knead the muscles of his neck.

She lifted her hands. "You wish to be alone?"

He reached for her. "No, stay with me."

She rose from her knees and felt for the small stool behind her.

"She was only eight years old," he said after a moment, glancing over at her. Her eyes closed as he spoke, and he knew she had begun focusing inward, creating from his words her own images. "With the white wings," he continued, "she did look like an angel. Except she was dead."

"What does this mean, Jimmy?" she asked, opening her eyes. "Before he was not taking the lives of children. What is there that is the same between a small girl and the men who died?"

"You have asked the right question."

"And do you know the answer?"

"No, Hanae, I do not."

✦

In the living room Hanae waited for her husband, standing again before the exposed pane of glass. The birds slept inside their covered cages. Taiko curled at her feet. She waited for her husband, attempting to empty her mind. For her, there was no day and no night. She lived according to her own cycles of time. It was night because Jimmy was home.

A headache had caused her to miss sculpting class this afternoon, something she did not like to do. But there was no help for it. She placed her fingers to her temples, still troubled by a remnant of pain pressing against her forehead. If she massaged and breathed in the correct rhythms, she could perhaps ease the tension. This unaccustomed discomfort, she hoped, had no real physical origin but resulted from the anxiety about keeping her pregnancy so long a secret from Jimmy.

She reached for the pins that held her chignon and shook her hair loose. Against her will the unformed image of the murdered child hanging in the church forced its way behind her eyes. She thought of her cousin's dream, the sound of her voice from the tape. Was the form, if not the substance, of Nori's nightmare a mirror of this death— a prophetic screen upon which the murder of this little girl was to be projected?

She heard the muffled clopping of Jimmy's geta against the tatami as he approached her. The scent of his soap settled in her throat as he moved her hair and pressed his lips against her neck. She could feel her pulse against his mouth. He turned her in his arms. Her fingers found his still damp hair as she pulled his face to hers. She had learned long ago that she could not remove her husband's pain. But tonight she would offer him whatever comfort she could.

Michael's apartment building was not what Willie had expected. She had known it was old, the top floor occupied by some member of the Llewellyn family since Michael's great-grandfather had had the building put up nearly a century ago, according to what Hanae had told her. What she had expected was a renovation. This lobby with its dead fireplaces looked as though it hadn't been touched by a designer's hand in at least the last six decades. It wasn't dilapidated or dirty. Its oddity was that it looked well kept and deserted in equal proportions. An abandoned movie set that might, at any moment, be put into operation.

She'd been waiting for over an hour when he came into the lobby. She had never seen him dressed as he was, in tight faded jeans, with a denim jacket lined in shearling, half opened over a flannel work shirt. Thrown over his shoulder was a kind of duffel bag she imagined held his carpenter's tools. In the mellow lighting he seemed to move toward her in a kind of halftime rhythm. As he came closer, she saw he needed a shave.

She stood up as he approached. "I thought you might want to take a look at these." She held out the three VCR cassettes.

"Come up," he said. He hadn't asked her what the tapes were or taken them from her hand.

"I'm exhausted." She shook her head.

Michael ignored her excuse, guiding her with a proprietary touch to the small of her back toward a narrow marble hallway. He worked the keypad of a private elevator. Then his hand found her waist again, directing her inside.

The elevator went straight to the top, opening onto a small foyerlike hallway with a single impressive door. Michael reached above the frame for a key. He unlocked the apartment, switching on a light just inside.

"Make yourself comfortable." He followed her in. "I need to grab a shower." He walked past her with the duffel, disappearing through a doorway.

She stood for a moment, looking around the huge living room. The space was architecturally beautiful with alcoves and elaborate molding. The few furnishings were quality. An Oriental carpet formed an island, where a glass slab of coffee table fronted a long sectional sofa and love seat. Audio and video equipment sat in a recessed wall, along with an impressive collection of CDs. And near the windows, a gym occupied the place where a dining-room set should have been.

She walked to the coffee table, where a book lay open. She picked it up and sat down on the sofa.

"I never took the bar." Michael stood backlit in the doorway, in jeans again, working a towel through his still damp hair. He moved into the room, took the law book out of her hand. She noticed he'd cut himself shaving.

"Would you like some wine?"

"Sounds good."

He took out a bottle and some glasses, then pushed the button on the CD player. Something bluesy came out, the wail of an alto sax. She was acutely aware of him, of the pressure of his body, as he slumped into the sofa.

"Why?" she asked.

"Why what?" He poured out a glass of wine and handed it to her.

"Why didn't you take the bar?"

"I decided being a cop was closer to the action." His face had become fixed, and it was quiet again, except for the music.

"Well, here's the action." She pointed to the cassettes she'd set on the table.

His eyes avoided them.

"We've had some developments," she pressed on. "The tapes are interviews with three men we're calling potential witnesses."

"Suspects," he said. His tone feigned disinterest.

She put down her glass. She hadn't been lying about being exhausted and was suddenly too tired to keep up her end of this.

He took a sip of his wine. "Who are these . . . potential witnesses?" He finally looked down at the tapes.

Now that it seemed her little mission might be successful, she felt strangely deflated, seized with a lethargy that had nothing to do with fatigue. Michael was waiting, the vacuum between them building again, along with her need to fill it.

"Are you cold?" He'd seen her shiver.

"No, I'm fine. But it is cold . . . outside, I mean."

It was a stupid thing to have said. She had the sudden giddy thought that walls were falling. She felt him move, sensed him edging toward her around the raw curve of glass. She turned her face willingly enough to his, but there was still the thrill of fear when he kissed her.

⁂

He had surprised her by coming so late. But Zoe had known he would come . . . eventually. She was in the shower when she heard the banging at the door. She scrambled for her terry cloth robe and looked through the peephole.

He was standing there, his collar open, his tie loosened. He held his coat flung over his shoulder. It seemed he hadn't slept in a week and needed a shave. For an instant she considered not answering the door. Then she flipped the dead bolt.

At first it appeared he was only interested in the drops of water sliding from her hair, down her neck into the gap of her robe. "Sorry about the dead bolt," she said finally, determined to play it as nice as she could for as long as she could.

Johnny held out his hand. The key to her apartment was in it. She met his eyes, then reached out and took it.

"You're a selfish cunt. You know that."

She nodded. "But you knew that from the beginning."

He looked like he wanted to hit her, but he wouldn't.

"Are you going to stand out there to finish this?" She moved away from the door, leaving him in the hallway. She pulled up on the thick collar of her robe, patting water from her hair. She heard the door close.

"Want a drink?" She turned, feeling her robe slip off her shoulder. She didn't bother to fix it.

"This isn't a social call." He threw his jacket across a chair.

"None of our meetings were social, Johnny. It was always business." The words oozed out. *Nice* was just not in the program.

His eyes darkened. She could count his pulse in the flesh at his neck. Then he smiled. "Except the whore got overpaid. The info was better than the pussy."

She laughed. "May I quote you?"

"Why not? You've quoted me on everything else."

"Come on, Rozelli, you gave me piss. I had to go after the shit that really counted."

He moved closer. She could smell his day-old cologne. "Now let me see," he said. "How did you manage to do that?" His hands were waist level. "I figure after I get the phone call about what's gone down at St. Sebastian, you get your tight little ass dressed and follow me." His fingers made contact with the knot on her robe's belt. "How am I doing so far?"

Her eyes tightened at the edges.

"Then you manage to sneak into the church, where you have a front-row seat. You keep your eyes and ears open. Hear about the wings. Make the connection between the kid and the fags. All the time watching us dumb fucks play detective. How's that?"

"Right on the button." She felt his hand yank the belt. The white robe hung open.

"You think this is just about getting a story, don't you?" His fingers were at one of her nipples. "Well, you're wrong, Zoe. This is about somebody's eight-year-old not breathing anymore." He twisted.

She grimaced.

"I admit I probably fed you. Enough for a couple of good bylines. Harmless enough. But you got way too hungry, baby, way too hungry."

<hr />

What am I going to see? he had asked her.

The television screen was now the solid blue of blank tape. But for hours Michael Darius had watched the interviews with Jimmy's three suspects to no discernible result. A bottle of scotch on the coffee table in front of him was empty. The ashtray was full.

I don't want to prejudice your judgment. Willie had denied him an answer. *And I've really got to go and get some sleep.*

She had looked tired when she'd left, with violet shadows haunting her eyes. But there was more than a lack of sleep, he suspected, behind her obvious need to escape. She'd been uncomfortable with that kiss, with what now seemed inevitable between them.

He had not spoken to Jimmy since the murder scene in the church, but the image of the winged child above the crèche had never left his mind and had now materialized on the cover of the *Post*, which Willie had left for him.

He rubbed his eyes and tapped a cigarette from the pack. He had not slept much since Saturday.

Despite all his objections, it seemed he could not escape this case. But if he had once had some special talent for investigation, he did not know how it worked. The process was a mystery that did, or didn't, occur. He could not turn it on like a faucet. A million years ago he had enjoyed that indefinableness. Now since Hudson, he felt naked and out of control, with instinct alone, a wild animal's instinct.

This was the real reason he'd left the force. The reason he'd tried to beg out of even an informal involvement in these murders. He felt suffocated by this case, unable to get a perspective. Although he knew he was less shocked than the others by the fact of Lucia's death. He had never been convinced that the homosexuality of the victims was the defining quality that marked them.

He had no idea what did.

CHAPTER

15

Did my invitation get lost in the mail?"

"You're up early, Counselor." Sakura secretly congratulated himself on his prediction. He figured Faith would corner him before he'd had time to brew his first cup of tea. "Tea?" he asked as he stood.

"Why wasn't I called in for those interviews?"

He smiled. "They're not suspects."

"Don't get technical with me, Sakura. The Mancuso girl was murdered in the priest's church. Paladino was her favorite uncle, and Shelton is a probable pedophile."

"And what about their connection to the other victims?" he asked.

"Lucia Mancuso is a good enough starting point for me."

"We're checking alibis."

This time Faith smiled, something cold and unfriendly. "Good." She extended her arm. "I want the tapes."

He looked down at her open palm. "I was planning to send them over this morning."

"I just bet you were."

He turned to his desk, reaching in a drawer for a copy of the videotaped interviews. He placed the cassette in her hand, closing her fingers around it.

"Thank you, Detective Sakura. The D.A.'s office always appreciates the NYPD's cooperation."

⚞

Rozelli's badge glinted in the fluorescent lighting falling on Sakura's desk. "It's yours. Take it," he said. Then he unholstered his weapon, laying the .45 next to the shield. "This too."

Sakura looked up.

"I'm your leak, Lieutenant."

Sakura shifted in his seat, leaning forward so that the lower half of his face was cast in a cold blue glare, his dark eyes in shadow. He touched the badge, then stood, walking to the single window in his office. The morning had risen in a thick milky-white haze, the air pregnant with the promise of snow. He turned. "Ms. Kahn?"

Rozelli's laugh was humorless. "Yeah."

Sakura moved back to his desk and sat. "Sit down, Detective Rozelli."

The detective took one of the chairs in front of the desk. "My dick got in the way," he said flatly.

Sakura reached out and picked up the jade piece. "It seems your penis has compromised this investigation."

Rozelli looked down at his feet. "For what it's worth, it wasn't intentional."

"How was it, then, Detective Rozelli?"

"Just small talk between the sheets. Nothing significant."

He kept silent, the jade moving smoothly between his fingers.

"I have no excuses. I knew what Zoe was."

"You underestimated Ms. Kahn."

"I'm sorry, Lieutenant," he said quietly. "There's nothing else I can say."

"St. Sebastian?"

Rozelli ran a hand through his hair. "She was at my place when the call came in. She followed me. Got in the church somehow. . . . I swear, Lieutenant, I didn't know."

He nodded, letting the jade slip from his hand.

"I expect IA will have to know," Rozelli said.

"Do you think anything productive can be accomplished by informing Internal Affairs?"

"Sir?"

"Keep your mouth shut, Detective Rozelli."

Rozelli stared. "Yes, sir."

"And, Detective, your weapon needs cleaning."

🙢

Snow hung, blue-gray, high in the sky, a mountain yet to fall—a frightening imminence that was also exhilarating. Hanae was glad to be in the park today, the redness of her wool coat vibrating in the white air, like an extra layer of warmth. It felt good to be outdoors and moving. The headache that had plagued her seemed at last to be in retreat.

"This has been fun," she said to Adrian. "I am glad you called and got me out."

"I was worried when you and Taiko missed class yesterday. I thought you might have caught a cold last week."

She shook her head. "I am used to cold weather. I grew up with it."

The wind, which had been silent, began to stir. Leaves skittered like bones on the pathway.

"I saw your husband's name in the paper again," he said.

"Oh . . . yes." She frowned. "Jimmy was unhappy the press revealed so much about his case. And, of course, it is so terrible about the little girl."

"I suppose they can't call him the gay serial murderer anymore."

"No," she agreed. "It is very puzzling."

"What does your husband say?"

"Jimmy does not talk very much about the case. But I know they are trying to understand how the killer chooses his victims."

A couple passed them on the path, young voices laughing.

"I really miss my wife this time of year," Adrian said. "She has her faults, but she really loves Christmas."

"Perhaps you will get back together."

"I know that's what Christopher wants, but it's never going to happen."

A complex of feelings colored his words. Longing, certainly . . . and bitterness.

"I'm sorry," he said.

She felt suddenly trapped, her headache again threatening. He had sensed his emotion embarrassed her. He reached out and briefly

touched her shoulder. Taikoi's harness jingled as he lifted and shook his head.

What happened next was unexpected, and yet forever a part of what the two of them had begun. Adrian reached out again and held her arm, stopping her on the walkway. His face bent over hers, the warmth of him beating at her skin as he moved to kiss her. Not a chaste kiss. Not a friend's kiss. But a lover's.

Without comment or apology, he was gone. She stood, trying out excuses, while she listened for his retreat along the path. But there was nothing. And no stirring in the leaves on winter grass.

⁂

Sakura watched Willie walk out of his office, working on her third cup of coffee this afternoon. Caffeine was high on the list of his former professor's dietary vices. He leaned forward over his desk and refocused. He could feel tension building in fine layers along his shoulders, but he wasn't ready to pull himself away from his notes on the three interrogations.

"Lieutenant Sakura?"

He glanced up.

"May I come in?" The face looked fortyish, except for the eyes, which could have been a thousand years old.

"Yes." He rose from his desk.

"Thank you." The man reached behind and shut the door. "I'm Edward Walsh," he announced. "Father Thomas Graff's attorney." He extended his hand.

Sakura reached out and shook hands, offering a chair.

"Thanks." Walsh began to remove a topcoat and a woolen scarf, which circled around his neck. If his visitor was going for effect, he couldn't have succeeded better. The stiff white Roman collar against the black clerical suit was a stark reminder of the immense power of Holy Mother Church.

Walsh caught his stare. "Not many of us wear clericals. I find they serve a purpose."

Sakura nodded.

"I presume you already know the question I'm going to ask." His smile appeared like one he'd practiced.

"I've had my share of visits from defense attorneys."

A laugh, only slightly more genuine than the smile. "So why is my client being considered a material witness in the serial-murder investigation?"

Sakura enjoyed how Walsh had correctly avoided the more incriminating term *suspect.* "His obvious connection to St. Sebastian"—he began the litany—"his relationship to Kellog, his friendship with the Mancuso family, Lucia specifically."

"I hope there's more for your sake." Walsh kept his tone congenial.

Sakura knew the rules. Knew he didn't have to say anything to this man. But there was no reason to make an enemy of Walsh. "As you know, we executed a search warrant for Graff's rooms at the rectory."

Walsh waited for him to go on.

"We discovered material that could be incriminating."

"Care to be more specific?" Walsh knew exactly what was in that secret room of Thomas Graff's, but he was yielding no ground.

"Photographs."

Walsh reared his eyebrows, waiting.

"Of nude men," he said. Then, because it wouldn't make any difference one way or another, "Our killer may be a latent homosexual."

"And when do I get copies of those photographs?"

"Give me a day."

"Thank you, Lieutenant Sakura." Walsh was standing now, beginning to put the scarf back in place, shrouding once more the stiff Roman collar.

"A question for you, Father Walsh."

"Yes?" He turned, an arm sliding into one of the sleeves of his coat.

"What's the Church's position on angels?"

"Angels?" Walsh was only momentarily puzzled. Then, "The wings . . ."

"Serial killers have fantasies. This one has angels in his."

Walsh nodded. "The Church on angels? I guess Catholics are supposed to believe in them."

"What about fallen angels?"

"Those too."

"And you, Father Walsh, what do you believe?"

This time the priest smiled for real.

"Angels . . . fallen and otherwise. A metaphor for good and evil?" He seemed to be testing the theory. "I recall reading somewhere that there is a great secret about angels. That the real action is not going on among us puny humans but between the good and bad angels. The real war, it seems, is theirs."

⚊

Hanae sat in bed, massaging the base of her neck where the pain now seemed to have settled. Her fingers moved across her face, measuring her features against her fixed internal image. Her hands, as always, were her mirror. The tips of her fingers moved to the hollows of her eyes. Around the lids there was a subtle tautness that rose to her brows, giving her, she imagined, a slightly startled appearance.

She allowed her hands to fall to her lap. Her face bore the effect of the war she'd been waging. Her happiness over her pregnancy fought with a sense of foreboding. The inner illumination had altered. The headaches intensifying from dull to stabbing. What was most frightening was that she had become a woman of secrets.

And now Adrian's kiss today embroidered upon the growing layers of her deceit.

The kiss? What did it mean? She was lost in this fresh betrayal of her flesh. There was no understanding beyond the deep pressure of his lips. Beyond his taste inside her mouth. Beyond the horror that she half enjoyed it.

Her anxiety over the baby seemed less important now measured against that kiss. Especially since Dr. Blanchard had been so reassuring. Told her she was in excellent health. She would deliver a healthy baby. A baby who could see.

For most of her life, she had accepted her blindness. Color and texture, shape and dimension, became her own particular inventions. The vision behind her lids constituted a universe that was both wholly real and intensely satisfying. That she had missed something, that she had been cheated, she had never accepted. She found no tragedy in her sightless eyes.

She reached down to the side of her bed where Taiko rested. "Tonight," she said, rubbing his muzzle. "Tonight I will tell Jimmy about the baby."

✣

Father Edward Walsh hailed from a large Catholic family with a tradition of giving sons to the Church. And though it had been fast
becoming unfashionable at the time, he had entered the seminary with
few misgivings. He was heart and soul an organization man, and no
earthly institution seemed to him more consequential, or deserving of
his commitment, then the Holy Roman Church. Educated to the law
at Harvard and Rome, he was a willing instrument in the hand of that
power, and as comfortable as it was possible to be as a human inside
his skin.

He sat for a moment behind the wheel of his car in the long, cir-
cular driveway of the Brooklyn retreat house, a three-story residence
of Georgian brick, solid and serene on its wooded acres. The air
tonight was windless, yet with a piercing chill. He took a last breath
in the warmth of the car and opening the door, dragged his coat from
the passenger seat as he stepped onto the sidewalk. He shot his
arm through a sleeve as he walked, swinging into the coat's protectiveness.

He had called ahead and was let in by the custodian with a mini-
mum of conversation, then directed down the hushed hallways to the
door of the room where he was expected. He did not bother to knock.
The door swung inward as he turned the knob and pushed. The man
sitting on the bed turned toward the motion. His expression, complex
and unreadable, passed in an instant to studied nonchalance.

"Want a drink?" Graff's greeting.

"Yes." Walsh took off his coat and sat down in the room's one chair
while the priest poured them each a scotch. It seemed typical of the man
that even under these circumstances, he was still breaking the rules,
the prohibition against liquor in this place. He accepted the glass as
Graff settled with his own drink on the bed.

"I met with Lieutenant Sakura today."

"And . . . ?"

"He didn't tell me anything. But I was mainly there to size him up.
Our contacts in the Department feed me all the information that we
need. The police don't have anything but those pictures."

"Dear Mrs. Tuminello"—Graff was smiling now—"the faithful housekeeper. Couldn't wait to rat me out. I'm sure she told anyone who would listen about my less than cordial relations with Father Kellog."

"Not important." Walsh shrugged. "The police knew the girl was the primary victim. Kellog just turned up in the wrong place."

"That's what's funny," Graff said. "I was probably in my room sleeping while most of those gay men were murdered, but my alibi is among the dead."

Walsh was silent, searching Graff's face. The studied self-assurance made it hard to tell when the man wasn't telling the truth. He imagined that he was as hard to read, hoped that he was, since he was so often lying. Like just now when he'd equivocated about the relevance of the enmity between Graff and his pastor. Certainly, the police must wonder if Graff had killed Kellog because of something the old man had suspected or learned about the first five murders. Such a scenario was not impossible, although it did not seem likely, since it still left the riddle of the girl. Why would Graff ever choose the Mancuso child as a decoy?

But that was a problem for others, as was the question of Graff's guilt. His job was to protect the client. And his client was the Church.

"Have you thought anymore about who could have killed them?" he asked. "Father Kellog and the girl?" He took a sip of the scotch.

"No," Graff said immediately. "I haven't the slightest idea who murdered them." He shot down the remainder of his own drink, got up to fix another. "So what happens next?" he asked.

"Nothing," Walsh said. "I don't see that the police have anything on which to order a warrant for your arrest."

"So, I can get out of here."

"No. It's His Eminence's wish that you stay put for a while."

"How long?"

"That's yet to be determined. The police need a scapegoat, Thomas. You've read the papers. It's getting ugly out there. We can protect you better in here."

Graff said nothing, but the expression on his face became intolerable, a contempt that went beyond mere cynicism. It called for a response. A little dose of reality.

"You could not expect that His Eminence would be pleased with the danger posed by those photographs," he said. "You threaten scandal to the Church."

Graff looked straight into his eyes. Amusement on the face now, an undertow of fear. "Do you care at all that I'm innocent?"

"Why did you become a priest, Thomas?"

The smile deepened but went out in Graff's eyes. "To save my immortal soul."

For most of the evening, Hanae had occupied herself making ornaments for the small tabletop tree, which Mr. Romero had helped her purchase. Her mind on nothing, her hands had seemed to move of their own accord, working in the long-memorized patterns. It had surprised her when the phone rang that her fingers had been folding swans.

"Hanae." Jimmy's voice had spoken to her from the receiver.

"You are not coming home." She had guessed. She had heard his breath. Hard wind through grass.

"Not until late. I can catch some dinner at my desk."

"I know you will not eat properly," she said. "I will have something prepared."

"Okay. But don't wait up. I can warm it myself. . . . *Aishiteru yo.*" He had said the words *I love you*.

"*Watashi mo,*" she'd answered softly, today's betrayal fresh within her heart.

She had not been sleeping when, at last, he had come home. The meal she had prepared for him had passed mostly in silence. She'd sipped at her tea, listening to the sound of his chopsticks. Now, while he prepared the bed, she stood inhaling the balsam scent of the small fir. She loved the smell, the sharp tiny prick of needles as the ornaments were hung. Christmas trees in Japan were largely artificial, public decorations placed in offices and department stores. The holiday itself was artificial in Japan, a grafted-on celebration, purely commercial, with gifts for children only. She loved Christmases in New York, had come to understand the spirit that lived inside the tradition. And yet the season remained a time best shared with children. Despite the distractions of his work, she must keep her resolve to tell him about the baby tonight. What better gift could she give her husband for Christmas?

She went to join him in the bed for what little remained of the night, kneeling beside him, her hands moving along the pathways of his back. Never had she felt the flow of *ki* within him more unbalanced.

"What is wrong?" she asked him.

His breath was a laugh that came in the form of a sigh. "I am tired," he said.

"It is more than that." She sank back upon her feet, her hands for the moment idle. "Is it the newspapers?"

He made a sound, a hard laugh now, but no immediate comment. Then, "We have three suspects."

"Is that not good?"

"I don't know. Two of them don't seem likely for the murders."

"And the third . . . ?"

"Is a Catholic priest."

She knew but little of the religion, but the power of the institution was clear. "Do you believe this priest committed the murders?"

"In some ways he fits Willie's profile."

"What does Chief McCauley say?"

Again that laugh. The harshness of it cut her.

"McCauley wants the commissioner off his back. The commissioner wants the mayor off his back."

Her fingers still rested along his spine. Something . . . involuntary, a phantom of apprehension, moved on the level of nerve and muscle.

"You are afraid," she said, "that you will be forced to arrest the wrong man."

He did not answer but rolled over beneath her hands. She felt his gaze, a tender pressure upon the curve of her face. It was now she must tell him.

"Jimmy," she began, "I have been thinking again about a baby." It was not the way to begin . . . with equivocation. A coward's mistake. She felt him stiffen.

"Please, Hanae, not tonight." His voice so infinitely weary. And had there not been, underneath, at least some edge of anger?

CHAPTER

16

The attorney and the comic were a mismatched pair as they filed into the interrogation room. Linda Kessler with her briefcase, severely chic. Shelton, loose and ostentatious. They sat across from Sakura and Johnson at the table.

Linda Kessler began with a rehash of the ground rules, which had already been settled on the phone. Her body language was hostile, and Sakura wondered why she had agreed to this second interview with her client. Neither the Church, in the case of Father Graff, nor Tony Paladino were being so cooperative.

"Thank you for agreeing to this interview, Mr. Shelton." Sakura turned to him as the lawyer concluded with a reminder that recording devices of any type were not allowed.

"I thought it might be entertaining," Shelton said. He half slouched in the uncomfortable chair, favoring Sakura with his persistent grin, pointedly ignoring Adelia.

"I understand," Sakura said, "that you're still working as a comic."

"I'm not headlining in Vegas. But if you don't mind the travel, there are plenty of small clubs." The mouth quirked cynically. "You'd be surprised how much money there can be in notoriety."

"I also understand you're being sued by the parents of the girls you exposed yourself to in the park."

"My client cannot comment on a pending case." Kessler made the objection.

"I am being sued." Shelton spoke as if he hadn't heard her. His voice started tight, but he smiled broadly and launched into what was clearly shtick. "It was the nanny who freaked out," he said. "The two little bitches actually laughed. I should be suing them for psychological damage."

Sakura knew he was intended to smile. "You have an apartment in Chelsea?" he asked instead.

"Yes, I bought it a while back. Paid cash."

"Own a car?"

"A Buick. My sweet old daddy would haunt me if I got a foreign job."

"Color?"

"The car? Red . . . like the hair."

"Do you do drugs, Mr. Shelton?"

"Don't answer that," Kessler said. She sounded like she meant it.

"Can it, Linda," Shelton said genially enough. "The lieutenant's not looking to bust me." The eyebrows bowed upward, making it a question.

"No, he's not," Kessler answered again, "but he is attempting to compare you to his profile of the killer. Which is why I've advised you against this."

Shelton's eyes during this exchange had remained on him. "Is that what you're doing, Lieutenant Sakura?"

"Yes." He smiled now.

"Does your killer use drugs?" the comic asked.

"You may infer what you wish from my questions, Mr. Shelton."

Shelton laughed, and for a moment the emotion seemed genuine. "I have in the past experimented in the usual controlled substances" was how he answered the question.

"Usual?"

He shrugged. "Pot. Designer shit . . . ecstasy."

"Cocaine?"

"Didn't like the stuff."

"LSD?"

He made a face. "A few times. But I gave it up."

"Why?"

"Bad trip . . . saw snakes everywhere. What do you think that means?"

He stared at the man. "I think, Mr. Shelton, that it means you're bullshitting me. Why are you doing this interview?"

The comic turned to Kessler. "Give them to him." His tone had turned bored.

The attorney opened her briefcase and took out several documents, which she passed across the desk. Now Sakura understood that Kessler's sour attitude was in part disgust with her client. She was a small-to-medium cog in a very large law firm.

"Those are affidavits," Kessler spoke, "from club owners in Dallas and Phoenix. They verify that Mr. Shelton was in their establishments performing when two of the murders took place."

"Thank you," he said to the lawyer.

"What I'm still unclear about"—he had turned back to Shelton—"is the progression in your activities. First, with the Davis girl, you look. Then in the park, you expose yourself. It's been some time since you were arrested for that. What's been happening since, Mr. Shelton? You *say* you never touch . . . ?"

It was purely a parting shot, but for the first time the comic's mobile features closed down, the spattering of freckles frozen in the Silly Putty face. For what seemed like a long time, he stared at him, apparently weighing the cost of what he wanted to say, the satisfaction relative to the risk.

"These clubs I work," Shelton said finally, the grin turned nasty, "a lot of them are on the Coast. Mexico is just a few hours away. There they don't care if you handle the merchandise. And whatever you want, whoever you want, you can buy."

✦

"What are these?" Willie glanced up from the papers Sakura had placed on her desk.

"Shelton's alibi," he said, pulling over a chair. "According to these, he was out of town when Carrera and Westlake were killed. If these are genuine—and Ms. Kessler's law firm has a reputation to protect—then that leaves Shelton out."

"The man is a total waste of human protoplasm," she said. "I wish it *was* him."

"It's not Paladino either," he said. "He did have a flat in the rain. But part of the reason he was so late getting to the dealership was that he had a passenger in the car at the time. He had to run her home first before he went to work."

"And this lady was . . . ?"

"His sales manager's wife. But we're keeping that confidential."

"My God, the man does seem to get around."

Sakura nodded. "His story about the neighborhood bar is also solid. He was there for the critical hours."

"What about Graff?" she asked him.

"Still holed up with his lawyer. They've sent over a list of parishioners that Graff visited on a couple of the dates in question, but the murders happened late. He'd have had plenty of time."

"And Saturday?"

"Claims he was in his darkroom when Lucia would have been abducted. But he has no witnesses. Nor for later that night when he claims he went for a jog and took in a movie."

"Mrs. Tuminello . . . ?"

"Can't confirm whether Father Graff was in the rectory while she was there. She claims she never saw him before she left that afternoon."

"So the bottom line is," she said, "that Graff has no viable alibis."

"Right."

"Have we gotten any explanation for those photographs?"

"No. The lawyer won't comment on that."

"Can we get Graff in for further questioning?"

He shrugged. "The Church isn't refusing outright, but they're saying that Walsh needs more time with him."

"Stalling," she said. Then, "What's McCauley think of all this?"

"Glad to have a suspect. Unhappy with the politics."

"And it's all bound to leak."

His face hardened. "We've been lucky so far with Shelton," he said, "but somebody's probably picked up on his being questioned today. Now at least we can have a prepared statement that he's been excluded as a suspect. It won't be so simple if the net gets tighter around Graff."

She nodded.

Since the discovery of the bodies in St. Sebastian, the story had gone national, with coverage on all the cable news channels. He'd seen the

Kahn woman on a FOX News show last night, and he could only imagine the impact when they finally had to confirm that the prime suspect was a priest.

"What's your feeling about Graff now?" he asked.

"I still have doubts about those photographs," she began, "and Lucia makes his guilt even more problematic. If Graff needed to elimi- nate Kellog because the pastor knew something damaging, then why select a little girl as the supposed victim? Why not another gay man? It doesn't make sense, Jimmy, because you know, as well as I do, that serials don't behave like that. Oh, they might change something in their MO to throw us off the track, but never something vital to the fantasy."

"The homosexuality of the victims seems critical," he said.

"I certainly thought it was. I don't know what to think now. Lucia had to be the primary victim that night. I mean, look at the trouble he went to, hanging her up there. That whole angel tableau, that's his fantasy coming out. I just can't imagine how Lucia could fit with the first five victims."

He'd picked up on her equivocation. "All right," he said, "if we can't say *why* Graff might have killed Lucia, maybe we better stick to some- thing more practical."

"Like *where* he killed her?"

He nodded. "Dr. Linsky says she was dead before the killer strung her up, and St. Sebastian was open for most of Saturday. So did he keep her in the rectory? Kill her there? It's a huge old building, and outside of the church itself, we haven't searched much more than his rooms."

"So the next step . . . ?"

"Take apart that rectory, top to bottom."

"Can you get a judge to extend the warrant on what you have now?" she asked him.

For the first time he smiled. "Let's find out."

⚶

Between the peak hours of breakfast and lunchtime, traffic in the café slowed. Detective Walter Talbot was one of less than a half-dozen customers. The waitress who brought his order had a name tag above the pocket of her uniform. It said TIFFANY in thin white letters on plastic sky blue. A tall, pretty blonde, who looked like she could stand to eat more of whatever the place offered. She smiled as she set the cup and the little pot of cream on the table. The gesture was midwestern expansive, uncorrupted as yet by a city that seemed to compact everything down.

"Thanks," he said, smiling up at her. "Could we talk?"

Her expression turned wary, appraising him, wondering no doubt if this was going to be a come-on. And whether or not she should mind.

"Talk about what?" she asked him.

"I was wondering how long you've been working here."

"Six months"—she shrugged to indicate it was approximate—"since I got to New York. . . . I'm trying to break into modeling." She'd tacked on the last, watching for his reaction. He imagined she told this to everyone.

"A man was murdered there." He nodded toward Westlake's building.

She stared past him through the window. "He used to come in here sometimes," she said. "Geoffrey. He was a model too. A really nice guy."

"So you knew him?"

"Not exactly," she answered slowly, embarrassed to have been called on it. "I waited on him a few times."

"Were you here the day they found him?"

"I saw them bring him out in the body bag," she said, still staring through the glass. "It was just like on TV. And then people started coming in and saying it was Geoffrey. I couldn't believe it."

"What people?"

"What?" She had turned back to look at him.

"You said some people came in . . . ?"

She studied him critically. "You a cop?"

"Yes." He turned up the wattage on his smile. "We're doing a little recanvassing."

"I was gone by the time the police came round that day to question everybody," she said. "God, I felt bad, like somebody should've been hauling *me* out on a stretcher." She flashed another look at him, wondering if she'd been too irreverent. "I was out for days with the flu."

"These people," he reminded her, "the ones who were talking about Geoffrey . . . ?"

"Regulars," she answered, "people from the neighborhood." She glanced back at the building. "Some of them live there."

"I'm looking for a tall, thin man . . . wears a baseball cap and some kind of big outdoor parka," he said. "You ever see anyone like that with Geoffrey?"

"No." She shook her head, but her attention seemed to sharpen. ". . . Not *with* Geoffrey."

"But you've seen him?"

"I've waited on him," she said. Then, ". . . He killed Geoffrey?" She had figured where all this was going.

He didn't answer.

"He was in here that morning," she said as if to prompt him, "that day they found the body."

"You know his name?"

"No . . . sorry." She looked truly pained. "He never talked much. Just drank a lot of coffee."

"Can you describe him?"

"His hair was blond . . . I think." She scrunched up her face, considering. "He always had on that cap. But yeah, I'd say blond."

"Eyes?"

She shook her head. "He wore sunglasses . . . always."

The detail of the glasses was significant, tallying as it did with the bartender's composite. And the blond hair. Thomas Graff had blond hair. "Age?" he asked her.

She frowned. "That's hard these days."

"Guess."

"Thirty-five, maybe older. But good-looking, what you could see of his face. And built too, but not in an obvious way. He didn't always wear the parka."

He smiled again, encouraging her.

"That's all," she said. "I guess I can't really tell you much."

"You did great, Tiffany. Have you seen him lately?"

"No. But you can ask the other girls. They might remember him."

"I'll talk to them," he said, "but first I'd like to know if you'd be willing to come in for a lineup."

"Like on the cop shows? One-way window and all?"

"That's right," he said. "You can see them. They can't see you."

"Sure," she said, sounding pleased with the drama of the prospect. "I want to help if I can."

✳

Zoe watched as Connie Venza backed out of the carport onto the street and drove away. She checked her rearview mirror, examining her hair, smoothing an unruly wisp into the tight French twist at the back of her head. Then she clipped on the small button earrings that matched the single strand of pearls circling her neck above the thin gold chain bearing a small crucifix. She fished out a pot of clear gloss and coated her lips. Her white silk blouse and navy wool suit were matron-simple. Along with the sensible leather pumps.

She had just returned from shopping for the suit, when she got the call about Byron Shelton being questioned in connection with the serial murders. In fact, this was a second go-round for the comic. She could really be pissed about missing out on this one, but her sources had it that Shelton would walk. His alibis were iron clad. The smart money was on a priest, but with the clout of the Church in this town, that was sure to twist the Department in knots. It was good enough to give her an orgasm—CATHOLIC PRIEST MOONLIGHTS AS SERIAL KILLER. Smoke that, Rozelli!

She stepped out of the rental car and walked across the street to Agnes Tuminello's house. A bleak one-story covered in faded yellow siding that made the exterior look dirty rather than cheery. Barred windows added to the overall effect of a life led in quiet desperation. A sad-looking Christmas wreath did nothing to dispel the general gloom. She reached into her handbag for the final touch. A pair of horn-rimmed glasses.

She opened the weather door and knocked. After a moment she heard the soft click of heels; then the door cracked open a fraction, restrained by a heavy safety chain.

"Yes." Agnes Tuminello sounded like someone used to turning people away.

"Mrs. Tuminello? I'm sorry to bother you, but I'm from *The Catholic Answer.* We're just a small Catholic newspaper. . . ."

A pause. The chain unhitched. The door opened wide.

"I'm Mary Katherine O'Malley." Zoe reached down and took Mrs. Tuminello's hand. She watched as the woman's eyes moved up from her sensible shoes to the gold cross nestled beneath the pearls.

"I was wondering if we might talk."

Even the crucifix wasn't enough to stanch the housekeeper's wary expression. "About what?" she asked.

"The awful tragedy at St. Sebastian." She looked full into the woman's careful eyes, compassion brimming in her own. "*The Catholic Answer* just wants the truth . . . and to help find the person who did this terrible thing." Her voice faltering on the last of her words.

Mrs. Tuminello nodded and held back the weather door. She led Zoe down a short hall and into a living room overcrowded with furniture. The heat was up too high.

"Please sit," the woman said, walking over and turning off the television. She pointed to a sofa. "You said you're with a Catholic paper?" she asked, settling herself in a chair.

"Yes, and we are deeply concerned about the violence that happened to Father Kellog and that poor little girl. Murder in the house of God." She sighed, shaking her head.

"That is because we nurtured a viper in our bosom." The words as righteously delivered as any Sermon on the Mount.

"A viper?"

"Thomas Graff."

"The priest who found the bodies?"

The woman nodded solemnly. "An evil man. I tried to warn Father, but he wouldn't listen."

"Such a misfortune. . . . What exactly did you try to warn Father about?"

Mrs. Tuminello's eyes closed as she rested her head against the chair's cushioned back. Her hand patted one of the overstuffed arms like the head of a faithful old mutt. "He had some of the ladies in the parish fooled, but not me," she said proudly. "I saw into his black heart." Her head lifted. "I knew what he was. An abomination." The hand quit its soft tattoo.

"What do you mean, Mrs. Tuminello?"

"He likes men. Takes pictures of them. Naked." She crossed herself. "He never wanted me to clean that room. Had a new lock put on the door. Kept the only key."

"What room?"

"In the same house with Father Kellog. Desecrating the rectory."

"What room, Mrs. Tuminello?"

"A darkroom. He developed his nasty photographs in Father Kellog's house. In that secret room of his."

Zoe had been leaning forward as Mrs. Tuminello told her tale. Now she sat back, took in a breath of overheated air. This was better than she'd hoped.

"They know about Graff," Mrs. Tuminello said quietly, "because I took one of his pictures. And my Connie gave it to them. They know."

"Who knows, Mrs. Tuminello?"

This time when she lifted her head, the housekeeper was smiling. A self-satisfied smile that said if she couldn't be rewarded in this life, she would surely be in the next. "The police. The police have all the pictures now."

"All the pictures?"

"Of Father Graff's naked boys."

⚜

Despite the overstuffed furniture, the living room of Vernon Norman's tiny brownstone had the feeling of a cloister. The air trapped inside didn't move. Overheated, thicker than normal, it blurred any color existing in the room and gathered in a graying mass like cobwebs near the ceiling. The walls were a yellowed white and bare, except for a large print hanging above a table of votives. Jesus stared out of the frame with an expression of painful bliss, one hand lifted to his breast, where a fleshy heart, circled in flame, hovered miraculously, pierced by a stout ray of light.

Sitting with Rozelli on Norman's sofa, Walt Talbot found that his eyes kept straying to the picture of the Sacred Heart. A psychology major, the detective had no problem identifying the underlying symbolism in the image. He doubted Vernon Norman was aware of it. At least on a conscious level.

"It's terrible that we have to keep the churches locked these days," Norman was saying. A small tight man in his seventies, he appeared lost in one of the worn brocade chairs that formed a group with the sofa. His faded brown sweater seemed meant for a larger man, or perhaps he'd been the one to shrink.

"We've been told you have a key to the church." Rozelli was smiling at the man, working him back to the subject.

"I do have a key." Norman smiled back. "I'm president of the Society for Devotion to the Divine Love," he explained. "We hold special services every week, and it's part of my duties to see that the Host is taken from the tabernacle and placed in view on the altar."

Rozelli nodded.

"I'm a deacon," Norman said to them both. "I took Orders after my wife died."

"Does anyone else in your group have a key?" Talbot asked him.

"Mrs. Delorio uses mine sometimes," Norman answered him. "She's our society's secretary."

"We're looking for a tall, thin man who wears a cap and a big outdoor jacket. Does that sound like anyone you know?"

"Father Graff dresses like that." Norman's eyes searched Rozelli's face. "I've heard the rumors," he said. "Do the police really believe that Father Graff might have committed these murders?"

"We have to consider everything." Talbot was the one to answer. "You said that Mrs. Delorio uses your key to the church, Mr. Norman. Is there no one else besides the priests who has keys?"

Norman's sad gaze shifted back to him. "Agnes Tuminello has keys," he said. Then, "A church has to be reconsecrated when a murder takes place inside. Did you know that?" He didn't wait for an answer. "We live in terrible times."

Talbot stood. "Thank you, Mr. Norman," he said. "It was kind of you to talk to us."

"Yes, thanks." Rozelli stood too.

Norman nodded. Pulling himself out of the chair by inches, he went over and picked up two little booklets from a stack next to the votives. The cover was a duplicate of the picture that hung on the wall. NOVENA TO THE DIVINE LOVE was printed in red at the bottom. "Our devotional services." He handed one to each of them as he walked them out.

Norman locked his door and went into his kitchen. The clock in the stove showed fifteen minutes past the usual time for starting his dinner. Since his wife had died, he had found that it helped to keep to a regular schedule. A schedule kept him busy. And idle minds, like idle hands, were the devil's workshop.

Still, variety was nice, and the policemen's visit had been interesting. He'd wanted to mention to them that he'd taught math for thirty years before he'd retired. Instead, he'd made a point of being a deacon in the Church. So what? He was not ashamed of his beliefs. They gave him his only comfort.

He stopped, leaving the food he'd taken out of the refrigerator on the counter, and went back to the living room. He sat on the sofa and pulled out the photo album from the dusty bottom shelf of the coffee table. There was a photo near the back that he suddenly wanted to see, a picture from about this same time a couple years ago when Ida Mae had still been alive.

The picture had been taken in the church hall, at the Christmas party that the ladies put together every year. He was there, posing for the group shot, looking uncomfortable, as he always did in photographs. But Ida Mae was smiling, still plump and pretty, showing no sign of the cancer that would kill her in less than six months.

He looked at the picture, at the predominance of old faces. Most of them would be dead soon, himself included. He looked at the youngest member of their group, come back for the party long after she'd moved out of the parish. Hadn't she once had a key to the church? The thought struck him for a moment but faded to unimportance. What could it matter? Marian, poor child, was already dead and gone, and for nearly as long as his Ida Mae.

⚊

The night was overcast and the street dark, as if the close humid cold had absorbed the glow from the streetlamps. Sakura, puffing clouds, left the rental garage and walked toward his building. He wanted more than anything to be home and at rest, but he feared it might be necessary to offer amends tonight. Hanae had still been sleeping, or pretending to sleep, this morning when he'd left, and he'd talked to her only briefly during the day, calling to tell her he would

once again be late and not to expect him for supper. He knew he had
hurt her with his abruptness last night. The case was taking its toll.

He thought of Faith. There had been no commitment between the
two of them. No love. But with Faith he'd never had to explain himself. In terms of their work, they had been completely in sync, compet-
itive and ambitious, but supportive in their separate spheres.

He had been reminded of that today when he'd called to bring her
up to speed on tomorrow's planned search of the rectory and the
lineup that was set for the next day. Faith had been approving, cutting
through the bullshit to his own bottom line. A witness ID on Graff
would go a long way toward covering his back. Proof his investigation
was making progress.

Of course, there was more than the politics. He hadn't forgotten his
conversation with Willie this morning. He trusted her instincts and
his own, and he shared her misgivings concerning Graff's guilt. But
instinct could be moot if tomorrow's search of the church grounds
were successful. If they found some piece of evidence that tied Lucia
to Graff.

He was getting ahead of himself. A bad sign, his needing a break this
much. It was unlikely they would find anything at all. If Graff was the
killer, he had left no physical evidence at any of the other crime
scenes. Still, Lucia Mancuso's murder had been an undeniable departure, and a change in MO increased the risk that the killer would make
a mistake. There was no penalty for hope. He stopped at the downstairs entrance and used his key. Walked up the stairs to the apartment. He entered the *genkan* quietly to the familiar greeting of the
marriage kimono. And a not so familiar voice. Coming to him clearly
from the living room. Speaking to Hanae. In perfect Japanese. A language he had not heard from those lips since the day of his grandfather's funeral.

He removed his coat. His shoes.

Isao Sakura rose from the sofa as he came into the living room. The
man looked as tired as he felt.

"Hello, Jimmy."

"Father."

Hanae stood, seeming to flutter in the silence.

"Your father would not let me call you," she spoke. "He did not wish to disturb your work." Her blind eyes were fixed on something behind his face. "May I get you something, Jimmy?"

On the coffee table were plates with the remnants of food.

"Nothing," he said. "I ate earlier. . . . Perhaps tea."

"I will make some fresh." Her eyes unfixed themselves. She bent to pick up the tray. He marveled as always at her grace, watching as she walked toward the kitchen. He felt his father watching him.

He turned back. "What are you doing in New York?"

The response was a smile at the brusqueness of his question. His father sat down on the sofa, waited for him to settle in his chair. "I'm in town for . . . a conference," he answered. "And also to deliver this." He brought out from the side of the sofa a package that was long and narrow.

He reached without thinking, accepting the gift, shocked by his certain knowledge of what the package contained.

His father was watching his hands.

He, too, watched as his fingers of their own volition worked the knotted cord and unrolled the heavy paper. It fell away, leaving the sword in his lap. He did not look up but stared at the embellished hilt and scabbard while memories rose like smoke. An image of Grandfather Nakamura nodding gravely, bringing out the sword from the chest where it was stored in its fine silk wrapping. Explaining to him once more the history and meaning of the family treasure, passed down from the time when a samurai wore this weapon as a birthright and called the *katana* his soul. Passed down to Isao as firstborn after Grandfather's death.

"Why?" He looked up at his father.

"I thought you should have it."

He was silent, forcing his father to say more.

"Your brother has no real interest. . . ." He'd been obliged to spoil it. "You are firstborn," he amended.

"Why now?"

Isao smiled, but there was nothing of humor or pleasure in the expression. His eyes were as Hanae's, fixed on his face, dark and searching. His father's lips moved in some mute gesture of communication, dismissing the smile with the barest sign of denial. A minute shaking of his head.

No translation for this silent script. He thanked his father for the generous gift of the sword.

Hanae returned with tea and fresh cups. She sat between them and poured, her butterfly questions filling space with replies from his father.

Susan and the children were fine. Paul had made a fine gastroenterologist and was an asset to the practice. Elizabeth had been happier since her divorce, and she was gaining quite a national reputation with her watercolors and *sumi-e*. It was possible she might have a showing in New York.

He half listened, giving answers when required to. He despised his reactions, the childishness of the feelings he still harbored. He did not know how to change them.

His father had something to tell him. That much he understood, but he was too exhausted tonight to try to clear some ground on which they might meet. He was infinitely glad when Isao rose, suggesting they see each other tomorrow before his plane left for the Coast.

Tomorrow was an eternity. He agreed.

CHAPTER

17

Coldness had plastered itself against the nearby window, an emanation of outdoors that came through in lieu of light. The finches, disturbed today for no discernible reason, chirped and fluttered behind their metal bars, while Taiko dozed fitfully at her feet. Hanae sat forward at her worktable, her fingers struggling with the clay. She had hoped that the bust of Jimmy might be finished before Christmas, but despite her efforts, she was making no progress. And the gift of his portrait seemed more than ever urgent.

She knew her husband. She clung to that. But more than her secrets, there were questions unspoken between them, which she had lately begun to acknowledge. Why had Jimmy chosen her? *Hanae. Damaged blossom.* Was it not in part that she might make the perfect wife for an American policeman? Japanese women expected to be neglected by their husbands. A blind Japanese woman was the child of isolation. She believed that Jimmy had married her for love. But was there not the assumption that she, of all women, might be satisfied with what he had to give? Had that, too, not been part of it?

His father's visit last night had further stirred these feelings. She had learned of Jimmy's childhood over the years, gently wheedling out the story. She understood something of his hurt. It was easy to believe that he had been attracted to her because she symbolized in many ways the path not taken, the life in Japan he'd been forced to abandon.

Little wrong in that. Men and women were attracted to each other for many reasons. Love had to begin somewhere.

The acknowledgment of her feelings was freeing. She took a centering breath, let her hands have their way with the clay. Their marriage
had been a bargain, as all marriages were. Was it not now unfair of her
to change the unwritten rules?

Unfair . . . yes. To Jimmy, whose love had so graciously opened a
world she had never thought to experience. And this new land where
uniqueness could be prized, her blindness a mere inconvenience. A
universe where all things were possible. Did she not owe everything to
him? And owing all, could she not justly be faulted for wanting more
than was truly offered? For wanting it all. A normal life—a family.

Jimmy's reaction when she'd brought up the idea of a baby had stung.
A wound she could only now bear to examine. Was it simply the pressures of this present case that had made him so unreceptive to even the
thought of a child? Was it his own unhappy childhood? Was her place
in his life to be nothing more than a companion for his loneliness, his
vision for the two of them so circumscribed that it could not bear a
third?

Perhaps it would help her own confusion if she could confide in
Willie. But Willie was Jimmy's friend too. Confiding in her would
seem like another betrayal. Like her friendship with Adrian . . . that
kiss. She could hardly believe it had happened. The memory of it still
pierced her with shame.

Jimmy loves me. The thought was a prayer, unfolding in her mind
the countless times her husband's gentleness and encouragement had
warmed her. His kindnesses beyond words. She felt heartened in these
memories, her doubts and fears half foolish.

I love him. The other half-equation.

She closed her eyes, fighting the headache that threatened, reaching
for that illumination that was her inner vision. It would be difficult to
express to Jimmy these things that troubled her. But she must have the
courage, a belief in the strength of their marriage. The baby she carried
was a fact.

She sat for long moments, willing a silence into her mind, a resting
place for heart and will to gather. She was surprised when she came to
herself to find that her fingers had continued their work. But it was
not her husband's face that had formed beneath her hands.

Pat Kelly could hear members of the task force and Crime Scene people upstairs. The ceiling overhead creaked and moaned with this surprise assault of moving bodies and equipment. An old soldier giving up the ghost. They were taking the St. Sebastian rectory a floor at a time. An army of officers attacking the enemy. Attic. Third. Second. First. Next was the basement in which Adelia Johnson and he now stood as the advance guard. The outbuildings would be last. The search warrant included everything, extended to the grounds. Precinct uniforms had been stationed outside to keep the neighborhood and press at bay.

"Cold as a witch's tit down here, Sergeant." Johnson's words came out in big puffs of frosted air. She rubbed her arms to get the circulation going.

"Yeah." If the attic had been secular, the basement was sacred. He looked around at the inventory of St. Sebastian's past, discarded into heaps and piles, remnants of a time when saints were in and the Mass was said in Latin.

"We'll need some light," said Johnson.

His eyes moved up to the row of stained-glass panes at ground level. With sunlight filtering through, he could imagine the blue-and-red diamond patterns erasing some of the gloom. Today the bleak December weather leached all color from the room.

"This place gives me the creeps." Johnson was examining a life-size plaster statue. A thin fracture ran down the forehead across the cheek to the jaw, splitting the face into uneven halves. She turned. "You Catholic, Kelly?"

"Not anymore." He watched dust motes spiral in a shaft of weak light, thinking of the last time he'd been to Mass. Somebody's funeral. He'd left before Communion and gotten drunk on his own wine.

"I'm Baptist and I sure as hell don't understand this stuff." She nodded toward the statue. "Who's this woman?"

He moved to where his partner stood. His latexed hand wiping away a tangle of cobweb that attached itself to the neck and shoulder. "I think that's St. Lucy." Once, he'd known all the saints. In his altar boy days.

"Why is she holding eyes?"

"They're her eyes."

"She was born with two pairs of eyes? No wonder she was a saint."

Kelly laughed. "The statue is St. Lucy once she got to Heaven. The eyes in the plate are the ones she had on Earth."

"Why is she holding eyes, Kelly?"

"Shit, Delia, I ain't the pope. I think it had to do with her not wanting to give it up, and the jerk took out her eyes. That happened a lot."

"What? Catholic ladies not wanting to give it up?"

"Yeah, the Church is full of virgins."

"Well, Sergeant, that was then and this is now."

"What you saying, woman? That there ain't no more Catholic virgins?"

Delia's whole body shook as she laughed. She patted St. Lucy's rear end. "You go, girl."

"We're ready to come down, Sergeant."

"Okay, Miles. You gonna need extra lights."

For over an hour CSU techs and task force officers took apart the basement. Everything was moved by section, according to a grid, carefully examined and cataloged. Hymnals, altar cloths, collection plates, glass votives, brass candelabra. The bowl of a marble baptismal font photographed and scraped for a questionable stain. A sample of holy water taken, a cake of Benediction incense bagged. The Infant Jesus of Prague and St. Jude, Patron of Impossible Cases, dusted for fingerprints. Nothing was spared.

"Hey, Sarge, you better get over here. I think we got something."

Kelly turned, saw Miles and another tech standing in a corner; a pile of blankets, like a mountain of old wool, was gathered near their feet.

"What you got?" he said, walking over, his focus directed toward Miles Turner's pointing finger. He looked down. Against the faded deep blue of the blanket, something gold winked like a tiny star in the arc lights.

⁂

Dominick Mancuso peered out the window of the brownstone, where his wife and children had lived quietly for the last twelve years, his father and mother for thirty-odd years before that. No one lived here quietly anymore.

The street for now was silent, though, the press people having given up for a while. The phone was silent too. The ringer turned off until the number could be changed to something unlisted. The message light blinked steadily, demanding that he wade through the voice mail for the legitimate calls from family and friends. Though they could be worse than the press, trading on their closeness for the secret thrill, as if, as the father of the murdered child, he had an insider's knowledge. As if the police told him much of anything.

Today was Thursday, less than a week since . . . He had no words for the black void that had swallowed up his life. Monday, he would return to his job as a foreman. He looked forward to what could be salvaged in routine, to an escape from this house. But he dreaded work too, for the awkwardness of every fresh encounter with his men. How long before anyone could feel free to laugh in his presence? How long before his own laughter might not be harshly judged? By himself, if not by others?

Truth was, he could not imagine a time when he would feel anything at all through the sucking blackness. He knew he could not feel love. Not for his wife, who lay upstairs in a haze of sedatives and grief. Not for Celia, packing in her room for the few days' escape to his brother's house in Queens. He could act on the strength of the love he remembered. He could show concern, a rough compassion that meant getting what was left of his family through the day. He could *feel* nothing. Perhaps if he could *want* to love, but that desire was gone too, ripped out by the monster who had killed his child, by a God who would allow it.

He walked to the table where he'd earlier thrown the newspaper. What was the point of anything, when the priest who heard your confession might be the killer who murdered your baby and hung her as a decoration in his church? He had thought there could be no more surprises, but the cover story in this morning's *Post,* naming Father Thomas Graff as the prime suspect in the murders, had still shaken him, despite the rumors he had already heard that the assistant pastor was under suspicion by the police. Shocking too that Agnes Tuminello, of all people, would give such an interview.

At least his brother-in-law had been cleared. He might hate the man's guts, might still want to smash his face, but there had been enough tragedy in the family without his sister's husband being named the killer. Barbara for some reason loved the man, so perhaps it was also true that Tony had never touched the neighbor's child. He hoped that was the case for Barbara's sake.

But what about Graff? Sophia had been crazy about the priest and had asked him here for dinner more than once. Could the man really be what Agnes Tuminello had said in the paper? An abomination? A viper they had nurtured? Had he invited into his own home the killer of his daughter? If he could still pray, he'd pray it wasn't so.

He tore up the front page, wadding it for the trash. He wanted no chance that Celia or Sophia would see it. Not that it was likely. Celia stayed in her room. And his wife had not watched TV or read any of the papers. Sophia expressed as little interest in the police investigation as she did in anything else. He doubted she'd remember tomorrow's funeral. Her condition was one of the reasons he'd agreed to let Celia stay with her cousins through the weekend. His remaining daughter needed the company of other people, a house that was normal. Monday, he would send her back to school.

The doorbell rang and he stiffened. Another reporter? Or perhaps it was only his brother coming to pick up Celia. But when he looked through the glass, a young man and a black woman stood on his porch, the woman holding up a badge.

"This is Detective Talbot," she said as he opened the door, "and I'm Adelia Johnson. We're sorry to have to bother you, Mr. Mancuso."

"No. Come in, please." He stepped back to let them pass. "You have some news?"

"We may have found something," the black woman said. She had put the badge away and now held out a small plastic bag. Inside was a necklace. Gold with a pendant heart. The implication was clear, they believed the thing was Lucia's.

"Where did you find that?" he asked.

"I'd rather not say just now." The black woman smiled. "Can you tell me if you've seen it before?"

"I'm not sure," he answered honestly.

"Perhaps your wife?" the male officer suggested.

He shook his head. Celia with her packed knapsack had come into the room. "Come here, CeCe," he said to her. Better than waking Sophia.

His daughter moved slowly, her eyes huge in her face. Celia looked scared, which had never been her reaction to the police.

"What's wrong?" he asked her.

"Nothing, Papa." Her voice was nearly inaudible, her gaze locked on the plastic bag in the officer's outstretched hand.

"Do you recognize this?" The policewoman pressed it forward.

The seconds went by. Celia didn't answer.

"CeCe," he prompted her, "is that your sister's necklace?"

The policewoman's eyes flashed a warning, but he didn't care. He wanted this over.

"Would you like to look at the locket more closely?" She reached for Celia's hand, placed the bag into her palm.

He watched as his daughter swallowed visibly, her fingers curling, pressing against the plastic to the tiny heart, where he now saw the letter M was engraved.

"Is it Lucia's?" He heard his voice harsh, his grief lashing out in impatience.

The policewoman sighed. There was another long moment when nothing happened. Then Celia's head began to nod, a marionette motion of short, sharp jerks.

"Yes, Papa"—her lips trembled over the words—"that's Lucia's locket."

"Is Crime Scene still at St. Sebastian's?" Michael Darius stood at the window of his apartment, looking out at the hard gray evening.

"I wouldn't be surprised," Willie answered from the sofa. "The techs are going over that corner quadrant where they found the necklace inch by inch, looking for hair, fiber, DNA evidence. Anything they can find."

"I guess the locket has kicked things up a notch." Darius turned to her.

"More than a notch." She sipped on the wine he had poured.

"It sounds like a witch-hunt to me." Darius had moved away from the window.

"That's not fair, Michael," she snapped. "You saw the Graff video."

He shrugged. "Not much moved me."

"Shit, Michael, this isn't voodoo." She set her glass down.

"And profiling's a science, Dr. French?"

She looked at him and laughed. "Touché. But you'll have to admit that finding Lucia's locket does make things look worse for the priest."

Darius slumped next to her on the sofa.

"It would have been easy for Graff to lure her into the rectory," she said. "Lucia passed the place going to and from the drugstore. She knew the priest. He'd had dinner with her family. She'd feel comfortable with him."

He shrugged, reaching for his wine.

"Graff could hardly murder her in her own bed," she went on, "or in his rooms. The rectory basement provided the privacy he needed—a place to hold her until he could take her into the church. The basement helps to explain *how* and *why* things happened the way they did. Transporting Lucia any great distance would have been awkward at best."

"Now it's convenient." He almost laughed.

"Think," she said, refusing to be intimidated. "If you're a priest making angels, which setup would more likely fulfill your fantasy—a bedroom or a church? If we accept that serials work up to speed, accept that they embroider on their fantasies, then suspending a body in a church would have to be more gratifying. This may be where Graff was heading all along. Working his way up to the church."

"But why a little girl?" Darius asked her now. "Why not another homosexual?"

She looked at him, remembering how it had felt when he'd kissed her the other night. How being with him was not like anything she'd ever experienced. Something incredible and frightening at the same time. He caught her staring. She looked away.

"I have another theory." She hated the way that sounded.

"I'm listening."

"Perhaps it's not the sexual orientation of his victims that interests the killer," she said, "but their appearance. None of the male victims were decidedly masculine. A change of clothing and hair—"

"Lucia was a very pretty eight-year-old girl," he interrupted.

"So were Carrera and Westlake—*pretty*," she said. "And Jude Pinot. Kerry and Milne less so. But all of them had appearances that could be sexually ambiguous." She paused. Then, "Lucia hadn't reached puberty. She was undeveloped. No breasts. Thin. Angular. Short hair. Lucia Mancuso could easily be mistaken in the right circumstances for a very attractive young boy."

"Is that what you think," he asked her, "that the killer saw Lucia as a boy?"

"I think the killer saw all the victims as sexually ambiguous," she answered. "Androgynous. Like angels."

The look in his eyes was neutral, which was encouraging.

"Remember, the killer's reality is his fantasy. He will think and do whatever it takes to make that fantasy work."

"And the names of fallen angels on the walls?"

"It would have made things a hell of a lot easier if he'd written names of *good* angels," she admitted. "I just don't know."

She looked at him. "One thing I do know," she said, "since Jimmy finally managed to get the Church to cooperate, agree to let us bring in Graff for a lineup, we just might get lucky and get a positive ID. Then I think we'll have enough for probable cause, enough for the D.A.'s office to make a case. And there's that partial heel print that the killer left in the church. It's not much more than a smudge, but we can at least match for size, once we get Graff into custody."

Darius shook his head, picking up the morning's edition of the *Post* lying at the edge of the coffee table. The headline read PARISH PRIEST'S PORN PHOTOS. "I need a cigarette," he said.

🙢

Welcome to the jungle. . . . Guns N' Roses wailed inside his head.

Sakura reached for the CD player's off switch and killed the sound, pulling away the earphones. He looked at the clock. *2:03* A.M. Why was he still here, sitting alone in his office? He got up from his chair and paced to the window that divided him from the squad room, where a few stragglers from the task force mixed with the regulars on shift. Not much to be done now but wait for the lab results on the accumulated samples from the search. He was hoping for the best—a hair or a fingerprint that would prove to be Lucia's, even a fiber that could reasonably have come from the clothes she'd been wearing that Saturday afternoon she'd disappeared. Something more substantial than that necklace's thin gold chain, which seemed too delicate to support alone the burden of Thomas Graff's guilt.

A witness ID would help, and both the bartender and the waitress had agreed to attend tomorrow's lineup. If either witness could make the link between Graff and Geoffrey Westlake, that would connect the priest to a second of the primary victims. Three of seven victims, counting Father Kellog.

He walked back to his desk and reached to pick up his cell phone, putting it into his pocket. His father had called this morning seeking to confirm their meeting, suggesting they have lunch together somewhere near the airport. Of course, he hadn't been able to go. Too much going on with the search. His work, the perfect excuse to cancel out.

He glanced back at the clock. His father's sudden appearance had canceled any chance he'd had to talk with Hanae last night. Truly, he'd been too tired for anything but sleep when his father had finally left their apartment. He'd be too tired again, if Hanae were still awake, for anything more tonight.

Just let me get through the case had become his silent mantra. *Let me get through the case . . . successfully.* Wasn't that the caveat? Defeat was the threat that tore at him, that distracted from all else. Until this case was successfully concluded, he did not have the luxury of worrying over his father's visit or what might have been left unsaid. No energy to spare for confrontation with his father. Or, even tonight, with his wife.

He was not yet ready to go home. He sat back down in his chair and recited for himself the samurai creed. "I have no parents; I make the Heavens and the Earth my parents. I have no home; I make the *Tan T'ien* my home. I have no divine power; I make honesty my Divine Power. . . ."

He went on, speaking each of the more than twenty statements carefully, finishing softly with the last two. "I have no castle; I make Immovable Mind my castle. I have no sword; I make No Mind my sword."

He was still sitting, silently now, in the chair, when Talbot, long past his shift, appeared at the door.

"I thought you'd called it a night, Detective. What are you still doing here?"

"I was going to ask you the same thing." Talbot drifted in and sat down. "I'm hoping we get lucky at the lineup tomorrow," he said in a moment, echoing Sakura's own earlier thoughts.

Talbot picked up the folder of Graff's photos, which lay at the edge of the desk where Willie had left them yesterday. He set the file on his lap, flipping idly through the stack of nude shots.

Sakura could see the detective thinking, watched his concentration sharpen as he flicked several of the photographs back. He picked up a black-and-white print, stared at it, and nodded.

"I've seen this. . . ." He was looking at Sakura now, pushing the print toward him on the desk, his finger jabbing at the image, at the dark and irregular blemish that ran out from the hairline like a stain.

"I know I've seen that birthmark," Talbot said. "And I'm pretty sure that I remember where."

⁂

Dreams had always plagued Michael Darius. His first conscious memory was of his mother snatching him up screaming from his crib, comforting him from some nightmare. His wails had been a child's, but not his understanding. Even in his crib his waking thoughts had been sharp and coherent, in contrast to his dreams. It was the sharpness that allowed him to remember so near to the beginning of his life.

An old soul, Margot had called him, smiling as she'd said it, regarding it as a good quality, one of many she had once claimed to find in him, before those days were gone.

It had become clear to him over the years that his marriage, like everything else in his life, had been doomed. That the happy days of his youth, punctuated as they were with his claustrophobic dreams, had been but a warning of the time when life and nightmare would merge into a seamless hell. His sister's murder had been the trigger of that melding but was not its cause. His own impotent rage, his parents' inevitable decline, the short reprieve of his marriage, were symptoms of some poison greater than his sister's death. Her senseless murder but a focus for what remained forever inchoate but potent in his dreams.

He had shut down completely after Hudson, had begun to believe that withdrawal was at least some protection against the poison that had leached into his life—the darkness from his dreams, which had claimed both his sister and his parents, would inevitably threaten any-one he got close to.

Was he crazy? A police department shrink might say so. Willie might say so. In the end it didn't matter. Crazy or sane, the threat remained. From himself, if not the poison.

He was dreaming now—though as the nightmares went, he'd had worse. Although not his waking self, he was at least recognizably the protagonist of the jumbled and fragmented scenes that spooled from his unconscious. A chameleon self that shifted and changed, slipping in and out of personae, like discarded layers of clothes.

For a time the impression persisted of his own eyes laughing at him from the faces of these strangers, as if the dream were a mirror, and the mockery an answer to a question he hadn't asked. But the screen went blank and was gone.

He was nothing. Centered on an apprehension that built on noth-ingness and flowered into sudden understanding. One brief instant he was light and unbound, but the certainty of the next moment was already a huge and hungry blackness. The agony of the plunge no less terrible for his knowing it would come.

He jerked awake and sat up in bed, sucking air like a man drowning. His throat had dried in the artificial heat of the apartment, and he ran his tongue reflexively over his mouth. There was a bitterness in the sweat that dotted his upper lip, the flavor of a memory that evaporated like the moisture from his body.

He was thirsty. He needed a glass of water. He turned, looked around the room. Where . . . ? Walls not white, but colored dark like decaying roses. The bed. Too high off the floor. He missed the odor of raw wood.

He remembered now. The restaurant. They'd both gotten a little drunk. He had taken her back to her apartment in the Village.

She was sleeping on her side. Turned toward him. A series of soft undulating curves under the thin sheet, her black unruly hair shadowing half her face. And the scent he inhaled was the smell of spent sex and Wilhelmina French.

CHAPTER

18

The week's nasty weather in temporary retreat, the morning of Lucia Mancuso's funeral dawned like a blessing. By eleven a crisp sunniness had peaked in the cold air, to glint and sparkle in the granite facade of the Church of the Blessed Sacrament. The local and cable broadcasters milling across the street seemed to catch this exuberance—reporters chatting briskly to their satellite pickups; shoulder cams patrolling the police lines like tigers, to flash and zoom on the mourners who gathered on the wide stairs of the church.

A delivery van stopped short of one of the barricades. "Flowers for the Mancuso funeral," the driver said, and the uniformed cop waved him through. Turning into a driveway located between the church and rectory, he parked in a paved area adjacent to a rear garage and got out. Opening the van, he unloaded a small potted fir tree decorated with teddy bears and bows. Walking back toward a side entrance, he removed his baseball cap before entering the church.

The driver looked around. The church was already three-quarters full. There wasn't much time, since Mass was scheduled to begin at any minute. Keeping his head down, he moved toward the central aisle, where floral offerings were being amassed to the right and left along the Communion railing. He stopped, giving the little tree a prominent place near the sanctuary. Then turning, he walked briskly down a side aisle, toward the confessionals at the rear.

Stepping inside, the driver took a deep breath. First untying the Nikes, then removing the khaki jumpsuit. The driver would have preferred to have worn a suit instead of pants and a blazer, but the borrowed uniform had made that impossible. However, the soft leather bag had fit comfortably enough across the chest. Now the driver opened the bag and removed shoes. The pins holding the hair flat came out next. A few quick strokes with a brush. Dark glasses in place. The uniform and joggers would have to be left behind. Straightening the lapels of the jacket, the driver thought that if everything continued to go as smoothly, the hundred-dollar bill was a small enough sacrifice to have bribed the original driver of Wonderland Flowers.

Zoe peeped out from between the confessional's heavy drapes. The coast was clear. Walking up the same side aisle she'd come down, she found a nearly empty pew midway, slid in as far as she could toward the center aisle, and knelt. A buttery smell came to her of candle wax mixed with fresh pine.

She looked through the ombré haze of her sunglasses. Near the front was a string of high-ranking clergymen, solid in black cassocks and capes. Magenta the only relief in a somber sea of dark. Close by were Sakura with Lincoln McCauley, along with representatives from the D.A.'s and mayor's offices. On the opposite side of the aisle, several rows were roped off. Dressed in the navy and white of a Catholic-school uniform were students of Immaculata. Their small faces pale against the white of their starched collars. Their eyes grave and frightened. Lucia's classmates, bussed in from St. Sebastian parish. Come to say good-bye.

In the front nearest the aisle was Lucia's teacher. Her back ramrod straight in the pale dove gray of her habit, her disciplined eyes on the altar, rosary beads pinched between long fingers.

Rozelli was nowhere in sight. Maybe he was outside, working the crowd. She'd spotted another florist van as she'd driven in, this one allowed to park near the entrance to the church. Surveillance taking pictures no doubt. Interesting that the task force was still actively seeking suspects. Which could mean Sakura wasn't completely confident that Graff was the killer. Or the lieutenant was just being scrupulous.

She looked around. Near the rear on the opposite side was Agnes Tuminello. In a dark hat, with a veil pulled over her face, she knelt praying. Zoe could just make out a slight movement of the house-keeper's lips. She turned quickly, securing the dark glasses on her nose. As far as she could tell, there were no members of the press among the mourners. She would be way out front with an exclusive on the funeral. But what she really wanted was something more sensational. A follow-up on her "priest porno" story. Except for the search of the rectory—and those results were still a big question mark—the riverbed had run dry. She needed to burst the dam.

The tower bell began to toll. Zoe stood with the congregation. Then, like a catch of breath in the air above their heads, the organ breathed, then boomed its opening notes. Zoe turned to the back of the church, where a trio of altar boys was leading the funeral procession. The first, a little ahead of the others, carried a large golden cross. Behind the boys came three priests. And next, pallbearers with Lucia's small flower-covered coffin.

The Mancuso family followed. Mr. Mancuso supporting his wife. The other daughter, eyes down, walking beside them. An older woman shrouded in black, a mantilla covering her head, moved slowly between two young men. One reminded her of Johnny, Italian handsome in his dark suit and even darker expression. A trail of aunts, uncles, and cousins.

Soon enough Mass began. Zoe sat and knelt and stood, mentally taking notes. Inside the leather bag a recorder was running. She'd have all the speeches verbatim, though she wished for a copy of the slide show that was presented in lieu of a eulogy—photographs of Lucia chronicling her brief little life. And nothing could replace film for family reaction shots, though she just wasn't close enough for that, even if she could have gotten away with a camera. She knew for a fact that MSNBC had been turned down flat on a live telecast of the funeral.

Time for Communion. Mr. and Mrs. Mancuso went up to kneel at the rail. Then the older daughter, Celia, her hands out to receive the Host, placing it inside her mouth as she turned. There was only the slightest hesitation, her eyes dark in the too white flesh of her face. A sidelong glance at the small coffin of her sister, stolen as though in secret. Then her lids shutting tight as she made the sign of the cross.

Zoe stood as her pew emptied for Communion and moved to the side aisle. She walked to the back of the church, still haunted by the look in Celia's eyes, as Lucia's little classmates began to sing:

> Let there be peace on Earth
> And let it begin with me.
> Let there be peace on Earth,
> The peace that was meant to be. . . .

It was way more than enough. She walked through the lobby, glad to push through the huge wooden doors to the outside. But the sunny morning had disappeared, given way to a leaden afternoon.

The lineup room was a glassed-in stage, fronted by a dimly lit hallway. Gil Avery stood waiting in the corridor-shaped room with Detective Walter Talbot. Avery's attitude was sullen, but an improvement on his mood when picked up earlier in the morning. It was Avery who had discovered Pinot's body, and Talbot who had interviewed the eighteen-year-old after his roommate's murder. He well remembered the boy's creepy self-possession at the time, a feral aplomb that held no quarter. *Jude is dead. I'm alive. So . . . ?*

Avery had been told nothing about why he was here now, or who he was expected to identify. Their best bet for an honest reaction was to maintain the element of surprise.

"Here they come," Talbot said unnecessarily as a door opened and five men walked onto the stage. Four were civilian clerks or cops, commandeered this morning for the lineup.

"See anybody you recognize?" Talbot searched Avery's face.

"Is that what this is about?" Sullen had become bored. "You gonna bust this guy for taking pictures?"

"Which guy are we talking about?"

"Number two."

No surprise. Graff was number two. The boy had verified what they knew.

"What are you saying exactly?" Talbot tied it down. "Where have you seen number two before?"

"He took pictures of me. Nude shots. But it wasn't my dick that got him going. The freak had some kind of weird thing for this." Avery fingered the birthmark at the side of his neck. He looked back at Talbot. "Since when is taking pictures illegal?"

"Is that all that happened?"

"You mean, did he ask me to suck him off?"

"Was there any kind of contact, sexual or otherwise?"

Avery shook his head. "He never even said much. Paid good and never touched me."

"Did this guy photograph Jude?"

Now Avery smiled, tight-lipped and self-satisfied that he'd finally gotten the point. He looked back to the lighted box, to where Graff still stood. The smile widened. "No way," he said.

"Number two didn't photograph Jude?" Talbot asked now.

"I don't know about that. I'm just telling you that nutcase didn't kill him."

Avery was taken away to an interrogation room for further questioning on what exactly had taken place in that photographic session. But it didn't seem now that they would be able to establish anything more than an indirect link between Graff and Pinot.

It was Tiffany Jameson's turn now. The waitress looked even thinner to Talbot than she had in the bistro, balancing on her thick high heels and wearing some skinny little dress. She fidgeted with her ponytail as she glanced around, all doe-eyed and anxious.

"That's my lieutenant down there," he explained Sakura's presence at the end of the hall. "He'll be observing. . . . You ready?"

"Sure." The ponytail got a tug.

He reached up and pressed the button on the intercom. "Send them out."

The five men walked out for a second time on the stage. All five wore dark outdoor jackets now.

In her high heels Tiffany shifted nervously.

"Take your time," he said to her. "And don't forget, they can't see or hear you."

"I know. But it's just . . . they seem so close."

"That's so you can really get a good look," he explained. "We can ask them to step forward or turn. . . . Whatever you think will help.

And if you need to hear a voice, we can get them to say whatever you want."

She nodded, then surprised him by walking right up to the glass. She moved the length of the line, one through five, and back again. He remembered she had told him she'd seen this *on the cop shows*.

"You know, I never actually saw his face." She had turned to him.

He nodded and hit the button. "Hats and sunglasses, please."

The men had been instructed on this earlier. In order to insure due process, no subject in a lineup could favor a witness description more than any other. All five took Yankees caps and sunglasses from the pockets of their jackets. Put them on.

Tiffany worked her way down the line again. "You said I could ask them to say something?"

"That's right."

"One and four," she said to him. "'Just a cup of coffee.'"

He hit the button again. "Numbers one and four. Step forward and say the phrase: *Just a cup of coffee.*"

"Could they say it with their jackets off?"

He nodded and relayed the instructions. Her face was completely earnest now, scrutinizing the two men.

"Let's hear that phrase again," he said, directing the men to repeat it a third time.

She listened with her head cocked, the ponytail swinging, then walked back over to him. She really was model tall, and the silly shoes put them on a level, eye to eye. Hers registered disappointment.

"I'm awfully sorry, Detective Talbot," she said to him. "I really wanted to help. I mean, it *could* be one of them . . . especially number four. But his voice doesn't sound right." She shook her head for emphasis. "I just can't be sure."

He smiled. "It's okay, Ms. Jameson. We appreciate your coming in. Detective Johnson's out there. She'll see you get downstairs."

She smiled back at him, and the midwestern wholesomeness showed through the trendy clothes. "It's Tiffany," she said. The doe look widened in her eyes, and then she was gone.

Sakura walked over.

"Sorry, Lieutenant." He shook his head.

"You did a good job, Walt. Sometimes it just doesn't happen."

Kelly poked his head in. "The bartender's here."

"I'll take it," Sakura said, "but stay here, Walt."

Jack Trehan walked in with an attitude, like the hallway was the real stage. He glanced briefly at the five men who were still in the box, then back to Sakura. "Hi, Lieutenant. Glad to be of service."

"This is Detective Talbot." Sakura introduced him.

A quirk of the smile. "These the guys?" Trehan was looking at the men now, still in the caps and dark glasses.

"Number four," he said, even before Sakura could answer the obvious.

"You need to be positive, Mr. Trehan," Sakura said mildly. "In your statement you said that you'd only seen the man who sat next to Westlake for a very short time. The bar was not well lit . . ."

Trehan turned away from him, looking back at the lineup. "Number four," he insisted.

This second time out in the lineup, position four was Graff.

⋔

Celia Mancuso was a ball of misery. She sat straight enough on the cold cement bench. But in her mind she was coiled tight, head down, legs drawn up to her chest, arms wrapping beneath her knees, hands anchored and clutching at her elbows. It was the posture she'd adopted for the last five days. As a physical fact within her room. Inside herself when anyone could watch, like this morning at Lucia's funeral.

What she wanted was to disappear. Or at least to be invisible.

"CeCe . . . CeCe," her cousins were calling. "Come on, CeCe. We're going high!"

Laura and Julia, bundled in their thick quilted jackets, were moving in tandem on the swings. Twin heads dipping and rising, their dark bobs flying out behind them, then parting and rushing like tasseled silk to sweep against their faces. Across the park her aunt Roslyn was occupied with the baby, that and gossiping with some friend.

"Be careful," she heard herself calling to the girls, and felt the black twinge inside. Stupid to be sent here to help watch her cousins. She hadn't saved Lucia.

"Hi."

She hadn't seen the girl approach, but she hadn't been paying attention. Seeing, but not seeing, as if the world, not herself, were fading.

"Hello," she answered to be polite. The girl, in jeans and jacket over a neighborhood high-school sweatshirt, was older than she'd thought at first.

"I grew up right down that street," the girl said, pointing. She sat down with her on the bench. "You live around here?"

She shook her head. "I'm visiting my cousins." She looked over to where the girls were still playing on the swings. Come to earth now, but twisting the chains and spinning.

"They're cute."

She smiled. The girl beside her was beautiful. She could look like a movie star, dressed right. "Your hair's really pretty," she said to her. It felt good to say something nice like that.

"Thank you. Yours is pretty too. In fact, you're pretty . . . ?"

"Celia."

"Neat name. But you look sad, Celia. Is something wrong?" The soft eyes probed her face.

She started to say no, that there was nothing, but the lie stuck in her throat. She didn't answer, looking over at her cousins instead. They were on the slide now. Laura climbing. Julia, already at the top, arms pointing straight, poised for the rush to the ground. Aunt Roslyn, still chatting away, was changing the baby.

She turned back to he girl. "Do you have a boyfriend?" The words came out of her mouth.

"I did." The girl's lips twisted. "We broke up. . . . What about you, Celia? I'll bet you have a boyfriend."

"Kinda . . ."

"What's his name?"

"Pete. Pete Fazio." And then without meaning to at all, she told the girl everything. About Lucia. About the necklace and how she had lied. Because Pete had given *her* the locket. The locket she had lost before she'd even had a chance to put his picture inside. Lost it the day they'd left the playground to sneak into the basement of the rectory.

It wasn't a sin, the girl said, if you really loved the boy to let him kiss you. And if Pete had tried to feel her up—well, that was just the way guys were, and she'd been exactly right to push him off and run away.

But what about the lie she had told the police? Saying that the necklace was Lucia's, to keep her papa from finding out about Pete. Her sister was dead, and she couldn't stand for Papa to hate her any more than he already did for catching the flu and letting somebody get Lucia.

The girl had been really nice and it had been good to cry. The girl had cried a little too and had said it was okay. And that she was sure that her papa loved her and didn't blame her at all for what some sick man had done to her sister. Only she hadn't said *man,* but a bad word. But that was okay too, because what had happened to Lucia made you want to say bad words like that.

The girl had hugged her before she left. And looked so pretty with her blond hair bouncing as she walked away, that for a little while she forgot to be sad. And only later felt guilty.

🔥

"Yes?" Adrian Lovett smiled vaguely at the stranger standing on his landing and watched as he shook off the rain that had just started to fall outside.

"Adrian Lovett?"

"Yes. May I help you?"

"Detective Pete Handy." The man flashed his NYPD badge. "I see you're headed out." He motioned toward the jacket he was holding. "Can I have a few words with you first, Mr. Lovett? I've missed you several times."

"Sure." He stepped aside, letting in the short stocky policeman, the wet still peppering the shoulders of his ancient overcoat. "I was just going out to pick up something to eat."

"This is some place you've got here." Handy moved in, looking in all directions at once. "I've never been in one of these renovateds. Do the work yourself?"

"Most of it was already completed before we moved here."

"We?"

"My wife and I."

Handy nodded, walked up to one of the walls that split the large loft into a maze. "This wouldn't be her?"

"Actually, yes."

The cop's pug eyes traveled over the black-and-white photograph. The naked woman appeared to be flying, her long legs split into a dancer's arabesque. Her arms, tangled in long curling hair, rose over her head in the unfinished circle of a half-moon.

"Beautiful woman."

"Yes, she was. She died some time ago."

"What a waste. Beautiful woman like that."

"Did you want to ask me something?"

"Oh . . . yeah." Handy turned from the dead wife's image, extracting a small notebook from the inside pocket of his coat. He flipped open the pad and pulled out a ballpoint. "This the kind of thing you show at the Milne gallery?" He pointed back at the portrait.

"Milne gallery . . . ? Is this about David's murder?"

"Just routine." The officer smiled. "Your name appeared on the gallery's list of artists. We're questioning everyone who might be able to shed some light on how Mr. Milne got to be one of this killer's victims."

"I have no idea. The newspapers say he's targeting gay men. . . . David was fairly well known."

"Do you know if Mr. Milne knew any of the other victims?"

"No, I wouldn't know that."

"How well did you know Mr. Milne?"

"I knew David professionally. I've exhibited at his gallery over the years."

The cop nodded, making notes. "Can you think of anything at all that might help us, Mr. Lovett?"

"No. . . . I thought someone was in custody."

"Not in custody. But we do have a numero uno suspect."

"That priest."

"Like I said, I've missed you several times and I need to tie up loose ends." Handy grinned. "You know how it is."

"Yes, of course," he said. "I wish I could help. I liked David."

"Well"—Handy snapped shut the notebook, passed him a card—"call me if you think of something."

He nodded, walking the policeman to the door. He could hear Handy's heavy footfalls as he moved across the short landing down the hall. Unconsciously, he'd been holding his breath, until he heard the swoosh of the elevator's gears, carrying the cop down to the ground floor.

⚶

Willie felt that the storm was inside her. Boundaries dissolving in explosions of lightning that boomed and crackled at the high-rise windows, igniting the bedroom into flashbulb brilliance that faded as quickly to black. And Michael, silhouetted above her, a shadow beating within.

She locked her legs around him, her hands against his chest, wanting to feel him solid. She felt his own grip tighten on her shoulders, heard him cry out. As the pleasure, unstoppable now, exploded in her spine, like weightlessness taking hold. A beast that shook her in its jaws.

For as long as she could, she lay still, waiting for a lightning flash to penetrate her lids, counting the seconds, listening for the thunder to crash and roll away. It was a game to fill her mind till she was ready to move, easier than listening to his breathing.

At the moment when she thought that he would reach for her again, she got up and walked to the chair where earlier she'd tossed her purse. She fished inside it for the aspirin. The headache she'd been fighting throbbed behind her eyes.

She swallowed the tablets dry. She hadn't looked at Michael yet, but she could feel him watching her from the bed, ready again to make love, or whatever he called what they were doing. It was amazing, his ability to perform again and again, each time with more intensity. Tempting to let herself believe that she was its inspiration.

Her clothes hung over the chair. She picked up her slip and pulled it on before she turned back to the bed. Michael was sitting up against the pillows, smoking. The glowing tip of his cigarette moved slowly from his lips to his knee.

She sat down and switched on the lamp. She could see him better now. The blue eyes still startling in the Mediterranean face.

"Are you going back?" he asked her.

"You mean back to my job?"

"To Quantico. Yes," he said.

"Are you asking me if I'm convinced this investigation is over?"

"I guess that's what I'm asking."

"Graff's photo of the roommate links him at least indirectly to Pinot, and the bartender positively ID'd him as the man who left Marlowe's with Westlake." She said it as an answer.

Michael took a drag on the cigarette. "The bartender wanted his face on TV."

No arguing with that. Since the lineup today Trehan had wasted no time giving interviews to anyone who'd listen. And leaks had begun to surface immediately that the man the bartender had identified as leaving with Westlake on the night of the murder was one and the same "Porno Priest" of the *Post*'s earlier exclusive. Negotiations were still under way with the Church, but it was pretty much understood that Thomas Graff would surrender himself to police custody sometime before the official announcement of his arrest was made. An announcement that was now set for the press conference on Monday.

"The suits are getting ready to take their bows"—Michael was apparently reading her mind—"but it's Jimmy who's going to be the scapegoat if another body turns up."

She sighed. She had her own misgivings.

"Life in the NYPD is shit," he said.

"You liked it once," she said to him. "You told me that you became a cop because the street was closer to the action."

"Yeah, battling evil." He reached over and crushed out his cigarette in the ashtray on the nightstand. "Isn't that what your work at Quantico is all about?"

"I don't think of it like that."

"How do you think about it?"

There was a darkness in his eyes that had deepened. She tried to remember what he looked like when he smiled.

"Protecting people . . . stopping the killing," she answered him.

"I'm hoping we'll learn enough about the development of serial murderers so we can detect them while they're still young."

"You don't actually think you can cure them?"

"Not cure, exactly. But if we could catch them in time. Break the
pattern—"

"What if they're just evil?"

"They're sick, Michael."

"Sick," he repeated. "Don't you believe in good and evil?"

She took a breath. How had they started this? "The universe is neutral," she said. "Good and evil are human constructs."

"So this killer we're hunting isn't *really* evil?" His tone antag-
onistic.

"Ethically speaking, he is, Michael. I'll grant you that. But ethics
only applies to human behavior. I don't believe that serial killers are
fully human. Their brains don't develop normally, don't operate in the
same reality. . . ." She stopped.

"What is it?" he asked. He had heard the hesitation in her voice.

"It just occurred to me," she said, "that LSD breaks down what we
think of as normal consensus reality, that picture of the world we all
agree on more or less."

"You told Jimmy that the killer was using the drug to try to re-create
his fantasy inside the victims' minds."

"I still believe that. I'm just seeing *why* he's doing it from a slightly
different angle."

He was waiting for her to explain.

"The killer's fantasy is like an adaption," she went on, "a substitute
for the normal psychosexual models that develop in a healthy mind.
The serial's way of relating to other human beings unfortunately in-
volves killing them."

"A hell of a relationship." His words still caustic.

"Don't you see how pathetic it is?" she tried again. "A serial knows
by observing other people's emotional responses that something is
missing in him. Our killer is intelligent enough to understand that he
doesn't really fit into our world. But with the LSD he can try to bring
some of us into *his*."

"He's killing people, for chrissake."

"I know. . . ." She fell silent. There was a void that trembled between them that words would never bridge. She turned off the light and went back to join him in the bed.

The room was cold and full of shadows, but the storm that battered Manhattan was miles away, and enough moonlight seeped through the curtained windows that he didn't need the lamp to write. Thomas Graff stared at the blank sheet of stationery he had found in the drawer of the bedside table, then dashed off the words. They seemed fuzzy on the page, indistinct. Not the bold scrawl he'd intended. He turned the page on its side, preparing to tear it in two, to obliterate what was at best insincere, at worst an unintended commentary on himself.

A picture flashed in his head. So clear. Kaitlyn speaking the fatal words.

I'm sorry, Thomas. It's for the best.

He could still see her face as she'd put the ring in his hand. That perfectly flawless face, which he'd thought to be his salvation. His mind had been racing as he'd looked at her, trying to figure it out, trying to understand who could have told her. He had always kept that part of himself so scrupulously separate from his normal life. And that last affair with the busboy had been over for a month.

"I've changed, Katie," he said. "You've changed me. You're my future."

"I know you believe that."

"It's true. I love you."

"I love you too. That's why I'm doing this, Thomas."

He hadn't believed her then. He'd been too angry. But she had been right. Even Katie in all her perfection could not have saved him. He understood that now, at least. He'd never learned who had told her. Maybe she had guessed that something was wrong and had set out to find the truth herself. He had been too arrogant then to believe that his cover was not perfect. So sure that his secret life was not his real one, its existence no more than an aberration to be controlled by an act of will.

The years blurred after that. A graduate degree in philosophy from Loyola University had prepared him for little but teaching. His secret life and all its dangers remained. From time to time he dated, but no other woman was Kaitlyn. They became his excuse for having sex with men. He would loathe the women who were less than Kaitlyn, rather than loathe himself.

Finally there was the Church, actively recruiting priests, since vocations from God had been increasingly falling on deaf ears among the faithful. It seemed to be the solution for the sterility of his life. Let the Church take Katie's place.

Why did you become a priest?

To save my immortal soul.

That was the plan, though not very well thought out. For surely he had known that in the seminaries there were others like himself. So the Church had not saved him, providing him instead with rationalizations. His little clique of seminarians had been very good at that. Justifying with technical arguments, and ecclesiastical dancing upon the head of a pin, that having sex among themselves did not constitute an actual violation of their vows.

He had allowed the arguments to seduce him, and had gotten along quite well. And then after the seminary, he had quit the affairs cold turkey. He had been so proud of that. Chaste at last. Faithful to his vows. The photographs had been harmless. An outlet.

And maybe that was just one more rationalization.

A sound, bitter, escaped his mouth. Walsh had warned him against agreeing to the lineup. But in his arrogance he had insisted. Get it over with. Enjoy their stupid faces when he passed with flying colors. He was innocent, after all. How could he have guessed that one of those nameless boys he'd photographed could be linked to one of the victims, or that he'd be falsely identified as being in some bar with another?

And still it might have come to nothing without that locket. How had the Mancuso girl's necklace turned up in the rectory basement? It seemed that he was being framed. By God, if not the killer.

He looked at the clock. Edward Walsh had called and left a message. He was coming here tonight, and soon. Coming to tie down the details for him to turn himself in.

He hadn't been allowed to attend the Mancuso girl's funeral today, nor Father Kellog's services at St. Patrick. There was still some talk of a defense, but the message was clear. The Church was giving him up. He'd run out of places to hide. He unbuckled the belt at his waist and drew it out full length. Then he looked down at the note he'd let fall to the bed. *I'm sorry.* He'd let stand what he had written. Let them make of it what they would.

Like this, they had not come together for too many nights. Together in their marriage bed, so completely as one, the great wedding quilt, a curling wave of silk and fine thread, rolled at their feet. The past weeks, too, rolled away, deep inside of her, out of memory's reach, where they could do no harm.

Her husband rested now in her arms, listening to the thrumming of her heart, counting beats, measuring rhythms. Hanae breathed his moist smell. The feel of his hair, cool and dense against her fingers. He sighed, a happy noise, like a small boy's. A sound too long absent from her ears. He moved his mouth to her breast, suckling lightly. She slipped a finger between his lips to feel the warm rough of his tongue. Only moments before he had poured himself full inside of her.

He rubbed his hand now over her abdomen. A small tremor shot through her, and she wondered if at last he would take notice that his wife had grown fleshy. He did not.

He lifted his head. "You are cold, my wife?" he asked quietly, and moved to unfurl their wedding quilt, gathering it snugly around them. "Better?"

"You spoil me." She whispered against the side of his throat.

"No, Hanae, I do not spoil you. I have not been such a good husband." She wanted to speak, but let the silence stand.

"This case has taken me away from you and that is not good." He turned her under him. She could feel his warm breath, his dark eyes on her. "I love you, Hanae." He kissed her softly.

"*Watashi mo,*" she answered.

He rolled onto his back, pulling her close, surprising her with his words. "I know you want a child. And it would be good for you."

She wanted to ask would it not also be good for him.

"I am afraid . . . ," he whispered into her hair.

"Afraid, my husband?" She rose up on her side.

"Of the evil in the world."

"Good cannot exist without evil," she said.

"But this job lets me see too much." His voice was almost angry. "I don't know if I want our child to come into such a world."

"This little girl's death stays with you."

"Yes." This time there was only sadness in his voice.

She lay back next to him, wishing for a better world. For her husband not to be afraid. That he would want this new life she carried. Her heart had already made a place for their child. Now she must pray that in her husband's heart there would also be a place.

"Jimmy . . ."

The ringing caused him to jump. He rolled over to pick up his cell phone from the bedside table. She heard him flip up the receiver. "Lieutenant Sakura."

She placed her hand against his back.

"When?" he asked.

She could feel the muscles tensing along his spine.

"I'll meet you there." He was already moving, his legs swinging off the bed. "I have to go, Hanae," he said. "The priest we were going to arrest is dead. Apparently a suicide."

She brought her lips to the soft curve of his back. "I am sorry, Husband."

She could hear him move into the bath, the shower running, then the water in the sink, the brush against his teeth.

"Go to sleep," he said softly, coming back into the room, his soap-sweet smell reaching her.

She heard the hangers click against the metal rod in the closet, the crisp sound of his shirt, the swoosh of his trousers, the slap of his belt. Then the jingling sounds as he filled his pockets.

He bent and kissed her. *"Aishiteru yo."*

He padded almost soundlessly across the *tatami* in his stocking feet. His shoes waiting in the *genkan*.

The outside door opened and closed. The sounds of his key in the lock.

Gently she exhaled, listening to the absolute stillness of the room. Then slowly, very slowly, she allowed herself to cry.

⁕

Asleep in the bed, Darius breathed in real time, but his consciousness was in dream time. He moved disembodied through lives half remembered, a ghost-snake slipping its skin. Whispers followed like footsteps. Words of the medicine man tickled his ear. An echo that thrummed with the blood in his veins. A truth that prickled his skin like the old fears, to halt the clicking sideshow.

In dream time he saw himself with fresh eyes, a boy upon a mountain, stripped down to breechcloth and moccasins, a small knife tucked against his hard young belly. He sniffed the air. Inside the heat he could smell the coming of autumn. Yet he did not trust his senses, hungry as they were for an end to summer and *o-kee-pa*.

Unlike the others, he would not give over his body to *o-kee-pa*. He would not hang in the lodge, suspended from rawhide ropes, hooks driven into his flesh with buffalo skulls tied to his feet, dangling until the spirits came. He would find his own way, he told himself, while cursing his weakness.

Listening with the boy's ears, Darius heard the chirr of an insect, saw it skitter beneath the rock, a black smudge against red. His brown fingers slid into the fissure, pinching the hard armor, plucking out the small, struggling thing. Twice the hot sun had risen and set, and no food had passed his lips. Yet even as he opened his mouth, his white teeth cracking the tough shell, his ears feeding on the sound, he cursed his weakness.

He understood that he was without whole mind, for he had not slept these two days, the sharp rocks between his toes and pebbles under his back had kept him awake. Sometime during the night, the skin between the first and second toe of his left foot had broken. Using clay and some of his own saliva, he'd fashioned a putty to staunch the bleeding, cursing his weakness.

Now in the high heat of the third day, the torn flesh throbbed. The sore would keep him from making a perfect dance when the moon rose again. He tried the song he would sing, but his throat was rust.

From the beginning he knew his body was his only possession. It was the only thing he could give. Yet his weaknesses defied this understanding. He looked down at his dusty feet, slowly loosening the hard paste between his toes. His dark eyes sought the ground. The sharp edge of a stone glinted. He reached, placing the rock between the first and second toe of his left foot. He squeezed until he drew new blood. The spirits must see he offered his flesh freely.

Still, the spirits hid from him on the third day, and once more he cursed himself for his weakness. He lay rolling upon the hard earth, his mind gone, wishing for the shade of a cottonwood tree. Then behind his eyes he saw the giant clouds split open the sky and the great wheel of sun spin, spiraling in upon itself, fire falling in straight paths from its great heart. He cried out only once, and when he came back to himself, the sun lay upon his chest, its fiery tongues branding him.

Darius jolted awake, his vision fading to ash. Beside him, curled like a child in her sleep, Willie dreamed on, untroubled.

He got up and moved naked and sweating from the bed to the uncurtained window. He'd been dreaming again, one of those nightmares that clung to near-consciousness like a virus. He struck a match, lighting the last of his cigarettes.

The first exhalation diffused his reflection into a ghost in the glass so that only the hot orange globe of the cigarette could clearly be discerned burning at his side. Slowly the image resolved, and he began to perceive the beveled outline of his flesh, looming larger, denser. Brighter than in life, his emerging form made a blinding contrast against the black slab of night.

CHAPTER

19

In the red environment of the darkroom, the man worked efficiently, despite the strangeness in perception that was an effect of the drug he had taken. He forced himself to concentrate, removing the nascent print from the enlarger, placing it in the tray. The blank white rectangle, floating near the surface, appeared bloody in the light. He pushed it under with the tongs, held it until the image took hold, blooming outward from its center like a flower. He did not fight his sorrow, which the drug painted as a violet shift in the air. He let it fill him, let it flow like dark music, like the grief he had felt over the loss of his wife.

He lifted the print from the fixative, rinsed it, and hung it with the others. The woman in his photos pulsed with life, the corporeal life of blood and flesh. Despite the lies that stood like a wall between them, she had touched him on some level that was yet human. Even with the LSD filling the receptors in his brain, he had to force himself to perceive in her Zavebe. That essence he had always known from before there was *before* or *after*. Known in that eternal *now* from which they both stood banned.

That was the real sorrow. He. Zavebe. All of the Fallen trapped in an eternity of what the Buddhists called *maya*. The illusion of matter. The seductive lie of warmth and happiness . . . and love. Warmth that grew cold. Love that died. Happiness fading to a sorrow that had no end. Over and over. Forever.

If not for the paramedics resuscitating his body after the accident, his own cycle of death and rebirth would yet remain unbroken, the memory of his true identity locked in the decomposing brain of what had been his human self. He could not waste this chance he'd been given. He was the only hope for the Fallen to regain what they had lost.

Which was why Kellog couldn't matter. Why the ghost of that girl in his bedroom couldn't matter. Nor, he reminded himself, should the other, the unfinished child.

He had always planned that Zavebe should be his last in New York. It was clearly time to move on. L.A. was the logical choice. "Los Angeles," he said the name aloud, letting the drug inflate and color the words. *Los Angeles . . . city of angels.*

The influence of the drug persisted, intensifying into a sensation of split time. He finished in the darkroom and went to fix himself a sandwich, sitting down in front of the television, which was blaring out commercials for insurance and soap. But he was also in the tunnel, reliving the fact of his death. All of it, here, now, then, complete and coexistent. The woman on the television chattering about whiter than white socks. Marian moving ahead of him, silhouetted in the light. And the moment of awakening that he could never quite encompass or hold. Only its pale reflection. And only when the drug was at its zenith.

He flipped to a local channel. As promotional spots since yesterday had promised, there was live coverage of today's police press conference. A bit of an anticlimax, since it was obvious from everything that had already appeared in the media that the dead priest was to be the anointed scapegoat. He felt bad about Thomas Graff, the second of his unintended victims. Another of God's little jokes.

He looked at the clock. The event was late getting started. The TV screen showed a still-empty podium, the fringes of a waiting crowd. He set down his unfinished sandwich. On the screen the shot had widened. He saw James Sakura emerge at the edge of the frame, ready to ascend to the stage. A dark-haired woman had walked out behind him, and merging with the crowd, someone else.

He was not prepared. A brilliance uncontained within the pixels of the screen poured like living phosphor from the set. He was off the sofa, moving to the light, bathed in the force of its radiance. On his knees, inches from the image, he tried to see, to penetrate to the human face that lay behind the aura. It was not possible.

No matter. It changed everything.

"Samyaza." He whispered the holy name, placing his lips in reverence against the fiercely glowing figure that lingered for a moment on the screen.

Pig in a suit. That's what Zoe thought Chief of Detectives Lincoln McCauley looked like today. His tiny porcine eyes all full of self-congratulation, if still wary. Whistling in the dark. If pork could whistle. He was up there now at the podium, patting himself on the back, taking the credit that "the terror was over." He should try for a job writing headlines.

She shot a quick look at Johnny, standing in the background with Sakura and other members of the task force on the stage. She'd caught him glancing her way early on, and pretended not to notice, preening in her turquoise suit that was going to shoot great on TV.

Television. That was her goal, the reason she'd held back from the paper on that little gem she'd picked up from the Mancuso girl. For all the high energy in this room today, what had come to be called the "Death Angel" story was basically dead. As dead as Thomas Graff. Oh, the media were all full of his being ID'd in the lineup and the dramatic discovery of the locket in the rectory basement. And everybody was digging for backstory on the Gil Avery connection. But it was really all over but the shouting. Unless another body turned up. Or little Zoe managed to shake things.

Which was just what little Zoe had in mind. A couple of appearances on cable had picked up some good feedback, but unless this story got new legs, unless the terror *wasn't* over, she would no longer be such a hot commodity.

On the stage McCauley had finished his statement. He was turning over the podium to Lieutenant James Sakura. The lieutenant would answer their questions.

Sakura looked less than thrilled. In fact, he didn't look a whole lot better than he had the other day in his office. Did he know the sharks were circling? Did he suspect that they had the wrong man? She felt a little sorry she was about to make things worse, tossing in the red meat at feeding time.

She raised her hand, but he went to the *Times,* courting the respectable papers.

"How specific was the suicide note?" Henry Jacobs wanted to know, echoing the rumors that they'd all heard, that Graff's supposed confession had been very vague indeed.

"The note is just one piece of the evidence against Father Graff." Sakura did a side step. "And his suicide, one might have to conclude, is as viable an expression of his guilt as anything he might have written."

The next questions went to local TV. The reporters nibbling at the edges, pulling at threads—loose ends that were intriguing, but nothing that seriously threatened to unravel the picture of Graff as the killer. Like a tennis match. Serve and volley. Sakura more than holding his own.

"Ms. Kahn . . ." He recognized her.

She stood. She'd made sure to get an end seat so that the pool camera in the aisle could get a good angle. She had thought a lot about her question, how to phrase it for the greatest impact, to sow the most doubt. She remembered to look elegantly grave. This was going out on cable.

"Lieutenant Sakura," she began, "I think it's fair to say that your most damning piece of evidence against Father Graff, the only real *physical* evidence that points to his committing any of these murders, is the necklace that was found in the rectory basement."

She saw him tense, thought for a moment that he might confirm the hypothesis in her statement, but he avoided that trap at least. She went on speaking, conscious of the camera zooming in, of all the eyes in the room.

"Chief McCauley confirmed for us today"—pin it on the pig if she could—"that the necklace found in the rectory was Lucia Mancuso's." She stared at Sakura. "But that's wrong."

She had thought her bald statement might have elicited an audible reaction from the gathering. It was better than that. Dead silence.

"*Wrong,* Ms. Kahn?" This time Sakura walked into her opening, fatalism in his eyes. It almost seemed that he relished this.

She took a breath. *Forgive me, Celia.* "Lucia Mancuso never wore that necklace," she said. "It belongs to her sister. It was the sister who lost the necklace in the rectory basement. She told me so herself."

Now the crowd breathed and murmured. Everybody making notes.

Sakura was cool. "We'll follow up on that." He smiled at her. "But it is, as you yourself suggested, only one piece of the case against Father Graff. We're still waiting for other evidence from that basement, including DNA."

It was as good a save as was possible. Especially the DNA bluff. She hoped the sharks appreciated it. As for her, it was mission accomplished.

⁂

Willie and Darius were waiting for him when Sakura returned to his office. They looked like conspirators. He didn't know what he'd expected when he'd brought them together, but it wasn't exactly this. He felt a small prick of jealousy at their alliance.

He greeted them both, sat down behind his desk, littered with surveillance photos from last week's funerals. "I didn't expect to see you here today," he said to Michael.

Darius remained silent. It was Willie who spoke. "It was pretty rough out there at the end. What do you think about this thing with the locket?"

"Ms. Kahn generally has her facts straight," he answered. "Johnson's headed to the Mancusos' to check if the sister lied."

Willie frowned. "Losing the physical evidence is tough," she said, "but it's not our whole case. We still have the bartender and—"

"And Graff's still dead." Sakura was aware of how he sounded. "No need now for probable cause."

"He did leave a confession."

"'I'm sorry.'" He quoted the note. "Graff didn't say for what."

"Would an innocent man kill himself?" She was playing devil's advocate.

"Maybe if he couldn't see a way out," he answered. "Circumstantial evidence piling up. He photos a guy whose roommate turns up among the dead. Gets ID'd by a witness who's seen some guy with glasses and a hat for two minutes in a bar. Not to mention he's been publicly outed and basically screwed with the Church."

"Might make me depressed." Michael had finally said something.

Willie shook her head. "I can't pretend that losing the necklace wouldn't be a real blow, and aspects of the profile still bother me. . . ."

"Nothing fits, Willie," Sakura said. "We've made it fit."

"I know," she conceded. "There's always been something wrong with how we've looked at this case. It's like one of those Magic Eye pictures, where the surface pattern hides the 3-D image. If we could change our normal focus somehow . . . look through the surface. That's where the real meaning is, in a place we haven't begun to imagine."

He had nothing to say to that.

"I had this idea the other night," she went on, "that maybe the killer is selecting the victims by their appearance, not their sexual orientation. Lucia could fit then, if you grant that she was something of a tomboy. And the men were all fairly effeminate. . . ." She let it die, thinking no doubt what they were all thinking. That time was running out for Jimmy. That the fiasco of the necklace would demand a scapegoat.

Willie stood. "I want to get some of my notes. . . . I'll meet you in the squad room." She looked at Michael.

He watched Darius watching her leave. "You and Willie seem to be getting along."

Darius turned to him, tilted back in the chair. "Yeah."

"'Yeah' . . . ?" he repeated the monosyllable.

"What do you want to hear, Sakura? That my intentions are honorable?"

"Willie can take care of herself," he said. "Maybe you should be careful."

Darius ignored the comment. Let the chair fall flat. "He's still out there."

They were back to that. He swiveled in his own chair now. A Kabuki dance. "Do you think I fucking don't know it?"

Darius's eyes narrowed. He reached in his pocket for his cigarettes, then seemed to think better of it. "I'd like to go through the files."

This was another surprise. "Give Kelly a call first. I'm leaving this afternoon. I've got a conference in Baltimore tomorrow."

Darius nodded and stood. "If I figure anything out—"

"You have my cell phone number."

The snow came down as it had long threatened, in tiny needlepoint flakes that blew in misty swirls through the plaza. The man stood his ground, not far from the ramp going down into the headquarters garage. He had been in this particular spot for a while now, watching the cars that drove in and out. He'd have to move on again soon. He didn't want the guard in the booth to spot him and wonder what he was doing.

He had gotten to Police Plaza as quickly as he could, searching for the man he'd seen on TV. Since he'd arrived, he'd remained outside the building, dividing his time between the ramp and the main entrance. Occasionally he'd gone indoors to look around, his camera bag at his shoulder, reprising his role as photojournalist.

The force of the wind increased, blowing stinging flurries in his face. He took it as a sign to move on, and pulling the drawstring of his hood tighter, he began walking around the building. A reporter, whom he recognized, started up the stairs as he approached. He slowed, glancing around at the crowds of bundled people moving toward the doors. He heard the reporter's voice ahead of him, calling to someone. Reflexively he turned and looked up at the man who was coming out of the building with the dark-haired woman at his side.

"Sergeant Darius." The reporter was backpedaling slowly down the stairs ahead of him, dancing in front of the man, attempting to stop his forward progress. "You back on the force, Sergeant?"

"No, I'm not. Just a private citizen." The man took the woman's arm, pushed forward and free, passing only feet from where he was standing. The light moved with him and lit the windblown snow, a blazing glow of milky incandescence.

Sakura leaned back in his chair, closing his eyes. Darkness lay beyond the darkness, a thick debilitating blackness that sucked air from his lungs, drained blood from his veins until he was no more than the vacated shell, surrendered by the locust he'd once kept as a child. Even now, he could see into the deserted bamboo cage, could hear the crackle as his seven-year-old fingers crushed the brittle exoskeleton into brown dust. The locust had escaped its old life. A perfect reincarnation that had left him sad and bewildered.

"I might be getting drunk after what happened at that press conference." Faith Baldwin stood in the threshold of his office, backlit by the squad room chaos. She closed the door.

"Where were you?" He brought up the fact that she had not shared the stage with the rest of the higher-ups.

"I was delayed, but arrived in time to hear Ms. Kahn's news. Quite the bitch, but I admire her tenaciousness. . . ." She had moved next to his chair and was looking down at him.

He felt himself straighten, the earlier darkness transforming itself into a liquid heaviness resettling in his gut. "One piece of evidence doesn't make a case. Or lose it."

She walked away toward the glass window separating his office from the squad room. "No, but I wouldn't have enjoyed prosecuting the good priest and having that locket bite me in the ass." She toyed with the blinds, finally closing them. "But it's all moot since Thomas Graff bailed out on us."

"Suicide points more to guilt than innocence." He stood, turning to make tea.

"We can't know that unless the killer strikes again." There was an edge of excitement in her voice, as though she were holding her breath, waiting for another murder.

"I'm leaving for Baltimore today." He turned and saw she'd sat down. The room's fluorescence had turned her legs to milk.

She raised her brows. "That's convenient."

He went back to the hot plate. "What do you want, Faith?"

She rose, moving to where he stood behind the desk. "You're no fool, Sakura. Don't let McCauley, or any of the others, force your hand. You know as well as I do that the chances of Graff's guilt were iffy at best. That killer's still out there. When you do get him, I want some solid evidence."

"I'm running out of time."

The green in her eyes shifted. Then reaching down, she slipped her hand between his thighs. A laugh curled in her throat. "I can still give you a hard-on."

His fingers tightened around her wrist, pulling her away.

She shrugged, then smiled. "But everyone knows it's only what happens above the belt that counts with James Sakura."

The ductwork in the apartment house was relatively new and spacious, and without his jacket the man fit easily inside the galvanized corridor that ran between ceiling and floor and within the skin of the building. He left his shoes with the parka and the camera bag next to the grille he'd replaced, and he crawled as silently as he could to the outmost lineal point, the junction between the topmost floor and this one.

He had followed the light. From Police Plaza to the subway. Then emerged behind the man and the woman at the station, tracking them through the streets to this building and its cryptlike lobby. He had waited in the shadow of a column, watching as they'd walked together past the elevators and the ornate marble stairs, to disappear into a discreet hallway. After moments he'd followed to find at its end a small private elevator to the top floor, its access controlled by a keypad.

Security was lax, and he was able to look around the lobby—a tourist with his camera, interested in old buildings—till the receptionist at the desk had returned to her novel. Then he'd slipped down the stairs to the underground parking he had noticed from the street. There were several vehicles parked in the designated spaces, including an SUV in a slot labeled DARIUS. He took his time checking everything out, then rode the elevator as far as it would go and, finding the stairwell locked, he made his way into the ductwork.

He braced himself now inside the metal walls, the leg he'd reinjured in the church screaming its protest. He ignored the pain, snaking upward the twelve-plus feet to the ceiling of the forbidden floor, crawling to an open grille. Below him was a hallway and nearby a door. He could see the top of its frame, where a spare key was hidden.

He was still there, watching and waiting, when finally the door opened and the man and the woman came out, the ineffable light of Samyaza spilling from the body bag called Darius. The woman was speaking, saying that Sakura would not be back from Baltimore till

Wednesday. In silence he looked on as the couple passed below him and took the private elevator down.

In minutes he was inside the apartment, and for a short time he just sat in the dark, breathing. *Inhale. Exhale. Inhale. Exhale.* The woodsy scent, *pine,* he decided, hung heavy inside his nostrils, flushed deep into his lungs. The top note. Lower, the molecules were sweeter. Fruity. He licked his lips and swallowed full. Then in the next inhalation he found the musk, elemental and defining. It clotted inside him. A solid knot. A nucleus of beginnings. And endings.

He stood, expanding his vision to take in the whole of the living room. Love seat. Table. Rug. Then like a mass of unformed flesh, a sofa in front of a bone white wall. *Leather.* He could smell the leather. Slowly he moved forward, hands reaching out like eyes. Touching. *Soft,* like new skin. Onto his knees he pressed his face into a cushion. *Ahhh,* his head falling backward. His musk here too. Soaked into the leather, a part of it now. His tongue stroked the pillow's edge, where the pieces of hide had been fitted and stitched. The darkness of the abyss parted, and Gadriel entered.

He collapsed against the floor, weak and shuddering with the deliciousness of his victory. He felt himself hardening, and he pressed the palm of his hand flat against his erection. With his head tilted back, he gurgled, the musky rawness bubbling inside his throat. Spittle ran down his chin, a single pearl landing on his chest.

Somewhere a clock ticked. He opened his eyes. Regaining his balance, he stood and walked to the telephone. He lifted the receiver. Trembling, he pressed the numbers and waited.

"Hello."

Her sweet voice. Zavebe's voice.

"Hi, Hanae. Adrian Lovett. Had to miss class this afternoon," he said. "But I hope we can get together before Christmas. I have a little something for you."

James Sakura sped along the turnpike. It felt like running away, even if it were true that his speech at the Law Enforcement Conference was something that had been scheduled months ago. He was glad at least that he hadn't booked a flight. It was better to be driving, despite the chancy weather. It gave him the illusion of control.

Adelia Johnson had called, catching him at home as he was packing his overnight case. Celia Mancuso had confessed to the lie. The necklace was hers, not her sister's, and had been lost in a make-out session with some boy. Without the necklace there would never have been enough for an arrest, or even the credible threat of one. Without the necklace Thomas Graff might still be alive.

He had managed to avoid McCauley before he'd left the office, which was a clear indication of the chief's avoiding him. Not quite ready to let the ax fall. Waiting, no doubt, for reaction to Kahn's revelation to develop in the press. For public anger to coalesce. A predictable anger that the monster, now preying on children, had not been caught, after all. That a priest, no matter how flawed, had been hounded to his death by an incompetent investigation.

He had seen it all before. The cathartic public rage allowed to peak before the announcement, which would inevitably come when the killer struck again. Lieutenant James Sakura would be replaced as the head of the task force by an officer of no lesser rank than captain. Proof of the seriousness of the NYPD in addressing public concern.

He had never failed before, not in any serious way. And he found himself wondering how he would react when failure had to be faced. This was itself troubling. A warning sign. He was observing himself like an object, as if emotion were divorced from mind. He had strayed from his path, from the Tao.

An image of Hanae sadly bidding him good-bye flashed like silver in his mind. His wife had been unhappy for weeks. He had sensed it clearly but had shut it out, allowing her to protect him from whatever was the trouble. He must be ruthlessly honest. The truth was, he did not accept that he could fail, either in his job or in his marriage. But such confidence was unrealistic. A mask for his fear.

He *could* fail. Any attempt to salvage his case must be based on this truth. He could waste no more energy on protecting his ego from McCauley, or from himself. When he returned from Baltimore, he would have very little time. He must make the most of it. And despite any cost, he had much to gain from a very long talk with his wife.

He was nearing the bridge now and he reached to turn off the wipers. The snow, which had seemed to follow him from the city, had ceased.

🔱

Michael Darius, standing in the hallway, reached above the door frame for the key to the apartment. It was foolish putting the key here. Probably foolish to lock his door at all, since only the staff and a very few people had the code for the elevator keypad. But he had always locked his apartment, a symbolic thing no doubt, as symbolic as the hidden key had become. It was Margot who had started leaving the key above the door. It had stayed here since she'd left him, in some half-unconscious belief that someday she might come home and need it to get in.

Darius opened the door and, as if in a gesture of mere habit, put the key back into its place. He moved into the dark apartment and, tossing his coat on the sofa, crossed the room to the long windows. The night he looked into was cold and still. The snow with its stinging fury had died away—a torrent of white gnats that had plagued the day, matching his mood. An anxious restlessness he could not shake, even here.

He moved to the cabinet and took out a bottle of scotch. Poured himself a double. The message light on his phone was blinking, the light too irritating to ignore.

Sorry for wimping out on going back with you to Jimmy's office this afternoon. Willie's throaty voice, distinctive. *Catch you there tomorrow. . . . Oh, and, Michael, bring my notes. I left them on your coffee table.* A hesitation before the click, as if she might have said something more.

He sank into the corner of the sofa. Downed half of the scotch. He had been glad today when Willie had decided not to join him. Glad that Sakura had already been gone when he'd returned to Police Plaza. He had hoped that his time alone with the files might produce some fresh insight. It had not.

He finished the drink and stared into the darkness. Something was not right. His restlessness was an energy that buzzed inside these walls. He reached and switched on the lamp, as if the light might annul its piercing frequency. But his tension only increased.

He stood. Knowing where he was going. But not why.

Their bedroom was as he'd left it. But not the same. Beneath Margot's heady lingering of civet and roses, his and not his, the odor of peaches dying.

CHAPTER

20

The weather was again worsening by the hour. Clouds like dirty woolen batts seemed pinned into place. Working all day with Darius in Sakura's box of an office, Willie felt a gray oppression that was more than a reflection of the sky.

She was tired, physically exhausted with this ten-day roller coaster since Lucia Mancuso had died. She rubbed her eyes, looking at Michael across the space of the desk. He might have been a million miles away.

"Ten days," she said to him in the silence.

"What?" He lifted his head.

"It's ten days since Lucia. There were twelve days between Pinot and Kerry."

"And it was two weeks after Westlake before he killed Pinot." Darius's voice was flat, sounding as tired as she felt. "There's no pattern. He killed the first three in less than a week."

"I know," she said. "I just can't help wondering when he'll strike again."

He didn't comment, going back to whatever he was reading, sinking in, oblivious.

She continued to watch him for a while. He was a natural speed-reader, plowing quickly through boxes of files. She imagined him devouring case law in just the same way. He would pass the bar easily, she decided, if he ever bothered to take it.

"I want to get through everything," he said, looking up at her again. "But you go ahead." He made the effort to smile. "You look tired."

"You're telling me to go home, Michael?"

"Not if you don't want to."

"No, you're right." She gave in without a fight. "I am tired, and I'm not doing any good here. But I would like to look at my notes."

"Sorry. I don't usually forget things. Here . . ." He wrote some numbers on Jimmy's memo pad. "You can stop by my apartment. This is the code for the elevator." He tore off the paper. "You know where I keep the key."

"Thanks," she said. "Call me if you come up with anything . . . or if you just want to talk. I don't care how late."

She reached for the note, felt his fingers wrap around her wrist. He pulled her toward him across the desk. That thrill of fear with his kiss.

The odor of raw wood and stale cigarette smoke assaulted her as soon as she opened the door. In the half darkness, the white walls of the living room seemed unfixed, undulating like sheets of clouded water. She flipped the light switch. Her notes were just where she'd left them on the coffee table. She began to gather up the papers but stopped midway, turning toward the dark eye of the long hallway. Hanae's words teased. *After Margot left, he'd sworn never to go into the room again.*

She would have liked to have been above such petty intrigue, yet she wanted to see the room Michael had once shared with his wife. She left the notes with the key on the table and moved in search of a solid face of closed door.

She paused outside his workroom. She could see wood stacked in neat piles, tools shimmering like trophies from shelves on the walls. She'd seen the models, since the room he slept in was next to the workroom. She walked in, pressing the button on a fluorescent lamp on his desk. The cold light fell across an open text, onto a glossy photograph of the French cathedral of Sainte Chapelle. Scattered around the book were bold renderings of the church, notations and measurements scribbled in the margins. On his worktable was the model. A small architectural puzzle. She ran a finger around the curved lip of an arch. For a moment she thought of Michael's hands working the wood, playing the surfaces like a musical instrument. Then she thought of his hands playing her. What he did to her in bed was something less than making love, but a great deal more than simple fucking. She set the model down and shut off the lamp.

It was the last room on the left. She turned the door's brass handle. A thin band of urban neon slipped in through a break in the drapes, slashing across one wall, creating a bright green scar on the face of a painting. The walls were the color of ripe eggplant, the wood floors crisscrossed with Orientals. A carved four-poster bed, thick with pillows, stood high off the floor. A brocaded chaise stretched in a corner, an abandoned fashion magazine nearby. Everything had a baroque quality, at odds with the stark simplicity of the rest of the apartment.

On a dressing table perfume bottles glinted. A silver frame stood to one side. Moving closer, she lifted a black-and-white photograph. A younger Michael Darius stared back at her. The smile he wore never reached his eyes. The eyes, ancient even then.

Suddenly she felt uncomfortable, guilty for what she was doing. Unaccountably, the hairs on the back of her neck rose. The hiss caused her to drop the photograph. And in the last moments before the gas filled her lungs, she saw his dark reflection tripled in the panels of the dressing table's mirror.

🔱

She came to, bound and gagged, staring up at him, lying flat against the cushions of Michael's sofa. He was nude. Tall and lean. But not frail. She remembered the viselike grip of his latexed hand as it had closed over her face.

He appeared to be young, although it was impossible to tell. She could only imagine his human face. Behind the gas mask, he resembled a kamikaze pilot from an old newsreel, the rubber hose curling down like an esophagus from his nose to the tank at his waist.

"Dr. Wilhelmina French." His voice was hollow sounding, filtered through the tubing.

Her eyes shifted from the mask to her opened wallet in his gloved hands, to the remaining contents of her handbag scattered on the floor.

"I apologize for any discomfort." Insanely, he sounded sincere. "But some things are unavoidable." He shrugged his shoulders and touched the valve on the oxygen tank, making a slight adjustment. "I wasn't expecting you."

She twisted her head, fighting the tape over her mouth.

"I'm sorry I can't remove that. Or the restraints. You understand, of course. But, still, I wouldn't want you to be in pain. Is the sofa comfortable?"

It had been the odor of the leather that had registered first in her reviving consciousness. That, and the strange halting sound of his breathing. She focused on him again. He seemed more humanoid than human.

He set her wallet down, picking up her folder of notes from the coffee table. He glanced at its heading; then with the tip of a finger, he reached and found a spot on her cheek. He bent over. The breathing hose brushed against her shoulder.

He stepped away from the sofa. "You know who I am?" His voice gurgled inside the rubber as he rose to his full height.

She nodded her head.

"I'm an interesting specimen, Dr. French, am I not?" His laugh reverberated inside the mask. He glanced down and began examining her notes. "But you do not understand." He looked up. "I do not kill them. I release them."

He came closer and squatted. "I do for them what they are unable to do for themselves. I awaken them to who they are."

Her eyes widened, asking, *Who are they?*

She somehow knew he frowned behind the mask. "I know it's been confusing—five men, one little girl. But they are all the same." He shook his head. "Human words are so inadequate."

She raised her brows.

He backed away again, withdrawing a page from the folder. "I see you have made some interesting observations, Dr. French."

She fixed her eyes on him.

He read aloud from her transcribed notes. "'A serial killer seems not to be able to distinguish himself as a separate entity. Cannot distinguish himself from other human beings. Cannot even distinguish himself from things. There are no boundaries. Bodies are objects. The act of murder is the disposition of flesh, not the taking of life.'" He stopped his recitation.

Her eyes remained on him.

"Does not apply, Dr. French." He allowed the page he'd been holding to slip to the floor.

He moved to stand before the window, where night fell hungrily. The room close to dark. He walked to a bag he'd left near the sofa and reached in for a sealed package. Quickly he tore into the plastic sheathing and pulled out a syringe.

"I meant it when I said I wouldn't want you to be in pain, Dr. French."

The office was quiet, and dark with the fluorescents turned off overhead. Darius closed the folder on the file he'd been reading and pushed it out of the yellow circle made by the cantilevered desk lamp. He relaxed against the chair back, tilting it into shadow. His hands rubbed at his eyes, tested the stubble on his cheeks. He was avoiding the squad room, and his coffee mug had been empty for an hour. He didn't want to see anyone. Didn't want to talk.

He bent down and pulled open the bottom drawer of the desk. The bottle of whiskey rumbled amid Sakura's tea things. He set it down with a glass and poured a healthy double, which burned liquid fire all the way down to his stomach. Food was what he needed. Food and sleep. But he didn't want to stop and break the continuity he'd established. It was a fact that the wide net cast by most serial-murder investigations took in the killer early on. The problem was seeing the important details amidst the sheer mass of data.

He poured another thumb into the glass. That weirdness last night in his apartment was a symptom that he was becoming obsessed. He was in danger of letting this case get to him in the same way that Hudson had, with that sense of something half recognized, some substrata of knowledge that nagged at him.

He sipped on the whiskey—this one had to last—and angled the lamp upward to the blackboard, to the close-ups of the victims that were tacked around the frame. He ignored the faces, permitting himself to see only anonymous white flesh. The glyphlike ash markings, broken bull's-eyes on the chests, looked like purpling bruises.

The thought was a charge that jerked him around in the chair, to the console that held Jimmy's books. In moments he had readjusted the light and was rifling through the standard text on forensics for the picture that had finally been triggered like a ticking bomb in his brain.

He almost laughed when he found it.

⁂

Darius relived it through the sudden haze. Rushing out of Jimmy's office, thinking that there was a trail to be followed now. Accident reports to be gathered. Cross-checks to be run with the witness and canvass lists. He had been eager to get home.

He'd wanted to think about it all some more before he talked to Jimmy. And Willie. He'd been hoping she might be waiting in his apartment.

He had known that she was, when the key was not in its place and the knob had turned in his hand. He had seen her almost immediately when he went in, bound and gagged on the sofa, her notes scattered on the rug. Her eyes trying to warn him. But the force of it had hardly registered before the sudden hiss. The gas hitting him full as he'd turned.

He awoke on the sofa, naked and bound. Not gagged. But there was no one else coming for him to warn. No one else on the floor to hear him. No one on any floor who could hear him, thanks to the building's construction.

Willie was now on the love seat, which had been pushed across the room. He could see only a small part of her. Could discern some bit of motion. He prayed she was still unharmed.

A man stood near him, nude like himself. His fingers, dipped in ash, were busy writing letters on the wall. On the coffee table syringes were neatly arranged.

He had never been afraid to die. Indeed, he had always felt a kind of unacknowledged eagerness that made him physically fearless. What he felt most now was anger for his carelessness. And what it meant for Willie. Lack of food and sleep was not an excuse, nor was the alcohol. These were decisions that he'd made. The sort of bad choices from which he never learned.

Discovering what he had tonight had proved a hollow triumph. Obviously, the killer had long ago discovered him. Had he not sensed a lingering presence in this apartment only last night, but ignored the warning? He had a morbid curiosity as to just how and why he'd been targeted as a victim. But he would hardly give the satisfaction of asking.

As if he'd sensed this, the killer turned to him now. He walked to the sofa and knelt down, taking his head in his hands. The grip was not cruel, but strong. Resistance futile. The man bent down, his eyes inches from Darius's own. "An interesting face," he said, letting go. Then, as if in answer to his question, "Your light fills this room."

Darius threw his head toward Willie, letting go his resolution not to speak. "And her light?" If there were any chance at all for him or Willie, it was to keep this bastard talking. Buy them a little time.

The man's glance had followed his. "Dr. French is not one of the Fallen."

"You mean she's not a fallen angel."

The killer smiled. "Completely human."

"So there's no need for you to hurt her?"

"She'll wake up in a little while with nothing worse than a headache."

"And you'll let her go?"

The smile became brighter. "What happens to her is up to you . . . if we're successful."

He ignored the ambiguity. "Let her go first," he said. "Once I know she's safe, I'll do whatever you want."

The man rose to his feet. "You still see only the shells," he said, ". . . body bags. But you'll understand soon. I promise." He reached for the plate of ash, began to draw.

Darius looked down at the pattern taking form on his chest. "Were you the one whose heart stopped . . . in the car accident?"

The question worked to catch the man off guard. He rocked back on his heels. "Yes." He was smiling again. "That was the moment of my awakening. . . . You know a lot," he said. He made a larger circle in ash around the smaller center. "But you know nothing." He stared into his eyes.

His own temper flared. "Goddamn you."

Laughter. "He already has."

The world was cold outside her window. Hanae could feel the chill beating like a bird at the glass, could imagine the snow. The phone was still in her hand. She returned it to its cradle and leaned back into the pillows on her bed. She had enjoyed talking to Vicky for as long as the call had lasted. Now it felt like nothing at all had been said, that the bonds between them had only further loosened.

And the restlessness that had prompted the call had not at all decreased. She picked up the phone again, dialing Willie's number. The machine answered with Dr. Jamili's voice, inviting her to leave a message. Willie was no doubt still at work, as consumed with this case as Jimmy. She did not want to disturb her friend at the office.

She hung up the phone. It seemed she had been fidgeting since yesterday, attempting to fill the hours since Jimmy had left with household chores. With books and music. Nothing held her attention. She might have tried again to work the clay, but she did not want to think about the bust. Or her call from Adrian Lovett.

But she had thought about it all day. His wanting to give her a present. She had not known what to say. She had felt a guilty awkwardness, the shame for allowing that kiss. She could avoid class next Monday, only a week before Christmas. But she must not be a coward. She must face Adrian and make it clear in the kindest way that there could be nothing between them.

She got up from the bed and went into the kitchen to fix the meal she did not want, hoping that Jimmy would call tonight, wondering what he might be doing at this moment.

A few days ago she had been at the point of telling him about the baby when the call had come about the priest's suicide. A sad death. But at least it had seemed the investigation was over, that she need be patient but a few days more. Jimmy would be winding down the task force, would at last be free of the pressures that had claimed so much of his attention.

But that had all changed with yesterday's press conference. She had listened to it on TV. She had realized from the moment that the woman reporter spoke about the locket that the case was not over at all and that her husband would be held responsible for what must seem incompetence.

A few hours later, Jimmy had come home, saying little as he packed for Baltimore. She had stood in the door of their bedroom as he'd moved to and from the closet, willing him to share with her something of what he was feeling. She longed for words, though the tenor of his silence was completely comprehensible. They were not to acknowledge that he could be hurt. She was not to bear any part of his burden. Such a hateful strength.

He had kissed her before he'd left. A real kiss that had softened her pain and kindled the hope she cherished even now, that on his return they would yet walk backward together to the place where their paths had been one.

The cloying incense woke her. Willie smelled it before she heard the voices. As wan and feeble as the light was, it had started pain throbbing in her head. She was lying under a blanket, still bound by tape—stiff and sore in the places where she wasn't numb. Whatever drug she'd been given had certainly knocked her out.

She squeezed her lids shut, resisting the urge to slip back into unconsciousness. The dull thudding in her skull had an edge of razor sharpness that shifted as she tried to change position. She reopened her eyes slowly, letting the pain stabilize in a tight band that anchored itself in her temples. Slowly, by degrees, she turned her head. Her arms were useless. She dug her heels into the leather, pushing herself upward, propping herself against the love seat's padded frame.

The killer was still in the room, bending over the sofa, yards away. The words she'd heard spoken had not been meant for her. Her brain registered that another nude man, his wrists and ankles bound, was lying on the sofa. Registered what her mind continued to deny, until the killer stepped away and forced her eyes to acknowledge—that Michael was the man on the sofa. She could see his face in profile and the dark sooty circles moving on his chest with his breathing. She wondered if he knew that she was here.

The man straightened, turning to the coffee table. For the first time she could see something of his face. It appeared an ordinary, even handsome, face. Composed and focused. On the wall above the sofa, foot-high letters spelled out *SAMYAZA* in ash.

She fell flat into the cushions.

I wasn't expecting you. The killer's words came back to her. He'd been hiding in the apartment, even before she'd arrived, lying in wait for Michael. Question on question crowded in her brain. Too many to sort out, and they weren't what was important now. She did not want to just lie here and wait for both of them to die. She fought against the restraints that bound her wrists and ankles, her hands searching over their short range for something, anything, that she might use to cut through the tape. But there was nothing.

She dug her heels again into the frame of the love seat, lifting herself, her head throbbing sullenly with the effort. The killer, with a syringe in his hand, was turning back to the sofa. She saw Darius stiffen and fought reflexively against the tape that held her wrists. She wanted to cry out, but even without the gag, any protest would be worse than ineffective. It could only add to Michael's pain.

The man began to speak, his voice entirely calm and reasonable. He was beginning the programming. It was the LSD that he had injected into Darius. Terrified as she was, she could not help her fascination. She listened as the killer droned patiently on, constructing the reality he wanted Michael to share, his belief that fallen angels were trapped in human bodies. Angels who must be awakened.

It seemed to go on for hours, but she had no real sense of time. Darius remained quiet, and she wondered what he was feeling. LSD could magnify every paranoid fear that floated in a subject's brain. He had to know, as she did, that he was going to die. The drug could only amplify that horror.

She was sunk again in the cushions, still fighting hopelessly with her bonds, when the killer's voice changed. He had begun a guttural chant, something vaguely Semitic. She dug in again with her feet and struggled upward. He had moved from his seat on the rug to kneel at the end of the sofa, and taking hold of Michael's feet, he kissed them.

The gesture was shocking.

Darius recoiled, his body writhing whitely on the sofa, but the killer crawled on top of him. She could hear the name Samyaza repeated again and again as he inched upward, touching his lips to every part of

Michael's body. The sensory stimulation would be magnified by the LSD. She was not surprised at Michael's erection.

She resisted the impulse to close her eyes. What had she to give him but her witness?

The ritual went on and on, until there was no resistance—the process, hideous in its madness, intended to prepare Darius for some imagined experience beyond death. The killer's monologue building and building, taking it further. Explaining, as if it were rational, what it was he expected from Michael.

Suddenly the flash came, through the fog of her fear and the pain that still throbbed in her head. She understood what it was that the killer planned.

At last the man sat up. She watched him reach for another syringe, his grip on Darius's arm . . . holding it.

"You know what this is." He held the needle to the light. "I don't pretend it will be pleasant. . . . Your heart will fight."

Again Darius resisted, but the needle went in. His body bowed upward. She heard him gasp, continuing to struggle. But the process, inexorable now, had begun.

Her body arced stiffly within the love seat's frame; she watched as the killer hovered closely, monitoring Michael's breathing. Then another syringe, the second a small and diluted dose of potassium. Waiting . . . waiting . . . his fingers on Michael's throat, checking the pulse in the carotid artery. And then the third injection.

The dying did not take long. Darius's breathing faltered, slowed to agonal. Fish blowing . . . one breath . . . two . . . three. None.

Something inside her stopped. She watched without real hope as the killer picked up the final syringe and plunged the needle quickly into Michael's arm.

🔺

The traffic, even for this time of evening, seemed abnormally heavy. Sakura drove tensely, his shoulders held flat against the seat, accepting, as if it were penance, the unnatural cold that seeped from the black vinyl to penetrate his coat. With the ice storm that was now predicted for the East Coast, he had left the conference early.

He peered through the wipers and the dirty fall of sleet beyond the windshield. He wanted to be home, was conscious of a need to see his wife.

He found his cell phone and punched in the squad room number. It was Kelly who answered.

"You still there, Pat?"

"What else? . . . Where are you?"

"On my way home. Anything happening?"

The answer was a grunt. Then, "Your partner was here earlier."

"Darius?"

"Yeah. And I don't know, but I think he might have found something. He passed through the squad room without saying a word. But . . . you know, he just had that look."

"Okay, Pat. Thanks."

He stared at the phone. It was possible Darius really had found something. He started to call but changed his mind. He should be in the city in a couple of hours. Better to go straight to Michael's apartment.

From inside the warmth of the Sakura apartment, Adrian watched slow cartwheels of snow descend, white pinwheels half suspended against the softer layers of deepening night. Small drifts, like cake icing, had already accumulated on the ledge. He touched the window-pane and felt the mounting cold. He exhaled, observing how his warm breath formed an exact circle on the glass.

He had heard surprise in her voice, mixed with—was it uneasiness?—when he'd announced himself. Had there still been a moment when she might have refused him? But in the end she had let him come up. Come in with his Christmas gift in hand.

He turned from the window. He still wore his parka.

"It's snowing again," he said.

"Yes, I know." She had come back into the room, carrying a small tray. Steam from a glazed pot of tea veiled her face like mist around a pale moon.

"You've been out?"

"No, I listened to the weather report this evening. Please sit." She had set down the tray.

"And how do you know I'm standing?"

"The level of your voice." She sat on one of the low cushions.

He moved to sit across from her, watching as she began pouring tea into small porcelain cups. "Everything looks different under snow," he said. "As though the world's hiding."

"Truth to be revealed in spring," she said.

He noticed that the center part in her hair made a fine white seam against the black. "I shouldn't have kissed you," he said.

She lifted her face. "It stands between us now."

"I'm sorry, Hanae."

"It is no one's fault." She handed him tea.

He took the cup, wanting to say more, but gave her his present instead. "I hope you like it."

She smiled, untying the bow, tearing away the paper. The tissue crinkling like thin ice as she dug deep into the box. "A hat," she said merrily, running her fingers around its wide brim.

"What color?" he asked.

She closed her eyes, her fingers resting lightly on the crown. "Blue."

"How do you do that?"

She laughed.

"Try it on."

She lifted the hat, anchored it on her head, and tugged a bit on the brim.

"Perfect. You look beautiful."

She lowered her head, removing the hat. "Thank you," she said.

"Is Jimmy happy about the baby?"

"Yes." She was looking up again, her dark eyes finding his. "Jimmy is happy."

He should have been pleased that she lied, but somehow he wasn't.

"I must give you your Christmas gift," she said, standing now.

With Taiko trailing, she walked to a small fir winking with white lights and dotted with red fans and paper birds. She held up a brightly colored envelope. "*Washi,*" she said. "In ancient Japan seeds and condiments were treasured. They were concealed in paper folds and given to special friends." She extended her arm, offering him her gift.

"Thank you, Hanae," he said, taking the envelope.

"*Arigato gozaimasu.*" She made a small bow.

He turned now, back to the window, unzipping his parka at last. "It's snowing harder."

"Yes," she said, her blind eyes following his. "It is making music in the air."

For the third time Sakura knocked, though he no longer expected an answer. There was a stillness emanating from the closed door that convinced him that Darius's apartment was empty. He admitted to a certain fear. Michael was quite capable of playing the lone wolf.

He stood where he was in the hallway and regulated the pattern of his breath. First calm, then thought. But quietness brought the smell of incense. The scent from the crime scenes had lodged itself in his brain. Perhaps it would always be there. He focused again, breathing slowly in and out, trying to convince himself that the unanswered knock did not mean trouble, conscious suddenly that the odor of incense was real.

The adrenaline was instant. He groped above the door, but the key was not where Darius kept it. He unholstered his gun and kicked. The door exploded into silence.

CHAPTER

21

The windows of the hospital waiting room were black-mirrored glass. Outside the snow still fell. Jimmy couldn't see it. The windows kept everything inside.

He felt trapped in unreality, his thoughts a loop that endlessly replayed. Willie and Michael stalked and taken by the very killer they'd been seeking. In the instant he'd exploded into Michael's apartment, time had ceased, burning into his brain a final sharp-edged image chiseled from the stuff of nightmares. Willie bound on the leather love seat, Michael laid out nude on the sofa. And on the wall, the letters *S-A-M-Y-A-Z-A*, in dark ash.

Then the ambulance, its wail adding sound to the horror, its running lights flashing cellophane red in the barely born morning. Michael taken out on a stretcher, lying in the well of the van, his face all but covered by a clear mask, his vitals closely monitored by one of the paramedics. And Willie in the back, wrapped in blankets, her hand reaching out to clasp his before the two white rectangles of doors closed.

And after, the CSU spilling out like small insects from a mound, crawling over Michael's apartment, leaving behind trails of fingerprint dust, the aftermath of explosions of light from cameras. He'd been pleased when Tannehill finally showed up. Not so comfortable when the precinct officers arrived. But they had had to be called, with a caution that the situation had to fly under the radar. Publicly, the attack could not be connected to the serial. The press had to be kept out.

The lack of a body would probably buy them some time. And then to Kelly, whom he'd left in charge as he'd taken off for the hospital sometime after midnight, with an appeal to contain McCauley as long as possible.

Now in the hospital, sitting still, waiting for hours, the mental picture had slowly begun to fade, melting into softer contours, colors bleeding into each other like a Monet painting. As he turned, watching Willie move toward him, a small specter in the loose white folds of a hospital robe, the image seemed never to have existed at all.

"Jimmy . . ." She walked into his arms, hugged him.

"How do you feel?" he asked, looking down at her. She appeared tired, shadows half-mooned under her eyes.

"I'm fine." She smiled.

"You don't look so fine."

"Thanks, Sakura, just what I needed—a critique on my looks." She laughed. "They want to do a more detailed blood screen. See exactly what it was the killer pumped into my veins."

"Michael?"

"He's conscious, but still pretty much out of it. I went into his room earlier for a moment, but I don't think he was even aware I was there. He was lucky, Jimmy. I don't believe there's any permanent damage, but they've still got him rigged up to a heart monitor."

"Feel like talking?"

"Sure." Willie moved toward a line of plastic chairs. "It was all pretty bizarre."

He pulled a chair close to hers.

"How did you know he planned to resuscitate Michael?"

"He talked about it all. . . . It seemed forever," she said. "I just didn't think he could pull it off. It's a miracle he did."

"Why didn't he let Michael die like the others?"

"Michael was supposed to take his place."

"Take his place? You mean *killing* people?"

She shook her head, curling up tighter inside the robe, pulling the cuffs over wrists already purpling. "In his mind he isn't killing anybody. He's awakening fallen angels. It's part of his fantasy. I didn't get it all. Some of what he said was in Hebrew, I think."

"Killing is supposed to free the victims?"

She nodded. "But it's a hell of a lot more complicated than that. That's why he's using the LSD."

"What about the LSD?"

"I was pretty much right about what he's doing with the drug. He's attempting to simulate for his victims his own near-death experience."

"His own?"

"Yes. Apparently, he nearly died himself. I don't know how or when, but that event could have been the trigger for all this. Some over-whelmingly traumatic experience that sent him over the edge."

He watched her pull on her hair, turning a strand of it round and round her finger. "Are you saying that a brush with death turned this man into a serial killer?"

She shrugged. "Remember, in his reality he's not killing them. What he wants is to force them to remember who they are before they experience death. Force them to remember they were once angels, kicked out of Heaven because they wanted bodies. The LSD is supposed to help them remember so they'll be prepared before he gives them the injections of the potassium chloride to stop their hearts."

"Prepared to do what?"

"Resist reincarnation as humans. Go back to being angels. Wait around to take back Heaven."

"Wait?"

"Behind some kind of barrier. He thinks if he can awaken enough fallen angels, they'll be able to force their way through."

"So, our killer thinks he's a fallen angel too."

"Yes."

"What I still don't understand is how he targeted Michael, or any of the victims for that matter."

"He said something about being able to see lights around the fallen."

"Lights?"

"Auras, he sees auras. And because Michael's was somehow brighter, he was the one selected to take his place. The killer had to bring him just close enough to death to remember who he was, but not let him die. With Michael, he had to alter the ritual. And since there wasn't going to be a kill, you didn't see any wings. Michael's doses of potassium to induce heart failure had to be well calculated. Everything was timing—the injection of the antidote to reverse the effects of the potassium, the mouth-to-mouth resuscitation. As I said, the killer wanted Michael to take his place. Which may be his way of telling us he's finished. Serials do that." She closed her eyes. "I told you it was complicated."

"You need to get back to your room."

"I'm okay. Have you talked to Hanae?"

"Not yet. She's not expecting me until later today."

"Probably best not to tell her over the phone what's happened."

He nodded.

"How's this going to play at Police Plaza?"

"McCauley will want me off the case."

"He can't do that."

"*Zanshin*. That's when a samurai's gut warns him something bad is about to happen."

"What are you going to do?"

His laugh was bitter. "Avoid McCauley as long as I can."

"And . . ."

"Kelly said Michael might have found something in my office right before the attack. I'd like to know what it was."

"So would I."

"I'll call you," he said. Then, "If you need anything, Adelia or one of the men will be around."

"You don't think . . . ?" She didn't finish.

"No." He shook his head. "But it's better to be careful."

Darius lay on his back in the bed, his lower body hemmed in by starched sheets, his arms free but wedded to IV tubes. Sensors attached to his chest fed a heart monitor, which bleeped cardiac contractions across a blue screen. A biography of electrical impulses. A life reduced to jagged lines.

Sakura moved to the side of the bed, placed his hand against the cool aluminum railing. Michael's face was clear, except for a green tube, forking into both nostrils, that piped in oxygen. His eyes were open, dark and immense, staring at something out of Sakura's reach.

For a moment he watched his chest rise and fall with reassuring regularity.

"Michael, it's Jimmy." He reached inside the fence of rails and clasped his hand. "You're going to be okay."

Darius was paler than he'd ever seen him, paler than after the Hudson shooting. A pallor that seemed manufactured, as though chalk had been rubbed into his pores. A whiteness that lay on the flesh rather than existed as part of it. Yet the black hair pulled back from his forehead seemed alive. A thing apart from the rest of the body. Like the eyes.

The eyes shifted now. "Willie . . ." Her name more breath than sound.

"She's fine."

The eyes closed.

"Michael, I have to know. What did you find in my office?"

The lids lifted.

"Kelly said . . ."

Darius's lips came together, struggling to form meaning. Jimmy bent over, felt Michael's fingers tighten around his wrist. But the single word was unintelligible.

※

Zoe walked into the marble lobby, looking appropriately grim. Hospitals gave her the creeps. But despite this aversion, she had carefully cultivated sources in every major facility in the city, staff people who could tip her off to celebrity and crime victim admissions. She had gotten more than one exclusive delivering flowers, even posing once as a grief counselor.

There would be no elaborate subterfuge today that might only get her spotted. She would simply walk down the hallway to scope things out. Hope for the break that she needed.

Since the now famous press conference, she'd devoted her byline to proclaiming Thomas Graff a police scapegoat. With his suicide, a sacrificial lamb. WHO'S NEXT? TEN DAYS AND COUNTING! were the headlines for today's cover. Zinging it home once again that the man who'd murdered little Lucia Mancuso was still out there, and that anyone at all could be the target of his homicidal rage.

Except that no one had.

Where was the killer? There had been lulls like this before, but something kept telling her that this wasn't the dry spell it appeared. Which was why she was here so early. She'd jumped at the tip from her source who claimed that James Sakura had been here visiting a patient.

And no ordinary patient. This one had been checked in under a "John Doe" and put into a private room. Security on the hall too, according to her man. Plainclothes. Discreet. Something important was definitely going down.

She took the elevator up and got out, avoiding the attention of the nurses at the central station. Visitors would not be allowed in for hours.

She stood frozen in the hallway as she saw him come out of the target room. He looked dead on his feet. Shirt opened at the neck. Tie pulled loose. He needed a shave. But none of it made him appear any less desirable. She hadn't realized just how much she missed him. She watched him shove his hands into the pockets of his pants and slump against the wall.

It had to be somebody important if they had Rozelli watching the door. Somebody connected to the serial.

She started walking again. The heels of her shoes registering as soft clicks on the polished tile. He must have heard her because he turned then.

For one instant he smiled. That patented smirk that flashed the perfect white teeth and made his eyes go slanty. A reflex, done without thinking, as though nothing ugly had passed between them. Then as quickly, his face emptied, went blank. She would have settled for anger.

"Hi, Rozelli. Long time no see."

He shifted, bending one leg so that the flat of his foot rested against the wall.

"How the mighty have fallen, if they have you pulling guard duty." She couldn't resist. "Unless . . ."

"There's nothing here for you, Zoe." His voice as expressionless as his face. Then the jingle of some coins in his pocket before his foot came away from the wall and he moved back inside the room.

She stood staring at the door. Shut in her face. But oh, how wrong he was. On both counts. She wasn't finished covering the investigation that had gotten her star billing on every cable news program in the country. And she wasn't nearly finished with Johnny Rozelli.

The Manhattan sky was still overcast as morning dawned. Sakura, on his way home, drove with the patience of exhaustion. It was snowing again when he reached the rental garage. He walked along the pavement in a cloud of tiny flakes.

White lights winked around the windows of several apartments, and a surge of holiday spirit hit him like a blunted punch. Christmas was less than two weeks away. He'd almost let the season slip. One of many things he'd neglected since these murders had started.

He shivered in the cold. He hoped Hanae had turned up the thermostat in the apartment. He imagined she would, if only for her finches. She preferred the cold. He smiled, thinking how she'd always given him the greater share of the goose down in their comforter. The image of her chubby hands kneading the fabric like dough flashed through his mind. How he wished he could crawl under that dense mound of feathers, if only for a couple of hours, pulling Hanae over to his side of the bed. But he'd have time for little more than a shower and a shave. He was determined to find what Michael had discovered in whatever time he had.

Which could not be much. Despite the debate that still raged in the media over the "debunking" of the locket, the public at large had taken comfort in the belief that Thomas Graff might still be the killer. That would no longer be possible when word got out of a new attack, an attack moreover on his own people. He was going to look a fool. McCauley would take pleasure in handing him his head.

He went into the building, up the stairs, and pushed his key into the lock.

Even years later, it would seem that his eyes had not betrayed him in that moment as he stood in the *genkan*—that the white silk of the ceremonial marriage kimono was in fact her pale naked flesh, that the long sleeves hanging from the pole were the bright unblemished wings of a swan. A portent that caused him to misinterpret reality.

"Hanae . . . ?" he called out, his voice distorted in his ears as he forced himself to look up, to see the kimono hanging in place as he removed his shoes in the *genkan*.

"Hanae . . . ?" He moved into the living room, his concern only growing with her failure to answer.

Taiko lay on the floor near the sofa. Not sleeping. Drugged. That was apparent in the dog's sharp and shallow breathing, the marked dilation of the pupils in half-lidded eyes.

"Hanae . . . ?" He was trying to remain calm. Trying to tell himself that she was asleep in their bedroom. That Taiko was not drugged but only sleeping, despite the evidence.

Hanae was not in their bedroom or anywhere else in the apartment. It was possible that Taiko had become sick. That the drug was something that Hanae herself had given him. He must call Mr. Romero. The driver would know where she was.

But Mr. Romero did not. Nor did the neighbors.

He moved about the apartment like an automaton. Searching for clues. For an answer to how long she'd been gone. A pain that was not physical tore at his heart and brain. He wanted to force back the clock. To make this not be. He sat down on the sofa.

After a moment he stood, not knowing what it was he was doing as his feet moved to the worktable and his hands removed the cloth that covered the clay. The bust that Hanae had been working on was shrouded in sheets of plastic. He began to remove the layers, like unwrapping a winding sheet from a corpse.

The face he revealed was cold and gray, but alive with the soul that his wife's fingers had imparted. If the bust had once mimicked the shape of his head and its planes the lines of his face, that had largely been lost beyond some lingering echo. He stood there, unthinking. Then moved without volition. Felt the nose explode beneath the bludgeon of his fist. He hit it again and again, smashing the face. The clay absorbing the force of his fury as it deformed beneath his blows, till the energy of his emotion was as blunted as the ruined features.

But the core of his rage burned inward. And remained.

✴

Terror shrieked like a living thing inside her brain. The force of it silencing her power to give it voice. She was seized by blackness. Suspended in the kind of void she had never been allowed to experience since her birth. Alone. Abandoned in the living darkness. Stripped. As if her other senses had followed in the wake of her sight.

She was naked. Physically naked. Beneath her, crisp sheets made a boundary.

Hanae seized on that. Curled. Wrapped her arms around her. Breathed consciously. In. Out. Finding her limit. A context for thought. A concept, a reference point, rose in her mind. The memory of the slugs in her grandmother's garden. Naked, quivering. . . .

The terror shook her, threatening her mind. She bit her lip. Tasted blood. Fought.

Slowly the void retreated. In her head a dull thudding ache. In her stomach a sick queasiness. Sound returned. She heard the fire, sap popping in logs. Felt the heat as a difference at one side of her face. A fireplace was a few yards away. The room that contained it was large. She experienced its size in the quality of the silence it contained. Beyond was a deeper stillness.

What has happened?

A flash through the haze. A sudden memory of walking, half supported, down the stairs from her apartment. Of being helped inside a car. An impression of motion that went on and on. The realization they were driving out of the city.

Adrian. She was remembering more of it now. She had let him come up to the apartment, despite her surprise at his unannounced appearance on her doorstep. There had been a moment's hesitation, but then she'd considered how she must face him sometime, tell him there could be nothing but friendship between them.

She unwrapped her arms and struggled up against the pillows, her hands searching outward at air, fighting the nausea, the pain in her head that sharpened and sliced through her stupor.

What has he done to me? To Taiko? The terror returned. Precise now. Fear penetrating her confusion. Fear and shame. *How could I let this happen? What will Jimmy think?*

And then the real fear as her helplessness came into focus, the depth of her danger.

She swallowed and breathed deep, trying to keep the fog from her mind. Tears welled in her eyes as she clutched with her hands at her belly. She wept for her child and was still. Listening now, gathering information in the quiet, till understanding wound like a serpent in her heart. She was not alone, nor had been. Adrian watched in the dark.

⁂

There were two James Sakuras now. The husband whose heart raced with the horror of things imagined, whose mind was screaming to hurry with the fear that even now it might be too late. And then there was the other, the automaton who meticulously, if fruitlessly, searched his apartment for clues to the identity behind the clay face. The robot without emotion already planning to hide the information that would absolutely bar him from a case in which he'd committed the sin of becoming both its subject and its object. The iron man scheming. The husband praying for the miracle that would make a rescue possible. For beyond the need for proof, he knew what others might not believe—that the attack on Michael had been but the first act in this suddenly personal drama, that the man whose face he'd destroyed in the clay had also taken his wife.

In the beginner's mind there are many possibilities, but in the expert's mind there are few. Suzuki-roshi's phrase had become insistent, sprung from some hidden reservoir. He had to leave behind the training that had not served. He must find again his beginner's mind, accept his own *suchness*. He was not so separate from the evil he pursued. The chaos, which he sought to control, breathed with his breath . . . was everywhere.

He watched himself as if from some far distance, returning to headquarters, avoiding the officers who were awaiting his address in the operations room. The mood was chaotic, the task force having been in a kind of limbo since Graff's suicide and the subsequent loss of the physical evidence that had tied him to the crime. He went straight to his office and ignored the messages on his phone demanding his presence in the chief of detectives' office.

Kelly came in, eyeing him strangely as if sensing some of what lay beneath the robot veneer.

"You have any idea what Michael might have been looking at last night?" he asked.

Kelly shook his head. "Like I told you, I didn't talk to Darius, didn't see him till he was leaving." He shifted subjects, saying what he'd come in here to say. "The chief's looking for you."

"I hear that too." He glanced down at his desk, his eyes hungry for the search. "Look, I need some time in here alone. No disturbances."

"Sure," Kelly said. "I'll pass the word along. You're not here, Lieutenant. Haven't even logged in yet."

"Thanks, Pat." He could see the questions in the vet's eyes. Understood that he wouldn't ask them.

Alone, the urgency flared. He scanned the desk, then down at the boxes of files still stacked on the floor. What had Michael been looking at? He turned back to his desk, where everything appeared much as he'd left it. Except for the book. The DiMaio text on forensics had been taken from the console.

He checked the index. Turned to the back, to the chapter on drug deaths. He went quickly through the topics, slowing at the sections on homicidal poisonings, but nothing stood out.

His phone rang. He ignored it. Something in this book was a clue to a fact they had missed. He forced himself to proceed logically, skimming the general topics. Then page by page, faster and faster, eyes scanning down through the text, moving quickly through the pictures.

He stopped turning. Flipped the page back. The illustration was in the section on nonpedestrian deaths. *Figure 9.5. Imprint of steering wheel on chest.* Concentric broken circles. Lines coming down. The pattern imprinted below the sternum. He read rapidly through the accompanying text to the paragraph that stopped him:

> Occasionally, one will have a motor vehicle accident in which the driver impacts the steering wheel and in which there is no anatomical cause of death after a complete autopsy and toxicological screen. There may be

> soft tissue damage to the chest and a fractured sternum
> or ribs, but not enough injuries to explain death. Such
> deaths are due to a cardiac contusion, with the mecha-
> nism of death being a fatal arrhythmia.

A fatal arrhythmia. The mechanism of death in the victims. So this
was what Michael had found. The ash drawings on the victims' chests
were meant to mimic the bruising that resulted from impact with a
steering wheel. The drawings were a clue to the killer's fantasy, which
somehow involved a car crash.

He remembered what Willie had said this morning about the killer
claiming to have had his own near-death experience, about some
event that could have been the trigger for these murders. A car accident? A wreck in which the killer himself had suffered a cardiac con-
tusion? According to the book, recovery was usual if the victim
received treatment in time.

He slumped back in the chair. The theory made some kind of sense.
It hung together. But it didn't explain everything. Like exactly how a
car accident linked up with fallen angels.

But that didn't matter. He didn't care about *how* or *why.* What he had
to know was *who.*

He cleared the space in front of him, pulled over the computer.
Thank the gods for Talbot and his insistence that everything be com-
puterized. With luck he would have what he needed, could access the
necessary public records.

He began with accident reports for the state of New York, compiling
a three-year period to include this one. Car accidents involving cardiac injuries. Then the cross-check. Run the list of cardiac injuries
against the master list—every name that had come up over the course
of the investigation from canvass reports, interviews, printouts, all the
DD-5's.

It took him longer than expected to set it all up. But finally he ran
the program . . . and waited.

There were several last names that tallied, but only one exact hit. A
name on the list of exhibitors from the Milne gallery matched with a
car crash victim. It took more time to pull up the accident report.

A Land Rover, an older model, had hit a disabled truck. The passenger in the vehicle, a woman, had died instantly of catastrophic head trauma. But the driver had survived multiple injuries, including an impact injury that had required resuscitation at the scene. He stared at the name: *Adrian Lovett.* Copied the address from the gallery list.

The phone was ringing. He could feel his heart beating again, steady as a metronome against its electronic bleating. He stood and replaced his issue weapon with the hideout gun from his ankle holster. Took out his badge.

Kelly stopped him as he passed through the squad room. "The chief's coming down."

He nodded, already moving again. "I left what he wants on my desk."

Hanae sat rigid, perfectly still at the side of the bed, clutching the bedclothes around her. She had been gathering the will to acknowledge his presence, to ask him the questions whose answers she feared, but Adrian had slipped from the room. She had tracked his almost silent footfalls as they moved on wood and carpet; heard the quiet opening and closing of the door, the latch turning, slipping bolt into lock.

How had she not sensed that Adrian was a threat? Why had the most dangerous thing about him seemed the kiss she'd half allowed? She had been reckless with more than her marriage. Her hands went to her belly, to Jimmy's child. How could she ever explain to him what had brought her to this place? If she died, she never would.

She stood, pulling the sheet from the bed, wrapping it around her. The room was warm from the fire, but her nakedness reinforced her vulnerability. She retraced Adrian's footsteps to the door and tested the lock.

She had a sudden flash of memory. Exploring her uncle's house. Hide-and-seek with her cousins. A favorite game in which she had excelled. Her blindness, in the end, an advantage. She was aware of sounds that sighted people missed, could sense even distant movement. She felt form and color in the energy that played against her

skin and beat at the tips of her fingers. She had sometimes wondered if the world in her head was more, not less, complete because she could not see, her information more widely gathered. This room, this space, was alien, but she was blind, not helpless. If there was a way out, she could find it.

The room's one window was large but fixed. Double paned, she was sure, against the outside temperature. Still, with her hands upon its surface, she could feel the outdoor cold. Her ear pressed against the glass, she could hear beyond the tide of her blood nothing but a deep rural stillness. Perhaps the stillness of water. *How far have we come from the city?*

She continued her search but found no phone, no clothes or anything else in the closet or the wide chest of drawers. The bedroom had been stripped of everything that might be useful. The bathroom, too, was empty beyond the bare necessities.

She returned to sit on the bed, her arms crossed to cradle her belly. In a few short weeks, she would feel this child move within her.

She fought the despair that tightened in her throat. Turned back the hatred for Adrian. The anger against herself. These would not serve her. She took a pillow and moved to sit on the rug before the fire. The flames were quieter now; the logs settled into a steady release of heat. She sat on the cushion, imaging herself before the familiar little shrine from Kyoto. Prayer would calm her mind.

He could not call it weakness, was not ashamed of his tears. He, Adrian Lovett. No angel of the Cherubim at this moment. But human. Mortal flesh that shuddered on the edge of the abyss.

Naked and stripped, he stood before the closet in this bedroom they had shared, he and Marian, his wife. Head back, eyes closed, mouth held open in a feral kind of inhaling. Molecules of scent, the carriers of memory, leapt from her clothing, invading his nostrils to mass at the back of his throat.

Beyond her flesh scent that still lingered, he could taste the flavor of their days. Candle wax and fresh bread. Coffee and burning leaves. They had been so happy here on those days stolen from the city, before

it had become apparent that the children for which Marian had abandoned her career would never, in fact, be born. And even with all their troubles, they had been happy still, laughing on the night she had died.

He reached on a shelf for her sweater. Fisherman knit. A soft creamy yellow. So wonderful a color with her hair. He must have photographed her wearing this sweater at least a dozen times. He held it against his chest, buried his face in the softness of its fiber. It was not weakness, this good-bye. Rather, it was a salute to the last of his lifetimes here on Earth, an affirmation of all for which he had so dearly paid. The rebellion might have been a mistake, but not a foolish one. What the life of flesh had meant to him, what Marian had meant to him, had to be acknowledged.

The *Fall* was a fall into time. The glory of imperfection. The possibility of change. The irony had lately occurred to him that he might be more instrument than opponent—that the rebellion had been anticipated, an immutable part of the Plan. And he wondered if his present mission to regain Heaven for the Fallen was less a continuation of war than the salvation of some principle beyond his understanding.

God works in mysterious ways.

The thought brought an anger that shook his human shell—a shadow of the discontent that had driven the Fallen to defiance. The rage of a cog that is all too conscious of the wheel.

He was tired of the present battle. Grateful that he'd succeeded with Samyaza. He had bet on his strength and had won. He could retire from the field with honor, having left the campaign to one much greater than himself.

He returned the sweater to the shelf. Marian was truly lost. The bond that was flesh would soon be broken forever. They could never meet again kind to kind.

But he was ready. Zavebe waited. He must return to her and begin the process that would strip away not her physical blindness but the truer blindness that plagued her. He would send her fully awakened to the place between. Then he would join her to wait together with the others he had sent before. Kasyade, Jeqon, Barakel. Asbeel, Rumel, Penemue. And the others whom Samyaza would awaken before he, too, came in glory to lead them.

✳

With the nose of his gun, Sakura tapped on the door of Lovett's apartment. He waited. Dead silence. Backing away, with his shoulder down, he rammed the solid expanse of wood. Once, twice. The third thrust caused the door to implode. For an instant he stood in the deserted hallway, waiting for the sound of the falling door to die, for the throbbing in his shoulder to ease.

The dull morning was fading into afternoon, and a weak stream of light reflected through the floor-to-ceiling windows, casting the loft in pale blue shadow, glinting off the chrome of gym equipment. He stepped in. The living area was a single undivided space. The furnishings were spare and modern, oversize to match the room's dimensions. The only color or pattern was a pair of matching Orientals on the hardwood floor.

His eyes made a wide circle, settling on a large black-and-white photograph hung on one of the support walls. It was of a nude woman who seemed to be dancing, her long hair swirling around her in a pale foglike mass. The dead wife? Killed in the auto accident?

From someplace in his mind, he was aware of his feet padding across a section of one of the rugs, then the woodsy *knock-knock* of his shoes against bare floor. A small kitchen was set to the right. To the left, a squared-off partition. He moved toward it, slowly snaking around its edge, gun drawn between his hands.

The bedroom's interior was almost in complete darkness, shades blocking the outer windows. The bed was a bloated white mound, too low to the floor for anyone to fit beneath. No closets. A single large chest. A bathroom wedged itself to the side. Pressing against the wall, he flicked the shower curtain with the leveled .38. Empty.

He walked across the living room back toward the kitchen. A small pantry door was fitted against the short wall. He shifted his gun to his right hand and swung the pantry door out. A tunnel of fluid blackness hit him. Instinctively, he stepped back. Listened to the silence. His free hand reached out, connecting with a switch. He flipped the lever. Instantly the space filled with red light. A drying line stretched out over him. Empty metal pans rested on a tiled counter. Bottles of developing fluid lined up in neat rows. A couple of cameras, like abstract sculptures, stood on a shelf. No photographs.

He clicked off the darkroom light, closed the door, and moved out of the kitchen back into the living area. From across the room the glass in the picture frame glinted dully. He moved toward the desk, abutting the back of the sofa. The photograph was a five-by-seven color shot of the same woman in the large black-and-white portrait. In jeans and a sweater, under a bowl of cloudless blue sky, with autumnal forest ablaze behind her, the woman smiled for a camera that clearly loved her. And just inside the frame, the weathered shoulder of a large two-storied home. He turned the frame over and unhinged the back. In a woman's hand, at the bottom of the photograph, an inscription: *In the country*.

He set the frame down and opened the center drawer. The usual clutter—pens, pencils, clips. He rummaged through paper but found nothing that could help him. He opened a side drawer.

They were scattered like pieces of a child's jigsaw puzzle, bright and colorful. All the snapshots were of her, taken that same day, against the backdrop of turning trees. Except for one photograph, taken of a man sitting astride a motorcycle, the shadow of a cap obscuring his face. And in the distance, against a flash of burnished leaves, its name just making it into the frame—*Chatwell*.

For a long moment he stared into the man's face, the letters of the town's name like runes thrown against the ground of his consciousness, the red leaves burning a fire into his brain. He had always known that his soul was bruised by the full force of his life in the city, by the brutality of the work he did. But he also understood that he endured because daily Hanae healed him. It was as simple a fact as he could know. He could not live without her. He opened his jacket and tucked the photos inside his breast pocket.

It was then he noticed it. At eye level, across the wide space of the room, a long screen situated against the wall that ran at a right angle to the kitchen. The screen rested almost flush against the wall. It was surprisingly light and he was able to move it easily. A blind door lay behind it. He raised his .38, reached out, and twisted open the door. Another door stared back. A highly polished steel door, like those fitted for walk-in refrigerated lockers. He reached with his free hand, feeling the door's resistance. He pulled hard and the grip popped.

Nothing human lay within, and he waited for the thick wall of refrigerated air he'd released to clear. There was shelving on either side of the locker. Boxes wrapped in freezer paper lined the metallic racks. Beyond, to the rear and overhead, suspended from aluminum poles were wings. Hung in pairs, they stirred in the dry frigid air.

⁂

Hanae opened her eyes to light. An explosion of light that left her exhilarated, fully sensible. Gone was the death-darkness. And with it the crush of crippling fear. She placed her hand over her left breast. Her heart moved in a safe, slow, and steady rhythm. She counted the measured beats, the accented-unaccented syllables, and numbered her pulse against her fingertips. How easily her breaths came now. Her chest, a gentle sea of rising and falling inhalations and exhalations.

She closed her lids. The light remained, but she was no more. Where once there had been Hanae, a distinct and unique separateness, there was *Kami*. No longer alone, a thing apart, but in the way of Shinto, part of the pure energy of all things. At one with the cushion upon which she sat, at one with the fire and the floor. Joined to the walls and the door of the room so that they ceased to form a prison against her. And in that same instant, joined to Jimmy. One with her husband in a completeness that her madness had almost caused her to forget.

But he would not forget. Nor would he forsake her. She felt a smile come to her lips and savored the joy that brought it. For she understood that beyond her confidence in the absolute goodness of his heart and mind, she could offer Jimmy the gift of time. Time to find her. It was up to her to remain safe until he did.

She had returned to the bed when she heard a small noise from across the room. The sound of the door opening, and then the soft padding of the flesh of his feet against the floor.

"Touch me . . . ," Adrian said, taking her hands in his. "Like before."

The skin of his face was as smooth as she remembered. But the planes were sharper now, so only the bone of his skull was left to define him. The eyes had fallen deeper into their sockets.

"You are thinner," she said, withdrawing her hands, making her voice calm.

"I have little appetite for food." He laughed then. And she thought the sound, like the feel of him, bore an acuter thinness, emanating from some airless place, resonating now through flesh as fragile as rice paper, bone as brittle as glass. There existed now an uncharacteristic emptiness that was not there before, and it seemed to her that he was in the process of slowly dissolving so that any moment he would simply cease to exist.

"Body and soul are one," she said. "You cannot starve one and not starve the other."

"What about Buddhist monks who fast for days?" He lowered himself to the edge of the bed. She felt the mattress give with his weight. A wave of wet warmth hit her, and she realized that he, too, was naked.

"They feed on spiritual food."

"Oh, Hanae . . . ," he whispered, bending over so that his chest rubbed against her breasts, his thigh against her thigh. "This body, this soul, you speak of, they are not one, but enemies who war."

"Adrian, why?" Her voice kept gentle, without accusation. "Why are you doing this?"

"This is not meant to hurt you."

"Taking me from my home hurts me, Adrian. This hurts me. . . ." She turned her head away. Hard, this was hard. "Taiko . . ."

"Drugged. He will be all right."

She turned back. "And Jimmy?"

"A most worthy adversary. But he cannot win."

Then like a dark star piercing the landscape of light, the truth came. And she understood. Understood at last exactly who this man was. Understood how carefully she must walk this dangerous path she had set for herself. How precious the gift of time she was offering Jimmy.

᭢

Willie got off the elevator and walked down the hospital hallway on her way to Michael's room. She had finally been discharged after her early-morning go-round with the doctors. She would never have stood for the delay, but she'd fallen asleep in her room, waiting for the paperwork to be ready.

She'd be a fool to deny that she'd needed the sleep. Yesterday's ordeal was not something you simply shrugged off, and Delia Johnson's earlier visit had turned into a detailed questioning that had further exhausted her. But that had been hours ago. Why hadn't Jimmy called since? Surely, they wouldn't be stupid enough to remove him from the investigation.

Well, she'd be at headquarters soon enough. Just a quick trip to the apartment for a shower and fresh clothes. Maybe this guy was ready to quit, but she wouldn't bank on it. And she wanted him more than ever now, wanted to get at the origins of that fallen-angel fantasy. It was hard to express the frustration she felt, having had him right in front of her. At least she'd survived the experience. And Michael had survived. A miracle, she'd told Jimmy. Miracle was an understatement.

Michael had come through with no apparent damage to his heart. But it was not his heart she was worried about now. An equally powerful attack had been waged against his mind.

The door was half open and she knocked softly, not really expecting an answer. For a moment she noted that Detective Rozelli was no longer in the hall, but as quickly the thought ebbed.

"It's me, Michael." She walked in and crossed to the bed. Awake, he didn't turn to her. His continued unresponsiveness was not a very good sign.

"Willie . . ."

She jerked around. He stood in the shadows behind her. "God, you scared me, Jimmy."

"I went to your room . . . came to see if you were here."

"What's wrong?" He looked terrible. The mask that he wore in place of his face actually made her fear him.

"He's got Hanae."

Her heart lurched in instant comprehension. "How . . . ?"

He shook his head, denying time for any explanation. "I think he's taken her to this house upstate." He handed her a photo. "I'm headed up there now." He took the picture back.

"What can I do?"

"I need a search of the property records of Orange County."

"You've got a name?"

"Adrian Lovett," he said. "Wife, Marian. Maiden name Chandler. The title could be filed under that."

Or this house might be rented or belong to a friend. But she didn't say it aloud.

"I left my badge for McCauley," he told her now. "You're the only one who knows about Hanae."

"God, Jimmy. You need backup."

"No." He was adamant. "That'll take too much time. Besides, there's no real proof that he has her."

She didn't argue. There was danger the mask might shatter and leave nothing at all of her friend.

He was leaving. She saw him throw a last look at Michael.

"Call me on my cell phone," he said, "as soon as you nail the location."

"I will." She wanted to say more, but his footsteps were already in the hall. She stood shell-shocked listening to them recede.

Michael hadn't moved and she wondered if he'd understood or even heard anything that Jimmy had said. She went to the bed. His eyes shifted, and for the first time they focused on her face. But not her gaze. Her eyes, he still avoided. But he spoke. One word. *Phaos.* She thought it might be Greek. His glance, never fully captured, slipped away.

"Are you warm enough, Zavebe?"

He no longer called her Hanae but used her angel name. *Her angel name.* He had spoken of death and rebirth. Of flesh and spirit. Heaven and Hell. Of awakening, not killing. How he'd craved understanding. How he'd wished her husband and the others could have clearly seen his path. And he'd spoken, too, of remorse for the priest who'd had to pay for his perceived sins. But such was the war. The war against the Ineffable One. On and on he'd spoken, spiraling off into another language. His voice now a bell, harmonious and soothing, then a loud and urgent drum. And finally a reed. Mystical and hollow. Adrian Lovett. The angel Gadriel. Jimmy's serial killer.

She understood now how he'd arranged to meet her, following first Jimmy to their apartment, then later her to Ms. Nguyen's studio, where he pretended to have been in class from the start. He was not a Web designer, as he had said, but a photographer whose wife had been killed in a horrible accident. There was no son. The boy on the phone was the nephew of a neighbor, bribed with the price of a video game. It was all a tissue of lies. The great irony, he said, was that Zavebe should be trapped in the body of the wife of James Sakura.

He brought his lips close to her ear now. "I asked if you were warm, Zavebe."

She nodded. "Yes . . ."

"I want to do nothing but please you." He brought his hand back into the water, sliding the sponge across the nape of her neck, down the ridges of her spine. Then over her shoulders, around the circles of her breasts. The white-flower smell of soap filling her lungs. Then he bent and kissed one nipple, and she felt it grow inside his mouth. Her heart cried out, but there was no place to hide her shame. She thought of *misogi*, the Shinto exercise of cleansing, how the act of bathing became a spiritual rite of purification. But not this, not this horror, this obscenity. In the still, unmoving water of the porcelain tub, she was defiled.

He sighed, lifting his head. "How sweet this human flesh. I shall miss it."

"Then do not leave it." Her voice was not her own.

"I am finished here." The bath stirred around her. "You and I go to greater glory."

"Wait. . . ." She found his hand under the water. "It is but a short time now," she said, placing the flat of his palm against her abdomen where the child grew. "Wait until after," she whispered, bringing her mouth close to his. "And we enjoy this flesh awhile longer."

He laughed softly, and she tasted his breath in the moment before his mouth closed over hers. Almost a chaste kiss. Then his hands were at her shoulders, pushing her gently back into the water. Her hair unwinding, floating outward. His fingers on the point where her sternum began, at the center of her chest, submerging her face, her mouth swallowing the wet pooling inside her, her nostrils flaring, sucking moist air.

✦

Yesterday's sleet had returned. The trees patterned with ice. The Hudson, a silver ribbon on the right, could be glimpsed now and then from the highway. Sakura saw nothing but the road ahead, moving as fast as he could in this weather, blanking the scenery along with every image that he'd banned from his brain.

The force of the sleet increased, little needles attacking his windshield. He looked out at his surroundings now, but visibility was limited. A white sky pressed the trees. He could not see the river.

Willie hadn't called. He glanced at the cell phone, which was lying with the photographs on the passenger seat beside him. He had disciplined his mind, but doubt was hammering the borders. He turned on the radio, scanning for a station that played his music.

The phone rang.

"Sakura." He shut off the radio.

"I'm sorry, Jimmy." Willie's voice. "I called Orange and the surrounding counties. None of them liked the idea of giving out information on the phone. I had to pull an FBI . . ." Her voice petered out.

"And . . . ?" He knew the answer.

"Nothing. No listing for Adrian or Marian Lovett. Or Marian Chandler either. I'm sorry," she said again. "Where are you?" she asked.

"Still on the thruway."

"Let me call Kelly. Maybe he can coordinate something with the locals. They might even be able to help locate this guy. Like I said before, I think Lovett's finished. He'll suicide, Jimmy. . . ."

The rest went unspoken. He would kill Hanae first. "Okay," he finally agreed, "call Kelly."

✦

A lotus in an uncertain wind, Hanae sat, shivering in the porcelain tub, water noisily draining. In the room no other sound. Legs drawn up, hands crossed over her breasts, she tried to quell her shaking. Tears mixed and fell with the beads of water that ran down from her face. She must regain control. She could survive her shame. What mattered was that she was still alive, still making time for Jimmy. Her shivering turned to rocking, a motion instinctive that seemed to calm. She stopped and returned to her practiced breathing.

Adrian's footsteps returning, bare skin spanking tile. She kept her breathing even, kept the air from rising in a sound of fear from her throat.

"This shell you inhabit is beautiful, but it masks a greater splendor." He had knelt at the side of the tub, his voice at her level. His finger made a gentle circle at the base of her neck. "You are afraid," he said, "but only because you cannot remember." His hands reached to remove hers from where they clasped her shoulders. He began to stroke her breasts.

"I want to remember," she said, keeping her voice steady. "Tell me again about the accident . . . and the tunnel."

His fingers ceased their motion on her skin. She sensed his smile, his eyes intent upon her face, as if he guessed that her purpose was delay. "It was in the tunnel I remembered," he began, and wrapping her in a large towel, he lifted her from the tub and carried her back to the bedroom.

She lay where he placed her on the bed, the towel spread beneath her. He turned her to face him, where he sat beside her, and began to rub her body with a warm and scented oil. He continued to speak—his hands kneading her skin—of the kinship they shared, she Zavebe and he Gadriel, beings of pure spirit who had once shared a union unimaginable to humans. A union they would soon share again.

She flinched when the blade touched her, moving first in the hollow of her underarm. She let his voice become a droning. Withdrew into the light. It was the light that glided above her skin with the razor. The light that purified the act, even to the shaving of her pubis.

The singsong of his recital stopped. The feel of the towel was raw reality. "You had little body hair." His words as he wiped her down, removing the residue.

He sat her in a hard straight chair, draping some covering around her shoulders, securing it under her chin. Words she could not believe whispered in her ear: "I will not hurt you."

She did not understand what was coming, her mind reaching for every bit of information, every detail she had gleaned of Jimmy's case. But it was none of that. Her only warning was the sudden grind of metal near her face, the scythe sound of the scissors beginning their harvest.

It was a kind of cleansing, he explained, this further mortification of her body. When he was done, when she was shorn, he brushed the clumps of hair from her neck and her cheeks, then removed the cover carefully from her shoulders.

"You are yet beautiful, Zavebe."

She nearly broke. Some part of her yearned for an end to it, to let go, to dissolve to nothing inside his madness. But in this moment she was still alive, the child within her still alive. In this moment, and in this moment . . . and this.

━━━✦━━━

Sakura had driven through the brittle sleet with a single string of words playing over and over in his head: *Let her be alive, let her be alive.* The precipitation had stopped, leaving behind an unwholesome stillness and a flattened sky.

He was losing sense of time again. But he knew it was well more than an hour since he'd left Willie at the hospital and moved out of the city onto the interstate, into the denseness of upstate New York and the Hudson River Valley. Kelly had checked in to say they were headed north and would expect him to call if and when he had an exact location.

He shifted in the driver's seat, catching a glimpse of himself in the mirror, the stubble of a beard grown darker, the fear in eyes barely recognizable. One hand clamped hard on the steering wheel, the other reached into the inside pocket of his jacket, withdrawing his handkerchief. No longer clean, he sought some remnant of laundered freshness inside the linen. Breathing deeper, he at last found a ghost of the starchiness Hanae had sealed into the cloth. Imagining her pressing perfect creases into the square, a part of him wanted to cry into the new worn and wrinkled folds, cry for the miserableness of his failure, cry for what in the end might be lost to him. As a small boy on Hokkaido, when he had felt most alone, he had cried. Had cried when he ached for a father, who kept between them land and ocean. But this pain, this anger, demanded more of him.

The wings in the locker had confirmed Adrian Lovett as the killer they had sought for so many days. Willie's witness proved it had been this serial who had attacked her and Michael. Yet he had no certainty beyond his instincts that this same man had Hanae. *But who else? And if so, why Hanae?*

Willie had tried to explain how Lovett selected his victims. *Auras,* she had said, *he sees auras.* So if he were to save his wife, he must accept that from inside his madness Adrian Lovett had seen an aura around his Hanae, believed her to be a fallen angel.

Or is Hanae's abduction merely revenge against me? With this thought he permitted self-loathing and guilt to join fear. Yet why had she not been murdered in their apartment? Was Lovett, as in Lucia's case, seeking greater isolation in which to draw Hanae into his fantasy, to take her life? And his own?

His headlights reflected off the sign. *Chatwell.* He glanced down at the photo on the seat and drove into the frame of the snapshot. Ahead, diffused illumination filled his windshield. A convenience store was open for business.

He pulled over, grabbed the photographs, and entered the store. A woman sat behind the register, reading a magazine. She looked up as he walked to the counter.

"Can I help you?" She worked a wad of gum.

"I hope so." He handed her the picture of Lovett astride his cycle. "Recognize this guy? Name's Adrian Lovett."

She drew up glasses from a chain around her neck and hooked them onto her nose. "Can't say as I do. But that don't mean nothing, since I usually pull the night shift. He a local?"

"No. Probably visits only on weekends and holidays. Has a place somewhere around here." He showed her the best shot of the house.

"Can't tell much from this. . . . Hey, Leroy."

A guy in his late twenties came from the back. He shifted the stem of a cigarette between his lips. The cashier handed him the two photos. "You work days. Know this guy on the motorcycle?"

Leroy grinned, showing off a mouth full of bad teeth around the cig-arette. "Would give my right arm for that hog."

"You know him?"

"Comes in to gas up the Harley once in a while. Dude's wife was killed a while back," he said, finally removing the plug of cigarette. "Filled up that Land Rover of his the day of the accident. Heard she was decapitated." He sliced a finger across his neck.

"Know where he might have a house around here?" Sakura shifted the photos in Leroy's hand.

"Big house." He angled his head. "But that figures. Rich guy like that."

"This would be a second home. Name's Lovett."

Leroy pressed the cigarette stub out on the floor. "My guess, it's on the lake. Lots of nice houses built 'round the lake. Primo real estate."

"How do I access the lake from here?"

"North end of the lake is fronted by a public road. You can catch it half a mile down. But that might not do you much good."

"How's that?"

"The big houses are around the south side. Head-on you can't see nothing but woods. Got to pick your way through. There's a gravel road that works its way in. But the offshoot roads are mostly private driveways. It's gonna be hit or miss."

"Will I be able to connect with this gravel road from the public access?"

Leroy nodded, handing back the pictures. "Why you looking for this guy? He in trouble?"

"Maybe. Thanks for the help." He moved to leave.

"Hey, mister. If you talk to this Lovett, ask him if he wants to sell that cycle."

⁂

The sheet and the blanket drawn up about her, Hanae sat in the bed and listened, making sure that she was really alone. She shuddered inside the covers, pulling the fabric tighter as if to blot his touch from her skin. But the shudder gave way to a trembling she could no longer stop. She had done what she had done. Had not resisted while he bathed her, shaved her, and cut her hair. Had been grateful for the water he had offered.

Adrian Lovett had been her friend. She still felt the connection. It would not help to deny what was true. She had played on their friendship, had listened to his madness. Patiently. Agreeing with him when she could. Not challenging, but reasoning against their imminent deaths, even offering seduction as the price for her life and her baby's.

But her strategy, she feared, was not working. Adrian was moving to his own internal clock, though he did seem to crave her understanding and consent. She must try, at least, to use that, to keep him engaged in explanation. A willing pupil who must be brought along.

If only she had told Jimmy about her new friend. But she had told no one because she had been ashamed of the way she behaved. . . . That kiss. She had been very foolish, but surely her life and the life of her child were too great a price to be paid. She loved Jimmy. She had never lost hold of that. She knew that he was searching for her now. She wound that belief around her as tightly as the covers until her trembling ceased.

The light remained within her, pulsing like a bright beating heart. Her blood beat and the child's. And Jimmy coming closer.

🜨

The owl flashed out of nowhere. Sakura had a sudden sense of it dropping, swooping in from the trees. Dark wings in a glide, talons grazing his windshield. Chasing something.

His foot hit the brake reflexively, and he swerved, nearly skidding off the gravel before he straightened out. His heart raced, not with the adrenaline rush of a near accident, but with the consciousness of time running out. How long since he had found Hanae missing? It seemed like days. There had been hours between Lucia's abduction and her death. He had to believe that he still had time, that his hunch about this house was correct.

If he could find the house.

He regretted not having his badge. He'd made up a story about being a representative for an insurance company to the few people he'd spoken to since the convenience store clerk. If anyone remembered Adrian Lovett at all, he or she remembered the accident that had killed his wife. None of them knew exactly where he lived.

The last man he'd talked to had sent him down the possibility of yet another branching road. It was a rabbit warren back here, the houses older and smaller as you moved away from the lake. And spaced much farther apart. But even here most homes stood dark and empty, owned apparently by "summer people" who wouldn't return for months.

He saw a light through the trees. A porch light. The rough-timbered house, set back from the road, was occupied. The multicolored lights of a Christmas tree filtered through the sheerness of a curtain.

He pulled into the drive and walked up the stairs to the porch. He could see now that the Christmas lights were the old-fashioned big ones, reflecting in silver-tinsel icicles that shimmered thickly in the branches of the fir. There was no bell. He knocked.

The door was opened immediately by a woman who seemed to have been waiting. Probably she'd heard the car.

"Sorry to bother you," he said, "but I'm looking for the Lovett house."

A young boy pushed through to stare at him. The cookie in his hand matched the baking smell, which was no doubt coming from the kitchen. Sakura smiled at him and the woman, waiting for her to say something—gearing up for the photo and the story about insurance.

"Down there," she said, pointing up the way he'd been going. "Gravel road turns back toward the lake. Big place. You can't miss it."

"Thank you," he remembered to say. He was already moving toward the car.

🔥

Adrian Lovett touched the shiny steel tip of the hypodermic needle, then ran his finger along the measured surface of the glass vial. A crystal cage that would at last release him from this earthly existence. No more cleaving to the flesh. No descent into corporeal mortality to move backward into space and time.

Even now, he had only glossy intimations of his fully realized nature. His most expansive trips on LSD could not return him to that instant of his awakening, to that absolute purity of moment when he understood who and what he was. So he had drifted into what might seem an addiction, a struggle to capture that time in the tunnel before resuscitation had clamped its iron jaws around him. Each time he took the drug, it had moved him closer to some infinite orgasm. Yet always he remained stranded and frustrated at the lip of the explosion.

He believed this veil that blurred his illumination would regrettably outlast the relinquishing of matter, his separation from substance. The return to full experience would have to await the others who came after, await Samyaza and the crushing of the barrier.

Or am I a fool? Was absolute actualization possible without union with that which he perceived as enemy? Could any one of the Fallen be an angel separate from God?

The two empty vials were not yet filled with the potassium chloride. He closed his eyes, imagining the pinch of the needle into spongy flesh, its jellyfish sting. The end of breath, the end of the *thump, thump, thumping* of the four-chambered heart. Then the flat-lining of the brain.

The edge of his thumb caressed the dark green velvet that lined the case where the two syringes rested snugly between small collars. How many months ago had he purchased the instruments? Relics from the past, they recalled a time when family doctors made house calls, their pills and potions, their devices and implements tucked like small jewels inside peeling black bags.

He snapped the case shut and looked at himself in the mirror. He was a freak. An unearthly thing trapped inside human flesh. A prisoner of desire. He reached for the straight-edge razor. Would that he could sever away the skin with the hair.

He ran his hand over the stubble of new growth. Each time less and less hair grew back. In some ways he was more than ever conscious of his humanness; in others, he had become more and more detached. The endless contradictions were damnable.

He smoothed the warm-scented oil over his body, though the ripeness of his own flesh could not be subdued. The straight-edge, like the syringes, was a throwback to the days before safety blades and electric razors. He flicked the side of the blade with his thumb. A fine line of blood erupted. Reflexively he brought his finger to his mouth and sucked. He gagged on the rich metallic flavor.

Over the mounds of his pectorals, across the planes of thigh and calf, over the slopes of his arms, inside his groin, he drew the straight-edge. His naked flesh shone like polished marble under the light. He had lost weight the last couple of weeks, and the tips of his fingers pressed through to the frame of ribs just beneath the muscles of abdomen.

He turned. In the mirror his shoulders and back were hairless. But there was the slightest trace of growth on his buttocks. He shaved across and between the shadowy crevice of his glutes. Then turning back, he observed the last vestiges of his primate nature. The hair on his face and head.

Oiling his scalp, he made even slices across his skull, then neatly shaved the taut angles of his face. Now he arched his brows, carefully manipulating the blade to follow the sparse growth pattern. He widened his eyes. Nothing left but the eyelashes. He reached for the tweezers. He flinched as he pulled the first lashes. They came out in small clumps, his eyes tearing as he yanked. Slowly plucking at first, then quickly, until he was finally as naked as an embryo.

✾

"Kelly," Sakura spoke into his cell phone. "I got a location. Where are you?"

"A few miles north of West Point."

"Good, this is what you do." He gave the directions from the access road to the gravel road that led to the house. "First driveway after the road turns back toward the lake."

"Gotcha. Stay put, Sakura. Wait for us."

Sakura turned off the phone and placed it on the seat.

The moon had yet to appear when he stopped midway on the narrow drive and got out of his car. A downy fall of snow had begun to loosen itself from a surprisingly clear sky, and somewhere another owl hooted. A plaintive call to its mate. In the distance the river flowed on, unknowing, in a bed carved from ancient soil. Beyond, the dark trees rose in impartial witness. He alone stood in dread.

He listened to the sound of his feet in the soft-forming drifts. *Memory does not so easily pass.* . . . He was nine the year his grandparents had brought him to Kyoto to celebrate New Year with cousins. The last day of the old year dawning unbelievably bright and blue. Now evening wrapped itself around the shoulders of the ancient city like a dark fur. In the chill, crisp air, the great bronze bell of Chion-in tolled.

He had run ahead, catching dancing flakes of snow on his tongue, his younger cousins, a parade of ducks waddling behind. Lights from overhead lanterns made warm smears on the blue ice, and the street in that moment seemed as still as a photograph. He remembered thinking that he had felt as new as the year.

He stopped. Somewhere between the time he'd arrived home from Baltimore and now, he'd laid down his overcoat and forgotten it. Yet the cold, as on that long-ago night in Kyoto, didn't register. Through the overhang of trees, he could make out the outline of the structure he'd seen in the Lovett photographs. The house was much larger than he had expected.

The place appeared vacant. No lights shone from the interior. But a white curl of smoke spiraled from the chimney. A dark recent-model car was parked to the side of a porch that ran from end to end of the house. The license plate glimmered like a small sheet of ice. He reached into his jacket and unholstered his .38.

He crouched as he moved up the winding drive. The structure was constructed of some kind of bleached wood, fitted with a high-pitched roof. A silver ghost in a sea of snow. Ceiling-to-floor windows broke up the exterior. A swing anchored to the gallery roof caught a sudden gust of wind. The metal chains moaned from their anchors. He stopped at the front door, pressing his ear to the wood, and listened. Silence.

⁂

The room smelled of myrrh and madness.

Hanae shivered, lying where Adrian had arranged her on the bed, bathed in the odor of incense and candles. Their buttery essence surrounded her, flickering and stirring in the warmth of their flames, cutting through the deeper odor of myrrh—tiny little tongues of scent, licking and retreating. She heard a match flare, another flame springing to existence.

It was the smell of the incense that seemed to frighten her most. She knew the place that it held in his murders, and she wondered if the letters that spelled out Zavebe were already written on the wall. She wanted to scream, felt hysteria rising. She had failed at last to keep him talking. Somewhere in his recounting of what he had planned, he had retreated into ritual. His stripping of the bedclothes from around her, his positioning of her on the bed, had been gentle. But she had no illusions of what resistance would bring. Adrian . . . No, *Gadriel* was in control.

He loomed once more at the side of the bed, returning again to his chanting. She felt his touch on her breast. His finger gritty with hot ash. The myrrh scent, overpowering, rose up from her skin.

His hand was moving. Making circles.

✠

Sakura reached for the door. It opened noiselessly.

The front room ran the width of the house, with vaulted ceilings like a cathedral. A large fireplace took up a third of the inside interior wall. Over the mantel was another portrait of the same woman, similar to the one he'd seen in Lovett's apartment. The glass covering the photograph absorbed a thin rivulet of light seeping in from one of the windows.

Then he smelled it. Drifting down from the stairs, ahead of a watery bubble of illumination. Incense. Sticking to the roof of his mouth, burning into the cells of his brain. And between breaths, his ears registering the voice. Soft and guttural all at once. Speaking now in English, now in some other language he didn't understand.

He grasped the banister, gun still drawn, walking slowly up the stairs, moving toward the voice from Hell.

✠

The singsong chanting ceased. Adrian slid in beside her.

"Zavebe," he whispered near her ear.

She said nothing. Her silence cried for Jimmy.

Adrian's hands were on her, his lips following. Kissing her. Everywhere. His breath moving on her skin like mist. She sought to retreat inside herself but could not. The violation was too real. She breathed, relaxed into the pillows. Accepting his touch. Forcing the lie that was the only hope for her and her child to live a minute, a second, longer.

He began speaking again. The words hypnotic. Slipping away from English.

Then his entry. Inside her. Sudden. A shock that stripped her senses. Eyes open, she fought for light.

A noise outside the bedroom. Footfalls like a cat's on the stairs. The soft *swish-swoosh* of breath. The *tip-tap* of metal against wood. And impossibly, the clear insistent beating of *his* heart, here and now, filling her, like water filling a vessel.

The hungry weight of Adrian's body easing in that blessed mixture of sound. In the pure realization that Jimmy had come to save her. That her gift of time had not been wasted. Then as quickly as joy came pain. At the heel of her spine, a serpent uncoiling.

She turned her head, her blind eyes finding him.

"*Kitsune . . .*" She heard his scream. His voice and the sound of the single gunshot reverberating inside her as she released the blood and water of their unfinished child from between her legs.

EPILOGUE

Sakura stepped off the mat, finished with his morning exercises. He had not practiced *Aikido* since his boyhood, but in the last few months, he had slipped easily back into performing the *aiki taiso*. The exercises, designed to restore a condition of harmony in the body's energy flow, were apparently ingrained like memory in his muscles. Still, he had progressed as far as he could without the commitment to a *dojo*. To go further, he needed a partner, *uke* to his *nage*. An assailant who was also a teacher.

He stopped in the bedroom on his way to shower, standing before the stepped chest that had once held his wife's clothes. A framed photograph still stood on the topmost level—a picture of the two of them on their wedding day in Kyoto. This was the photograph he wanted to remember. But it was Lovett's photographs that he could not get out of his mind.

Among the pictures of Hanae and the other victims found packaged in Lovett's freezer were also photographs of him, surveillance shots trailing him from the Westlake crime scene back to Police Plaza and eventually to this apartment.

While the media had made much of Lovett's stalking him, it was not likely that he'd ever been a serious target. What was clear to him was that he had failed to protect his wife, that he had been the instrument of Lovett's attack on Hanae. The greatest of his many failures.

They might have gotten an early break in a routine cross-check, with Lovett's name surfacing on both the Milne Gallery list and the list of clinic patients. But the clinic staff had resisted what they regarded as an unnecessarily broad intrusion on the privacy of their patients. The investigation had not been given a copy of Kerry's appointment book or even a complete list of clinic patients. Would Hanae . . . Would his unborn child have been spared, if only he'd pushed harder?

And then there were his other transgressions. Going it on his own. Taking a department vehicle. The list went on and included the wounding of a suspect who had not been armed. Amazing what the department could overlook when the public needed a hero. And the media with few of the facts had judged his actions daring, had credited him with saving his wife and stopping a vicious killer. He wanted to shout that he was a fraud.

But his badge had not been accepted. And there were those he still respected in the department who made it clear that his work was valued. Without the accompanying paperwork his gesture remained just that, though he knew McCauley was eager for the day he requested the forms that would make an early retirement official. For now, he was on leave and had not made any decision. In truth, his career was the furthest thing from his mind.

He realized he was still staring at the wedding picture, and now he picked it up, as if somehow it could bring Hanae closer. She had been very weak those first few days in the hospital, having to be reassured about Taiko, about Willie and Michael. Eventually he'd had to allow her official questioning. Detective Johnson had done that, with him sitting in the back of the room.

His wife had asked Adelia what she had not asked him, about Lovett's condition. She had been told he was recovering from the single bullet that had penetrated his shoulder. She had simply nodded and told Adelia her story. He could still see her face, her emotions clear projections on its pale translucent screen. Disbelief . . . horror. Guilt. *Why did he choose me?* The last question had been hers.

It was the question that plagued them both. For beyond the obvious suppositions was something so haunting in Lovett's photographs of her. In her own portrayal in clay of the man who'd befriended a blind woman. *He* had once been the stranger who'd befriended her. And he could not get out of his mind a movie that played there—

Hanae's long fingers moving with their slender grace over the face of a killer.

Why did he choose me? The question remained unexamined. A thing that stood between them.

The baby was another. He had been such a fool. So unseeing. The one who was truly blind. He had tried to explain his sorrow. She had spoken no words of blame. But for the first time since they'd met, communication was difficult.

I will only be gone for a while, she had said, and it was six months now since she'd left for Kyoto. Many times in those long weeks, he had thought of his grandmother. It was many years since she had died, and yet he could recall her in a way that went beyond simple memory. Summoned, he always felt her presence. Her wisdom had spoken to him on a thousand occasions. Indeed, it spoke to him now.

It was not this way with Hanae. Though his memories of their life together were sharp and clear, and would always remain so, Hanae herself seemed in danger of slipping beyond his reach. And were he to allow that to happen, he would never again in this life, or in any other, be whole.

And yet he understood that he must not act too quickly. His preparations must be only within his heart for now. A Zen poem came to him, and he spoke the words aloud:

"Sitting quietly, doing nothing,

"Spring comes, and the grass grows by itself."

In New Orleans even breathing was an effort in summer. Days under the relentless sun paralyzed, and evenings lay heavy and seductive like a narcotic. Only cicadas stirred with any purpose in the thick night air.

A pale skink appeared lifeless against the bone white stucco of the lower Garden District home, resurrecting itself from a dark wedge of aspidistra. There was a faint smell of wet, but the rain had failed to materialize. Willie French pushed her bare feet against the wide planks of porch, arcing back and forth in the wooden rocker, humming notes that didn't fit any particular song. The last of the ice had melted, diluting her gin and tonic. She brought the glass to her lips and pinched the lime between her teeth, eating the pulp, then tossing the rind. Something skittered across the green water inside the huge black cauldron, where slaves had once boiled sugarcane to syrup.

She pressed the cool glass between her breasts. There was no relief for the heat, but she spurned the damp air-conditioning inside the house. It froze something inside her. The heat only made her listless. She took another swill.

She had stayed on in New York after Lovett's hearing—there had been no trial—hoping that he would eventually talk. Her dream case study. But that never happened. She eventually told herself that she remained in the city to help Jimmy tie up loose ends with the investigation, help him come to terms with Hanae's miscarriage and her decision to return to Kyoto. But none of it was the real truth. The case had been put to bed officially, and Jimmy was quite capable of handling his life, both professionally and personally.

She had remained in New York because of Michael Darius. Trying to understand, to find some answers for what had happened between them. The intensity of the murder investigation seemed to have blunted her reasoning, had kept her in a state of unreality. Only Michael's brush with death had finally forced her out of her stupor. She remembered his kissing her good-bye at the airport. It was dark and cold. A light snow fell. She had shuddered in his arms as his mouth covered hers. It had felt like a kiss that was meant to last a lifetime.

Her brother's request begging her to come home had been a reprieve. Flying first to Virginia, she'd quickly settled things at Quantico and closed up her apartment. And so she had returned to New Orleans, to the house of her childhood, to reunite with ghosts she'd forgiven but never forgotten.

Once the seat of imperial power, Kyoto was a city of contradictions. Of ancient ways and modern energies. Of mountain and sea. A place whose heart measured its course in the rhythms and colors of the seasons.

From behind latticed walls, Hanae heard Mrs. Kawabata sprinkle water across the narrow pathway that fronted her own home and the home of her parents. A common ritual that kept dust from rising in the summer heat.

She moved from the elevated *tatami* room where she slept, down into the main room, Taiko at her side. As she passed the *tokonoma,* she could smell the fresh blossoms her mother had arranged earlier this morning. She knew a small card, placed in the alcove the day of her arrival, rested still against the vase. On the square of rice paper had been written a prayer, offered in thanksgiving for her safe journey home.

It had been January when she'd returned, after the New Year celebrations, and the sky shivered, releasing ghosts, moving in white flurries of snow. Her own heart and mind frozen. At first she had allowed her parents to indulge her, her mother feeding her warm bowls of miso, insisting on long afternoon naps. Her father spoiling her with his funny stories and the sweet cakes she'd loved as a girl, buying her combs to pull her shorter hair back from her face.

Her parents had asked few questions, respecting her privacy, believing that what she most needed was time to heal from the loss of the child. In the mornings she sat in their small garden. In the evenings she walked with Taiko through the neighborhood as far as a small Buddhist temple, then back home again.

She bent now and gave Taiko a scratch on his muzzle. Twice she and her dog had been blessed with good fortune. First the shepherd had suffered no ill effects from the drug he'd been given that day she'd been taken from the apartment. And then later in Japan, the authorities had allowed her to keep him with her during the required two-week quarantine. Settling in with him, however, had been more difficult. A small home that had once made room for her birds had at first found it difficult to accommodate a large dog. She heard the tattoo of his tail on the *tatami* as though he'd read her thoughts. "Yes, Taiko, even Mama-san you have charmed."

It had been almost six months since she'd returned home. But still, she saw few friends or relatives, except for Nori, who came to visit regularly, often accompanying her on her evening walks or to the store to buy art supplies so she could start sculpting again. Unlike her parents, her cousin refused to stand on polite convention and asked question after question. Though most remained unanswered, Nori chattered on.

Jimmy called often. Always mentioning coming for a visit. But never a plan. And never asking when she might return. Not since the first time he'd asked and she'd answered he would know when the time was right and would not have to ask.

When she'd first returned to Kyoto, she had not been able to think of Jimmy. Her thoughts a cold dark pool, moving in endless, useless circles. Then after a while she had been able to do nothing but think of him. And that was worse. Her thoughts like glassy heat rising from a desert. Then one evening she tied Taiko to a willow and made her way inside the small temple she regularly passed. Resting on her knees, she sat back upon her heels, her arms on her thighs, palms up, her index fingers joining thumbs to form circles. Slowly the pool became calm and the desert cooled. Her mind stilled and she emptied herself. In that moment she was able to think clearly about Jimmy. And Adrian Lovett.

Why had I ever doubted that Adrian Lovett could harm me? Was it a wish to believe I could not have misjudged him? A wish to believe he was not what he was? Syringes with potassium compounds and LSD had been found in the bedroom of the house in Chatwell. A pair of wings. And she had inhaled the burning incense, felt his fingers rub it into her skin. He *had* meant to kill her. And himself.

Her instincts had failed her. And so had her heart. The man she had befriended in the park had been Jimmy's serial killer. Adrian Lovett had killed those men. Had murdered the little girl. Had taken Willie and hurt Kenjin. And twisted inside this horror was her betrayal of Jimmy, and the death of their baby.

Alone now in the house of her childhood, she wept, a shadow of *monoganashii* inside her heart, the beauty of something precious slipping from her grasp.

🔺

Michael Darius parked his car in one of the spots reserved for visitors and walked up the paved drive to the entrance. The evening was still hot, and he could hear the splishing sound of an underground sprinkler system at work. Mueller was on the desk, and he flashed him his identification. Merely a formality now, but still a necessary ritual in these kinds of facilities.

The building had undergone extensive renovations the past few months, and a bank of new elevators had been installed. He entered a car, pressing the button for the top floor, watching the lighted digits pop one after another, waiting for the freeze-flash of his number. The car glided to a stop and the doors sucked open.

Along with the new elevators, all the interior walls in the building had been resurfaced and painted a matte institutional white. The floors had been retiled, and glass and stainless surveillance cages had been constructed on each floor as part of the overall face-lift. He moved up to the cage now. Hodges rose to his feet.

It was a fairly short walk down the hall. There were only twelve rooms on this floor, and at present only three were occupied. Hodges walked ahead, aiming toward the last room on the left. When he stopped, he glanced momentarily through the small window cut into the steel door. Then he turned and gave him the go-ahead nod. Michael stepped up and looked inside.

Only Lovett's eyes remained alive now, and only when they rested on him, his one regular visitor from the outside. And then they were the eyes of a child, or an animal, who wants to understand why it has been so betrayed.

Severe withdrawal, Willie called it, a not unusual outcome in a subject whose psychosis was as deep-seated as Adrian Lovett's. The surprise, she'd said, was the degree to which he had functioned normally outside the parameters of his delusion. An atypical paranoid psychosis was her diagnosis. And with no violent episodes prior to the head injury he'd received in the automobile accident, it was a condition that might have been at least partly explained by damage to his brain.

Willie's expert assessment made a lot of sense. Michael accepted it all. Except in his dreams, when once again he pushed against the barrier toward the light, and in one slow instant between heartbeats, he remembered what it had meant to be Lucifer, *who wore them all as a garment, transcending all in knowledge and in glory.*